PROLOGUE

"There are hunters and there are victims. By your discipline, cunning, obedience and alertness, you will decide if you are a hunter or a victim."

~General James "Jim" Mattis

In life, there exists a balance between civility and anarchy; security and chaos; right and wrong. A thin line separates the wolves from the sheep who occupy each end of the spectrum, and in between those two sides are men who skillfully navigate that thin line. These men operate in the shadows with precise competency, and without caution for consequences. The men who secure the line are anomalies – mythical if you will. Their bravery, forged in the fire of survival is suppressed beneath normality, outwardly hoping to never surface, but inside screaming to be released. In the face of violence, these men can be seen confidently being drawn toward death and destruction like a magnet, while all others flee for their lives.

This type of soldier is scarce – not many men embody the strict moral code that guides the violence required to destroy the evils of man. These men are similar to their adversaries; they are both mad; their psyche, if analyzed by professionals are virtually identical. The only difference is the men who guard the line have the fortitude to balance their mental dilemmas. They control their inner demons and harness their monstrosity on-demand to protect us at all costs.

Men like Silas Gray represent a minority among us. It has

been said that a monster is defined as a man without a conscience. It takes a monster to embrace, engage and neutralize wolves who dare to cross the thin blue line. You sleep comfortably at night knowing that the line is protected by men like Gray. Rest assured that when anarchy arrives, there will be men who silently maintain composure, suit up and thank God for their time to balance out the spectrum. The quiet protector with ice-cold eyes and adrenaline in his veins was born for that moment and will cut through the souls of evil men so that you sleep secure yet another night.

Christopher Galvez

For Grampa.

COLD NIGHT'S HEIR

Currie Rankin

Frigid conditions of the evening contradicted the fire in lungs and the acid in his blood. His heart raced and his nerves steeled after nearly three days of intense investigation. *It was time this came to an end.*

His thoughts ran to the pain in his knees and the weight of vest, but the mission came first. He was in good condition, but it could always be better. Rapid footsteps and heavy breathing were the order of the moment. *Too many of these moments.*

The figure in front of him was the object of his desire. His obsession. His curse. Nothing could've filled the void in his soul like this figure. The love and hate that he had for this singular being was nothing he felt before. Graduations, wedding, birth of his first child; Nothing compared to his hunger for catching his prey. That's what it was, a hunger.

Shit, another turn. This guy must run marathons! My knees can't take this shit!

As he made the turn onto the next street, he realized one thing: I am alone. Unsanctioned. Unplugged. No backup. *Just me, my nemesis, and our respective weapons.* His weapon, a Sig 1911, at the ready. Eight rounds of department issued .45 ACP ammunition with one in the chamber. It weighed just over two pounds, but he just ran five blocks. She might as well be a bazooka. The SureFire light attachment added to the weight but provided the advantage of 800 lumens of white light. Scan, dismiss, scan again. *Night becomes day, you son of a bitch.*

Another block made; another intersection. So many hiding spots in this area: an art center; a parking garage; a glass building attempting to stay modern but showing its true age. Historic "Downtown Lafayette" provided a business atmosphere on workdays and a party paradise on the weekends, but on this day, it is still; it's eerily still. He attempted to catch his breath and believed that his target eluded him. The annual Christmas decoration hung from restored streetlights as they did every year. The glow of the holiday offered more light on this cloudless night, but this provided no advantage in locating the demon he pursued. He is exposed; open to his prey.

A loud crack, almost like a firecracker, but without the echo. No sound like it; no feeling so ominous. The sudden impact felt like a freight train hitting him in an area the size of a pencil eraser. One shot, one kill; one of phrases drilled into him at Fort Benning's Sand Hill when he was a younger man, but he never thought of being the victim of that statement. A second impact as he fell to the cold concrete floor of the urban landscape. No soft landing as his body weight and selected accoutrements forced him onto his left side. Vulnerable and unable to move. *I'm still here, asshole.*

The Artist emerged from a parking garage near one of the corners of the intersection. The object of obsession is within his grasp and in his grip is a gun. His vest stopped the bullet from piercing his heart, but the pain he felt was a possible cracked rib, maybe two. The fire in lungs escaped and his panting gave way to his lungs being paralyzed. We wanted to breathe, he needed to breathe, but for a moment his body couldn't perform a simple function. Lying on his left side was uncomfortable, but he still held onto to his lifeline, his ace in the hole, his weapon. *Breathe, but don't move, god damn it!*

His adversary approached him; each step more deliberate, a

slow approach. There was no sound as he inched forward. The ominous figure was bathed in faint holiday lights, but darkened by the shadows offered by the surrounding structures. Savoring the moment when the hunter was now the hunted. Two predators, now one. Nothing like the kill. The thoughts of the man that caused his premature demise flooded his mind. He'll be hailed as a hero. An officer felled gloriously upon the field of battle. They will name a school or street after him. Create scholarships in honor of his sacrifice. Folded flags and a 21-Gun salute to honor him. Valkyries will escort the warrior into the Great Hall. Valhalla awaits. *Fuck that! Just wait for your moment. You'll only get that moment.*

The prize is now over him. He raised the blued steel that paralyzed him temporarily. No face. No sounds. *Now!*

His adrenaline surged and a familiar clarity entered his mind; clarity that only battle can provide. His thoughts were untainted by family, friends, policies, procedures, commendation, or criticism. Only instinct and discipline remained. The mission comes first. Clear objective. Clear line of sight. Clear threat. All force is authorized, even the kind that the media would decry as too aggressive. Right and wrong, good and evil, antagonist and protagonist meet in the ultimate duel. In this moment there is only one outcome: one dead, one alive.

Action beat reaction. His mental clarity and his training become one. As he rolled to his right, he guided his weapon. *Stable platform*. Aim for the sweet spot on the target. *Center mass*. The bazooka in his hand became a handgun again. *Sight picture*. Two pounds of steel. *Sight alignment*. The thumb safety disengaged without conscious thought. The trigger squeeze was fluid, but rapid. *One, Two, Three.* Recoil of the weapon managed through thousands of practice rounds. *Four, Five.* Sound was non-existent, but his vision as sharp as ever. *Six, Seven.* His once piercing blues eyes now black and empty; no remorse, no feelings, just the mission. *Eight, Nine, Slide Lock, Reload.* The metal meeting the meat wasn't like the movies, it never is. The searing copper jacketed hollow-points entered flesh at just under 1000 feet per second and devastated anything in its path, but his target didn't fly backwards. This wasn't a Quentin Tarantino movie where the blood spewed forth like a deranged water fountain; just a slight pink mist. His target fell to the ground, collapsed more like it. Forward and to his right. No words, not even a grunt. Just silent death. A warrior's death. Quick and efficient.

A deep cleansing breath filled his lungs. The clarity he had in the previous moment gave way to the fog of modern society. Humming streetlights, sirens in the background getting louder, and the engines of cars in the distance. The thoughts of his wife and son rush in and grab him like a mother consoling their child. His prize lies on the ground motionless, but in respectful tranquility. A red liquid pools around and under the body of the fallen. A warrior's blood. A worthy adversary. Death came for them both, but only one would be escorted by Charon over the river and into eternity. By living, he assumed the role of storyteller and now the story of this moment was his alone. Only one other possessed the capacity to understand their game and he was no longer for this world. *Goodbye, "old friend." I'll see you in hell.*

Gaining full control of his senses allowed him to stand. He was shaken, but steadfast. He didn't gloat or curse or anything related to celebration. He stood there, quietly and respectfully, staring at the crumpled mass, still unable to see the visage of his fallen foe. He had taken lives before, but it was never personal. He felt the weight of it, but never to this extent. He was both proud of what he accomplished, but sad that the chase was over. His opponent took him beyond the limits of his mental and physical fortitude and now there was only the numbness of the moment and the inevitable aftermath; internal affairs asking the same questions over and over, scores of police officers and psychologists asking if he was feeling O.K., public information officers preening themselves for the inevitable live press conference, and cameras hoping to get a glimpse of the bloody aftermath. For now, there was peace; peace that only death could bring.

He thinks of the last three days and utters two words under his breath, words that have a new meaning. "It's over."

He reengaged the thumb safety and holstered his weapon as he had done so many times before. He gazed at his trophy as the blue and red LED lights became brighter and sirens increase in volume, memorizing this moment like previous times before. Every smell, sound, and nuance etched themselves into his memory. The taste of iron still hung in the air where the mist once existed. Thoughts are, in this moment, his own and there is silence. His stillness would be broken by a familiar phrase and tone.

"Drop your weapon and get on the ground!"

He's heard these words before, said them many times. He felt the barrels of weapons trained on him. The fog of previous events is completely gone now. He's off the grid and just shot a man, or someone who likened themselves to a man. Reality was different and the aftershock would be immense. He turned toward the order, slowly, hands visible.

The deputy repeated his order but now sees the face of who stands before him and the word emblazoned on the front of the vest worn by the man in front of him: POLICE. Still he didn't register it immediately and began to repeat himself.

"Drop your weapon and... It's Gray! Hold your fire!" Mental registration is complete.

Sirens are still blaring at this point and all the lone figure could do was crack a slight smile. *Someone always forgets to turn off their siren.* The storm was behind him and a growing storm before him, but that wouldn't be his concern. Still, the concern of years past weighed heavily on him.

THREE DAYS PRIOR

DAY ONE

"The fury of a demon instantly possessed me. I knew myself no longer. My original soul seemed, at once, to take flight from my body; and a more fiendish malevolence, gin nurtured, thrilled every fibre of my frame."

-Edgar Allen Poe, *The Black Cat*

I.

December 22nd

02:31 AM

327 Highland Hills Drive

Blood was everywhere; spattered across the spacious living room like a sadistic Jackson Pollock painting. Bodies of three, maybe four people strewn about the open space. It was hard for the demon to remember how many he slaughtered in the previous hours. The chaos of the previous evening filled his mind like a sweet dream – pleasurable, but hazy.

This sinful figure collected the heads of the recently deceased and laid them in a row on a coffee table. *One, two, three, four*. Two men and two women. Each face had different expressions on them, but they all bore the sight of death. Each pair of eyes were empty, mouths open, tongues removed. The detached bodies laid on the floor in a row in the same order as the heads, but in a shape familiar to the properly initiated. It was a carefully, deliberately placed message to one. *Detached, but still together*. It was a gruesome sight for those that didn't understand the beauty of death or the glory of their final moments. *They will never know what they did for me, and I thank them for their generosity.* Each body suffered a tremendous amount of trauma, but they remained alive until they were decapitated. It was only after their demise that the message was perfected.

After pridefully viewing his newest canvas from an open, raised walkway connecting a staircase to upstairs bedrooms, the budding artist decided to take a shower. He brought with him a black trash bag containing a full change of clothes. He picked up the "brushes" that he used to create the art prior to making his decision to wash up. The sharpened steel and serrated edges were covered with the paint of his choosing. He couldn't help but be infatuated with the mixture of blood and water as it filled the basin of the shower.

"It's magnificent," he said to himself. His tanned frame filled the shower; tall and muscular. As the water drained, he searched for any signs of dark hair and if he found any, he placed it in the plastic bag that he brought with him. *No evidence for the detectives to find.* As he searched, he thought back to his night.

Two couples, obviously family members by blood and marriage. Sipping drinks at a local watering hole: Fracture. None had any idea that an artist was in their midst. They smiled and laughed without a care in the world, enjoying the holiday spirit, as it were. He went unrecognized, as was his nature for the moment. He wished to remain unseen by his canvases until it was time for them to experience his mastery of the arts.

"Ah, I found you," he muttered as he found a small hair. He picked up the small object and placed the hair in a plastic bag typically used to seal sandwiches, but on this day holds a deeper meaning for it. His hands were no longer excitedly shaking as they had during his work.

The men were fit and young, the women beautiful and well-toned. Obviously, they cared about their appearance. Those around them taken in by their exteriors. They prepared themselves for his brush strokes.

"And another." He performed the same process with this hair as he did with the previous one.

They entered their luxury sedan and drove away. Most likely still laughing and preparing for a good night's rest. The driver manipu-

lated the vehicle well, for the most part. Obviously, there was some influence from the night's levity, but well, nonetheless.

"Scrub, scrub, scrub. There can be no paint outside of the studio, my dear." The brush was also retrieved from the black plastic bag, obviously new. The Artist always supplied his own ways of making sure that everything was perfect. Opportunistic material could prove unacceptable, especially when viewed by those knowing what they are looking for.

The recently departed driver parked his car on the roadway, legally but slightly crooked. He obviously did not see the black car behind them, nor did he see where it parked. No situational awareness and completely unaware that greatness was going to reveal itself.

The remainder of what happened prior to the master's first stroke was blurred, partially by uncontrollable desire and primarily from deft movements. Both men immediately incapacitated with well-placed blows to the head and both women screaming from within the luxury home. I love rich paints. They always have good soundproofing. Flashes of knives cutting skin, bodies tearing, and bones breaking relieved him of the depression of the completing the work. Tongues being cut out in order to work in a tranquil space and for their transgressions. This was what he lived for; creation after chaos.

"What shall I do, today," he said to himself as he reached into the trash bag and retrieved a vacuum sealed package containing fresh folded clothing. "Shall I go for breakfast or go home for rest?"

As he dressed himself, he admired the physique that he created. Countless hours of training, both in the gym and in violence, molded the man he viewed in the mirror. This admiration was constant, but necessary in his mind. Imperfection had no place here and he must remain vigilant for the fights that were to come.

"I am ready for this, but is he?"

The devil inside urged him to give into the necessary functions for life. This would serve a dual purpose: replenishing expended calories burned from his evening frivolities and looking for new canvases. The rational side told him to rest and not expose himself after his stroke of genius. Besides, his canvases were already chosen and a deviation from his plan would imply lack of control. *That will not do, not for me.* Caution and fatigue won the battle within him.

"I have food at the house, my dear. A hearty home-cooked breakfast and rest would do some good."

He would leave his studio several minutes later, his newest masterpiece to be enjoyed by all and being careful not to step in the "paint" left over. The grim study of these bodies would terrify and confound the mass of uniforms that will eventually descend upon this house, but for now there is prideful reflection. He knew there was no evidence to find. He was careful, mindful of who his potential opponent would be. *An old friend. He'll understand my message and know that I have been thinking of him.*

"In all my travels I have never beheld such beauty, my dear. This will be my finest work." The bodies before him were beautiful in life, more beautiful than any other canvas before. In silent rest they were magnificent. Born anew in his vision for them. He stood motionless for a moment and was nearly brought to tears by the impact of it all. His first piece completed. His masterpiece started. Before leaving his studio, he left a small opening in one of the splendid window drapes. This was his final touch for this work before leaving.

"Whew, it's getting colder." The Artist entered the real world again. The air was crisp and the forecasted cold front in full force. He dawned his jacket and began to walk away from his macabre work, grinning from ear to ear like the Cheshire Cat. He parked his vehicle in a darkened area further down the street. An empty, new construction where day laborers worked for a pittance of the potential selling price. No cars, no people, just a town peacefully sleeping off the remainder of the evening. There were other houses in the area, but none lit by the life of their occupants at this early hour.

His vehicle is as luxurious as his "art material's" vehicle, a black Mercedes E-Class. The push button start offered the convenience of not only starting the engine, but also adjusting his seat upon ignition. *I deserve this after my show.* His radio is constantly on talk-radio. He loved hearing the pundits and the talking heads spew forth political ideology. Gay rights, transgender bathrooms, white supremacy, abortion; all of it was tantamount to court jesters entertaining the king. He scoffed as one special guest congresswoman stated that she cared about the abortion issue and the most important issue is women having the freedom to choose.

"You don't give a shit about that! You really think that women are so stupid as to be single-issue voters! You just care about walking the party line and reelection! God, I hate fake people," he yelled at his radio, as he so often did when he knew someone was dishonest. Honesty was his domain. He never lied to anyone unless it was to reveal the truth later.

Another fool of the court then responded with the preservation of life argument. Every life is sacred. This enraged The Artist because he knew that this buffoon was a puppet for the special interest, required to make an argument for whatever side paid her the most.

He again yells at his radio, "You charlatan! No better than a prostitute flaunting your body on a street corner!" Angered by the voices on his radio spewing purchased sincerity but unwilling to turn the dial. *I know there is music I could listen to, but today's music is pure shit.*

Contempt for the illusion of truth. Truth, to him, was the most important aspect of humanity. He couldn't respect a person that would make an argument using other people's plight. He remembered a conversation where a young man made a stand on the legalization of marijuana based on people with medical conditions and he told the college student that he could respect the position more if the pupil admitted that he wanted to legally get high with his friends and didn't care about people with glaucoma or cancer. It would've been a terrible reason, but at least it would've been honest.

He saw through the hypocrisy and the lies, but he knew that there was only one person who never lied to him. He knew that he and that man would be reunited soon. Connected in viciousness and always pure in word. The trauma of future events cascading into an inevitable duel between two honest men. The Artist versus The Saint.

My old friend, Silas.

****

The world slept, but not the same as he did. He drifted away earlier in the evening and dreamed of days gone by. The violence of his past haunted him, but he welcomed it. Some would say that he suffered from a condition, but he saw it as building strength for the fight before him. The demons that came for him every night held no sway. He wouldn't be startled from his resting place. He would fight them on the physical battlefield as well as the mental and the imagined points of engagement. He was a peaceful man and slept as such, but this peace was purchased in blood. A better statement would be that he chose to be a peaceful man, and, in that choice, he buried the darkness within him every day only to be met by that darkness in his dreams. The battle within him raged. He wouldn't succumb to his demons on this night or any other.

Hell awaited him, but for now there was only rest.

II.

8:02 AM

Beep, click

Admission into the brick building was always secured. The key card in his wallet allowed him access to just about everywhere, save the most sensitive areas and the commanders' offices. A short walk through the city council chambers and then another secure door.

Beep, click

Another notification; another confirmation of still having a job to do. *First door on the right and then to my chair.*

Beep, click

Success! I still have an office. The plaque next to the door had two names: Detective Silas Gray, Detective Sean Guthrie. Nothing fancy, just a holder with a piece of paper sandwiched in between two small glass panes. Easily changed, easily moved. He never liked the name Silas; too old school for his taste, but it was a family name. He preferred to use Gray as a moniker. Something that he got used to when he was in the Army serving as an infantry officer.

He entered the well-worn office and couldn't help but notice the wall art. His side contained a mix of undergraduate and graduate academic achievements and a few important law enforcement milestones. An officer of the year plaque, his law enforcement certification, and a canvas picture of a winged police officer holding a child's hand. The latter decoration was given to him by his son who looked at his "daddy" as a "vampire slayer." Even at the young age of six, Gray's son knew that his father battled monsters, he just didn't know how accurate his youthful description was. His partner's side was more eclectic but contained just as many professional accolades. Hand-drawn pictures by children – nieces and nephews – intermixed with pictures of random objects: a bayou campsite painting, a rabbit missing an ear, a photo of military men in company formation. This was a cop's office, no mistaking it.

He sat at his desk and stared at his computer screen for a moment, as was his habit, and sipped his coffee. He read the e-mails from the previous patrol shift. Some public disturbances, a few thefts, traffic accidents, and several public contacts to let people know that we were there for them. He always held high regard for the public contacts. Some of the names were the same and they were people or businesses always on the list. Other names were new and in more blue-collar areas. Contentment entered him when reading these highlighted areas of concern. Happily accepting the opportunity to work in the low-crime town of Broussard, Louisiana. This was a welcome reprieve from humanity's darkness, his darkness. Nothing exciting, at least not in comparison to his previous experiences.

Two doors down were the clerk's office and another secure lock. Gray liked to talk to the clerks in the morning. He knew that if he was nice to them, then they would help him out when he needed it, but moreover, he also enjoyed the morning banter. The banter was usually innocuous and unrelated to police work.

Beep, click

"Good morning, ladies!"

The response was something out of a *Charlies Angels*, but neither Gray nor the clerks were alive during the show's original run.

"Mornin', Gray," two of the three responded.

"Mornin', Sally. Beard's looking a little grayer this morning," said the third. This was an inside joke that started about a year prior when a victim asked for "Sally Gray" and then referred to him as the "Old Detective."

"Anything interesting today, ladies?" Gray asked without thinking. The answers were a mix of funny stories from the previous night and "nothing really." The conversation lasted a few minutes and consisted of laughing, mostly. He didn't pay much attention to the content. He just enjoyed the light-heartedness.

"Well, back to the dungeon. Call me if you need me." Before departing the company of the ladies, Gray raided the candy drawer for Tootsie Rolls. The ladies knew that he had an affinity for this candy and would purposely place them at the top of the box holding the sweet treats.

"Success, yet again," Gray said with a coy smile, "No treat is safe."

Gray walked back to his well-worn chair and unwrapped his pilfered treasure. He then began plucking manila folders out his stack. An endless supply of misdemeanors, some felonies, and headaches. This particular case has a cat stolen from the complainant's yard. According to the report, this was a "special" cat that supplied the owner with an endless supply of fried pork chops. Gray laughed at the insanity behind the complaint and the sarcasm that the report had intermixed with pertinent facts. He couldn't make this up if he tried. If it's on the page, then it happened. A subsequent phone call to the victim confirmed the story. *I'm a long way from my old agency, but people are still crazy.*

The investigations were seemingly mundane, but Gray was content. He was an investigator for a larger agency about two years before this day and saw more than his fair share of excitement. Robberies, rapes, drugs, and homicides were common and the workload exhausting. Kicking doors and heavy body armor were an everyday thing, but not anymore. Nine years of "skull-cracking" took its toll, physically and emotionally. Four years of military service before that. He still missed the excitement, but not the hassle. Deciding to go to a department of 36 officers serving 11,000 people was a far cry from the hellscape of a city and parish out of control and 320 officers doing everything in their power to keep the wolves at bay. He was still healthy at the age of 37, but his body took the brunt of combat – "Over There" and in "The Streets." Still in good shape, his taller than average frame held up a powerful structure. Broad-shouldered with a penchant for fitness, he maintained a honed dexterity and a layer of softness, particularly in the love handles. Blunt force trauma meeting agility meeting gumbo and potato salad. He enjoyed the cuisine of "Cajun Country" too much to concern himself with ripped abs. He believed in being strong, quick, and enjoying the simple things. His calmness would often defy a tense situation, but this was his way and his way served him well throughout the years, much to the irritation of his superiors at times.

This is my new normal and I welcome it!

****

10:08 AM

His partner, Sean Guthrie, always comes in well before his allotted time of 10:30. Task-oriented, to the point, but always pleasant, at least to Gray. Sean was a prior service Marine, but an atypical Marine. Eclectic, some would say eccentric, intelligent, and mission-driven. He didn't speak or act like a man of his experience but was proud of his service. Standing slightly taller than Gray and built like a runner. You wouldn't know it by looking at him, but he was a martial artist and usually carried a variety of blades on him at any given time and offered combative instruction to anyone who showed interest. If Gray were the hammer, then Sean was the scalpel. High energy, nimble, fluid, and precise would be the best way to describe Sean.

"Hey, hey!" Sean's typical greeting. "How was your night?"

Sean walked in with an arm full of papers and a laptop. Gray tried to keep Sean from bringing work home with him but to no avail. Gray hid the laptop once, but, as detectives usually do, Sean found it.

"Good, until I fell asleep and woke up having to come to work."

"Well, it's better than the alternative," Sean said without missing a beat, "You could've woke-up having breakfast with your ancestors." His statement had a hint of gallows humor, which both men shared. Their time in the military and on the streets molded a dark sense of humor, some would say inappropriate, but it was always good-natured.

Gray responded, "True. They were boring, anyway."

"How's the wife and kid?".

"They're good. They left yesterday afternoon. I'll be joining them in the next few days."

"Awesome, send them my best when you talk to them." Sean was a laser-focused individual, but always had time for pleasantries. With Gray, this extended to friendship.

"And you," Gray asked. "What are your plans?"

"See my mom and my dad, my brother, and his wife and kids. Drink a little. Still loving the bachelor lifestyle and I save money this time of year."

"Yup, I remember those days. I had money and freedom," Gray said with a smirk. "But I wouldn't trade it for the world."

Each man sipped their coffee at their respective desks and shared information about what they were doing that day. Each had a plan, but rarely did the day go the way they wanted. This was a small department. Something was always going on and someone would inevitably disturb the plan. Neither man minded the distraction, but it would become bothersome at times, almost annoying. When annoyed, just go to plan B: shut the door. It was a subtle way of telling people to "fuck off" and this tactic worked most of the time. They liked the freedom to do what they pleased and didn't want to answer questions about their cases. That information would be conveyed to their supervisor, then to their supervisor's supervisor and so on. *Let us alone to do the job, just the way we like it!*

Gray and Sean appeared to be opposites. Gray's desk was orderly to a point of OCD. Sean's desk was full of papers and Post-It notes. Despite the appearance, both men trusted each other implicitly and shared the same thought processes when investigating a case. They were generalist investigators, and, individually, they were proficient at their chosen fields of expertise – Gray with violent crimes and financial crimes and Sean with violent crimes and sexually-based offenses. Together, they were a force to be reckoned with. Sean was not as experienced with violent crimes but had a knack for it. His attention to detail was impressive. Gray admitted this fact on several occasions, but whatever he lacked in this talent he made up for with knowledge. Both men complete gentlemen and friends and both capable mentally and physically.

The two men performed their assigned functions like a well-oiled machine: a follow-up phone call here, a report there, a visit from the clerks or other officers. The best part about the holiday season was that demand for their services diminished as Christmas Day neared. Each man had their theories and each theory plausible as to why crime declined during this time, but the reason didn't matter. They wanted to walk into their extended holiday weekend with as little excitement as possible. The cold weather and reduced need suited them just fine. Little did they know that this holiday would bring them to the brink of their respective mental and physical capabilities and strain their relationship.

Friends, partners, brothers.

III.

Noon

Worry slowly crept into the mind of The Artist as he wondered if anyone found his newest creation. He was not worried about being found out, that was inevitable given his fellow combatant. He worried about his work losing the full assault on the senses of those who gazed longingly at it.

"I hope they find it soon. I would hate for one of the five senses to lose out on the experience, especially sight and smell," he said to himself as he sipped his coffee and gazed into the cityscape that he adored so much.

Although animalistic in nature, he enjoyed the finer things in life. His vehicle was luxury. His seventh-floor studio apartment also luxurious. High ceilings, comfortable furniture, exposed wooden beams, the artwork was strewn about the interior, stainless steel appliances, and well-placed knick-knacks and complimentary decorations filled the space. One could say that it was a high-end bachelor pad, but this was a connoisseur's retreat. Artists do not live like this and he was nowhere near starving, as the saying would have you believe.

"I have rested as much as I care to, my dear. I believe that I will go to the gym." He spoke as if someone were in the room, but he was himself the only occupant. *Am I insane? No! I am special and soon everyone will know it.*

He grabbed prepared gym and garment bags and allowed

himself a quick look in the mirror. Many would say that he was the picture of health, but he always saw room for improvement. Today, he was repulsed by the small amount of fat under his chin, something that he could not help because of genetics. He exited the abode and walked a well-trodden path, reaching the stairwell and descending it to the parking garage. As he walked to his car his determination to rid himself of imperfection replaced his worry for the glory of his creation. A short drive and he would be improving himself. *How can my work be so perfect when I, myself, am imperfect?*

Entry into the gym was restricted to members only. A key fob allowed entry for only those worthy of paying the steep monthly price Gymnase de Lafayette. *They do love their French culture here. Peasants!*

"Good morning, sir! Good to see you again." The perkiness of the desk clerk annoyed him as he entered. He knew that this was false and forced.

"Good morning, my dear," he responded as the smiling beauty behind the desk handed him a white gym towel. *Always white. Never anything fitting a man of my talent and discerning tastes.*

"Please let us know if there is anything that we can do for you today!"

His irritation with the perfectly tanned, beautiful young woman grew with every disingenuous syllable. "I will. Thank you." *She would make a perfect canvas, but I dare not harm her, such a young woman. She's only doing her job.*

He entered the locker room and was disgusted by the sea of humanity that filled these hallowed halls of improvement. Imperfection, as he saw it, everywhere. This was a far cry from the beauty he created just hours before. Sagging skin and beer bellies repulsed his delicate sensibilities. He did not care that they were there to change themselves, he only cared that he had to see it.

"Mornin, gentlemen," he said entering this palace of flawed flesh and using common words, which he hated. He received the usual pleasantries, but no time for small talk. Changing into his well-worn gym clothes, only one thought entered his mind: perfection awaits.

He observed "his kind" in the free weight area. Men and women of perfect symmetry and tone. Young and middle-aged, all beautiful. Muscles bulged with every repetition and tendons strained with every movement. This was his peace, his Zen, his work in progress. *No time to talk, just work.* Approving head nods and chin raises added to his sense of self. Approval from his fellow practitioners of perfection. Another day and another opportunity to perfect himself and show others what a pure body can do.

His routine began with the insertion of earbuds. Classical music played as he lifted weights that would crush lesser men. He never paid much attention to the music, only the work, but he knew that only master strokes of musical perfection were on his level. He was a man possessed. Repetition after repetition, set after set. No time for rest, only work. "Tourists" watched the man jump from exercise to exercise without missing a beat. His form, perfect. His repetition count, high. His determination, undeniable. Every movement was accompanied by a new bead of sweat. *Imperfection leaving this body. Truth in pain.* He received several glances from "his people," both male and female. Some gazed upon him with minor curiosity and others with lust in their eyes. He coveted the attention but hated that they admired his physical form and not his skill.

He finished before the end of Mozart's *Requiem.* This was, however, the second long-form musical selection that he enjoyed during his "improvement" time, following Brahms' *Piano Concerto No. 2.* Sweat soaked his clothing and glistened on his exposed skin. An almost angelic glow. As he finished, he began to clean the respective machines and benches that he used on his last set. Most would look at this as courtesy for others wishing to use the equipment, but he found this assumption absurd. *They are not worthy of my improvements, even if it is imperfection leaving my body.*

"Have a good one guys," he said as he exited the weight area. Again, he despised the ordinary tongue, but this made him more accessible to potential canvases. The unqualified love believing that they are on the same level.

He entered the locker room and observed, yet again, what he loathed. There was no outward reflection of repulsion, but he thought it. *Social graces are intact.*

He showered and changed into clothing befitting a man of his gifts. Fitted medium gray suit, perfectly tailored, with a white shirt. Shoes and belt complimenting the two-button Italian silk ensemble. White gold watch. Fashionable, yet utilitarian. Dark hair perfectly coiffed in the latest style. No need for a second look in the body mirror near the exit, he knew that flawlessness needed no such reassurance. *I must seduce those that wish to model for me.*

The towel given to him by the perky blonde at the front door was discarded in a bin near the entrance.

"Have a great day, sir," the young lady said without missing a beat, "See you tomorrow."

"You too, my dear," he responded with irritation beginning

to set in again, "I'll be seeing you."

He felt a sense of anger as he turned away from the receptionist. Exiting a temple of imperfection and false acceptance annoyed him. Truth cannot be found in this structure where so much emphasis is placed on improvement. People here are more counterfeit than the lips and breasts of some who occupy this sanctuary of flawed existence. *My inner sanctum.* Fake hellos, fake goodbyes, pleasant dispositions for by the almighty minimum wage, and constant reminders of those that exist to be rejected as his future "works" antagonized him. Despite his deep contempt for this false idolatry, he would return again and again, to improve upon his flaws, however minor they may be, and search for those worthy of his attention. Return visits also steeled his resolve against the hideousness of the physical world. He knew this was a contradiction and justified it as a necessity. *I wonder if my old friend will figure this out. I'm sure he will.*

Leaving the parking lot was a welcome occurrence and, as usual, talk radio acting as the white noise for his drive. Today's topic was improving Louisiana's educational system. His responses to the topic at hand were as pure as they could have been; a mix of carefully selected profanities and indictments of those claiming to purvey truth. He alone knew the truth, but these people were inferior and undeserving of his truth. Only one deserved his pure certainty.

"Have you found them yet, my friend? Are you on your way? Do you appreciate what I have done for you? I hope you appreciate how much care I took to create this for you," he says aloud as the pundits are silenced by commercial breaks.

Reveling in this day will be a welcome reprieve from previous days without his friend.

IV.

The radio crackled with a new "adventure" for uniformed patrol. The two officers receiving the call read the comments offered by the computer aided dispatch system, CAD as it was commonly called. One officer determined it to be something that administration needed to know, so he created the necessary e-mail notification.

High Priority Call

Location: 327 Highland Hills Drive

Incident # 19-007895

Signal: 107C – Suspicious Circumstance

Details: Neighbor walking her dog saw a vehicle partially in the roadway. Believes that the owner of the vehicle may be hurt because he never parks his vehicle in the roadway. Tried knocking on door, no response. Looked through front window and saw someone lying on the ground.

EMS and Fire en-route.

The messaging system for the department notified the command staff and detectives of circumstances that may require more attention. This system proved to be both annoying and helpful. Annoying in that it would wake you up in the middle of the night and helpful in that you got the heads up if something "really" happened. Anything from traffic incidents to major crimes was sent through this system.

Responding officers arrived at the house about two minutes after dispatch. The town was large enough to accommodate most needs but small enough to arrive promptly. As they approached the stucco coated canopy, they had a moment of levity. They spoke about something other than the job at hand. This was their way to prepare for what may be inside. Soon, this moment would sour, but for the moment they were oblivious to what awaited them.

They saw what the neighbor who, at this moment, felt like Nancy Drew. The neighborhood detective in a jacket, yoga pants, and the all-important comfortable walking shoes. *They grow on trees in this town.*

"I called it in officer," she stated as the officers approached the luxurious residence. "Brian never parks his card in the road, unless he's had too much to drink, and I saw a person lying on the ground. I only saw a leg, but it was weird. I think he passed out."

"Thank you, ma'am," started the younger officer, "We'll check it out."

The younger officer commented on the neighbor's attire to his partner as they approached the house. "It's definitely too cold for those pants, but I'm sure she's not wearing those to stay warm."

The older officer cracked a smile. "Yup, definitely trying to get noticed. It worked!"

The younger officer laughed a bit and slyly looked at his partner, "Well, you're old, not dead, I guess."

"Smart-ass," the more season man retorted without a second's hesitation.

Both men approached the door cautiously and, in a manner, that their respective training officers would be proud of. Two generations of police officers but working as one. They knocked and announced. No response. This pattern repeated two more times. The older officer then approached a window with a slight opening in the curtains.

"Body," he said forcefully. They both knew that this would be considered an exigent circumstance because they needed to get in immediately.

"Comm, I have one lying on the ground, no movement inside of the house. Residence secured. Forcing entry."

"*10-4,*" was the reply.

Both officers drew their weapons and braced for entry. The younger officer's kick was perfect: boot just under the doorknob. The heavy wooden door opened with incredible velocity but slowed when it hit the wall. Textbook forced entry under these circumstances.

The sight of it overwhelmed the senses. The Artist knew that he would receive nothing but praise in the form of gasps and curses. It was his plan.

Panicking at the sight, the younger officer exclaims, "Uh, Comm, I have a situation here! I need additional units ASAP!"

"*Are you Code 4?*"

"Negative, Comm. We have, um, multiple people down at this location." Composure could not overtake the shock of it all. "Revise this to a...uh... homicide and have a, uh, supervisor and
detectives respond."

The concerned neighbor peaked inside. Taken by the scene she let out a scream that curdled the blood of anyone within earshot. Her legs gave out from under her and, for a moment, all faculties left. The overwhelming sight was too much to bear, but not enough to look away. Instantly, she was warmed by the sensation of fear. Her pulse raced. Her jacket became a furnace stoked by Lucifer himself.

"What....h-h-h-happened?" the neighbor asked. Her words sounding more like a child than an adult.

"Ma'am, I need you to go to the front of my car and don't move from that spot," the seasoned veteran yelled back. She was obviously in shock but did as she was told. The officer was just as horrified at the sight, but more experienced to the job. His composure came with the gray hair peppered in the sea a black. He was no stranger to stress, but this shook him to his core. Four bodies carefully placed under four severed heads. Each body partially dismembered and twisted into a recognizable pattern. The blood on the walls formed Christian and Satanic symbols, whimsical flowers and birds, and phallic and vaginal references. These were the ornate borders of this well-thought-out invitation. This was his version of a greeting card or, more appropriately, a return visit announcement.

The officers proceeded to clear the house of threats to their safety. They walked up a stairway that led to a raised walkway over the living room. Luxury knows how to make an impression. There were many gatherings here, no doubt, and this raised area would allow the hosts to view their guests from a position of authority. A common tactic for those maintaining status above someone else. After clearing bedrooms and bathrooms on the second floor, the officers proceed back from whence they came but only the senior officer glances down at the revulsion below him and is instantly frozen. He sees what was meant to be seen and does not comprehend the meaning.

"I think it spells something," the older officer calls to his young partner who is now at the bottom of the staircase. "It's a word."

It wasn't a word; it was a request left by the host of this last gathering. Intentional and gruesome. Limbs positioned in unnatural ways to form the letters specific to the occasion. The revelation would prove too much for many to comprehend, but some – the properly initiated – would understand its singular connotation.

V.

"I hate High Priorities, man. They always make a big deal out of things." Sean knew it was necessary, but it was not high on his list of favorite things. Far from it.

"Just wait until they have something. Probably a drunk that passed out from too much fun the night before. Hair of the dog and shower will cure it."

Both men were immune to the "emergency" notifications and went about their business. Still, they both raised the volume of their radios and listened for anything that may spur them into action. This was their practice for everything that didn't come out as a serious call. They listened for certain signals that would call for an immediate response, but for now nothing. No response was necessary.

Another sip of coffee and another chirp from the radio.

"*Uh, Comm, I have a situation here! I need additional units ASAP!*"

"*Are you Code 4?*"

"*Negative, Comm. We have, um, multiple people down at this location. Revise this to a…uh… homicide and have a, uh, supervisor and detectives respond.*"

Gray and Sean immediately looked at one another but said nothing. Each prepared themselves for what was about to happen. Action now, think later. Both men run from their desks, making sure to grab their keys, cell phones, and radios. Everything they needed was in their police vehicles.

The men responded to the residence quickly and without hesitation in Sean's department vehicle. Years of police work in this area taught them the roads to use at certain parts of the day to arrive quickly to emergency calls. Beyond that, each man prepared themselves for the horror that was to come. There is no "getting used" to a homicide scene. These scenes are usually the worst to recover from, some more than others. Some are bloody and some are clean. Regardless, they had a job to do and they would fulfill the mission.

Crime scene tape surrounded the house and the lone witness, "Nancy Drew," was sequestered by one of the responding officers. The older officer had a clipboard and a crime scene log. Only those living can write on this page. The gaze of the discovery officer was affixed to Gray as he waited to place his John Hancock on the page, but Gray's focus was getting into the house and not on people that he knew. After scrawling their illegible signatures on the official document, the men enter the house, fully prepared for what they were about to see. Or so they thought.

"My God," Sean said upon entry, "This looks like a Rob Zombie film."

Gray gave no outward response but agreed with his partner. He analyzed the broken bits of humanity in the living room and the profane wall decorations for what seemed like an eternity. His eternity only lasted for several seconds. His senses immediately heightened. He smelled the unmistakable aroma of dried and drying blood. Decay was not set in, too soon and too cold for that, but rigor was in effect. The previously living now permanently fixed in their respective situations.

"They were alive before he cut the heads off," Gray finally stated. "The arterial spray patterns are unmistakable. They were tortured and then murdered. One by one. Each one seeing what their future held." *Fucking monster!*

He dared not touch the bodies before the coroner and crime scene technicians from a neighboring agency arrived. Initial examinations of the scene only. Initial pictures only.

Sean observed the minutia of the scene. Looking closely at the images on the walls. Crosses, pentagrams, penises, vaginas, flowers, and birds. The blood now dry, but the trails of crimson following gravity's direction toward the floor.

"Satan worship," Sean began. "Possibly sexually driven. But the other images are a bit of an outlier."

Gray came to the same conclusion but wasn't convinced of the motive. He'd been here before and yet this was new territory. He felt a familiarity with the scene. This was not random. It was not without thought. This was planned, every detail of the scene held meaning. They were on display, but for what reason? Who is the intended audience? At this moment he realized that there were rhyme and reason for this passage, but what? He was missing the big picture at this moment. Something he rarely did.

Both men left the residence and awaited the inevitable search warrant for the house to be approved by a judge. The electronic submission system allowed easy work of putting everything together. Probable cause was undeniable for this situation. Finding a person of proper education and election was a different story, but on this day the response was almost immediate. A judge signed the warrant that allowed for evidence collection. *Thanks, judge! Freezing my ass over here.* The army of officers waiting for entry was just as relieved. Jackets and knit caps offered no protection from the wind and humidity that arrived with the most recent arctic gift.

By the time entry was made into the house, Gray and Sean were accompanied by their supervisor, Lt. Rodney Malcolm Castile, or "Rod" as "his guys" called him, Lt. Castile to everyone else. He didn't mind the nickname given to him by "his guys" and rather enjoyed it because of the potential juvenile humor associated with such a nom de guerre. Rod was tall and an overt physical presence with a freshly shorn head covered by a wool knit cap. He spoke with a bit of a Cajun accent but showed a level of intelligence far beyond what some would assume he had based on his use of common vernacular. He never pushed his intellect on others, but rather enjoyed being underestimated. Formidable would be the best adjective to describe him. He cared for the guys under his command, often urging them to do the job and damn the consequences and at the same time knowing when to "pump the brakes." Rod gleefully took tongue lashings from his superiors when his guys did something perceived to be careless, but if it worked, he took such berating with a sly grin and would explain why it was done that way. If it didn't work, then he still had the sly smile and would let such things roll off his back. He could speak to anyone and calm down any situation with no effort, a skill learned over two decades of law enforcement. A true leader and one that his guys would follow into hell. *Don't sweat the small stuff, because everything is small stuff.*

"Well, fellas," started Rod, "What kind of heinous fuckery did you step into this time? Especially you, Silas."

Gray sarcastically responded, "Hello, gorgeous. Welcome to the shit show."

Gray never said anything about Rod calling him by his "government" name. It showed familiarity and a segue into eventual humor between the two.

"It's all Gray's fault," added Sean, "He told me earlier that he thought it was going to be a quiet day." The Q-word was not allowed in this business. In law enforcement, this small word was akin to a full moon or a black cat crossing your path.

Without missing a beat, Rod responded, "Fucking, Gray!"

No response from the victim in this onslaught, just acceptance. *I'm a shit magnet, I know it, I accept it.*

Crime scene detectives from the area's Metro Crime Scene photographed the scene and collected evidence as the three men – Rod, Gray, and Sean – exchanged words, mostly humorous jabs at one another. This process took the most time and was tedious. The three brothers in arms would wait for the all-clear to examine the bodies after evidence was photographed and collected. For now, there was lightheartedness amid death.

"Detectives!" A stern, concerned voice emanating from the house. "You might want to see this."

As they approached, all felt the chill of excitement run through their veins. They initially believed that they were about to view the lynchpin to an investigation that just began, a Rosetta Stone if you will. The face on the crime scene tech told another, grimmer story. A cold stare in Gray's direction and a familiar suspicious look told Gray something was amiss. He knew the man making the discovery well or at least well enough to know something wasn't right.

Rod took the camera and viewed the genesis of the group's beckoning. His usual jovial and inquisitive demeanor devolved into concern. A concern that a parent would have for a child or a friend for another friend in need.

"Gray, I need you to come with me." The statement was filled with concern, but unmistakably an order from a superior.

"What's up, Rod? Whatcha got?"

"Silas." Gray knew that it was serious at this moment. "Have you ever been to this house?"

Confused, Gray responded, "No. Never had a reason to come here."

"The situation here has changed. You will not be working this case," Rod's demeanor somewhat softened hearing Gray's denial of being at the house, "Sean will take it from here. You're out."

"What?! Hell, no! What happened? This is bullshit, Rod! Sean and I are a team." Gray protested as any good partner would do. Sean provided a similar protest, but this was a fight that neither would win.

Rod then turned the camera's LCD screen toward Gray and showed him what caused his dismissal. Gray stared at the image of the broken, battered, and bruised bodies for several seconds then looked at Rod, and again affixed his gaze on the screen. More confusion. Questions. Fear. A very real fear after seeing the image. The murderer's signature penned in the atrocity before his eyes. He felt warmth in his gut that could only come from the possibility of punishment. It was a feeling foreign to him, yet very close. His work, up to this moment, never yielded much by way of discipline. A scolding here and there, but never the feeling of a child punished for an action.

"Let's talk at the office," Rod said as he walked ahead of Gray and both men entered Rod's department-issued SUV. Sean stood in stunned silence next to the crime scene tech, confounded as he watched his friend, his partner being whisked away from a scene that they both should be working together.

****

"I'm Maria Gomez for KNAC Channel 4 News."

After receiving the all-clear, the reporter retreated into the warmth of the news vans. Hot chocolate would warm the body and a cigarette would warm her soul. She only opted for the drink in her hands as she was trying to quit such a nasty habit. Her body craved nicotine.

"What's next on the agenda, Tom?" she asked politely. "Please tell me it's something better than ducks getting a new crosswalk."

Chirp

"Uh, Comm, I have a situation here! I need additional units ASAP!"

"Are you Code 4?"

"Negative, Comm. We have, um, multiple people down at this location. Revise this to a...uh... homicide and have a, uh, supervisor and detectives respond."

Chirp

"Did you hear that?! Let's go!"

"Maria, that's not our beat," Tom said.

Maria shot back, "Don't care, get your ass in here, NOW! I'm driving!"

Maria wasn't accustomed to following the rules and adhering to invisible lines of demarcation. She knew that the only way to get a good story was to be first and to be accurate. She was young but old-school. She learned the craft from her father who was a producer for television news stations for 35 years. She remembered her father directing her toward a different path and, like her father, did what she wanted to do. At 28, she was very accomplished as a journalist. She investigated corruption in a neighboring parish's clerk of court office and won several awards for uncovering truths that were supposed to remain hidden. Beautiful, intelligent, and driven. Her father wished that she would settle down and give him grandchildren, but that was not her path for now, if ever.

"You know that we're gonna be in some deep shit, right," Tom explained as Maria broke every traffic law in the book and a few criminal laws. Tom knew that his words fell on deaf ears. She had a story and it was going to be hers. "I can't believe I let you have a police scanner installed."

No response, just a grin. She decided early on in life to do what couldn't be done. She only stood five and a half feet tall but commanded adherence to her will. Lesser people would recoil at her obvious nature, but many just acquiesced in hopes that they would not incite her fury.

"We'll be there in 15 to 20 minutes, Tom. Get everything ready."

"Just don't kill us. I have a wife and two cats that depend on me," Tom nervously replied as he crawled into the rear of the van and began prepping. Deep down he hoped that this was a joke, but he knew Maria couldn't resist a hot story and resigned himself to living in Maria's world as an unwilling resident.

"This could be considered kidnapping, Maria," Tom yelled

from the back of the van, "I am officially being held against my will and transported to a place that I don't want to go! You're committing a criminal act and that is what I'm telling our producer when he fires us."

Maria giggled at the statement.

"Tom, you're being "kidnapped" by a woman half your size. That should make for interesting talk around the office. If anyone asks, tell them I threatened to break your legs. I'm sure they'll believe that."

Tom smiled and nodded. He knew that if it became an issue that he could say that, and the higher-ups would believe it.

"Fine, Margo," Tom yelled back, "I got your back on this, again."

Maria knew that Tom was all-in when she heard his term of endearment for her. She detested any kind of pet name, but from Tom, she accepted it completely. These two were partners, but more than that they were friends, fast friends. They believed in backing each other's play, even if it was constantly Tom backing up Maria in whatever hairbrained situation that they both found themselves in.

Traffic was surprisingly light for this time of day. This was primarily due to schools being shut down for the Christmas holiday and people wishing to remain indoors as much as possible in the cold weather. South Louisiana was not acclimated to the cold. The sub-tropical climate dictated t-shirts and shorts most of the year, but this cold snap force people to seek warmth as quickly as possible, especially with the wind blowing as hard as it was.

As she arrived at the home on Highland Hills, she couldn't help but notice the customary sights of an active crime scene.

Marked and unmarked vehicles flashing blue, some with blue and red. Officers wearing white full-body coveralls, masks, and gloves. Obvious administrative and command personnel guiding the scene's trajectory. A command post where responding agents could obtain supplies, coffee, or just a place to warm up. Her observation was then diverted to something unusual. Two men, one larger than the other entering into a large, black SUV. One obviously in deep thought and the other with a look of concern on his face. Neither man dressed like patrol officers, obviously investigators. Her eyes met with the dark-haired man following the man wearing the wool knit hat. All she saw was a steel blue gaze that seemed to pierce right through her. She also saw concern and confusion; her years of interviewing people honed a skill that helped her sympathize with people. She instantly memorized the face and knew she recognized him from somewhere but could not place him. Casual encounter? News story? *Why are they leaving and how do I know him?*

Maria dismissed the event but could not dismiss the look from the man stepping into the passenger side of that black SUV. Still, she had a job to do and news to report. Little did Maria know that she would become a part of a much larger story that spanned geography and time. She couldn't have known that her life was now intertwined with the grand plan that The Artist had envisioned. If she DID know, would it have changed her response? Probably not. She lived for this. Needed the action, more so than the physical desire for a cigarette.

"Ok, Tom. Get everything going. Get the lead out of your ass."

"Moving as fast as I can, woman," Tom jibed. "Not everyone is five-foot nothin', and 1oo and nothin'."

"Then lay off the po-boys and fries," she said playfully.

After a few minutes of prep and glancing in the rear-view mirror of the van, she was ready. The wind picked-up velocity by the time Tom settled the camera into its tripod. The viewing area was about to receive breaking news from one of its most trusted journalists; a journalist known for her intense work ethic and unwavering integrity.

Tom raises his hand and the silent countdown began with three fingers, then two, now one…

"This is Maria Gomez with KNAC Channel 4 and we are live at a very active crime scene on Highland Hills Drive in Broussard………"

****

The mood was solemn on the ride to the office, both men concerned about the outcome of what they just saw. Breaking the silence would have been helpful, but neither man dared breach the needed tranquility of the moment. They arrived at the office and Rod parked his vehicle in a parking spot designated for him; backing in the vehicle as law enforcement officers are known to do.

"I know you don't want to be away from this case, Silas," Rod stated breaking the silence and reading Gray's reaction, "You have to trust me on this. It's for the best right now."

"I do trust you," Gray responded. "But why me? I don't understand what's going on. I feel like Alice falling down the rabbit hole." *I don't want to play this game, but now you have my undivided attention.*

Soon, both men would be at odds with people that they trusted. People that they called friends and colleagues. The

Artist's deed was done, and men would become undone by the symbolism of a singular portrait.

VI.
4:07 PM

This is Maria Gomez with KNAC Channel 4 and we are live at a very active crime scene on Highland Hills Drive in Broussard. This typically very quiet street is buzzing with activity. Not much is known at this moment and we are awaiting confirmation from staff with the Broussard Police Department, but we can confirm that this once quiet area of Broussard is now the scene of a homicide. Unofficial reports suggest that there may be more than one person dead. A live news conference...

As he muted the television set in his apartment, he couldn't help but feel elation that his work, his talent was now appreciated. He also wondered if his friend found the message left for him. If he appreciated the care in which those bodies were placed.

"Oh, my friend. We will soon be reunited," he remarked as he watched the beautiful brunette delivering the news, albeit no words could be heard. *She would make a wonderful canvas, but I digress.*

He found himself in a state of ecstasy, filled with a bliss that could only be described as orgasmic. He knew that this would bring him closer to his master plan and that his friend would be there to see it to fruition. He hated that he would not be able to deliver this good news to his friend and had to keep it a surprise, but it was for him. Everything up to this point was for him. *My generosity knows no bounds.*

"Now to put in play the remaining characters in this masterwork." Again, he spoke as if someone were listening and, again, he was alone.

The Artist sipped his cold drink, just a club soda with lime as he detested polluting his body with alcohol and walked to his tastefully decorated kitchen island. The black granite countertop held several items, the most obvious of which was a black leather satchel that obviously contained something of great importance to him. He opens the elegantly handcrafted bag gleefully, almost childlike, and removed three folders of various color: green, yellow, and red. Each bound by a black silk ribbon and a wax seal. *Only the best will do!* The seals bore a single image of the Ankh, an image synonymous with the Egyptian civilization. The ancient pharaohs bore this symbol and research suggested that it was offered as the breath of life for the god-Kings of long dead ancient dynasties. *I am no god, but I am worthy of this symbol.*

The green folder was first to be opened. It was about a half inch in thickness, they all were, but the contents held something that could not be defined by initial appearance. The masterpiece of all masterpieces. Rembrandt, Da Vinci, Michelangelo, Bernini, Durer; none held such regard as he soon will.

His attention is again drawn to Maria. *My God she is beautiful.* Still no words, but he was struck by her obviously confidence and beauty.

"I must get to know you, my dear. We should meet."

He gave no mind to her slightly disheveled hair, it was, after all, a windy day, and couldn't care less about her news report, only that it was reporting the beginning of his creation. He knew the truth and he was sure that she would do everything in her power to report what she knew. *Focus, Creativity has no time for romance.*

The contents of the previously sealed folder were strewn about his immaculate granite countertop, ordered and each page in its predetermined place. One group of papers held bank account information for the next element of his design. These documents provided a map of purchasing habits. Habits previously confirmed and reconfirmed over the course of study of his next message. One habit he found most helpful was that his target appeared to extract a large sum of money on the first and third Thursday of every month. This pattern repeated consistently. His studies led him to a bank and then to several high-end establishments that sold food, wine, and extravagant gifts. The end of observations led him to a well-maintained and secluded nest where a beautiful, younger blonde woman from his canvas' office would await the arrival of her *amore*. She was obviously married to someone else and he the same, but this passion could not be quelled with the occasional lust-filled glance.

Two additional piles held medical records and business holdings information. Medical records told him very little, but the business filings held the secret of his hideaway. Filed as a business retreat from his previous life as a powerful executive, the romantic getaway was held in escrow by a shell company that offered the ordinary onlooker nothing but a dead end. The final page from the folder had a single photograph. His newest canvas. The image was neither young, nor his flavor. He deviated from his normal selection due to the power that this man wielded. Power is just as suitable a canvas as beauty and this man's influence was undeniable. This was a power move, a move that only he could make because those inferior to him would shudder at such a direction. Not this artist. Never this artist. He believed in bold strokes of his brush when it was needed to entice the wits.

Again, his attention is drawn to the muted television screen. The urge to gaze upon this woman overwhelmed his desire for focus. *This is twice that this woman has distracted me from my work.* He felt a sudden rush of intoxication at the very sight of her. Her dark hair, her deep brown eyes, her perfect olive complexion. Every inch of her face presented to him in high definition. It is said that the camera will show every flaw, but there she was: flawless. Dutifully braving the frigid cold that enveloped this state in order to pursue her professional duty.

"Maybe I should deviate slightly, my dear. Would hate to deprive you of such wonderful company and I would hate to be a terrible host."

The thought of losing himself in her eyes excited him. *This connection that we have is undeniable.*

He lost himself for a moment imagining their rendezvous. *Would she wear something as tasteful as he would? Where would they meet? Will awkward silence be followed by more awkward conversation?* He dismissed all these notions. There is no time for such inferior thoughts as he knew that their connection would be instant. She is a woman of good breeding and obvious drive and intelligence. He is a specimen of humanity with gifts the likes the world has yet to see. *Our joining will be effortless, but I must attend to my paints before our desires can be realized.*

The photograph that stood in the way of true love was distinguished, obviously posed in a typical manner befitting his stature. Behind him stood two flags: one bearing the very recognizable stars and stripes and the other the blue and white of Louisiana. The man's full head of silver hair was impeccably seated to his face and not a single bit of it out of place; classically cut and groomed. The tailored dark blue suit emphasized the shoulders and reduced the slightly visible midsection. The white shirt and power tie complimented the simple but elegant ensemble. *This is a man of taste and style.* Finally, there was the lapel pin, typical of a man in his profession. An appropriately sized acrylic seal of Louisiana. *Your paints will provide the power strokes of my vision.*

"Mayor Duplantis, it will be a pleasure to make your acquaintance. You will soon be immortalized for far more than your terms in office."

The cat-like smile returns, foretelling what is to come but revealing no specific detail. This won't take too much time; he is a weaker, but worthy canvas and he had a special brush stroke for his canvas' liaison.

After, I will court Ms. Gomez.

VII.

6:17 PM

Gray was lost in thought whilst sitting among the decorations of Rod's office. Rod offered him words of encouragement, but Gray didn't hear a single syllable.

"It's been over two hours, Rod. What the hell am I still doing here?"

"Sean is doing his "Sean thing," and you know how that goes."

Gray nodded and replied calmly, as was his nature, "I mean what am *I* still doing here? Obviously, I'm off the case and there's no information coming from the crime scene. Whoever is responsible for this is trying to get me involved and I'm off the case. Now I'm in the case."

"Calm your mind, baby," Rod said forcing his slight accent to become a bit thicker. "I know that you want to be out there, but you understand the big picture. This needs to be done without you or else this guy gets away. You know some slick-shit defense attorney will use every possible angle to turn this case around and some sympathetic judge will buy what they're sellin'. So, calm the fuck down before you have a stroke. You're making me sweat, and Big Homie don't like sweatin' unless it's with Big Momma, ya dig."

"Do I not look calm to you?"

"You do," Rod knowing that his previous statement was purely in jest. "I just wanted to see if I could make those crow's feet a little bit deeper."

Gray couldn't help but be amused by Rod's words. He knew that Rod was right and in this moment the image that exiled him from the case left his mind. *You always know what to say, you rotund bastard.*

Rod's desk phone gave the tone of an external call. He set his phone to ring one tone for internal calls and another tone for external calls. Gray spent lunches and breaks with Rod, so he knew the difference between the two.

"Lt. Castille," Rod answered. "Yes, Chief. He's sitting in front of me." Muffled words followed. "10-4, Chief. I'll let him know. Good-bye."

"What, Rod?"

"Sean just got removed from the scene, too. A conflict or some shit. The Troop showed up and took over the entire scene."

"Troop," Gray said, somewhat confused, "When did they start picking up local homicides?"

"I guess today. Either way, monkey off our backs."

"What did Chief say about me?"

A slightly concerned, but pleasant demeanor shown on Rod's face, "They wanna speak with you. Ask a few questions. Two of them are on their way now."

Gray held certain members of the Louisiana State Police in high regard, mostly the troopers working in investigations. He knew many of them that worked in the area and served with several over years, mostly on task forces or assisting whenever they required more manpower and local intelligence. There were some, however, that he didn't like. The reasons varied from personality style conflicts to those who tarnish the badge but were never caught. He hoped to encounter the former, rather than the latter, as he had no patience for God complexes and people who had no business "revealing" to him right and wrong. Small talk and more amusement were shared by Rod and Gray as they awaited the arrival of their state guests.

Beep, click Security, security, security.

Two voices were heard down the tiled floor hallway, but the sound of footsteps revealed many more; that and the internal camera's live feed on Rod's computer.

"Three blue boys," Rod said with a hint of surprise, "And the chief. How nice. The blue boys are pretty, baby."

Gray knew two of the three troopers well: Lt. Kaplan Rodrigue and Sgt. Tyler Fontenot. They all served on a violent offender's task force for the region. Both were seasoned vets of law enforcement and knew the practice of law enforcement well. Kaplan, or Kap as he was known, was Gray's age and of similar build. Tyler was a bit younger, shorter, carried a more muscled physique, and was just as proficient in the execution of his duty as any that Gray served with, albeit with a much more laid-back style.

"Well, shit, Gray! You look terrible," Kap said, his demeanor pleasant toward an old friend.

Tyler followed suit, "Looking old, Gray. Broussard must be stressing you out."

"If you two are the guys that I have to talk to, then please accept my resignation, Chief."

Broussard Police Chief Roger Desormeaux smiled at this comment as he knew Gray well and appreciated the lighthearted comment in moments of stress. Desormeaux was well versed in law enforcement and insisted on being involved with his guys. His salt and pepper hair, green eyes, and weathered skin told stories of his time as a military man then as a sheriff's deputy and police officer and, now, police chief. His average height and build may not have seemed imposing, but his presence in a room undeniably commanded respect. His most distinguishing feature, if not hidden, was a scar on his left forearm. A gift from an armed robbery suspect he encountered on a traffic stop many years before this day. Only one man was able to tell that tale after the encounter and Desormeaux wouldn't rehash war stories. All that remained was a closed case and a grand jury decision. Gray and Desormeaux knew each before the latter's ascension into high office, still their friendship was always tempered by their respect for each other's positions.

The third trooper, an apparent on-the-fly addition to the reunion, excitedly introduced himself to Gray. "Detective Gray, I'm Senior Trooper Gary Donaldson. I just need to ask you a few questions regarding the crime scene." His delivery was quick and efficient, but somewhat rehearsed. "Please follow me."

"If you need me, I'll be watching the monitor from Rod's office," Desormeaux advised Gray somewhat apprehensively. *Worry, that's not like you, Chief.*

Gray, Kap, and Donaldson left the now crowded office and entered an interview room that Gray knew well. He obtained many confessions in this room and made hardened criminals cry like children. It was home field advantage, but the away team had the ball this time. A switch on the wall was flipped, a light turned on, and the DVR began to hum.

"Detective Gray, or do you prefer Silas?"

"Gray is fine." *Jesus, junior! Relax.*

"Ok, Gray. When was the last time you were at the house on Highland Hills, prior to today?"

"Never," responded Gray.

"So, you've never been to that house before?"

"No, never had a reason until today."

Donaldson reached into a bag that he had carried into the room with him. Gray hadn't noticed it until now due to his greeting his fellow law enforcement veterans. The leather satchel was well-used, but solidly built for daily work. Donaldson reveals that he'd brought photographs of the crime scene and begins to place these photos in front of Gray in a very specific order; the order in which they were found. Until this moment, Gray put these images out of his mind and wished to never see them again, but Donaldson, being young and imprudent, believed in shock value. Patience in interviews came with practice.

"Rick Lanier, twisted into the first letter." Donaldson places the first picture on the table in front of Gray. "His wife, Sarah, posed on her side, arms and legs fixed." Photo number two. "Colby Lanier completely dissected from his groin to his collarbone. Entrails connecting the two almost separated halves." The images in front of the interviewee nearly completing the singular word. "And his wife, Samantha, almost the opposite of her husband, dissected from where her head should be to her belly button. Upper body ripped apart." The word was complete and more disturbing up close.

Gray's dread at seeing these images in photograph quality megapixels was more disturbing than ever. He realized that this was not a dream and he hadn't fallen down the rabbit hole. This was happening and moving to a place that he didn't like. He provided no outward indication that the images disturbed him when he viewed the individual pictures and saw, in detail, what was done to them. Bones protruded from skin in angles that would make the most flexible gymnast scream in pain. Incisions extended from one part of a body to another. He felt sympathy for the victims, but more than that, he felt hatred toward the person who snuffed out innocence. The deeply held sense of right and wrong superseded his duty to the legal and illegal. He knew that he would find the thing responsible for this showcase and no one, not even friends and colleagues, would stand in his way. Previously forgotten days of night would follow, days that he believed were behind him, and he was comforted by what he knew needed to be done.

You pushed too hard.

****

In the previously crowded office, Rod, Desormeaux, and Tyler, watched a television monitor that provided the live feed of the interview. All three men focused on the word spelled out in front of Gray. It was mesmerizing and repulsive.

"This animal will not turn my city into a killing field," Desormeaux said resolutely. "All means necessary, Rod."

"Roger that, Chief."

"Do you understand what I'm saying, Tyler?" Chief's anger beginning to flash in green eyes that beheld most of life's wonders and carnages.

"Yes, Chief, I do." Tyler again stared at the screen. "This is something new. Something, I've never seen before."

The men are again fixated on the carefully crafted and grotesque design that held so much curiosity. Each held on to perspective of what they were seeing, and each held on to the hopes that this amounted to nothing more than coincidence or randomness. They analyzed each body-borne letter that collectively created a name they all knew, a name they trusted:

GRAY

VIII.

7:38PM

Sean arrived at the department and quickly entered his office, boiling from his dismissal from the case. His protests at the scene fell on deaf ears as his Chief made the decision. He understood, but that was beside the point. A later conversation with his ultimate superior calmed him, but it didn't deter his path. *Chief knows I'm not going to stop.* His drive wouldn't allow him to stop, regardless of what he was ordered to do. He would cooperate, but he wouldn't offer any information unless specifically asked. This was he and Gray's way of doing things: forgiveness, not permission and let the chips fall where they may. It wasn't often that he felt rage consume him, but he was there and on fire. Not even the single digit wind chill could squelch his inferno.

He marched his way toward Rod's office and saw three men, two he knew well and one he knew in passing, fixated on the monitor of Gray's interview.

"Pull up a chair and stay a while," Rod said. "Watch junior get his ass torn into."

Chief gave Sean a quick, but fact of the matter look. No words, meaning understood. Each held the same secret but no one else would know until it was needed.

Sean seats himself in one of the two chairs in front of Rod's desk, but this time he was without the occupant of the other chair. The other chair reserved for the man being questioned by a novice.

"How's Gray?"

"Oh, he's good," Rod stated. "I can tell that Scooter's line of questioning is beginning to piss him off. This is gonna be good."

Tyler then asked, "You think, maybe, someone should tell him?"

"No guys. Everyone has to learn some time," Chief Desormeaux added, "Hell, if I had to, then no one is safe from this teachable moment, not even young troopers."

Sean, paying no attention to the monitor, started playing with his phone and smiled because he also knew what was about to occur. Anyone within earshot was in for a treat.

Each man in the room knew and experienced these moments and each man was better for it. Gray could tolerate unskillfulness as this was usually due to lack of training or time in the field. What he could neither abide by, nor tolerate was the combination of intentional ineptitude and arrogance. Gray held firm in the belief that arrogance was the anesthetic that numbed the pain of ignorance – a paraphrased line he once read in a passage many years prior to law enforcement. In his view, the lack of knowledge could be remedied if one is willing to recognize their own unawareness and seek improvement. Unfortunately, Donaldson was about to experience a "Come to Jesus" moment that everyone knew was foreseeable, except for the Donaldson.

****

Donaldson talked more in the interview than he should have and Kap sat quietly and awaited the inevitable. Even he wasn't immune from teachable moments, even as a State Police sergeant.

"You claim you've never been to that house and yet your name is literally in the crime scene. Bathed in blood and you are going to tell me you don't know anything about it. Your alibi is that you were home all-night sleeping, but no one saw you because your wife and son are visiting her family up north. Your phone's GPS was turned off by you years ago because you didn't like to be tracked by a huge conglomerate. I find that hard to believe."

Careful, child, your treading on thin ice. "Yes, that's what I'm telling you."

"All of your stories," Donaldson using his hands to do the universal air quote sign, "are shit. Pure shit and I don't believe you. I think you knew these people and that you have someone in mind that did this. Why else would they write your name with their bodies?"

That's it, you called out my integrity. "Listen, Ronaldman or son or Dunbar or whatever the fuck it is." Gray knew his name, he just wanted to get him worked up. "I don't need to tell you shit. Me sitting here with Kap is a courtesy that he's earned over the years. You, on the other hand, I don't know, nor do I have to extend this courtesy. What I won't do is have some pencil dick wannabe cop sit in front of me and tell me about a crime scene that I could've read in seconds if allowed to do my job. I don't have time to carry your little cop baby nuts around and spell it out for you so you could write a report and fuck it up. Now, if you'll allow the grown-ups to speak for a minute, then maybe, just maybe, you'll learn something that would prove useful in the future of this investigation. If you don't shut the fuck up, then rest assured I'll ram you and your half-shaved-testicle millennial haircut through that wall and sit your unconscious nut sack looking ass down at the children's table until this is over. Fuck you!"

The laughter from the office near the interview room could be heard through the "soundproof" material immediately, albeit very muted. Kap was not immune and cracked a smile, thankfully he was seated to the right and slightly behind Donaldson. Gray, previously believed to be incensed, was now in full "Gray Mode" after his profanity laced oration: calm and composed. Donaldson, on the other hand, was as red as the famous Louisiana hot sauce from Avery Island. He'd never been spoken to like that before and had never been put in his place so bluntly, especially by another police officer. Most just acquiesced, but not this man.

"You mother..." A hand stopped Donaldson before he said something that would prove his undoing.

"Stop. I'll take it from here Donaldson. Go get some coffee."

"But, sir!"

"That's an order that I won't repeat, Donaldson," Kap said sternly, but softly. Donaldson was done and Kap didn't want to add to the embarrassment. He wouldn't, however, give the order twice. Donaldson glared at Gray as he petulantly picked up his leather bag and stormed out of the interview room.

"Bye, Junior," Gray said as Donaldson exited the room.

Donaldson's walk down the hall would lead him passed Rod's office where, to his knowledge, only three men occupied the space. Little did he know that Sean arrived and offered a fourth witness of Gray's assault on Donaldson's delicate sensibilities. All four still had tears in their eyes. Where Donaldson went after he exited the building was neither known, nor did anyone else care, but Gray's astute observations of the previously puffed-up young trooper was as accurate as it was hilarious. No man in that building would forget what they saw at the scene, but now they had another story to share around the bar top when this case was over. Donaldson would not be invited to reunion.

Kap and Gray finally stopped smiling long enough to continue the interview. "Gray, how many times are you going to do that? He didn't know."

"You knew I was going to do it and you didn't stop it, Kap. So, I gave everyone what they wanted and made a point the he won't soon forget." Gray then looked into the closed-circuit camera in the corner of the interview room, smiled, and gave a wink. He knew others saw the whole thing and surmised that they were still laughing about Gray's newest initiate.

"Everyone has to learn some time, I guess, but you could've chosen someone other than the governor's nephew." Kap then burst into laughter. He could no sooner stop Gray from being Gray than he could stop the cold front that slammed into Louisiana.

"Eh, fuck him if he can't take a joke," Gray said, joining his friend in the hilarity.

"Listen, we've got your statement and I know you had nothing to do with what happened," Kap stated reassuringly, "You realize that you have to stay nearby for the next few days in case we need you."

"I figured as much. You know that the wife isn't going to like that. I'm supposed to meet them at her mom's house tomorrow." This was the first time throughout the interview that Kap saw real concern on Gray's face.

Kap then looked at Gray empathetically, "Sorry, brother. You know how it is."

"Yeah, I do, unfortunately. Can I at least get a note or something?"

"Nope, you're on your own, Gray."

"Thanks," Gray said, the sarcasm undeniable, "You're a real friend."

Both men then stood up and shook hands. Gray extended his warm wishes to the Kap and his family and the words were reciprocated to Gray's family. Not only did the two men work together, but Kap introduced Gray to the woman that would later become Mrs. Gray, Charlotte, or Charlie for those that knew her. Two things that Kap never questioned: Grays loyalty to Charlie and their son, Simon, and Gray's devotion to his work. Donaldson was out of line, everyone knew that, but his assumptions about Gray were a volatile mix of youth, arrogance, and inexperience. If he knew the man, then he never would have questioned him the way he did. Kap understood the man standing in front of him, as did everyone else currently in the building, and that alone was enough to take Gray's word as gospel.

Gray and Kap exited the second "murder scene" of the evening, the victim of that scene already left in a mood. Gray passed Rod's office and told all in the office that he was going home and to call him if he was needed. No one tried to stop him as they knew making him stay would be impossible given everything that happened this day. He wanted to put the day behind him. He wanted the comfort of the familiar. He wanted an adult beverage and rest. His mind was exhausted, his body beginning to ache from the cold front interacting with old injuries that reminded him that he did stupid things as a young man. Still, he wondered what was next. *This isn't over.*

"Bye, baby," Rod said hoping to induce a laugh or smile or something, a response that wouldn't come. "Well, ok, then. Grumpy ass."

"Call me later," Sean added. No response received from is partner, but he heard it.

"Do you need critical incident response for your feelings," yelled Desormeaux.

"Got it covered, Chief," Gray yelled as he walked toward the exit, "Dr. Daniels and I have a recently scheduled group therapy appointment. G'night." Gray didn't drink much, but tonight would be a one, maybe two finger evening.

It was already 8:03 when Gray entered his unmarked unit,

a silver Charger, and the radio immediately turned on as he pushed the button to kick over the engine. He didn't feel like listening to talk radio as was his norm and settled for a playlist that he created on his I-Phone.

"Hey, Siri," he prompted, "Play music, random."

"Playing music, shuffled," the impersonal robotic voice confirming the order. *Random, shuffled, whatever?!*

The song and band were a favorite of his, *Devil* by Shinedown. Gray smiled a bit and couldn't help but notice the irony in what was chosen by the device's computer.

"How appropriate, Siri. I'm beginning to think that you listen to my conversations," he muttered. Gray felt an awakening in his soul that he believed was gone, a darkness that, if left unchecked, would consume him. It was a familiar embrace.

Gray's drive was only about fifteen minutes in duration, give or take, but on this night, it would take a bit longer. The roadways were slicker because of ice forming and Louisiana doesn't have salt trucks to help with the situation. He didn't mind the extension, Charlie and Simon were away and he was getting hungry.

A quick stop at an open fast food place and then to the house.

****

"Sean," Desormeaux snapped, "You can't interfere with the investigations that Troop is conducting! Do you understand?!"

"Chief, this is bullshit! Troop is in our city. This makes us look like little brother asking big brother for help! Gray and I can do this!"

The argument between Chief and Sean went on for several minutes after Gray announced his departure. Neither man backing down, nor giving an inch. This was an impassioned professional disagreement, not personal, and Chief insisted on brutal honesty from his most trusted officers. Nothing held back just so long as it was respectful, for the most part.

Rod intervened between the two men, "Gentlemen, both of you need to stop before I get my round ass out of this chair and put both ya'lls noses in the corner! Both of you, shut up and sit down!" Rod's accent was decidedly thicker when irritated.

Rod earned the respect of his subordinates, peers, and superiors and they knew that he meant no lack of respect when he spoke plainly and bluntly. It was his way to get everyone on the same playing field. No one better, no one worse, each equal regardless of rank. He was old school. What some may perceive as contempt for rank was an offering of common sense. The two combatants take seats in front of Rod like kids facing down a principal, ardent contention now replaced with silent expectations of wisdom.

"Chief," Rod began, his face softening, "This is a tense situation and everyone in this room knows it. Sean is looking out for everyone, as he normally does. He's the momma hen in this situation, protecting his partner at all costs. It didn't help that "Douche Canoe" Donaldson basically accused Gray of murder. By the way, fuck that guy!"

Rod then turns his attention to Sean, "And you! Talk to Chief like that again and It'll be me, you, a closed door, and no cameras, *comme ca*! Chief knows the situation and he knew why this decision had to be made. Besides, I'm sure that the look Chief gave you before Donaldson's verbal annihilation at the hands of the "Saltine Supreme" has a hidden meaning. My guess, you guys aren't out, but I'm telling you that if you don't include me, then Big Homie gonna get mad and make a gumbo of whoop-ass with your names on it! Extra spicy, emphasis on the whoop-ass!"

Chief and Sean didn't realize that Rod saw the glance as both, they believed, were out of his purview. The façade of anger on both their faces is then replaced with amused smiles,

smiles that only "Rod-isms" could create.

"How did you…" Chief started.

Rod interrupts, "Big Homie sees all, Chief, and whatever it is, I'm in."

Rod's intent in this mediation was not to put the men he trusts in their respective places, but rather to remind them that they were on the same side and that one of their own was in a world of trouble. If Donaldson has his way, then Gray would be the man left on the battlefield. *Leave no man behind.* Rod also knew that Gray could handle himself. He knew of Gray's past, even if he never spoke of it. Seeing Kap and Tyler earlier in the evening reintroduced memories of news articles that never seemed to end and an investigation that changed the trajectory of Gray's life. Gray and Rod spoke of it once, but never again. It was a revelation that, in this moment, made Gray the most dangerous man in this or any department, and Rod would do anything to help the man that trusted him with such disclosure.

May God have mercy on whoever did this, 'cuz Gray won't be so merciful.

IX.

8:07PM

"Right on, time."

The Artist was impressed with the former executive, attorney, and now politician's, sense of timing. He waited for him for about thirty minutes, but he already knew that he would arrive between 8 and 8:30, as was his habit. The popular public figure was nothing if not predictable. Two to three minutes dedicated to finishing whatever phone conversation he was having, then five to ten minutes to haul the overgenerous foodstuffs and gifts from his city issued Suburban, then another ten to fifteen minutes to clean up and prepared the love nest. What his next canvas didn't know was that a master was in his midst, already prepared, waiting to show off his new studio. *He will appreciate this as much as I will.*

His new canvas exited the overcompensating vehicle and retrieved two bags from the read storage area. He had his keys at the ready before approaching and then stopping at the door. *The trap is set.* The door opens and keys are tossed into a bowl near the doorway, a no-look toss. He's done this many times before. Heavyweight paper bags are set down near the bowl and a light switch is flipped. *You'll enjoy this, my dear.*

"What the hell?' Shock entered as Roger Duplantis beheld his future. "Who's there?"

Before him was an antique wooden chair, and in front of the chair a mix of The Artist's brushes: knives and machetes, hacksaws, piano wire, box cutters, assorted medical tools that looked to be nothing more than wires, and four tourniquets.

All the chosen brushes were of high quality and glimmered in the incandescent light of the hideaway. The rest of the tasteful furniture and decorations were position around the room in a way that resembled a box, a framework if you will. *Go!*

The Artist emerged from a darkened hallway and raised the plastic device. A quick pop and 50,000 volts delivered into the body. He didn't faint or pass out, that's movie fiction. He let out a warbled yell as he fell to the floor. He had to move quickly as he would only be incapacitated for a few seconds. *Plenty of time for someone of my skill.* He was immediately on top of his canvas, savoring every moment of physical contact. The cloth gag skillfully wrapped tightly around the politician's money-maker and solid hit to the temple.

"Welcome, Your Honor. You are now my gift to my friend, Silas."

He took his time preparing his canvas. He didn't worry about the next arrival, no need. The Artist visited her before she prepared herself for the evening's activities. *Exercise and a shower, that was her habit.* She wouldn't, however, miss the grand opening of his newest gallery and would find herself as the first patron to the supremacy of his creativity.

Crack, sniff

The smelling salts worked to assist the Duplantis with regaining his mental faculties. Vision blurred but sharpening quickly. Hearing muffled slightly. Smell of iron in the air. He felt a chill fall over his body and numbness in his arms and legs. As his vision refined, he viewed a familiar sight seat before him a comforting sight at one time, but now only fear. Nothing else but fear. He then took account of his own predicament. Naked and unable to move because of the heavy-duty cable ties that bound him to his expensive antique chair. A gag in his mouth and tourniquets on each limb, tightened to the point of circulation loss. The fully conscious, beautiful woman before him similarly imperiled, but in a standing position, strapped to a rudimentary stake-like structure. Both exposed, both helpless. He then noticed that he had a deep incision in his right thigh, bright red blood pooling in a slow drip underneath him; arterial blood.

The Artist emerges into their respective lines of sight wearing brand new white overalls, nothing else. No shirt, no shoes. His muscles glistened with perspiration achieved from hauling both into their situations. This is where his mastery would soon begin.

"I apologize, your honor, for the cut on your leg. I needed to make sure that my brushes were suitable for such tender skin." The Artist smiled after the explanation, an explanation that he felt he had to give as a matter of course given the mayor's position.

He turns to the woman, seemingly intrigued by her.

"Behold, my dear," The Artist explains to the finely crafted woman, "The object of your carnal desires. A man of power and wealth, much like your husband. You two must travel in the same circles. If you had paid attention to your surroundings and not each other, then you would have perceived me at the same gatherings. But alas, my dear, all you craved was his embrace."

His eyes, jet black eyes, then fall on Duplantis, "And you, sir. You are a man of excellent taste. You chose your conquest well. Look at how she prepared herself for you. Her tone, her perfect skin, shapely in every way that a man could desire. She is beautiful, stunning, and not yours to have. Your libido couldn't stop the growing pleasures that played out in your mind and you blindly walked into my newest studio. I do hope you like it. It's such a beautiful studio."

The Artist moves to the woman before him. She bore no signs of trauma, at least none that the honorable man could see. He removes her gag and she began to ask questions of who and why. Questions that only add to the lovers' sense of fear; a fear that fed The Artist's creative juices. The words fall on deaf ears as no response is given.

"Shall I take her breasts? Her eyes, her beautiful bright green eyes? What about lips? Hmmm?"

Fear now evident in both canvases. The woman's terror more evident than before. The Artist was asking serious questions, albeit many would think it was for dramatic effect. He was inspired by the dread exuded, the smell of it, the look of it. He was drunk from it.

"I have a better idea," The Artist said in a moment of creative lucidity.

He attacked the woman's face with a carefully selected brush from The Artist's palette: #10 surgical steel scalpel and hemostats. The whole ordeal last seconds and Duplantis couldn't make out what he was doing to her. He yelled to stop during his lover's attack, but the gag prevented the spoken word from exiting with any clarity. When the savagery was done, there was blood. First a drop, then a splatter, now a constant drip. Blood and saliva.

"That's better," The Artist proudly stated as he observed the meat in his hands, back still to the formerly composed man. "What do you think, sir?

Duplantis' eyes filled with tears and rage as he saw The Artist face him. Blood on his exposed neck, chest, and the previously unblemished overalls. He recognized the form in held in this man's hands, a mass that once brought auditory and physical pleasure to him. He is now fixed on the mouth of his lover, crimson flowing from her once perfect expression. Crimson and saliva now mixed with tears.

"You see, sir, I am not a destroyer. I am a creator of that which invokes emotion in all who view it. This is nothing personal against you or this lovely creature, or should I say for-

merly lovely creature. I couldn't care less about political position or charitable works or drainage projects or platitudes.
This is a gift to a friend; *my* gift to *my* only friend. A brother,
if you will? You are the power of my movement. She offers
more paint to accentuate your substantial addition. This will
be a shared legacy and your significant others may be angered,
at first, but grateful for what I have done. Immortality, Mayor
Duplantis, is the gift that I will give you. My generosity will be
known to all, but only meant for one. Shall we begin, sir."

The Artist dropped the severed tongue at the feet of the
recently attacked and begins his work. In his ears were newer,
now partially red Bluetooth ear buds. Tchaikovsky's classic
Christmas staple, *The Nutcracker*, playing. *I must remain in the
spirit of the season, how could I not with a master in my ears.*
The pain his canvases felt was excruciating, to be sure, but
The Artist felt only the pain of inspiration. Each attack more
savage than the previous. He alternated attacks between the
two, letting each watch as their limbs were removed bit by
bit, each stroke of his brushes deliberate. He made sure to
take extra care of Duplantis. He wanted Duplantis to remain
in the now, watching his and his lover's bodies become more
detached with every brushstroke. The intensity of the attacks
remained constant and as relentless as his exercise regimen.
The Artist finished his newest effort as the beginning of the
Pas de Deaux, the second to last movement of the Tchaikovsky masterpiece. Clean up and a new set of clothing retrieved
from his "luggage" and he was walking out of the door, a pride-
filled look at his newest creation made before shutting the
door. Again, no evidence. *Oh, Silas, maybe this will help you in
your time of need.*

He was driven by a timetable. He had a date with the
10:30 news. *True love could not wait.* His schedule didn't interfere with his vision, it just sped up realization slightly. His
placement of his paints still perfect and his conditioning
and strength allow him to work quickly and efficiently, his

physical prowess allowed swift effort. *No wasted movements; perfection achieved.* His canvas offered very little by way of challenge. There were a few moments were the pieces didn't seem to fit just right, but a little shaping and, *voila*, a stroke of invisible genius set in its proper physical place. This stroke will be undeniably studied, not because of who one of the paints were but because of the intellect involved in his vision's culmination. He walked to his luxury vehicle and again thought of the appropriateness of his steed. Talk radio and the inevitable yelling at guest clowns would ensue. The time: 10:01 PM.

"More than enough time, my dear," The Artist says with delight in his voice. A boyish fixation now drives him. Work is done for now and it is now his time for romance.

I won't miss a single minute of you.

X.

"Damn it, Maria," the producer exclaimed. "That wasn't your beat!"

"So, don't give a shit! Got the story and it's mine now."

The producer recoiled at Maria's words, knowing full well that she was right. It was hers and hers alone. Further argument would only incite Maria's wrath, and no one was ready for that hurricane.

"Fine, what do you have."

Maria responded, "Not much so far except for what was said at the press conference. Four bodies found in the house, no suspects, and the Chief requested that the State Police handle the investigation. I don't understand the last part, but I think it has something to do with a man being escorted from the scene.'

The producer looked puzzled. "What man?"

"He looked familiar, but I couldn't place him. The department has a website and he is listed as one of their detectives. A, Silas Gray." Maria still couldn't place the man she saw.

"Wait, Silas Gray? You know who he is, or at least his work." The producer found it funny that the name didn't ring a bell with Maria. He savored her temporary unfamiliarity because it was a rare occasion, indeed. "He worked the Tri-Parish serial killer a few years back, they called him the Bayou Teche Butcher, and was on the task force that eventually brought him down. He cornered the killer and a gunfight erupted in the middle of New Iberia. He supposedly saw the man in a bathroom or something and decided to arrest him without backup. He was the only man left standing. Officially, he shot the suspect in self-defense when the suspect raised a gun at him. Unofficially..."

Maria interrupted, "Yeah, unofficially he shot the guy after he had thrown down his weapon. The grand jury found it to be a good shoot. Rumor had it that he retired or left the state after that. What was the nickname the media gave him? Shit!"

"Judge Gray, Maria," the producer smiled, "Looks like the rumors were just that. Rumors."

Maria didn't know the connotation of the nickname, but the producer did. It was play on the *AD 3000* series of comic books initially released decades before her birth. It revealed to the reader a dystopian future where law and order was placed in the hands of one group, the Judges, who would perform their law enforcement function and immediately cast judgement on the offender, up to an including summary execution. The imagined image of fallen men surrounding a singular dark, still standing figure made the sobriquet apropos.

"Regardless, is your tape ready?"

"Yep, just finished the edit." Maria now smiled, very pleased with herself after winning an argument that she knew was hers at the onset.

"Don't do it again. And for God's sake don't string Tom along. He's a ball of nerves as it is."

"Hey, Tom is his own man. Go easy on him," Maria wisecracked.

Maria left the production room and found her desk at the end of a row of cubicles. She never much liked the studio; too safe and comfortable for her taste. She preferred the field. The newsroom was for those that wished to live the boring life, the life bereft of accomplishment but full of people recognizing you on the street. Her desk was usually a mess, filled with sticky notes, papers, and half written articles for the media outlet's website. She was constantly under the gun to complete an article, but never missed a deadline. This was her normal and she enjoyed driving everyone crazy. Maria grabbed her purse and jacket and made her escape from the office. Her car was in a well-lit area of the parking lot. Little did she know that she had an admirer.

****

Good evening, breaking news from Highland Hills Drive as the investigation into what has now been reported as a quadruple homicide is still ongoing. Officials have reported that four people, all family, were found inside of house in the affluent Broussard neighborhood. Our very own Maria Gomez has the story.

The Artist watched as Maria, the newest object of his desire, appeared on the screen before him. He, now undistracted by his canvases, listened intently to every word and hung on every syllable uttered by the beautiful woman. He didn't care much for the words, but how she said them. How her lips shaped themselves to create the words that the unworthy viewer hung onto. The dimples that formed when she spoke. The way her head tilted to add emphasis on the importance of the previously or currently spoken word. She was, in his view, perfect.

"You, my dear, are everything I could want in a woman. You have broken my concentration on my work. This is a sign, providence of what is to come."

The smile previously reserved for his work appeared, only this time without the sinister look. It was boyish, filled with emotion that he hadn't felt toward anyone else, except for one. Unlike his previous interest, Maria's gift would be romantic love, not brotherly love. He was filled with excited confidence at the thought of giving such a gift, the same excitement he felt when he determined to give his other gift to his friend.

"The two people that I love the most will receive everything that I have to give. There is no greater love than this, my dear. You, my love, will receive by heart, and the other my soul. We three will be bound together for the remainder of our lives." The thought of sharing what he held so dear made him beam with unbridled joy.

As Maria's pre-taped newsreel ended, he became more entranced with the mysteries hiding behind her deep brown eyes. *What secrets will she share with me and I with her? What future does she see for us?* He was able to rewind live television and viewed Maria again and again, becoming more obsessed with her. The wonder that consumed him soon gave way to dedication. She would be his and he would be hers. He would give himself completely to this woman, but only after an appropriate courting period. He believed that this period was important as it would reveal the perfection that he knew she held. *She is worthy of me. So many have believed this, but only you are selected.*

The Artist could not help but feel the warmth of love as he engaged in his compulsion, warmth that would give way to a certain chill when she no longer filled his senses. He would start the cycle repeatedly and see light surround her, an angel's light, if such a notion existed. Once she was gone, the light dimmed, and he was now in cold darkness. His concentration is suddenly broken by something, a subtle clanking sound and a creaking of a door, and the sound of brushes scraping a hard surface. He turns to look. A certain thrill filled him instantly.

"Have I been discovered prematurely? Impossible! I was perfect."

His heart begins to pound and blood courses through his

veins as his excited attentiveness is piqued beyond anything that he has felt, outside of his canvases, of course. He remembered the term hypervigilance – an enhanced state of sensory sensitivity accompanied by an exaggerated intensity of behaviors whose purpose is to detect activity. Every minute detail is now focused. Eyesight sharper. He could hear his heart beating out his chest. He feels the cold rush that accompanies the state of mind. The object of his current state reveals itself and he is again consumed by exhilaration. *Is this what Silas experiences when he does his work?*

"Maria, my Maria." No sweeter words could have been uttered at this moment

He watched as she exited the news station and walked to her car. Memorizing every fluid motion of her body as she travelled through the parking lot without a single wasted movement. She retrieved her keys from her purse. His newest muse well within a distance that he could cover in seconds. He watched as she entered her fully restored '69 Chevelle SS. *A woman of classic tastes as well. She is too good to be true.* He engages his vehicle's engine as the powerful muscle car flies out of the parking lot and onto the roadway. He follows, matching her path out of the parking lot and beyond.

"We will meet tonight, my love," he states to himself determinedly, now ignoring the talk radio that typically entertains him. "My heart will be yours."

XI.

10:45 PM

He breathes a heavy sigh as he walks along the familiar corridor. A corridor that usually led him to a place that he loved. Tonight, however, was different, evil entered and remained.

"Damn it, Norm," Gray spoke in a rough tone, "How many times have I told you not to poop on the floor? I just let you out! That makes no sense."

Two eyes looked at Gray as he picked up the refuse with a bagged hand, the eyes of his greatest challenge to date: a Boxer puppy. His fawn colored foe watching his every movement, analyzing what his master did in every detail. Victory was his for the moment, but Gray would win the war of wills.

"You're lucky your cute and that Charlie and Simon would notice you're missing. Turd!" Norm stared his master, tongue out, and seemingly pleased with himself.

Gray was irritated with his pet and didn't like to be reminded that the house-breaking process was just that: a process. His frustration was only compounded by the hour-long conversation with Charlie. She and Simon expected Gray to meet them tomorrow and he had to explain how the situation changed. Charlie wasn't happy and made it clear, abundantly clear. Simon, however, was just happy to hear his dad's voice after a day of chasing "vampires." His family didn't sign up for this, but they endured. His wife knew what Gray was when they married and accepted it. Long days, at times, and the threat of becoming a widow must have been hard to suffer. Still, he loved her and she him, always. Their love was real, as real as anything that this world could offer. A love that only intensified as the years flew by.

Knock, knock

The rapping at Gray's front door didn't startle him. Confusion, yes, but startled, no. He looks through the blind-covered window and sees someone. A woman. Stunning, with dark hair, about five foot six and 110 pounds, wrapped up in winter clothing. He then notices the vehicle in his driveway: classic and Detroit built.

He opens the door and is greeted by the woman he saw arrive at the Lanier's house before he was dismissed.

"Detective Gray, I'm Maria Gomez with…"

"Yes, I know who you are Miss Gomez. It's late. What can I do for you?"

Maria noticed the package in Gray's hand and giggled a bit. "May I have a moment of your time after you put that shit away."

Gray stared at the plastic bag and closed the door in Maria's face. After disposing of Norm's gift, he returned to the door, grabbing a hooded sweatshirt from his laundry room. Gray would not have another woman in his house without Charlie there. It wasn't his way. He was devout in his love for his wife and wouldn't allow even the slightest intrusion of the opposite sex without Charlie's knowledge.

The door reopens and Gray joins Maria outside on the well-lit front porch.

"What can I do for your, Miss Gomez?"

"Maria, please."

"Miss Gomez, it's cold, I'm tired, and I have no patience for unannounced visitors, especially those that were not invited and have press credentials. Forgive me if I'm being blunt. It's been quite a day."

Maria couldn't help but notice Gray's piercing blue eyes aflame with impatience. She found him handsome, in a rugged sort of way. Not the rugged that was flaunted in fashion magazines with men wearing skinny jeans and fitted shirts. It was a roughness brought on by a life full of tragic experiences and doing what needed to be done to survive. She was attracted to him, but that's where it stopped.

"Are you alone, Detective?"

"Yes, my wife and son are away for the holidays. Please get to the point, Miss Gomez."

"I just have a few questions concerning the incident on Hillside Drive. Would you be willing to give me a few minutes of your time, preferably inside where it is warmer?" The last statement contained hope of warmth. Maria was freezing.

"First, Miss Gomez, this is a line. A line that shouldn't be crossed. I'm at my home. Where my family and I live. I know you have a job to do, but that jobs ends at the beginning of my driveway. Second, at no time will you come into this house when my wife and son are away. That's never going to happen. Now, if you'll excuse me, I have to not talk to you right now. Good night and safe driving."

At this moment, Maria realized that she made a mistake. She wanted the story so badly that lines, real or imagined, didn't seem important. She was struck with the calm, yet indignant tone that Gray used with her. Maria knew that she was wrong, something she rarely admitted to herself, let alone in public.

As gray turned to enter his home, Maria said two words that he believed he'd forgotten, "Judge Gray!"

Gray froze instantly. His quiet indignation about to be loosed into an overt rage. The traffic of vehicles passing his corner lot home disappeared. His blood began to boil. Time, as it were, moved slower as the anger within him mounted. These two words reminded of him of his darkest days as a law enforcement officer. Days filled with endless questions, funerals, and angry family members wanting answers as to why their loved ones were dead or injured. He turned to face Maria.

"Pardon?"

"Judge Gray, Detective," Maria repeated, "That's what they called you."

Maria knew she hit a nerve with this name. She saw his attitude switch from mildly annoyed to instantly feral. Outwardly, he was calm, but his once steely eyes became as black as the cloudless night sky. This side of him was visibly terrifying, but she was drawn to it. She couldn't help but be entranced by man in front her. A man that was a saint to most and a demon to others.

"Please leave, Miss Gomez," Gray said, wishing that he never heard those words again, "There's no story here. Again, be safe. Monsters are out tonight."

Gray was back in the warmth of his house after saying his goodnights to Maria. Maria was left standing in the cold, lit by the LED glow of high efficiency outdoor lighting. She dwelled on the last words that Gray spoke to her before he left her in the cold. *Monsters?* His delivery when he said it was ominous. Maria needed relief, a strong drink would be the perfect medicine for the ailments of guilt and fear.

Gray retreated into his peaceful place and was met at the door by his pup. He walked to a small closet near the kitchen and opened the door. This closet held memories of "glory" days. Days where five men and a woman were united by the bond of battle in the streets. Chasing only the most violent that society had to offer. Murderers, rapists, human traffickers; none were safe from this membership of righteousness. Those taken by this crew were instantly transformed from predator to prey. Those that resisted their force met with inevitable destruction and those that came peacefully instantly realized that the personification of fear wore a badge and knew know jurisdiction. Three now gone away, two working for the State Police, and the last one a detective in a small town that experienced their first homicide in over a decade.

I'm sorry guys, I failed you.

Another glass of whiskey and bed. The new day awaits.

****

"Well, that's a surprise," The Artist watched in amused bewilderment. "This exchange must have been interesting."

He watched as Maria and Gray, his two most cherished people, traded words. He was not jealous of Maria's choice of destination, far from it. He awaited the moment that all three of them would be together. He couldn't join them, of course. He had work to complete and a proper reunion to plan. Still, he was confused as to what Maria said that changed his friend's demeanor so. He knew the look that Gray had and knew it well. It was a look of savage violence in conflict with overwhelming control. He, too, shared this in common with his friend, or so he believed. *We three are forces to be reckoned with.*

Maria left the front porch and again entered into her chariot. She was not as quick to leave this lot as she was the previous one but this was a residential area. She was deliberate and careful.

Her potential suitor followed.

XII.

11:20 PM

Maria found herself at a trendy watering hole near her home in the neighboring city of Lafayette. She was neither a stranger, nor was she a fixture. She was just, there, sipping on a glass of bourbon, straight up. Nursing her drink was her nature, especially since this particular bourbon was ultra-premium at $13.75 a shot. A few guys in the bar showed interest and one even attempted a pick-up line.

"What the fuck does that even mean," Maria said to herself. "His mother. Angels. Clouds. Jesus, men these days are fucking insane."

"Amen, sister," the tattooed bartender, Sasha, replied. "I don't know what they think about when they try something like that."

"I have a question, Sasha: Why are men the way they are? Sometimes they are exactly what they appear to be and other times more complicated? You know."

"Anyone in particular this time, Gomez. The subject of a story you're working?" Sasha always insisted calling her patrons by their last names, just a habit that Maria assumed Sasha picked up while in the military. Sasha's tattoos gave away her time in the service, namely the Marines. No one ever complained, though. Sasha was tough but beyond that she held the keys to liquid jubilance.

"This cop, a detective. Real hard case. He did some shit in the past that made him a minor celebrity for about two minutes. He's approachable, but at the same time very closed in. Earlier, I thought he was about to rip my head for bringing up the topic. The look in his eyes was animalistic, terrifying, and then, poof. Gone. Back to himself."

"Sounds like you have a thing for this guy, Gomez."

Maria smirked a bit at this comment, "Please! He's a story, plain and simple. The centerpiece of a much larger story that only he can break open. I mean, I may have crossed a line by showing up at his house, but no story without risk. Right?"

"Can't help you with that," Sasha said while wiping down a portion of the bar. "I gave up guys a long time ago, but maybe you should've just called. Just a thought."

Sasha was right. Maria's imprudent act may have damaged any potential information that she could have gotten from Gray. She often forgot to look before she leapt and the consequences be damned, but this was the first time that she ever showed up at the front door of a cop's house. She knew it was a violation, but she was driven by the story and adherence to proper decorum played second fiddle.

"Hey, Gomez. Front door. He looks interesting."

Maria the saw him. Dark hair. Well-built. Clean shaven. Tall. Dressed properly for the bar and the outside elements. She stared at him for a few seconds, but those seconds seemed like minutes. He didn't greet anyone as he walked in and took a seat at the bar, several chairs from Maria.

"Excuse me," the stranger directed to Sasha's bar mate, "Club soda with lime, please. Thank you."

The stranger received his drink just the way he requested, making sure to tip the bartender generously for the prompt service and attention to detail. He then glanced at Maria, who was still staring at him, and raised his glass in response to her look and quickly attended to his drink. He sat in the chair:

confident and comfortable. A man easy in his own skin. No need for boisterous friends. Just he, his drink, and whatever was playing on the televisions set up above the bar. He appeared to be a loner, just like Maria, and in that there was a kinship that almost compelled conversation.

****

As The Artist sipped his fresh drink, he knew that eyes were upon him, namely Maria's. How could she not notice him? He studied human nature in order to select his canvases and used this skill to know what Maria would find interesting. He was not looking for muses tonight, he was in the mood for romance.

"Another, please," The Artist requested. The bartender dutifully prepared a new glass and placed the glass and a fresh napkin down in front of him. Again, another generous tip. *How long will it take for her to approach me? Not too much longer, I'm sure.*

****

"Either go talk to him or take a photo, Gomez. Stop being so obvious."

Maria felt drawn to this man but resisted. "You think I should?"

"Listen, even my ovaries jumped when he sat at the bar. I know yours are probably screaming at you right now. Besides, what's the worst that could happen? You guys don't hit it off and you go home. Alone." Sarcasm is the language for Sasha at this moment, "So tragic, yet familiar for you."

Maria loved Sasha's direct take on life. "You bitch," she joked, "Maria Gomez does what she wants, when she wants, and gets whatever she wants."

"Oh, third person. Must be feeling yourself tonight, eh, Gomez."

Maria finished the rest of her drink and Sasha quickly re-filled it. "Liquid courage. On me."

She scooted out her seat and walked toward the stranger at the bar, fresh drink in hand. Closer and closer. Nervous, but composed. She smelled his cologne, pleasant and tastefully applied. The man didn't seem to notice her approach and appears slightly amused by the tap on his shoulder.

"May I," as she motioned toward the seat to his left.

"Of course. Please," the stranger responded with a delight-ful tone and a slight hand motion to the empty seat next to him.

The Artist was now sitting next to the love that he craved, if only for one evening. She was more rapturous up close. He wasn't stunned by her approach except that her inevitable line to him took far longer than he thought. *She is a strong one, but not strong enough to resist me.*

"Maria," she said as she stood next to the mystery man.

"Adam, pleasure to meet you." He nonchalantly sipped his drink after the brief introduction. His attention now focused on her face, particularly her eyes.

"So, why are you alone tonight, Adam." Maria's attempt at small talk was not as natural as an interview on the street.

"Just needed to get out of the house, I guess," The Artist replied in response to the obvious ide-breaker. "Last working day of the year for me and I wanted to celebrate it. By myself, but now with you." He feigned a slight laugh as he said it and Maria reciprocated it. *This is a good sign.* "And you, Maria. Why are you here nursing a bourbon into infancy?"

Maria's smile widened as his last word struck a humorous and observant tone. "You saw that, huh? I guess you could say that I also wanted to celebrate the working day, except mine was more disastrous."

"Care to talk about it," The Artist sincerely asked, "I'm a good listener."

"No," Maria coyly said, taking another sip of her bourbon. "Reliving mistakes is something I've never done. Learn from it and move along."

"Well, here's to mistakes never remembered." The Artist raised his glass and Maria concurred with her glass. Sasha saw this and grinned, knowing that "her" Gomez was on the right road with the first man in years that made her question her sexuality.

The conversation between Maria and Adam became more effortless as time went by. Ten minutes became twenty, then thirty. Both engaged each other on a seemingly genuine level. Maria smiled as much as her companion. Sly glances became soft touches of the hands and thighs. Maria believed that she had found someone that was not complicated, and The Artist found joy previously unknown to him. Maria looked at her watch and saw that it was only minutes to midnight and saw potential for the rest of evening. Adam was engaging and attentive and she needed more liberation from her day.

"So, Adam, where do you live?"

The Artist knew the question was coming, he generated this whole meeting. "About three blocks from here. A studio not too far from the courthouse."

"Why don't you show me your studio?" Maria's question was softly asked and more of a demand, but she didn't want to appear pushy.

The Artist stared deeply into Maria's eyes. She was disarmed at this moment and he knew it. He was similarly disarmed but had to remain in character. "

What shall we do when we get there?" *Play the game, she is yours!*

Maria leaned in closer to Adam, softly grabbing his left and with her right hand, and whispered into his ear, "Make mistakes that we won't relive, at least if we don't want to."

"Sounds like a terrible plan, Maria, but I'm willing to add to my slipup count for the day."

Maria bid Sasha the usual see-you-later farewell and Sasha just nodded her head, knowing what was about to happen. Another love connection made at the end of the bar. Adam left another considerable tip for the great service and received a generous thank you from the barkeep that refreshed he and Maria's beverages that evening.

As they walked to parking lot, The Artist stopped for a moment and retrieved a pre-paid phone from his jacket pocket, the ones that are used by the criminal element. He had romance in his heart, but work on his mind. He needed to set in motion specific events for his friend. *Always time for you, Silas.*

"One second, I have to take this," The Artist faked an incoming call. Maria nodded and proceeded to her vehicle which was, not so consequently next to his car. *And now for the next gift for my friend.*

Ring

9-1-1, what is your emergency

Voice now much lower in pitch and with a slight accent, "I'd like to report an injured person. 4536 Pelican Park Road. I'm not sure, but I think they're bleeding. Please hurry."

Yes, sir. And your name and call back number.

Click

The Artist, now with his back to Maria, then broke the cheap phone in half and placed both pieces into his pocket. Maria didn't see the move; she was feeling the need for further companionship and if she had to wait another ten seconds, then so be it. He retreated from the cold and was again in the cockpit of his car, talk radio as usual greets him as he shifts into drive. Maria follows.

He stares at the heads-up display – 12:02 AM – and sees that that the new day has come. "Oh, Silas. The new day brings fortune for both of us. You get my work and Maria my passion. Fortune shines on all of us this evening. Sleep well, my friend. Today will find us all in a state of frenzy."

Welcome back, "Judge Gray."

DAY TWO

"Whoever fights monsters should see to it that in the process he does not become a monster. And if you gaze long enough into an abyss, the abyss will gaze back at you."

-Friedrich Nietchze, *Beyond Good and Evil*

I.

December 23rd

"Romeo Three to Romeo One"

"Go ahead, Romeo Three."

"Suspect is approaching the northwest corner of the building. Green shirt, blue jeans, white shoes. No weapons observed."

"10-4, Romeo Three. You and Romeo Four maintain position. Romeo Five and Six, take position on Main Street at Iberia. Romeo Two and I will hold near the plaza exit. All units direct."

"Direct"

"Direct"

"All units direct, advise movement when necessary."

Gray released the grip on his throat mic and transmit button. He'd been sitting in this vehicle for three hours and his behind was beginning to feel numb. The weight of his equipment weighed on him and the heat was almost unbearable, even this late at night. His only comfort was that he was not alone. He had Marlene with him, or "Mags" as she was known to the team. The streetlights in New Iberia's historic district illuminated the quaint shops that sold goods during the day and the bars on the city's main drag open that evening was surprisingly slow.

"So, Gray," Mags started, "Do you think I should or shouldn't."

"Really, Mags? Why don't you just say yes and stop overthinking it. Jimmy is a good man. Stop torturing him."

Gray and Mags knew each other for years prior to this night.

Toughest woman he'd ever met and easily the best friend that he had on the team. Both entered law enforcement at the same time, he with Iberia Parish and she with Lafayette Parish. Same academy class, SWAT training schools, high risk warrant schools, investigations. Their time in this business paralleled. They were close and trusted each other without question. Now they were assigned to coveted positions with the Rapid Emergency and Preparedness Response Unit – a local/state/federal interagency task force that investigated and tracked the worst criminals the state of Louisiana had to offer. They used the call sign Romeo and a number, but those in the know had another name for them: REAPERS. No boundaries, no jurisdictions, just cops doing their jobs. Six driven individuals working as one.

Mags smiled, knowing that Gray was right. "I need a maid of honor, Gray. Do you think..."

"Sorry, girlfriend," Gray playfully interrupted, "Dresses really aren't my thing. They make my hips look too big. Try Tyler or Kap. I'm sure that they might be able to pull it off."

"Control to Romeo One. Control thinks Mags should say yes. Over."

"Romeo Three and Four to Romeo One. We agree, and neither one of us will be wearing dresses."

"Five and Six to One, Ditto."

"Romeo one and two are direct on that traffic," Gray responded, his finger now off the transmit button. "It's official, Mags, top on down. You have to say yes and none of us will be going strapless."

"Really, Gray," Mags playfully pushed Gray on the side of the head and referred him to a mental health professional, albeit roughly, "Everyone heard that! I'm gonna kill you."

"Hey, now you have to say yes. Even Jacques and Tony approved, and that's saying something because they don't like anyone. No pressure, Mags," Gray said with a childlike smile on his face and ob-

viously pleased with himself.

The banter continued until Mags asked Gray if he thought Charlotte would stand next to her on her potential big day. Gray assured her that Charlotte would be ecstatic, but she had to say yes to the proposal, first. Mags couldn't help but love these guys. They were her family, her brothers, and they treated her like a tough as nails sister. They were right, she deserved a good man and they all met Jimmy and gave their separate approvals, independently of course and in their own way.

The radio chirped.

"Romeo Five, Romeo One. He's exiting the building."

"Direct. All units hold position and wait for my go. Ready?"

Mags pulls the charging handle for her Colt M4, loading a round into the chamber and Gray simultaneously loads his H&K UMP. No words are said at this point. The target is within their grasp. A reign of terror about to end, either with an arrest or a hail of gunfire. The unknown heightens their senses.

"Romeo One to all units, standby."

The suspect, known to them as Garret Boudreaux, had a different name given to him by the press: The Bayou Teche Butcher. He was linked to at least nine murders in a three-parish area. all his victims tortured, strangled, and dumped into the Bayou Teche – a river that's name may have come from the local Native-American word "tenche," or snake. His last victim saw the serial killer graduate to rape and forensic examiners were able to get a positive DNA confirmation. Additional investigation revealed that the killers cell phone pinged at the last location of a body dump. The probable cause for the arrest warrant wrote itself and a district judge happily signed and subsequently sealed the details of the warrant.

Three two-man teams watched as the killer walked into a restroom facility located in the plaza near the bar. The building had a front and rear exit. This was their opportunity and the window would close quickly. No civilians to worry about, but the area was somewhat darkened by the shadows of decades old buildings and a centuries old oak tree, still it was the best chance the team, had to end this menace, one way or the other.

"Romeo One to all units, go..."

KNOCK, KNOCK, KNOCK

****

Gray is startled by the pounding at his door. A cop's knock, unmistakable. He looks at his phone to see the time: 1:49 AM. He was no longer with Mags and his team. A realization that saddened him. A loss still felt deeply. He fell asleep on the couch in his living room shortly after talking to Maria. Norm was a ball of fur near his feet.

KNOCK, KNOCK, KNOCK

"ALRIGHT," Gray shouted. "I'm coming!"

He looks through the window blinds the same way he did when he first saw Maria, but this time it was two men, Donaldson and Sean. "What the hell!"

The door opened and Donaldson's face glares upon the man that chastised him earlier, still seething from the verbal beatdown he received hours earlier. Sean, on the other hand, looked worried.

"Donaldson, Sean. What can I do for you?"

Sean begins to speak, and Donaldson lifts his hand to stop him. Sean complies with the gesture. *Something's wrong.*

"Detective Gray, you need to come with us," Donaldson says with a modicum of satisfaction. "There's been another incident."

"Where?"

"You need to come with us," Donaldson repeats, "I won't

ask again."

Gray was impressed by Donaldson's audacity in thinking that he, of all people, would be intimidated by the thinly veiled threat. *This kid has balls.* It was then that Gray noticed three Lafayette Parish deputies accompanied "Dapper" Donaldson, all of whom Gray knew. Gray only then realized that Sean was there to preserve the peace. The newfound confidence Donaldson seemed to have was false, apparently bolstered by people who have fought battles on the street. *Never mind, dickless.*

"Sean?"

"You should come, Gray."

"Ok." Gray glared at the now smirking Donaldson. "You're lucky Sean's here, junior. I'll get dressed."

Donaldson then tries to walk into Gray's home but Gray stops him with a hand to the chest and fury in his eyes. "You stay out here. Sean can come in." Donaldson's face is now filled with anger, the childlike anger that Gray saw earlier.

"If you think that I'm going to…"

"You'll do what I tell you or you'll never have the use of your legs again," Gray said calmly, but now obviously irritated with Donaldson's presence and the presumption that he was worthy to enter Gray's refuge from the outside world. Donaldson withdrew several steps from the front door. Despite his false daring, Donaldson knew that crossing this line would mean his destruction, at least physically. Bravado, for the time being, gave way to Donaldson's self-preservation instinct. Sean enters Gray's home, smiling at Donaldson like a boy that knew the secret password to the clubhouse. *You're not invited.* The door closes and the two partners are alone and speak in quiet tones.

"What happened," Gray asked Sean as he retrieved belongings for a cold night of law enforcement.

"Mayor Duplantis and his mistress. They were found on Pelican Park Road. Both dead."

Gray looked confused, "What does the Lafayette mayor have to do with me?"

"There's another message," Sean added, "It's for you. Donaldson got a call and a text from someone at the scene."

"Rod and Chief?"

"Both at the scene right now, waiting for you," Sean responded. "It's bad, Gray. Donaldson is convinced that you're involved."

"Fuck him," Gray adds, holstering his weapon and inserting magazines into his belt slide carrier, "What do you think, Sean?"

"I think someone wants you on this case and this is their way of guaranteeing that it happens." Sean sounded concerned and confident with his answer. He knew Gray couldn't do anything like this and knew that Donaldson's axe to grind was more personal than professional.

"We need more intel, Sean. We need to know what Donaldson knows. Get with either Kap or Tyler and tell them that I'm calling in "that" favor, but only when I say to. They'll know what it means. I know they'll try to keep it quiet, but Donaldson strikes me as the type that'll find out what we're trying to do."

"Gotcha. I'll run with it on my end and see what I can find out."

Gray's irritation then gave way to concern, "Be careful. Whoever this is has an agenda. Donaldson has an agenda. This has personal written all over it."

Sean smiles at Gray's apprehension, "Stupid shit is your job.

I'm the good one, remember?"

Gray finished getting ready for new day's adventures and he and Sean met Donaldson at the door. Neither man acknowledged the existence of their shared pain in the ass. Gray and Sean approached Gray's department vehicle and began to seat themselves in the car.

"What do you think you're doing," Donaldson excitedly yelled, "You're coming with me."

Gray shot back, "The only order your giving is my coffee order, junior. Black, two sugars. Sean likes his with cream. See you at the scene, sweetheart."

The assisting deputies couldn't help but be amused by the display and each left in their respective marked vehicles. Donaldson ran to his vehicle and attempted to keep up with the two insubordinate detectives. His anger grew with each mile travelled. He felt that Gray was holding back on him and Sean was assisting with the secret. Shared or not, both men would feel his wrath when this was done.

II.

4536 Pelican Park Drive

Gray and Sean arrived at the sequestered scene on Pelican Park Road, each still amused by the dumbfounded look on Donaldson's face when they fled Gray's house. Gray had more fun with Donaldson as he switched lanes repeatedly and took nonsensical turns in order to frustrate his pursuer more. Both were quite pleased and expected Donaldson to be irate when he met with the two troublemakers.

As they exited the Charger, they were met by a familiar voice. "Well, look at Frick and Frack. Where's your boyfriend?"

"Hey, Rod. I think we lost him on Highway 90. Somewhere around the airport," Gray said. "I'm sure that someone will give him directions."

"Really? Good to hear. The less I have to look at him the less my indigestion will act up," Rod replied with a proud look on his face. "Watcha think about that, Chief?"

"I think you boys need to focus on the task at hand," Desormeaux said sternly, "but a few minutes without that intolerable sumbitch works for me."

The four men spoke quietly as the crime scene techs did their work. *Déjà vu*, set in for all of them as they watched photographers, evidence collectors, and command staff performing their respective functions. This was a scene that would garner far more attention than the previous as the man inside had considerable power and influence. Calls would be made from the soon to be appointed interim mayor to people with stars on their shoulders. Favors provided by the governor and neighboring municipalities and parishes. No stone unturned would be the rallying cry for every agency involved. Condolences would come later.

An SUV arrived and parked beside Gray's vehicle entering the busy scene at a high rate of speed. Donaldson emerged from the vehicle nearly foaming at the mouth. Uncontrolled anger was abundant.

"Chief Desormeaux!" Donaldson making his presence felt by one and all. "I want that man stripped of his credentials and his weapon taken from him. I'm listing him as a suspect in this case!"

Chief ignored the demand, somewhat disgusted with the presumption of receiving an order from another well beneath his post.

"Well, hello sunshine," Rod said whimsically, "Got lost?"

At this point, Donaldson had it with their disobedient and irreverent attitudes toward him. He flew into a fit of rage that began signing checks that his skinny pants couldn't cash. All four watched as he became more consumed by his growing dislike for the men, especially Gray.

"Detective Gray, you'll surrender your firearm and badge until this is complete. Do you understand me?!"

Gray, now more defiant than ever, answers his demand, "Did you bring my coffee?"

Donaldson made a move for Gray's waste, presumably to take the firearm his holster. It was move that could have been made easily as Gray's jacket was open. The motion was met by a reflex, reflexes honed by years of training and experience. Donaldson near fell to his knees as he felt every bone in his hand close to the point of being crushed. A second hand grabbed his wrist and he was suddenly jerked forward. The whiplash in his neck was met with a sudden thud of gravel meeting his face. Gray's knee now firmly placed in between Donaldson's shoulder blades. He was now at the mercy of his better and he knew it. The pain intensified as he now felt his wrist and shoulder at the point of no return.

"Are we learning yet, youngster," a calm voice said to Donaldson as the pain intensified, a voice he had only recently become familiar with. "You will not assume to order anything. You are nothing. You will demand nothing. When you reach for a man's weapon you had better be right in your judgement. If you're wrong, then be willing to suffer the cost of underestimation. Now go do your work before I break your shit off and beat you to death with it." *I've had enough of you, you little bastard!*

Relief swept through his body when Gray released him from a pain that he's never felt before. A pain that this man had presumably caused to many. Donaldson stood up from his prostrate position, defiant but obviously outmatched. He brushed himself off. Twigs and rocks fall from his previously spotless attire. He is almost nose to nose with Gray when he stands but his defiance gave way to fear and that fear kept him from doing anything else. The others presently watching this event knew to stay out of it. Donaldson steps back, no words, no direct eye contact, only humiliation.

"Thus ends the lesson, junior."

Gray's words to Donaldson finally seemed to sink in and the vanquished adversary turns his attention to the house. He didn't walk away infuriated like he had before. He was humbled. Moreover, he was humbled by a man, more than a decade his senior, who seemed to be astute to acts of detached violence. Gray's reputation, at least to Donaldson, was well-founded and he would not make the same mistake twice.

"That went well," Rod added. "Now, if you're done playing paddy cake, what say we try to figure something out. Something like, I don't know, the murder of the most powerful person in the parish and how that relates to you being Donaldson's prime suspect. Sound good?"

The four men were not allowed in the crime scene this time. Not their jurisdiction. They had enough connections to solicit some information from those they trusted, but the information was sparse, at best. From what they could determine each victim was bound at the time of their respective attacks. Various instruments were used, and it was believed that a sword or machete was used most. The tongues were removed, and the bodies' dissected pieces placed in a specific pattern. Rod, being the less threatening of the four, was able to get most of the information but it wasn't enough to figure out what threw Donaldson into such a frenzy.

"They lips are tight, tight tonight, baby. It's ok, someone will talk," Rod's accent thickening.

Sean looks to Gray, "Call?"

Gray just nodded, responding with silent affirmation.

Rod and Chief looked puzzled, but then again, they knew that Gray and Sean had ways of getting information. They never asked from whom or where they received their intel, only that it was solid.

"Let me know what you find out," Chief said, looking at his two investigators, "I'll run interference with the brass from the other agencies. Report to Rod what you find out. And Rod, that thing we discussed, put it in motion."

"You got it, boss."

Gray and Sean understood the instructions. Chief wanted to be in the loop; however, reporting everything they found out wasn't in their nature and they wanted Chief to have deniability in case something went sideways. Rod was a different story. They told him everything and he would buffer. Need to know information provided to those that needed to know. Chief walked away from the three compadres and began his usual offers of assistance to his peers.

"Alright, gentlemen," Rod now staring at Gray and Sean, "I don't care how you do what you do. Who you must break? Not my concern. Sean, make the call that is obviously important to Gray. Go." Sean retreated to a quiet spot near Gray's vehicle and dialed the phone number previously given to him by his partner.

"Silas, first off, you assaulted another law enforcement officer and that can't go unpunished."

"Rod, really? He came at me."

"Put your hand out, Silas. Go on."

Gray put his hand out, palm down, and Rod slapped it as a mother would a child when the child was caught taking a piece of candy without permission.

Rod added the warning, "Don't do it again. At least not today. There, you've been counseled. Now, Go and investigate something. I have to take care of a "thing"."

Gray knew better than to ask what Rod meant.

"Rod be careful. This is…"

"I know, baby. Don't you worry about Big Homie."

There was no mystery between these men, but for now it was imperative to compartmentalize. The right hand not knowing what the left hand was doing kept them from having to answer questions from those that claimed they wanted to know, but really didn't.

"Gray," Sean spoke up from his position, "You need to see this."

Gray left Rod's side and approached Sean. He didn't know what to expect, all he knew is that Sean's face told a ghastly story. He saw something that unnerved and confused him. Something that would soon unnerve Gray and resurrect demons that were long believed to be dead.

As he made it to Sean, Gray's phone vibrated in his back pocket. It was a text message from Kap. The message only contained two words, but they were a powerful, ominous communication:

"Leave, now!"

****

The Artist looked at Maria as she slept is sweet repose. She was more beautiful than he had imagined. The previous hours saw the two of them engage in their carnal desires and he was more drawn to her. He dared not wake her. She needed her rest. This new day would bring more excitement, excitement that "his" Maria couldn't resist. He excused himself from her presence, albeit reluctantly, and retreated to his kitchen. She would be asleep for a while and he had work to complete now that his romantic desires were satiated. The black granite met him as he approached his destination and, on that granite, the handcrafted leather bag holding the mysteries of his next canvas. *Work enters where love once stood.*

The yellow folder makes its appearance, bound and untampered with. The information held within was like the previous one. Documents and a photograph. His thoughts turned to his friend.

"This canvas will be the nuance of my masterpiece. The stroke that causes all to fall in awe of its bold subtlety. Silas, more than anyone will, understand. Such gravitas." He was pleased with himself as he said this, knowing that his previous work was being appreciated at this moment by all privileged to see it.

He chose this piece because of the elegance that exuded from her. She was charming, well-read, privileged, and full of social graces. The belle of the ball, so to speak. Men loved her, women loved her, society love her. His reports also included a darker side: an addiction to opiates and sex. This addiction nearly consumes her every moment and still she can function within white collar society. Stints in luxury rehab. Cash payments to dealers of the upper crust. Anonymous trysts through high-end matchmaking connections. All there, in black and white. His information, as usual, up to date and perfect. *I'm a detective with the heart of an Artist.*

"Hello," soft voice is heard from the bed area. "Adam?"

The Artist quickly places the file in its proper order and places the now unbound folder into his bag. Maria is now in view, wrapped in a blanket that shielded her body against the cold. He didn't understand why she would hide such a wondrous creation, but decency, as it were, must have taken over.

"Hey," The Artist responds in kind. "You were sleeping, and I didn't want to wake you."

Maria smiled, "What are you doing up?"

"Just looking at a file from work. Something was gnawing at me with one of my accounts. It was nothing."

Maria appeared pleased with the answer, the answer and the memory from the previous encounter with Adam. She couldn't explain it, but she felt a connection with this man. Physical attraction aside, she was taken by him. It was like he knew her and she him, but there was still a mystery hiding in his calm and approachable demeanor.

"You said you didn't have to work anymore this year," Maria reminded him. The Artist defeatedly smiled, a playful smile.

"You're so very right," he said, agreeing with her observation.

"Let's, you and I, go back to bed and see if we can make more mistakes." Maria approached him and kissed his lips. He was more than happy to oblige.

As Maria led him back to the bed, she saw a small object lying near the kitchen island. She knew what it was but dismissed the item quickly. She'd seen the object before, most as a necklace or a tattoo, but never in wat she believed to be soft plastic. She was too engaged in this enigmatic man that seemed to know her and didn't bother to concern herself with the seemingly innocuous, yet random image of an Ankh.

She wouldn't share him this evening with anything. Work and an ancient symbol be damned.

III.

02:58 AM

"Are you finished, yet?! Jesus Christ, you guys are fucking killing me!" Donaldson's impatience was boiling over. He was not used to waiting for anything, let alone crime scene techs that were below his stature. The previous humility instilled in him by Gray had, apparently, faded rapidly.

"Impatience and crime scenes are not a good mix," Tyler said bluntly, leaning against a wall not covered in human remains. "Calm down and let them do their job."

Donaldson didn't like the tone, "With respect, this is my scene and I will decide the pace of this investigation." Donaldson only added "with respect" because Tyler outranked him, and he knew that some insubordination could be forgiven with that statement. He didn't mean it. Tyler was not the kind to back down, especially to Donaldson's type, but he wasn't stupid. He appeared aloof at times but was very experienced and skilled in his way. The kid had connections that other Troopers could only dream about. Still, his urge to rip into Donaldson built with every word uttered.

"Donaldson!"

Donaldson whipped around expecting to see someone he could berate without consequence. He was met with disappointment. He should have recognized the voice, but his ego prevented his brain from functioning properly.

"Outside, now!" Kap was in a foul mood.

The two men met outside of the house, where none of the

crime scene techs could hear them. Tyler, on the other hand, stepped closer to the entryway. He wasn't going to miss this.

"Sir, it is imperative that this crime scene be processed quickly. We have a prime suspect and potentially more victims. This is..."

"Shut up, Donaldson," Kap barked, his tone undeniably authoritarian. "Silas Gray is not a man to trifle with. I thought you would've learned that by now. You have no right to demand his dismissal from shit! You're goddamn lucky that he didn't send you to hospital with that little stunt you pulled before I got here. And guess what? You would've deserved it."

"Sir, he attacked me!"

"After you tried to disarm him, Donaldson! Have you lost your fucking mind?! Trying to disarm any cop, let alone someone like him. If you pull anything like that again, I swear that your connections won't mean shit! I'll have your ass transferred to policing tow truck companies for Department of Transportation violations. Am I understood?"

"Yes, sir. Understood."

"Get out of my sight and do your job. And stay away from Silas Gray!"

Donaldson turned from Kap, defeated and much calmer than before. He reentered the house and was now more polite with the crew working the scene. Tyler saw the confrontation and couldn't help but enjoy the show. He and Kap were now just inches from each other and speaking just outside of Donaldson's range of hearing.

"Did you send Sean the photo?" Kap asked.

"Yeah, Kap. Taken care of." Tyler sent the picture to Kap. He knew it was important that the information make it to the right people at the immediately. "Did you send the message?"

Kap nodded, indicating that he, in turn, sent the message to

Sean. Both men finally started putting the pieces together and soon Gray would join them in their conclusion, if he hadn't already.

"Donaldson will start putting the pieces together. He may be an ass, but he's smart enough to see what's in front of him," Kap said. A little research and it would leave the underlying story exposed. It'd been a while since Gray and Sean left the scene to parts unknown, both now radio silent until they decided to reemerge. They knew that Gray could handle the pressure and they knew Sean to be capable, but Gray wouldn't allow Sean to follow him. He couldn't take the responsibility of placing another in harm's way, at least not for him.

"Jesus, Tyler. I thought this was behind us. It was over."

"Someone has another plan, brother. But what's the reason and the endgame?"

"Damned if I know. Keep me in the loop. Let me know what Donaldson finds out. We have to be ahead of it."

"And Silas?" Tyler concernedly asked.

"Silas is going to be Silas, Tyler. Let the chips fall where they may."

Tyler silently agreed and dreaded where this was going.

****

"What does that picture mean, Gray? What aren't you telling me?"

Gray and Sean were in a park near the university campus. The university was only a few miles away from the crime scene. The park was desolate at this time of the morning. If anyone else were present, then they wouldn't have concerned themselves with the two. A few ducks paddling in the pond was the only company they kept at this hour. Gray stood there, silently analyzing the photo that Tyler sent Sean. Sean sent the picture to Gray before arriving at the park. He was trying to discover any evidence that would link the scene to the killer. A shoe print, a handprint, anything at all. Nothing. *This guy is a pro.*

"Damn it, Gray! Say something!"

"Sean, this has nothing to do with you. Whoever this is knows me and wants me. I don't know how they know me, but they do."

Sean was taken aback by the statement, in part due to the assumed lack of trust.

"That's a fucked-up thing for you to say to me, Gray! I'm your partner, good or bad, I'm gonna back your move. I just need to know what that move is."

"I don't want you to get hurt, damn it! This will not end well. You're out!" Gray knew Sean wouldn't like the tone. It would only incense him.

"That's my choice to make, not yours," Sean shot back.

"You don't know the whole story, Sean. Don't assume anything, especially wanting any part of this."

Sean became defiant, "And you think you do? You think you know why this psycho is doing this. Why he's doing this to you? Donaldson apparently knows what's going on, at least enough to consider you a suspect. Tyler and Kap appear to know. But I don't. That's bullshit!"

Gray only revealed details of his reasons to transfer to his current department to one other person, Rod. A person that he knew years before coming over and only when he had a bit too much introspection. He sat on the front end of his car and quietly contemplated the gravity of revealing to his partner what this newest message meant. He knew that Sean, of all people, deserved to know this story and its effects on recent events. Still, he is hesitant to bring Sean into his world. A world filled with darkness. Darkness that only Gray and two other living souls were able to escape. More so, he was worried about the impact of this revelation on what Sean would do. Would it serve to motivate Sean into finding the truth? Would it injure him, or even kill him? The responsibility of command was nothing new to Gray, but the darkness within him wouldn't be contained from Sean for much longer. Gray returned his attention to the picture, analyzing the way that the separated body parts that formerly belonged to a powerful man and his lover formed letters. A combination of letters that has haunted him for years.

Sean joined Gray, sitting against the front of the car. His tone softened as he noticed how this new message affected him. He'd never seen Gray so somber.

"What does that word mean, Gray," Sean asked, deep concern evident by his tone, "Who or what is MAGS?"

"That's my burden, Sean, and mine alone. Please, don't push."

Gray trusted Sean and he hoped Sean knew it. He only kept the information from him because he cared too much to involve him in something that could prove fatal.

"You'll tell me when you're ready, I guess. I'm gonna walk."

Gray stops Sean, "Where are you going?"

"To figure things out the hard way," Sean said. "Apparently I'm not worthy of the "Great Silas Gray's" past."

"Hey, don't take it personal!"

Gray only saw Sean's back and the universal "fuck you" hand gesture as the man he trusted most walked away from him. Gray was overwhelmed with fatigue, physically and emotionally. He decided to rest for a bit. Rest that would most likely traverse time and location. The Lanier's, Duplantis. He was putting the pieces together and kept Sean at arm's length for a reason. He didn't need to be drawn into this.

Pandora, let loose from your box the iniquities of man.

IV.

03:14 AM

Chief Desormeaux finished his high-power meeting with other chiefs and parish officials. All thanked him for the offer of assistance and accepted it as a matter of course. He never felt comfortable in these meetings, too much street-cop residue in his nature. Still, he understood the importance of the gestures. He found Rod not far from the meeting area.

"Where's my boys?"

"They went dark, boss. Doin' their thing, I imagine."

"And that other thing I wanted you to take care of," Desormeaux asked.

"Done. Everything you need will be at the office in three hours, or so I've been told."

Chief was amused, "It isn't for me, Rod. Go to the office and wait. Hold onto whatever is given to you and don't ask questions. You'll know when you have to use it."

Rod was a bit confused, "Well it better not be for me. I don't even know what it is. You told me to call a guy and say a single word: Cerberus. And then the phone hung up. Who the hell is Cerberus?"

Rod couldn't help but be intrigued. The "Old Man" still had tricks up his sleeve and apparently inconspicuous connections. Chief excused himself from the crime scene and left Rod in a state of confusion. There was a reason that he asked Rod to call in a favor from someone that Rod never met. This person would soon deliver a care package for the Chief. That was Rod's function right now, to retrieve the package and hold on to it.

"Rod," Chief said before driving away, "If Gray needs anything you make sure to help. Whatever it is?"

"No prob, Chief," Rod said as he watched Desormeaux drive off. "Well, I'll be damned! Gray and Sean are gone. Chief being mysterious. I'm here talking to myself. Ain't that a bitch!"

Rod walked to his SUV and sat in the driver seat. Leaving the scene was a welcome occurrence. The morning wasn't getting any warmer and he needed to defrost. Still, he was concerned about what would await him in the next few hours and resigned himself to a catnap in his "comfy" office chair.

****

Donaldson was still overseeing the scene when another detective approached him with a handful of papers.

"Thank you," Donaldson said dismissing the detective. Donaldson read through the documents and became more interested with every page. Intently devouring the words. Each syllable containing an answer to the mysteries of the past day. Tyler watched as Donaldson feverishly flipped through pages.

"Son of bitch," Donaldson said with shock in his voice.

Tyler became more interested, "What's that?"

"Silas Gray's history. Academy class rank, assignments, task forces, military documents, training, it's all here. Who is this man? Look, there's a gap in his records. Four years before he arrived in Broussard. Nothing. It picks again up when he joined his current department."

Donaldson handed the documents to Tyler and observed the redaction in documents. What Donaldson didn't know was that the same redaction would be found in both Tyler's and Kap's personnel folders. This was sensitive work dealing with the obscenest criminal element. Undercover operations, felony takedowns, statewide manhunts. This was information that was sealed after the incident that dissolved the REAPER unit.

"Maybe it's an error. It happens. This is the state, you know," Tyler said attempting to lead Donaldson away from the obvious.

"No, sir," Donaldson responded with a somewhat sinister look in eyes, "This feels intentional. this feels like someone trying to cover-up an embarrassing episode. Something that would reveal why these murders are happening."

"That's a bit of stretch, Donaldson. You're talking about people well above our paygrades. Hell, I'm not even too sure if they would even have that much stroke. Just focus on what you have in front of you and you'll be ok. Don't lean on conjecture." Tyler handed the documents back to Donaldson and assumed his leaning position against the wall.

Tyler usually treats me with contempt. Donaldson heard the words come out of Tyler's mouth and instantly became suspicious. Tyler was a man of few words, sometimes no words. This long statement felt out of place and his delivery was informative, almost fatherly advice. He couldn't firmly capture why the sudden change in tone. *There's something to my theory, play it.*

"You're probably right. Just a data error. I'm going to get coffee, want some?"

Tyler shook his head, "Nah, I'm good."

Donaldson took this change in word count as an affirmation of his theory. The sudden change in Tyler's delivery and tone only strengthened his resolve in finding out who Silas Gray was and how he is connected to six victims. To Donaldson, Gray's victims. Donaldson retrieved a hot cup of coffee and then removed himself temporarily from the crime scene and began typing a phone number. *It's time I use my connections. This will make my career!*

The phone rang and a raspy voice answered his call.

"Hello."

"Hey Uncle Luke, It's Gary," Donaldson's voice somewhat childish. "I know it's early in the morning, but I need to ask a favor."

"Sure, son," Governor Lucas Dubois said, "I'm sure it has something to do with that case you're working on."

"Yes, sir. Just need to ask a favor and keep it quiet. No sure who I can trust over here."

"Whatever you need, son."

****

Tyler watched as Donaldson talked on his phone. He may have left the crime scene, but he was still new to the covert areas of the job. *Newbies.* Tyler correctly assumed that the call was to one of Donaldson's well-placed connection, maybe even the governor. It was only a matter of time before the truth would be found out and he and Kap would be off the case, possibly suspects themselves. Tyler then made a call himself.

"Kap, we have a problem. Donaldson is making a call."

A muffled voice on the other end responded.

"No, I'm sure he doesn't know, yet. Gotta go."

Donaldson returned to the crime scene, "Anything happen while I was away?"

"Nope, they're still dead," Tyler responded.

****

Kap became more concerned after Tyler's call. Donaldson was sniffing very close to a truth, unfortunately it would be a truth with several gaps that only he and Tyler could fill. This could become problematic for Gray as Donaldson would spin this as motive for what happened to those found in gruesome circumstances. Kap was still at the scene and chose to stay away from the house's interior. He wasn't averse to murder scenes, he just wanted to be where the information was. This required him being around people he didn't much care for, but his mission was important: proving a friend's innocence.

"Gentlemen, anything new?"

Kap was met with several responses, but nothing of substance. The detective that provided Donaldson's reading material began talking to another fresh-faced officer on the scene. Kap intently listened to the conversation, albeit inconspicuously.

"Man, that file was thick," the detective started. "This guy Gray was a beast before he burned out. High-risk operations, narcotics, homicide, violent offenders, and that's when the file ended. Four years off the grid and then, bam, back at it. Donaldson seemed pleased, maybe I'll get better treatment, but not holding my breath on that one."

The emotion to come unglued when the rookie detective called Gray a burnout was subdued by his need for information. It wasn't this kid's fault that he didn't know what Gray had done to preserve his Kap's and Tyler's lives, let alone their careers. Gray bore the brunt of a terrible situation and paid a tremendous price for it. A debt that Kap knew he couldn't repay. Kap did glean one bit of information from the not so discreet investigator: Donaldson had Gray's "official" file. Now it was on him to keep Gray's real history hidden for as long as he could. If discovered, then it would prove his, Tyler's and Gray's potential ends.

This thought haunted him for several minutes and he decided to make a fateful decision. *God help me.*

V.

"Romeo One to all units, go..."

Mags and Gray exited their vehicle and moved as one, each covering the entrance of the rest area in the plaza. Tyler and Kap approached from their position and the second team, Tony and Jacques covered the rear exit of the facility. They had the murderer cornered and the advantage of surprise. Their odyssey of tracking this monster was almost over.

"One and Two, up."

"Three and Four up."

"Five and Six up."

"All units up, proceed on my go. Three... two...."

A sudden barrage of gunfire erupted from within the brick structure. The sounds were deafening and rapid.

"Comm, advise shots fired! Shots fired! GO, GO!"

Gray entered first, followed by Mags, Kap, and Tyler, flowing into the room as one and splitting into designated roles. They saw shell casing lining the floor, but no body. The target moved to rear of the building toward the Tony and Jacques. Each covered a portion of the interior and held position.

"Five and Six, report!"

Nothing. Gray's heart sunk; a dark feeling came over him.

"Five and Six, report!"

Still nothing.

"*Romeo team on me!*" *Gray led the team to the rear exit and saw their teammates. Gray saw the extent of their injuries as he exited. Their bodies riddled with bullets. Each with well-placed final shots to the face. Jesus!*

"*Romeo one, control. Officers down! I repeat, officers down. Fulton Street behind the restrooms area!*"

Gray felt their necks for something that would not be found, first Tony and then Jacques. Mags, Kap, and Tyler held security positions around their fallen brothers.

"*Control, rescue to my location ASAP!*" *He knew they were gone. The final shots only cemented that fact.*

"*Movement front,*" *Mags yelled. Kap and Tyler focused their weapons toward Mags' call.*

Gray's fury boiled over and he felt a new emotion: hatred. He hated this man unlike any other before. He would find this man and show him true justice, street justice. Nothing could be done for Jacques and Tony. He didn't want to leave his brothers, but he knew that the mission came first. Medical would tend to them shortly.

"*On me,*" *Gray yelled back.*

The remainder of the team moved rapidly on a sidewalk lining street, each member watching for any subtle motion that would give away their target's position. The team approached a stairwell that led to a raise platform used for gatherings and bands. This area was the high ground and they knew it.

"*Kap, Tyler. Up.*" *Gray's hand motion indicated their direction, the opening at the top of the stairs.*

The two men followed the order and knew it to be sound. The high ground offered advantages that they needed. The area was higher than most of the surrounding terrain and the openings in the wall provided a position for overall security. Kap and Tyler reached the pinnacle of the stairwell and were met with an empty open-air room, complete with shadows.

"What do you see, guys."

"Romeo three to Romeo one, clear up... wait!"

****

Gray's phone triggered his consciousness. It wasn't his usual alarm tone. It was a phone call; a call from Rod. Gray only meant to rest for a moment, but that moment lasted for three hours. He looked around to reestablish his bearings and discovered that he was still in the park. The sun was still hiding beneath its blanket of stars, winter's morning just as eager to remain asleep as he was, despite his nightmares. At least in his nightmares Tony, Jacques, and Mags were there, if only for a moment.

"Hello."

"Mornin' sugar. What it do?"

"Hey, Rod. What's up?"

"Oh nothin'. Just looking at a package that was just delivered by someone who looked really suspect. He dropped it off, called me and said it was here, and left. For some reason, it has your name on it. Care to expound upon this unusual phenomenon?"

"You tell me," Gray said. "I'm not expecting anything. The office is closed, and I don't think that the ladies ordered anything."

"I was told to hold onto it until it was needed and right now it appears that you'll be the one needing it. Just sayin'"

"What are you talking about, Rod?"

Rod's accent was about to get thick again, "Boy, you more dense than my pecker on Viagra! This package is for you, dummy! I'm letting you know that I got it when you need it! Jesus, Mary, and Joseph. You gonna make me have to go to confession."

Gray's mind raced as he knew that he didn't have a clue as to who would deliver a package for him or why there was a package waiting for him.

"What does the package look like, Rod?"

"It's a black case, about two foot by four foot and about a foot deep," Rod stated. "It has your name on it and a symbol. Looks like a seven or something."

Gray immediately knew what the case meant. It meant that someone was watching out for him and that whoever it was is one of the few remaining people that knew every detail of his past, including emergency protocols.

"Rod," Gray began with apprehension in his voice, "Could the seven be a sickle?"

Rod paused before speaking, "Yeah, it could be. That's pretty morbid."

"Hold onto it until I come get it. Don't open it or let it out of your sight."

"Will do," Rod responded, "Big Homie's security service got it covered. Besides, the box is locked up tighter than candy at my house. I'll see you in a few."

Gray started his car and let the engine warmup. The temperature continued to drop and this morning it was in the teens. He wondered where Sean ran off to or if he damaged their relationship beyond repair. He'd lost people in the past and didn't want to lose anymore. Sean was smart though. He would figure something out and put the pieces together without Gray's help. Gray only hoped that he could stop this madness before anyone of his friends became victims.

The drive to the office was uneventful and traffic lite. Most of the area observed the unofficial "winter days" off. The university was a ghost town. Only essential jobs were on the streets this morning and even they knew to park their cars when they could. The bustling town of Lafayette was sleeping in this morning. Peaceful. He felt relief when he finally parked at the familiar brick building. This was a haven away from the monsters lurking the streets, except when he and other officers invited those monsters in for a chat.

Beep, click

Gray walks a path of which he is familiar.

"And he arrives," Rod boisterously announced. "No need to thank me, the mystery man in the blacked-out truck already gave me a tip!"

Gray walked into Rod's office and sitting in front of him was his past and his future. Rod couldn't help but see Gray's expression go from the calm that he was used to a morose happiness. He saw his friend study every inch of the box and likened the experience to seeing an old partner. Rod was quiet during this reunion as he knew this was something special to Gray, special and deadly serious. Still, Rod couldn't help but wonder what this meant. Gray told him about his past, but this was never part of it.

"Silas, whatever is this box is for you and you alone. I just have to ask a question before you take it. The man who dropped it off left a note on it. The note said to only give the case to the person who had the correct response to the challenge word."

Gray ran his fingers along the name inscribed on the container, his name: S. GRAY. He studied the worn white spray-painted sickle covering a large portion of the lid. It showed signs of wear commensurate with years of being taken in and out of vehicles. Three padlocks sealing its content from the world and Gray was the only man with the key. It was just as he remembered it after closing the lid for what he hoped was the last time. *How many times have I opened you? How many times have I sealed in your secrets?*

Rod provided the word, "Challenge: Phoenix."

"Response: Gladys," Gray said, never breaking eye contact with the object before him. *I haven't opened this in years. I thought I never would again.*

Rod sat back in his chair and placed the card containing both terms in an envelope. This wasn't a time for questions as answers would prove impossible to get from the man in front of him. It was a time for his friend to reflect for a moment.

"Do you need help carrying it out," Rod asked politely.

"No thanks. This is my cross to bear. Listen, I owe you an explanation. There are some things that...."

"Stop," Rod interrupted, "You don't owe me a damn thing. You'll tell me whatever it is when you're ready. You told me what you wanted to tell me once and now there's more to it. That's all. I still got you. No matter what."

The two men shook hands and Rod watched his previous charge lifted by the man that knew its importance more than any other. No words were spoken between the two friends as Gray disappeared into the hallway. A door opening and closing confirmed that Gray had gone, hopefully to his house. Rod knew the story, or at least what Gray told him about the story. This event brought to life a new twist on a man he thought he knew. Rod couldn't help his friend and a religious side overwhelmed him. He did what came naturally during times of adversity.

Rod opened his desk drawer and retrieved a worn medallion bearing the patron saint of police officers.

"Holy Michael, the Archangel, defend us in battle. Be our safeguard against the wickedness and snares of the devil. May God rebuke him, we humbly pray; and do you, O Prince of the heavenly host, by the power of God cast into hell Satan and all the evil spirits who wander through the world seeking the ruin of souls. Amen."

Rod began crossing himself, but then quickly added a post-script, "Oh, and Mike, please keep Gray from burning the world to the ground. That would be great! Amen, again."

Rod replaced the medal and walked out of his office. It was a long night and an even longer morning. He needed to make a call.

"Hey my love. Just gettin' off. I'll be home in a bit." Rod walked out of the building with a smile on his face after hearing his wife's voice, a little bit of a strut accompanying his positivity injection. Still, he knew this wasn't the end and he would be needed again in short order.

VI.

7:00 AM

The smell of breakfast filled the studio apartment. The Artist in his persona as Adam was making a traditional meal for his guest. She needed the sustenance after their previous night together. He flipped eggs and whistled holiday songs. Coffee brewed. Breakfast sausage sizzled. In all, a very normal breakfast scene. *She will awaken soon.* The news that morning contained the usual broadcasts for this time of year, with extra emphasis on the cold font that saw temperatures drop every hour. Holiday parades, last minute gift ideas, police officers urging the public to imbibe responsibly. All of it orchestrated and usual. He hated this, but "Adam" loved what Maria loved. If Maria loved the holidays, then so did Adam. *Sounds of the season, I loathe simplicity.*

Still, no word on his latest work. The address was right and his message clear.

"They're probably concocting a story befitting a man of his importance, my dear. They also need to explain the presence of another. Maybe a meeting or Christmas party away from the office for close office staff. I wonder?"

"Adam, who are you talking to?"

A thrill runs of The Artist's spine. *What did she hear?* Maria is again in his sight as beautiful as last night and a few hours earlier. His breath taken away at this moment. She is wearing his shirt from the previous evening and he thought, in this moment, that he may have found some modicum of peace.

"Adam? Hello."

"I'm here. Sorry, just talking to myself. Reminding myself of what I have to do today." The Artist composes himself long enough to offer coffee and breakfast.

"A man that can cook. Impressive, but you didn't have to do that," Maria said with a smile on her face.

"No, ma'am. My momma wouldn't approve of a guest going hungry," The Artist doing his best southern gentlemen act to remain in character.

"And would she have approved of, you know?"

"Absolutely not, and that's a bit weird to bring up." Both laughed, and Maria was a bit embarrassed by the question. It was awkward and she knew it as soon as she said it.

The two shared coffee and breakfast together. Again, their conversation flowed as effortlessly as the previous evening and a genuineness between the two emerged. Maria enjoyed the conversation. Adam, as she knew him, was a man with no pretenses. He lived in the moment and loved this way of life. A confirmed bachelor with no family, obviously driven to succeed and a perfect gentleman.

"How is it you're single?"

Adam slightly blushed, "I tried once, but the world is sometimes cruel. After that, I tried a different path."

"I'm sorry," Maria added, "I don't mean to pry."

The Artist placed his hand on the Maria's hands and softened his tone, "Nothing to be sorry about, Maria. There's no secret there. Boy meets girl, boy and girl fall in love, girl leaves. Shit happens and you move on, eventually."

The Artist always knew that the best characters always held a hint of truth. This was a true story from his past, but the meat of the story was removed. Maria didn't need to bother herself with the specifics of a failed relationship.

Breaking news this morning this morning out of Lafayette

Maria breaks with the conversation. She recognized the voice on the television from work.

* Mayor Roger Duplantis, the first term mayor of Lafayette, was found dead this morning of an apparent homicide. *

Maria was fixated on the newscast. The Artist, outside of Maria's field of vision, only smiled. *My friend got my message, I'm sure.*

*KNAC reports that the bodies of the Mayor and his personal aide were found inside of a residence located on Pelican Park Road. The mayor's office confirmed that the popular first term politician and former prosecutor held a Christmas party for his closest aides and colleagues the previous evening and an anonymous call led police to the location. Walter Gauthier has more at the scene. *

"Well, that's an interesting way to start off the morning," Maria said while watching the news report. The Artist said nothing and enjoyed the show, mostly enjoying Maria's reactions. She was very fact of the matter and seemingly unmoved by the scene of people behind the news anchor.

"Political rival," The Artist posited.

Maria turned for a moment and smiled, "I don't think so. Word on the street was that he had affairs a plenty. I'm thinking a jealous husband."

Maria refocused her attention on the scene. The live shot was now on the men and women in the background. Crime scene techs, command personnel, uniformed police. The scene was obviously not as active as it was several hours ago, but they were going to take their time with this one. She sipped her coffee and again her attention focused on a singular individual.

"I know him. I've seen him before," Maria said aloud as she

approached the television screen. "He was at the house yesterday."

The Artist smiled but remained in character. "What guy? What house?"

Maria pointed to a well-dressed young man, obviously someone that held some regard at the scene. "This guy was at the house on Highland Hills. He showed up about an hour after I got there. He was out in charge of the ..."

The Artist stared at Maria with a forced blank, but amused expression.

"... and you have no idea what I'm talking about."

"Maria, I wish I did. I don't watch T.V. very often. Do you have to go?" The Artist lied to his beloved. He knew what she was talking about, but Adam did not.

Maria felt that she was being a bad house guest, but she saw that Adam knew this meant a lot to her. She couldn't help herself.

"I'm so sorry, Adam."

"Maria, you have nothing to apologize for. Go do what you have to do."

Maria ran from the kitchen area and quickly changed into the clothes she wore the night before. Adam stood in amazement watching speed and efficiency in motion. He also prepared a to-go cup of coffee for the intrepid reporter.

"Would you like to shower or something," Adam asked.

"No thanks," Maria said while putting her last shoe on, "I'll grab one at my house."

Maria walked over to the man she shared the evening with and thanked him for the "mistakes" that they made. He handed her the cup of coffee and wished her luck. She kissed him softly and turned toward the door.

"Oh, by the way," The Artist stated, "My number is on the cup." Maria looked on the side of the cup and saw the digits scrawled in permanent marker. She smiled at him and said nothing as she walked away, closing the door behind her. *She'll call, they always do.*

With his love away for the foreseeable day, The Artist could be himself. No more pretending to be Adam. Sensitive, Adam. Adoring, Adam. Adam was boring. The Artist needed to be himself. He needed his canvases. His newest canvas awaited his kindness, but more importantly his dear friend needed his undivided attention. His attention was now focused on the television as he placed the live newsfeed in rewind. He wanted to see what Maria saw and finally found the man that she spoke of.

"This is the man in charge of the investigation? He's is a child playing a man's game. There is no way that he could fully comprehend this excellence, my dear. Dear God, what is he wearing? This is not the attire of the initiated. This fool may have to be dealt with in short order lest my gifts be unappreciated."

He gazed at Donaldson with mild irritation. "You will not spoil my chance to amaze Silas, infant! This is his gift, not yours! You will come to know me."

Foolish boy.

****

Sean found himself wandering the streets for most of the morning until he found a 24-hour diner that serve coffee by the gallon. This diner was not typically his scene, but the morning's weather forced him to seek shelter from the cold and bitter winds. The Marine in him was furious with Gray for not trusting him enough, but the cop in him forced him to realize a singular truth: Gray is looking out for me. He thought he knew his partner, they shared an office for two years and talked about everything, or so he thought. His anger was mitigated by the way Gray spoke to him about getting hurt. He'd never seen Gray like that, and this worried Sean more than the words spoken hours before.

The bell above the door indicated that another soul seeking refuge entered the diner. A shuffle of the feet and the expected sounds of a jacket rustling accompanied. Sean didn't look up to see who it was. He was still burning from his argument with Gray.

"Mind if I join you?"

Sean looked up and saw a familiar face, "Of course, Chief. How'd you find me?"

Desormeaux sat himself down and motioned for the waiter to bring coffee.

"This is one of my usual spots, Sean. I like it here in the mornings. People watching is a hobby of mine. What brings you here?"

"Gray and I had a falling out of sorts."

Desormeaux was intrigued by this statement. "How so?"

"He doesn't trust me, Chief. Everyone seems to know what is going on and I am on the sidelines. This has something to do with Gray's past and he won't tell me what it is. He won't let me help him."

The coffee arrived and both Desormeaux and Sean prepped the steaming drink to their liking.

"Sean, you and I are opposite sides of the same coin. You're all passion and I'm all analysis, both of us want to help Gray. The main difference is that I know that he'll ask when he needs it and you're wanting to force it. Just let it ride and trust Gray. Believe me, he knows what he's doing."

"And I don't, Chief," snapped Sean. "I'm just as capable as he is. He's my partner and I'm out. No offense, but you, Gray, and Rod are not making any sense and none of you are being up-front about what's going on."

Chief was impressed by his young investigator's tenacity. Impressed and somewhat annoyed. Sean had proven himself capable in many ways and Desormeaux appreciated this. It made him an outstanding investigator. Despite his skill, Sean was also young in the violence game. A game that Gray knew all too well. There was no doubt that Sean would match blow for blow with anyone, but this level was beyond him. This game was mental.

"Sean, I have a question for you. What if you could rid the world of an evil so great that if it lived it would soon consume everything around it? Would you get rid of it?"

"Absolutely," Sean answered immediately.

Chief then added, "What if this evil was a person lying on the ground, wounded, and could be saved? No one around. Just you and that person. Would you still get rid of it?"

Sean couldn't answer that question immediately. He didn't know what his superior wanted to hear. If he said yes, then he would be a murderer. If he said no, then he would allow evil to live.

"Chief, I..."

"Silas Gray can answer that question, Sean. Further, he can live with the decision that was made. He's not worried about what happens to him. His code allows him to sleep at night knowing that he did what was necessary to preserve inno-cence, but when he sleeps, he relives his decisions. He's not worried about you doing your job and believe me, he trusts you more than you know. He is trying to save you from the having to make decisions like that. He cares enough to let you live your life without having to live with the consequences of making that choice. You think its lack of trust and not caring to let you in. It's Gray's way of keeping your soul intact."

Desormeaux finished his coffee and placed a few bills on the table.

"Chief, this isn't one of your usual places. Tell me, how'd you find me?"

Desormeaux smiled, "You see, that's why your one of my detectives. You know when someone is lying. By the way, your department phone has GPS and I have the password."

Sean laughed at the statement, "Then tell me, where's Gray right now?"

"Don't know," the Chief said reaching into his pocket and retrieving a phone, "He slid his department phone in my pocket about four hours ago. See ya around."

Sean was left sitting at the table, alone with his thoughts again. His conversation with Desormeaux aided his understanding of his partner but did not lessen his firmness in helping his friend.

VII.

7:45 AM

Gray arrived home thirty minutes ago and, again, faced a gift from Norm. His usual frustration with his pup aside, he was happy to be in the embrace of the familiar. He'd slept roughly four or five hours in the last day and his body craved rest, but now wasn't the time for rest. He prepared coffee for one and as it brewed, he felt the weight of being alone. The house was still and the usual noise of his wife and son were now being enjoyed by his wife's family two states to the north. He missed them terribly at this moment. He missed his little boy running up to him in the morning and having morning coffee with his Charlie. These were the moments that kept the darkness at bay, that allowed him normalcy in a lifetime of extraordinary events. He lost himself in thought.

His concentration was broken by a knock at the door. The knock was forceful, but not a "cop knock." As he approached the door, he couldn't help but notice the large black container in his living room. It remained sealed for now. It taunted him, but he resisted. He arrived at the door and looked through the blinds, as he had done so many times before, and saw the unexplainable.

"What the fuck? Really!"

As he opened the door he was confronted by a new familiar face.

"Ms. Gomez, I see that our little chat earlier did nothing to drive the point home. Let's be clear. My house if off limits. My family is off limits. Everything you are doing right now is off limits. If that is in any way unclear, then please allow me to elaborate."

Maria understood, but this was important, "Detective, I know the man leading the investigation and I know why he is here. Please, five minutes of your time and you'll never see me again."

His anger with Maria was understandable, but he admired her tenacity. He broke with his irritation long enough to feel the bitter cold filling his home and to hear the coffee maker beeping. He decided to break his rule against certain guests being in the house when the misses and son were away. He needed the information that she had, and a kind gesture would further his need for clarity.

"Five minutes, Ms. Gomez. Please, come in. It's very cold."

"Thank you," Maria gladly accepting refuge from the elements.

"Would you like coffee, Ms. Gomez?" Gray was nothing if not a gracious host.

"No thank you, Detective."

Maria studied the room and obviously noticed the black box in the middle of the living room. She studied the pictures of Gray's family. Mothers and fathers, sons and daughters, friends and colleagues, all the normalcy one would expect from this quiet part of the world. The house was decorated as one would expect from a small family: an odd combination of a usual suburban art with a child's touch. This house was a home, filled with the trappings of a family man.

"You have a beautiful home, Detective. I'll say that the black box with a scythe on it throws the room off a bit," Maria said, trying to endear herself to the man approaching her with his cup of coffee.

Gray smiled at the comment, "Thank you. Please sit, Ms.

Gomez. You have until the end of this cup of coffee to explain why you're hear, again."

"Detective…"

"Gray, please. This is my home. Leave work at work."

Maria believed this to be a sign of acceptance, but it was a disarming method that Gray used many times in interviews with suspects. *What is she up to?*

"Ok, Gray," Maria started, "I believe I know why they brought the young guy to investigate the case."

"To whom are you referring to, Ms. Gomez."

"Maria, please." Gray nodded and Maria continued her thought, "Gary Donaldson."

Gray was impressed. Her sources were top notch, still he showed nothing. The less Maria could glean from him the better this will go.

"Gray, Donaldson is a well-connected and usually brought in for political reasons. His connections to the governor's office are well-known. He's basically an attack dog for his uncle. If you were dismissed from the case, then there is a deeper reason for it."

Gray quietly sips his coffee. "And what reason would that be, Maria."

"His last assignment was investigating cops and officials Jeff Davis Parish. Half of the people investigated were found to have violated any number of laws, but no arrests were made. Oddly enough, the parish pulled for his uncle in the governor's race a couple years ago."

"I'm not interested in politics, Maria," Gray said flatly, "I only care about doing my job."

"That's my point. Any number of people could be here right now, but Donaldson is here for a reason. He finds things that people don't want to find and has the stroke to blow it wide open or twist it toward someone's favor." Maria couldn't help but look at the black elephant in the room when saying those words.

Gray saw Maria's look and took another sip of his coffee, "Is there something here you find interesting, Maria."

Maria felt the overwhelming urge to confront Gray. He wasn't fazed by anything she said and appeared to carefully select every word. She also knew he was a seasoned detective that analyzed her every syllable and body movement.

"Word on the is that street several years ago was there was a group of officers that worked outside of the law. Vigilante-types. They went anywhere they pleased and enforced the law the way they saw fit. I interviewed a few people that were snatched up by them. One of the guys I interviewed said that he was by himself one second and the next thing he remembered was the he was being dropped off at a jail. He never saw who grabbed him."

"Really, that's very interesting, Maria. What did the guy do to gain such attention from these people," Gray asked, sipping his coffee, again.

"He killed a family of seven, four of them children under the age of 16." Maria saw a hint of smirk from Gray as she said this. *She has balls for interviewing that guy; he was psychotic and fought like a rabid dog before Mags knocked him out with brass knuckles.* She began to believe that the man before her was more complicated than he appeared, or at the very least more secretive than she once thought. She again looked at the container. Nothing from Gray.

"Maria, you came to my home to tell me that Donaldson is a pawn and to tell me about a bunch of out of control cops. The box that you are looking at is an old army footlocker that I pack my clothes in. I'm leaving to meet my family on Saturday. That's my luggage. Is there anything else that I can do for you, Ms. Gomez?" *She's getting too close to this.*

Maria expected more but knew she would get nothing from Gray. He was a seasoned law enforcement officer and she was a reporter: the two hardly go together. She naively believed that he would tell her something about the investigation or at least provide a detail, but she got nothing. If anything, she gave Gray too much.

"No, that's it."

Gray finished his coffee. "Thank you for the information. Please be safe driving home or wherever you're going." Gray stood up and approached his front door, placing his hand on the doorknob.

A disappointed Maria stood up and thanked Gray for his time. She was taken by him more now than ever, but the attraction was not remotely reciprocated. Gray opened the door for his guest.

"Maria," Gray stopped her in her tracks. "Some people are called to confront demons. When that time comes, you call upon broken angels that stand unafraid."

"Who said that, Gray?"

Gray looked down, hiding his sadness, "An old friend that I miss very much." *Mags always had a way with words.*

Maria handed gray her card, "Call me. I have ways of getting information."

"I'll keep that in mind. Good morning, Ms. Gomez."

Gray closed the door and pocketed Maria's card. His focus was now on the vessel before him, the sickle emblazoned on the cover. He selected the proper key from his key ring and began to manipulate the padlocks that prevented trespassing into this sacred sarcophagus. Each turn of the key forcing a piece of his soul to tatter. His darkness would soon consume him. A darkness that he felt comfortable navigating. He needed to be that man again in order to stop the madness overwhelming this area as of late. He didn't ask for this present, but someone felt this was necessary. The monster called him out and he felt forced to answer this challenge.

Broken angels who stand unafraid.

****

Maria walked to her car and was more convinced than ever that she was close to what was going on. She also believed that the man inside of the house behind her was as dangerous a man that she'd ever met. His control stunned her, and she was convinced that he was a good man that hid a dark side. Gray is a good cop and seemingly unphased by anything in his path. He sat in front of her sipping his coffee and hardly moved from his original position, except for when he spoke of an old friend. There was, however, something deeper. Something that terrified her. A cold calculus with every word he uttered, and action taken, or not taken.

She drove away from Gray's home and felt she needed more information from a trusted source. She retrieved her cell phone and called her partner in crime.

"Tom, its Maria. Find out everything you can on Silas Gray. Job histories, family, anything you can. Something isn't sitting right with me. Oh, and see if there is anything with his name that I associated with a sickle and look up quotes for broken angels. Sounds crazy, but just take a look."

Tom protested, as was his usual, and reminded Maria that this wasn't some politician taking bribes or a criminal that sold drugs on the corner. This was a cop, a cop with an outstanding reputation. Maria didn't listen to Tom and made her demand again and Tom was powerless to stop her. Maria's drive placed her in many precarious situations. An expose' of a corrupt city manager that embezzled millions, a crime lord with ties to the district attorney's office, human trafficking rings that included payoffs to former and current state and federal agents. Nothing was off limits for her, but Silas Gray was a mystery. A man that could disarm her with a look. Maria was sure that Tom though she had lost her mind and she didn't care. She was hunting for a story and the story came first. She felt the thrill of the chase.

****

Kap and Tyler cleared the crime scene and both men were famished from their evening's adventure. Both barely slept a wink before being called to Pelican Park Road and both needed a recharge. As they drove to the nearest breakfast spot, Kap felt a heaviness in the air. Thankfully, Donaldson was not with them and did not add to the already testy situation.

"What do you think, Tyler?"

"I think that skeletons will be revealed and then sealed again," Tyler said while looking out of the passenger side window. "We definitely underestimated Donaldson."

Kap agreed. "Yes we did. What about Gray?"

"Gray doesn't underestimate anyone. I'm sure he's done or is doing his homework."

"Why now," Kap asked. "Who is going after Gray and why wouldn't they come after us, too? This obviously has something to do with the team, but we don't seem to be the targets."

"Who knows," Tyler said. "All I know is that we have to find out who else was involved and see if we can get to them before this psycho or Donaldson do. It won't be easy."

"No, it will not."

The two men's fates were intertwined with Gray's. If Donaldson discovered the connection between the victims before they could contain it, then all three would fall. If Gray put the pieces together, which they were sure he had, then there would be hell to pay. All they could hope for was that Donaldson's connections would be stalled by red tape and bureaucracy.

VIII.

10:00 AM

1201 Rue Royale

The Artist arrived at the posh gallery in time for the receptionist to greet him as the first guest of the day. Art surrounded the man as he entered; pieces that moved the eye and soul. He was taken in by the atmosphere. This was a luxury business specializing in interior designs. He thrived in such conditions, conditions that befit a man of his tastes.

"Good morning, sir," the young man greeting The Artist said pleasantly. "Welcome to Maison de Luxe. Do you have an appointment?"

"Good morning. I have an appointment to see the Ms. Claxton. Tell her Adam Singleton is here to see her." The Artist handed the well-dressed man a card bearing his nom de plume and the young man accepted it with a smile. *Again, fake smiles everywhere.*

"I will announce you to Ms. Claxton, sir. Please follow me."

The Artist was led into a room decorated to receive those of refinement. The table before him appeared handmade and held a selection of refreshment. Gourmet treats that tempted the strongest of wills and Kopi Luwak freshly brewed held in a fine silver pot. The Artist poured himself a small cup of the expensive coffee but dared not partake of the sweet delicacies. He would not pollute himself with refined foods, even if they were disguised in exclusivity. All of this impressed The Artist, but he knew he was still amongst amateurs in the field of art.

This luxury was built on lies and the foundation was no more dry sand. His canvas would join him shortly and he would behold that which would further refine his masterpiece.

During his wait, he observed that the proprietor of this museum of excess had a fascination with the ancient and the modern. Works created by street artists in the same vein as Banksy filled some sections and murals of ancient battles the other sections. Masters' facsimiles meeting aspiring vagabond originals. The Artist couldn't help but be attracted to images of torture and desire and sculptures that bore sharp points that reminded him of his brushes. He smiled and thought fondly about his own creations.

The door opened and a woman in her forties entered; her dutiful receptionist excusing himself and closing the door behind her. The woman before him was professionally dressed in the latest business fashions. She maintained her looks through a combination of moisturizers, exercise, and plastic surgery – the latter being more of an assumption to most, but The Artist knew better. Still, she was very attractive, well put together, and her business acumen top notch. She created this business a little over two years ago, but her family's influence and money assured the business' place in select society. She wasn't his physical canvas type as he preferred the natural look, but her elegance presented an irresistible opportunity. *Silas will enjoy this.*

"Mr. Singleton," Rosemarie Claxton exclaimed, "It's such a pleasure to finally meet you. Your donations to my charitable foundation have been very generous. I hope that I haven't kept you waiting for too long."

"Not long at all, Ms. Claxton."

"Rose, please."

"Only if you call me Adam, Rose. I see that you have quite a selection of works here."

"Anything in particular that catches your eye," Rose asked, her obvious attraction to The Artist written in her eyes.

"This piece," pointing to a large sculpture bearing beveled edges and sharp turns. "I like how the sculptor used everyday items to create it. The curves of the artwork harken to the curves of a lover and the sharp edges remind me of how a lover can cut deep. It's truly extraordinary."

Rose was enthralled by his analysis, despite her seeming inability to see what he saw. The way he spoke to her, pointing out small details and intricacies to support what he took from the piece only increased her desire to have him.

"You see all of this, Adam. Something tells me that you're a romantic at heart. Tell me, does it remind you of someone."

The Artist smiled, knowing that the hook was baited. "It does. Someone that I felt very deeply for, but the feelings were not returned in kind. That was some time ago, but still the feeling of unrequited desire stings upon reflection."

"I know what you mean," Rose responded empathetically and placing her hand on his as a form of consolation. "We all have desires that need fulfillment."

"I couldn't have agreed more with that statement, Rose."

Both continued to exchange pleasant words and Rose showed The Artist the finer points of luxury interior design. It was more of an art than a science, something that he could appreciate. What he couldn't appreciate was the woman before him. False in every sense of the word and striving to maintain a youthful existence despite her obvious failings, albeit many of those failings were self-inflicted. He studied her movements prior to this moment and her luxurious lifestyle held a darker side that required her mingling with the dregs of society. Degrading herself for her next fix of oxycodone or whatever she could get her hands on. He felt repulsion every time she would grab his arm and escort him through the gallery. *You sicken me, but this is a means to your end.*

"Please tell me that you received my invitation," Rose said as she and The Artist fixated themselves on another sculptor's work.

"Invitation?"

"To the charity gala tonight. Here at the gallery. You must come, Adam. It is the event of the holiday. Only the most elite will be here tonight."

The Artist knew this fact. "No, I can't say that I have."

Rose's eyes flashed with the delight of offering a personal invitation, "You must come as my guest. I won't take no for an answer."

"I would be delighted to come, Rose."

Rose nearly shrieked with delight at his acceptance of the invitation. She was also not immune to The Artist's overt attractiveness. She was taken in by the conversation and his physical attributes and needed to have him before anyone else could.

"Adam, is there a Mrs. Singleton in your life?"

The Artist forced a blush, "No there isn't, Rose. Never felt the need."

Rose's expression changes slightly, a look that The Artist knew all too well. "The gala starts as 8pm. Would you care to join me for drinks after the gallery closes?"

"What time does the gallery close," The Artist asked.

"Today, we close at noon. Holidays and all. Employees and other staff will be gone by 1:30."

The Artist saw the hunger in her eyes. Rose wished to have him, how could she not. He was an exquisite example of humanity. Physically a specimen to behold. Cultured in many ways. His prowess legendary. She couldn't resist him, much like an insect couldn't resist the sweet nectar from a Venus flytrap.

"Rose, I would love to join you, but I must remain discreet."

Rose could barely contain herself, "Discretion is my forte', Adam. There are no security cameras in the gallery as many of my guests value privacy. Here, take this." Rose handed The Artist a keycard. "This will allow entry to my private elevator. The entry is near the rear exit of the gallery. You'll have all the discretion you could hope for. Just you and I. How does 3 sound?"

These were morsels of information that he knew. The final piece, secret access, was now in place. He was given free reign of the gallery, the private elevator, and the canvas' private quarters. Quarters that witnessed many forms of debauchery over the years.

"I look forward to your hospitality, Rose." The Artist held Rose's hand in his and extended a kiss to the appendage. "Until, then."

The Artist turned toward the entrance and felt the gaze of all who saw him. He knew that he would not soon be forgotten by anyone occupying the space, male or female. He always left an impression wherever he went. As he entered his vehicle, he felt the need for self-improvement. He would visit the place that nauseated him in order to achieve the perfection that he craved, that he held within him: Gymnase de Lafayette. The short drive prepared him mentally for the imperfection held within the hallowed halls of fakery. *False pretenses offend my sensibilities.*

He parked in his usual spot far from the entrance. He wished to be seen as he walked in with his usual accompaniment of a gym and garment bag. *Everyone deserves to be blessed by me.* His phone rings as he gathers his belongings. His heart nearly bursts out of his chest and he is distracted from his mission. Only one could have this effect on him.

"Hello," The Artist answers, barely able to contain his excitement as he heard Maria reciprocate the greeting, "I wasn't expecting to hear from you so soon."

****

Maria blushed as she spoke to Adam. The previous evening and the early morning hours ran through her mind like a daydream and she felt invigorated by the thought of seeing him again.

"So, what are you doing this evening?"

"I'm meeting an old friend earlier this afternoon," The Artist said, "but if you'd like we can go somewhere this evening."

"What did you have in mind," Maria asked.

"Do you like Christmas parties? I have an invitation to a gala tonight and no one to go with. Don't think of it as a date. More like you'd give me a reason to leave early."

"Who's party?"

"It's the gala at Rosemarie Claxton's gallery. I've had to go stag every year and every year had to stay much longer than I wanted to. Please say yes. Don't make me have to be around those people all night."

"How do you know her," Maria was obviously impressed with is connections. "She is very, um…"

"She's a snob, Maria." Maria's laughter could be heard throughout the newsroom after hearing that comment, "A snob that happens to be one of my clients. She always invites me, and I am obligated to go in order to keep her business."

"Adam, that's not really my thing."

"I'm not beyond begging," The Artist said. "Think of it as

charity for the needy, like I need an excuse to have to leave so I can spend more time with you."

Maria couldn't help but give into Adam's logic. She agreed to his terms and promised that she would find a way for both to excuse themselves before the evening became too tedious for their tastes. Still, while talking to Adam she still thought of Gray. She realized that the other man in her life was more mysterious than the man she was speaking to. This intrigued her. Here was a man that she knew was an open book and could talk to him and get an answer. On the opposite end was Gray, a man undefined in her eyes.

"Where would you like to meet," The Artist asked Maria.

Maria thought for a moment, "How about the usual spot? I'll let you figure that out."

"Really? No clues." The Artist knew that she referred to the bar where they met. The place that promises good service and where Sasha would always offer liquid courage.

"You're a smart guy," Maria teased. "You'll figure it out."

With that sentence Maria hung up the phone. The Artist was pleased that she reached out, beyond pleased. He would join Rose for drinks in a few hours, meet with Maria, and hopefully his art would be on full display for the upper crust to enjoy. He only regretted that his friend Silas wouldn't be there at the big reveal so that he could see how far he was willing to go for him.

"This will not do, my dear," The Artist said to himself while walking into the gym. "We must figure out a way for my friend to enjoy the evening's festivities."

He was met by another familiar face as he entered the facility, the blonde with the perfect tan. He received the usual greeting that came with her meager paycheck and a white towel awaited him as he graced the building with his presence. Soon he would be in the rapture of masters as he strove for perfection. His selection on this day included Mahler's *Symphony No 4* and selected pieces of Chopin and Debussy. The masters would guide him through the pain of excellence and his own artistic contribution would serve to feed the masses yearning for the visceral.

This will be a good day.

IX.

Romeo three to Romeo one, clear up... wait!

"*Romeo three and four?!*"

Again, silence. "Romeo one, control. No response from three and four. Where the fuck is my support?!"

"*Control, Romeo one, response two minutes out.*"

"*Fuck it! Mags on me, cover rear." No verbal response from Mags, but Gray knew she would follow. Tyler and Kap weren't responding and family never leaves family.*

Gray and Mags proceeded up the same stairs, Gray's weapon focused on the opening that his team entered and Mags trained her weapon behind them. Back-to-back they climbed the stairwell and silently hoped that their brothers were still alive. They didn't hear any shots fired and no screams were heard from the open-air area above them. Mags adjusted her position behind Gray once they reached the top of the platform leading into the darkness. Entry would be quick and fluid. The lights mounted on their weapons would prove useful in the shadows. A firm squeeze on Gray's shoulder and both were in. Quick and efficient, no wasted movement.

Kap was midway through the room when he fell and Tyler several feet from him. The area provided concealment for their prey. Gray saw that both appeared to be injured, blood covering their faces, but they were breathing. He couldn't determine what happened and, for a moment, his focused shifted to helping them.

"*Mags, move to Kap.*"

Gray and Mags again moved, sweeping the room with light. As they reached Kap they saw that he was breathing normally. He was unconscious. Tyler was next and in similar condition. Tyler's injuries were more severe, and his handgun missing. Next to Tyler was another handgun, the slide locked rearward and seemingly devoid of ammunition.

"Romeo one, control. I have two down, injured. ETA?"

"One minute, Romeo one. Hold position."

"One minute," Mags said. "A lot could happen."

"I agree. Defensive position around Kap and Tyler and wait for response."

Gray remained near Kap and Mags near Tyler, both knowing that they were exposed. The team's element of surprise was compromised, but how? No one knew the mission except for the team, control, and selected individuals that would provide cover stories in case something went wrong. This would be one of those times, unfortunately.

"Gray!"

Gray turned toward the voice and saw Mags, obviously taken by surprise by the man they were stalking, except now they were the target. Mags was capable and they swept as much of the area that they could before their attention diverted to Kap and Tyler. Mental mistakes forced upon them by the emotion of the moment. Gray's light showered Mags and at this moment he wished he were blind.

"Drop the gun," Gray demanded. He saw the weapon's muzzle pressed against the right side of Mags' throat. The look of distress covered her face. An image that would later haunt him.

"Who the fuck you think you're talking to, asshole?!" The Butcher stood defiant knowing that he held an Ace in his hand.

"Gray," Mags said, "Shoot this motherfucker!"

"Really, bitch," the man holding Mags yelled, "Fuck you!"

Gray's light shown the eyes of Mags's captor, eyes of a beast with *a taste for blood. He then saw Mags' face change from fear to peace, a resignation to the situation. Mags knew something that Gray did not and faced this knowledge with the same determination that catapulted her into the ranks of the elite. He again viewed the suspect, his animalistic appearance now mixed with fury. It was almost as if he fed on the fear of others and hated that Mags showed none.*

Gray raised his weapon to the target. No feeling. No remorse. Only the mission.

BANG

****

He believed he'd fallen asleep, but that was not the case. He was back in the place that haunted him. Back with his team. Their last mission together. The last thing he remembered before his journey into the past was opening the sickle laden container and emptying its contents. The only item in his hand when he awoke from his past was a picture of the REAPERS. All six of them in their gear, filthy and smiling. Their faces with splotches of mud and dirt. Tony, the big man of the group, stood behind them all and his wingspan nearly encompassed the breadth of the other five. As always, Gray and Mags stood by each other in the middle of the picture, bookended by Tyler and Kap. Jacques laid on his side in front of the group, one arm propping up his head and a leg in a triangle as if he were posing on the beach. *This was a great day.*

Gray retrieved his personal phone from the stand next to him and saw that he had a text message from Rod. As he saw it, Rod was checking in on him. Gray never liked texting, too impersonal. He preferred a voice and per his preference decided to call Rod.

"It's about damn time you called me. What were you doin'? Never mind, don't tell me. I'll hate myself if I don't like the answer."

"Hey Rod," Gray answered. "What's up?"

"What's up? It's one in the afternoon and Big Homie ain't heard shit about shit. I'm feeling a bit unloved at the moment, almost like we had a good time last night and you now you won't return my phone calls."

"You didn't call, Rod. You texted"

"Don't get smart. You know what I mean. Heard anything from Sean or Chief?"

"Nope, and I'm not planning on it. Sean and I aren't seeing eye-to-eye right now and Chief is, well, doing Chief shit."

"I hear ya. Listen, Chief said to give you what you need to move this train along. So, if you need anything let me know and I'll make sure it's taken care of. Think of me as your Big Homie Allstate agent. You in good hands."

"You know, I could use something," Gray responded.

"Damn, that was quick! Whatcha need, baby?"

"See what you can find out about Donaldson. I came into some information about him being a merc for the governor's office. I know his connections are deep, but position and lack of experience leads me to believe that there is more to little bastard."

"So, you want me to look into a guy who is more connected than Verizon. The same guy that listed you as a suspect for some heinous shit and send you that information as quietly as I can in hopes that no one will find out. That's what you want me to do?"

"Yes, Rod. That's what I want you to do."

"OK. Just making sure I heard you. Gimme a little while to pull out the stone tablets from my ancient connections and I'll let you know."

"Be careful," Gray told his friend.

"Stop saying that! You're worse than Big Momma. Don't tell her I said that. She'll kill me."

Gray placed the phone back from whence it came and saw the items laid out before him. He was reminded of the training and missions that accompanied these items, especially the vest. He inspected them for any signs that they would fail him in the near future. Nothing, not a single fault in the equipment. Just the way he left them years ago. His hard armor; perfect condition. His equipment on his belt still in the same positions. His holster in working condition. All the items showed the usual distressing caused by scores of street incursions. He then gazed upon his uniform. It had been some time, but he remembered every inch of it, particularly the shapes of the stains left on it from his final mission. He couldn't bear to clean it as it would remove the remaining signs of Mags', Tony's, and Jacques' existence with the team. Every drop was precious to him and every reminder painful. He was the only eyewitness left to all three's bravery. Kap and Tyler were there for Tony and Jacques, but Mags' story was his to tell and keep sacred. The rest were mere spectators to an aftermath. Underneath was a dark gray folded t-shirt with the sickle and crosshairs. No words, just the image. Only six were ever made and worn and only three had the honor of being able to wear it today, although none of three ever did.

The final unwrapped gifts were his well-used H&K UMP and a black case that held his second most trusted friend: Gladys. He opened the case and saw her sitting there in cut foam, the smell of gun oil filled his senses. The manufacturer called her a Sig Sauer 1911. Gray referred to her as his mistress. She laid there in the same condition that he left her. Never failing him when needed. Every minute detail known to him. The forbidding reunion of man and machine now complete as he held her for what he hoped would be their last mission together.

****

The Artist's return to his apartment was met with much delight to himself. He felt as if he could move mountains. His exercises were met with the same awe and curiosity as so many times before. His dress and style were impeccable as always. A deep blue suit and selected items that would accentuate his wardrobe and affluence. Today was different, though. He had two important dates this day: the first with his canvas, Rose; and the second with his love, Maria. Today's procession would ultimately lead to his only friend, Silas. The stars aligned for The Artist like no other time before. He would soon be amid his own genius and what he held dear, simultaneously. He knew Silas would figure this evening out and would most likely join he and Maria. *Only Silas is worthy to read into this.*

"Oh, my dear! This day couldn't be better! Only my finest brushes will do for this evening. The adoration of the masses awaits me and my loves. I would not attempt to beguile them with inferior work. Only the best will do!"

He prepared his brushes by inspecting them. Edges were clean and sharp. Teeth were perfectly aligned, or unaligned depending on the brush. Bondage materials were new and unused. All were placed in his black trash bag, but on this day this bag would be transported in a canvas satchel. Also enclosed was his typical vacuum sealed bag containing high-end clothing.

"We cannot be suspicious, my dear. Eyes may be upon us, despite the promised discretion. This will be a night to remember for some and impossible to forget for most."

There was still time before his rendezvous with Rose. He thought he would grab a late lunch at a restaurant near Maison de Luxe.

****

Rod was good to his word. He pulled out all the stops for his friend and quietly asked people that he trusted about Donaldson. What he found was a mix of political connections and seemingly classified work performed on behalf of the state. Some of his contacts were unavailable at the time of his calling and he left messages for each.

"Well look at that," Rod said as a ringtone of AC/DC's *Back in Black* played. "Hello."

He exchanged pleasantries with a high-ranking member of the State Police, a man that he trusted could keep things quiet. Questions were asked about Donaldson and promises made to keep names out of the limelight. Rod observed that even the mention of this kid's name sent shockwaves through even the stiffest of spines. Many of the known facts about Donaldson were bad enough to keep tough men out of his sights, but some of the more secret facts were terrifying. The governor's office, blackmail of state and federal judges, politicians bending to his will at every turn were just the start of Donaldson's clout. Rod took notes on all of it. The source was credible and beyond reproach in Rod's eyes.

"Appreciate it, I owe you." Rod hung up the phone and viewed all the information that he'd written. It was daunting seeing the words before him. *How did this guy get so much?*

Rod became more worried about Donaldson and that worry translated itself into worry for Gray. He knew Gray was a force, but Donaldson was the immovable object in this scenario. Still, Gray had something that Donaldson didn't: violence. If Rod read Donaldson correctly, which he was sure he did, then the tiebreaker between the two men would be who could commit more violence upon the other. Donaldson was mostly mouth and Gray mostly action, but the former was still a relative unknown. Rod was still uneasy about a final conflict between the two, but was sure that it would end with one man on the ground.

X.

2:40 PM

Sean entered the bar and saw that the late lunch crowd seated in what he assumed was their normal position. The building had a faint smell of stale beer and cigarette smoke, but he wasn't there for the atmosphere. *Hostile Downtown* wasn't his typical social scene, but he was never one for partying until all hours of the night. Some would say that this was an "alternative lifestyle" bar, but Sean knew better. He accepted people for who they were. No judgements. He was there for information. Behind the bar was his source, Bryan, or Bianca as she liked to be called.

Sean and Bianca had a connection, albeit professional. About three years prior, Sean was working a patrol shift and saw what he believed was a woman being beaten by several men. Sean exited his patrol unit and intervened in the merciless attack, definitively defeating the assailants with a mixture of martial artistry and police-approved techniques. At the end of it, four men laid on the ground, three of which were unconscious, and Sean tended to battered woman. Even after it was revealed that Bianca was born a man, Sean rendered aid as he would've anyone else and sat by Bianca's bedside that first night and visited her as often as he could. At first it was part of the job. He needed a statement from her. Latter visits were friendlier, but always professional. He couldn't fully understand Bianca's tribulations, but he would be there for her triumphs.

During the trial of those men, Sean sat next to Bianca in

the courtroom and assured her that no harm would come to her. She had physically mended from the beating, but mentally she was fragile and bore scars from that fateful night. The men on trial also bore the scars of that night. A gift from Sean and a reminder that their behavior was unacceptable in every sense of the word. These men attempted to intimidate Sean and Bianca using icy stares in their direction. Bianca was cross examined by an unscrupulous defense attorney that used several homophobic and transphobic slurs toward her, but still she found Sean in the gallery and fed off his silent composure. His blank expression toward the men would fade when Bianca needed strength to continue after the attorney's onslaught. Day in and day out, Sean would provide an ever-present specter of menace toward those that feed upon the innocent. She always said that she owed Sean and Sean always told her that she didn't owe him anything. Still, Sean knew she was a great resource because of her proximity to people in the know and would ask her, on occasion, for information.

"Hey, Bianca," Sean said, taking a seat at the bar.

Bianca immediately recognized the voice and spun around to greet her friend and one-time protector. "Officer Guthrie! It's been too long. How are things."

"Please, call me Sean. Things are good. You seem to be doing well."

"Oh yes. Business is great!" Bianca was the bartender and owner of the establishment. Her assailants came from very well-off backgrounds and the subsequent civil suit bankrupted a couple of those families and bankrolled her place of business.

"I see that. The place looks great. I'm glad to see it."

"You know, I'm always looking for security on the weekends if you're interested. Pay is great and it's only a few hours a night."

"You know I can't, but I appreciate the offer."

Bianca always offered when they met, and Sean always politely refused.

"Well, it'll be there if you ever change your mind. What brings you in today?"

"Bianca, I'm working something right now and I need some information. You are basically in the heart of the area so you're in a perfect position to keep your ears open for me."

"Sean, no need for flattery. You know I'll do what I can. What do you have?"

"I'm looking for someone with a flair for the dramatic."

Bianca laughed at this, "Honey, that's just about everyone that walks in here." Sean couldn't help but agree with the hilarity of the statement.

"You got me on that one. I'm thinking it's a male, possibly new to the area, and possibly a fan of art and religion." Sean was smart and figured that the wall art at the first scene gave an insight to the murderer's psychopathy.

"Anything else?"

"He'll be physically fit, most likely someone who keeps himself in shape."

Bianca was intrigued by this statement. "Does this have to do something with the murder on Highland Hills?"

Sean was impressed with how Bianca put that together so quickly. She was sharp and this statement proved it. "Why do you say that?"

"Sean, give a girl a little credit. A murder happens in your neck of the woods yesterday and now you're sitting at my bar asking for information. It doesn't take a rocket scientist."

"Your right, as always, Bianca. Just call me if you get anything and be careful. This is a very dangerous person."

"I'll be fine. Bundle up, it's getting colder outside." Bianca appreciated the concern and her concern for Sean was returned.

Bianca watched Sean leave the building and began her way of gathering information. First, she sent a text messages and then sent a message to her private social media page. She was discreet with the description of the man and let her friends and followers think that the man left his credit card at the bar the night before. Her contacts, both personal and social, would work their way around. A few thousand sets of eyes were better than her pair. She would also keep an eye out for someone matching Sean's vague description; a task that could prove a bit daunting. Her business was frequented by many matching what Sean described. The relative needle in a stack of needles.

Sean walked back to the vehicle he retrieved earlier in the day. He was bothered by Gray being alone on this and more bothered that he had to ask Bianca for help. The reason for this feeling was because he knew that Gray and Bianca could be in danger and he could only help if he was with them. Gray knew the risks of the job, but Bianca was an innocent. His protective sense was in overdrive and the only thing he could do was wait.

Sean drove around the city for a while searching for something. Peace, revenge, time. Only he knew what he was looking for and he didn't know what he was looking for. In times like this he leaned on his partner, his brother. This wasn't an option to him at this moment. His anger toward Gray overwhelmed and subsided like waves.

****

"Why the Lanier's and Duplantis," Donaldson said to himself. "I'm missing something. Something only that bastard knows. Why the gap in his service records?"

Donaldson slept very little between the time he left Duplantis' crime scene and this moment. He knew that Gray was involved and held the key to ending this, a key that Gray would never give him. The thought tore through him, consuming him as he continued to dwell on a man that was immune to him. *Doesn't he know who I am?*

A tone from his phone would soon answer his questions. An urgent e-mail sent via a secure server. It looked to be a court case: *State of Louisiana vs. Silas Gray*. The proceedings were sealed. It was a grand jury decision dated years before his introduction to the man he had come to despise. He hastily retreats into his home office. The office looked like a spreadsheet of mayhem. Pictures of the Lanier's on one end of a large white board and Duplantis' and his lover's dismembered bodies adorning the other. Among the collage of barbarism were pictures of four men: Gray, Sean, Rod, and Desormeaux. Gray's photo took a prominent position above the other three. He opened the e-mail on his computer and began reading. His appetite for the information was voracious. Names that should have been redacted were not. This was an unaltered copy of sealed court proceedings. No one should have this, and the information was obviously sent from a singular source. *Thank you, Uncle Luke.*

Donaldson believed that he'd found the cornerstone for his case with this information, but it would take him hours to read through it all. His obsession was worth the hours that it would take to consume. The goal for Donaldson was not justice for the six people slain by a monster. His goal was taking down Silas Gray, by any and all means at his disposal.

****

Rose's employees left for the remainder of the day and would not return for several days. Christmas holidays proved to be useful is keeping prying eyes away from her business and her private apartment above the gallery. She was expecting a guest, Adam Singleton. She bathed herself with the finest soaps and shampoos and only used the best lotions to keep her skin youthfully supple. She desired to have Adam and what Rosemarie Claxton desired she got. People couldn't resist her. She was upper class, refined, and seemingly envied by all who knew her.

Her moisturizing regimen included every place that her hands could reach, including her feet. It was only at this point that she would pause and look upon her past. She was an opiate addict and that addiction led her down a dark road: heroin. She wouldn't allow her arms or legs to show the years of abuse and chose to inject the potent poison between her toes. Each gap between digits was pierced by a needle at some point and it was one incident that caused her transition from heroin to pills. Rose's point of enlightenment occurred when she witnessed a murder or what she believed was a murder. Never in her life had she viewed such violence, except in movies. But this transformative moment wasn't a movie. It was her life. She was a bit hazy on the details due to her coming down off of a high, but she would have to relive that moment at least one other time in the form of a formal recorded statement. Her family would ensure damage control afterwards. That was when she decided to "get clean" and refuse a substance meant for the lower class. She was more refined, and refinement was for the upper crust. She finished her routine and proceeded to select something special for her gentleman caller.

"What shall I wear for Adam?" She selected several garments that would entice the eye and selected one for a man of his stature and taste. "He'll love this."

She waited patiently and hoped that he was as punctual as he was desirable. She prepared herself a glass of white wine and left a second empty glass near the electric wine chiller. Wine was as top shelf as she was. A 30-milligram tablet of oxycodone recently acquired by her loyal receptionist accompanied this glass of high-end vino. Rose's addiction, as it were, could never be halted, only polished. She checks her watch: 2:57. Three minutes until she and Adam would see each other in a way reserved for very few.

****

The Artist always arrived on time for his appointments and this appointment deserved his reliability. He parked his vehicle in a covered garage hidden from view by anyone but those that knew where to look. The elevator was exactly where Rose said it would be. He saw a white Range Rover near the elevator and presumed it belong to his canvas.

"She is a woman of taste, my dear. But I will say that her selection of vehicle is somewhat disappointing. Not all canvases are perfect."

He retrieved the key card from his jacket pocket and held the canvas bag in his free hand. As he saw it, Rose wouldn't ask many questions about the bag. If she did, she would receive a prepared response. This wouldn't be a lie, The Artist loathed liars, but it wasn't the complete truth. *Truth will be realized during her contribution.*

Beep

He swiped the card and the spacious elevator door opened. Rose was expecting him. As the doors closed behind him, he observed the walls covered in mirror and another door immediately in front of him. One side led to her apartment and the other to the gallery. The panel on each side decided where the end point would be. This was obviously an elevator that could transport people or artwork or both. The mirrors were just a narcistic touch. He couldn't help but admire his physique, his clothing, his overall appearance. Beyond that was his intellect and sophistication. An Artist's intellect. He saw things that no one else saw. Used mediums never before attempted. All this for one man, his only friend.

Ding

The doors opened into a large living area and before The Artist was Rose with desire in her eyes.

"Good afternoon, Adam."

"Good afternoon, Rose."

XI.

Rose was a vision to The Artist's eyes, albeit one he was repulsed to see. Every curve of her toned body shown through shear white night attire, only undergarments worn were silk panties that were barely there. She dressed as a young woman would and The Artist could barely contain the urge to rip her in half. He detested the falseness of her outward form; all aspects of it. To many, she would be a vision of perfection, both natural and manmade. To The Artist, she was what he loathed. *I must stay in character.*

"I see that I'm a bit over dressed for this meeting," The Artist said. "I believe that I'll change into something for the occasion."

Rose walked to an antique chair near the elevator and watched as "her" Adam removed his clothing. She marveled at the chiseled frame before her. It rivaled many of her sculptures in the gallery and would tempt the goddess' themselves, if they were real. Every muscle in The Artist's body exuded form and prowess and Rose wished to have every inch of his form on hers.

"What's in the bag, Adam?"

The Artist smiled. He was surprised that she hadn't mentioned it before now. He figured that pills she took earlier affected her observation skills. From the bag he retrieved a brand-new set of white overalls.

"Adam, you are an artist," Rose exclaimed. She enjoyed the

sense of irony that she would be taken by an artist in her gallery. "I should add you to my exhibits, only you're not for sale."

"Everything has a price, Rose. You just have to be willing to pay for it." These words were never truer than now. Rose was too filled lust and opiates to understand the impact of such a profound statement.

The Artist now stood before Rose adorned in his painting attire: overalls with nothing underneath. Rose could no longer contain her desire and stood up from the ornate support. She walked to The Artist and touched the exposed portions of his chest and shoulders. She felt how powerful they were. She then ran her hands down his arms. Every carnal desire flooded through her mind and it warmed her intimate places. The Artist, still in the character of Adam Singleton, looked at her with approving desire. Secretly, every touch from this woman fed his rage to tear her apart for what she had done. Rose takes Adams hands and places them on her surgically perfected breasts. She nearly raged at his touch on one of her most intimate places. She felt like one of her painted heroines bathed in the love of the gods. She was, however, mistaken.

"What shall we do now, Adam?"

"Take me wherever you'd like and take me as you'd like," The Artist responded. These words appeared to send shockwaves through Rose as she looked deeply into his eyes, his black eyes. All he saw was Rose's mood of extreme euphoria and pinned out pupils. The Artist also smelled the presence of wine on her breath. He no longer had the patience for this charade anymore and needed to begin this canvas.

Rose turned, Adams hand now in hers, and led the man toward an open room. They walked through a spacious and beautifully decorated sitting area. The antiques alone were worth more than some houses in the neighboring high-end subdivision. The artwork tastefully placed and in themselves worth a small fortune. The Artist was ready to perform for the present masters.

"Rose, stop."

Rose turned and looked at The Artist. "What's wrong?"

"You will be my finest work to date," The Artist conveyed, smiling as he said these words.

Rose blushed and believed that this was his way of showing her sexual feats that would rival Aphrodite or Eros. She again turned to lead Adam into her personal space. It was at this moment that Rose felt nothing. No sounds. No pain. No motions. No sight. A flash of light and then, nothing. She was there in body and spirit, but no longer present.

The Artist must attend to his gifts.

****

Maria decided to meet a friend before going back to her apartment. She found herself at a familiar place sitting in a familiar seat. In front of her a friendly bartender with military tattoos and the attitude to match.

"So, Gomez? Are you gonna keep me guessing or what?" Sasha was always to the point when she needed information and she would not hesitate to torture those who held it. Her torture consisted of keeping the gates to fermented paradise closed.

"It was great, and I'll leave it at that."

"Damn it. The first time in years that I almost switched sides and you're holding out on me. That's just cruel."

Sasha poured herself and Maria a shot. They were about to down the shot when Sasha noticed a new face in the bar. She'd never seen him before but noticed a glaring trait that was hard to miss at any distance: piercing blue eyes. His dark hair was covered with a knit cap that was removed immediately upon entering. To Sasha this meant either military or manners. His beard had a hint of gray at the chin. He removed his jacket and revealed a relaxed t-shirt and jeans style with a powerful frame. His walk was confident and bore the stride of a man comfortable in any environment. He scanned the bar immediately and dismissed everything non-threatening instantly. This was a wolf among sheep; a hunter.

"Hey, Gomez," said Sasha as she motioned to the man that just walked in.

"I'll be damned!"

Sasha couldn't help herself, "You might indeed at the rate you're going." Sasha walked to the opposite end of the bar and tended to other guests.

Gray walked to the seat next to Maria, "May I join you?"

Maria was stunned. Here is a man that wanted nothing to do with her just hours before and now this man is asking to sit next to her in a bar.

"I'll take your silence as a yes. Even if you said no, I would still sit here. You came to my home. The least I could do is interrupt your alone time."

Gray motioned to Sasha and asked for a club soda with lime. Maria fixated on the drink order. It was the second time in as many days that a man next to her ordered this drink. No, it wasn't an uncommon request, but she couldn't help but think of the irony of this moment. Gray sat and stared at the television above the bar.

"Are you gonna say something or just sit there?"

"Should I call you Gray or Detective," Maria asked.

"Gray is fine."

"What are you doing here, Gray? I know most of the people

that come here and you're not one of them."

"What can I say, Ms. Gomez? I missed you." Gray sipped his drink, never making eye contact with anything but the television. His attitude was different. He was different.

"No, really. How'd you find me?

"I am a detective, you know. It's kinda what I do," Gray said, grinning a little as he always found this kind of question somewhat ridiculous. Maria's response to this comment was what he expected: acquiescence to a valid fact.

"Is there something I can help you with?"

Gray still didn't make any motion to face her. "What would you do if someone provided truth, Maria? Would you be willing to go to jail? Lie? Die, if it came to that?"

"I would do…"

"Don't answer this question without really thinking about it. Truly think before you speak, or should I say think before you act. What I'm asking will determine how the rest of this unfolds."

Maria though for a moment and wondered what her father would say at this moment; the man who introduced her to the world of journalism. Even though he was a producer, he knew the power of the informant and what it may take to keep them safe. It was something that she learned at a young age and it served her well in her career, even if it got her into hot water at times. Maria didn't realize it yet, but she misunderstood the question.

"I will protect you, Gray."

Gray smiled, "I'm not worried about protection, Maria. I don't care if I'm found out. I need the facts to be given as they are. No hyperbole. No embellishment. The story is sensational enough and doesn't need the flare that some in your profession seem to enjoy. The truth is more often shocking enough without the drama."

"You have my word, Gray. Facts only."

Gray turned and looked into Maria's eyes for the first time during this meeting. He heard determination in her voice and saw conviction in her eyes. Her answer was concise and used the appropriate amount of words to convey the message. Gray often used this tactic to gauge his targets. A concept referred to as reticence – using more words when less will suffice. He knew at that moment that she would do everything that she could to hold true to her word. He needed her at this moment. Not as a friend or confidant, but as a means to an end. *I have no doubt that you will.*

"Well, here it goes."

****

The Artist stared at Rose's unconscious form and was proud of the work that he was able to perform without waking her. It had been an hour, but to those in the throes of creation it seemed like minutes. She would remain in this state if not properly revived. The well-placed blow to her head and the opiates she previously ingested would prevent immediate consciousness, regardless of what he did to her. As always, he carried a supply of smelling salts and used it to reengage her senses. He opens the packet and places it under her nose. A reflex action and she was coming around. Her vision was blurred and her hearing somewhat muffled, but she was with him. He worried about the blood loss, but his tourniquets worked as advertised and the loss minimal.

"Welcome to my newest studio, my dear."

Rose's awareness was coming slower than other times before, but The Artist had time and he figured that her opiate addiction played a role in this. He waited for her full attention before returning to his soliloquy. Rose felt a tightness around her abdomen, chest, and forehead as though she was immobilized against something. Her mouth was dry and filled with an unfamiliar fibrous material.

"You know, Rose. It kills me that I had to ruin parts of this magnificent Persian rug. I truly apologize for this, but art must know some sacrifice in order to mean something to others."

Rose could still feel the air circulating through the room on her exposed body. She was exposed more than she was previously. The temperature was a bit colder that she was used to. Her eyes moved around the room rapidly, but her scope was limited with her being unable to move her head.

"I also apologize for the using this beautiful sculpture as your resting spot. It is a moving piece. The angel with outstretched wings was a perfect way to add to the glory of this movement. You, Rose, will be appreciated by all who view you."

Rose's senses recovered and she realized that she was in her apartment's living room. The select pieces of artwork and the description of the room by The Artist confirmed this fact. She tried to speak, but she was unable to utter an intelligible word. Her vision was gained more clarity, but at this point she could only see a blurry image of the man she thought would bring her to the pinnacle of pleasure. She was still able to make out what she believed were smudges on his clothing.

"Can you see me yet, Rose? It'll take some time, but you'll soon see me in my glory."

A few rapid blinks of her eyelids revealed the man she knew as Adam Singleton still dressed in white overalls. The dark maroon smudges on his attire didn't match the bright and deep red on his exposed skin. His face bore the handsome features of the man she saw earlier with smears of the red liquid on it. His eyes were wide and filled with wonder.

"Allow me to remove this." The Artist lifted one of his brushes, his trusty scalpel, and cut the object that prohibited the spoken word. She breathed deeply as the fabric fell from her mouth.

"Adam, what the fuck is going on? Why are you doing this?" Rose's elevated tone and tears were understandable. The Artist expected this.

"Now, Rose. Maintain a civil tongue or I'll remove it. Rudeness is unacceptable, especially in another's studio," The Artist responded.

"Adam, what are you doing? What's that on your clothes and skin?

"This is my paint, my dear. You are the next chapter in artistry. This masterpiece will be unforgettable. You will be immortalized. Isn't that what you want, to be immortal. You certainly do enough to maintain yourself. Moisturizers, exercise, and a nip here and tuck there. Your regimen is stringent and your surgeon top notch. Your real fault is your drug use."

"I haven't used in..."

"Don't," The Artist yelled. Rage could be scene in his paint stained face. "Don't you dare deny what I already know. You will be held accountable for what you have done, and you will be accountable for the words that have hurt others. Others that I care about. Others that did not deserve your lies. Your addiction forced this upon you!"

The Artist then left Rose's limited scope and returned, holding something in each hand just below her peripheral vision. Whatever was being held didn't seem to weigh too much, but Adam was a powerful figure. Not much would pose a challenge.

"These were the tools of your treachery," The Artist said as set them down. He left again and retrieved another item. Rose dared not utter a single word as her tears continued to fall.

"And these are what brought you to this place and so many

places that contributed to your lies." He laid what he re-trieved below her. Still, nothing to indicate what these important items were.

"Adam, I have no idea what you're talking about. Please let me go. We can fix this, whatever it is," Rose pleaded, but those pleas would fall on deaf ears. "I have money! You can have it all."

The Artist's anger consumed him at the notion that he was someone that would worship the almighty dollar. This, to him, was blasphemy. He didn't commit to his art for monetary gain. He did this for the person that he loved and cared about. This was the gravest of insults to his sensibilities. He walked to Rose until he was face-to-face with his canvas. He raised his brush and let loose the ties that bound her head from moving around.

"You have no idea of the man I am, Rose. You have mis-judged me greatly."

The Artist backed away from Rose and allowed her to see what he wanted her to see. Rose was in stunned silence as no words could come. All she could do was look upon what was done. She viewed Adam's items lying on the ground before her and then looked to her left and right. Disbelief entered her mind and at this moment she wished this was a dream. A scream was then let out when she realized that this was her reality. Her arms and legs were no longer where they should have been and in full view below her. Her screaming was music to The Artist's ears. He was now electrified by the out-pouring of appreciation.

"The master's would be proud of the emotion invoked by this work. Let us continue?"

XII.

5:00 PM

Gray unloaded the atrocities that he saw, and Maria listened intently. Gray left out the part about the message left for him at the scene. That wasn't her business, but he described how the Laniers' bodies were broken and torn to pieces. He told her how Duplantis and his lover were systemically dissected, and every piece was placed in a grisly order. Maria heard how the walls were decorated with the blood and guts of the deceased and that these decorations looked like a child's finger paintings. The detail of the tongues being cut out was saved for last, as if the previously described images weren't grisly enough.

"Why remove the tongues?"

"My thought," Gray began, "If the eyes are the windows to the soul, then the tongue is the outlet. Some gangs use this as a symbol that the dead person was a snitch, but this isn't gang hit. Besides, the tongues were never found. Usually it would be left at the scene or on the body."

"Wait! The tongues weren't at the scenes?"

"Nope."

"That's a little weird."

Gray chuckled, "No. It's insane, Maria. Whoever did it is insane."

"What about Donaldson?"

"Donaldson was designated by the Troop to take over the

investigation when Chief requested that we be removed from it. His selection is beyond me. He's a prick, but he's no idiot. Someone is very interested to find out what happened. Someone way up there."

"He is the governor's nephew you know."

"I know. Still didn't save him from needing to learn manners, though." Another grin crossed Gray's face as he said those words. He took a bit of pleasure in conveying that little tidbit of information.

"Why did your boss request the state in the first place?"

She's sharp. Maria was stepping into dangerous territory with this question. If he revealed the truth, then it would potentially reveal the messages left at the scene and put Kap and Tyler at risk. It could also reveal the existence of the REAPER unit. This was a secret that he wouldn't reveal to Maria. The team was family, and Maria just another acquaintance at this point.

"You'd have to ask him."

"Ha," Maria scoffed, "Getting answers from that man is harder than getting answers from you. Hold on. Why are you telling me this? This is inside information and your reputation is one that doesn't exude a sense of cooperation with anyone, especially reporters. Didn't you punch a reporter for asking you a question at a scene once?"

"No, I never punched that insolent bastard. I gently reminded him that an active crime scene was not a place to ask family members about their recently departed loved one. During the conversation he accidently slipped and fell on a curb. Repeatedly. Poor guy should've watched his step more closely than he did."

Maria smiled, "So you're sticking to that story."

"The family backed up my account, Maria. Cleared of all

wrongdoing. Still, I can't say that I was disappointed in seeing him fall." Gray gave a sly look toward Maria. She knew that that was all he would say about the incident.

"So, back to the original question. Why are you telling me this?"

Gray turned himself in the chair and stared a hole through Maria. His eyes aflame with conviction. The stare immediately broke down any defense that Maria had.

"Because there is right and wrong in this world, Maria. The right thing to do would be to tell the story. I saw how the politicians spun the mayor's death and how the Laniers were quote-unquote "found" in their house. The integrity of the case be damned! Two scenes connected to one another and both were deserving of the same attention. Obviously, the politician got all the press and more concerted efforts and the Laniers quickly forgotten. That's bullshit. They deserved the same treatment and got less. The people have the right to know that there is a monster out there."

Gray's indignation was convincing, but it was mostly an act for Maria's benefit. She needed to see that rage again, if only a small portion of it. His words held partial truth. He despised how law enforcement was at times used for political gains and absolutely detested the preferential treatment that some people received because of their position or influence. He saw how mothers would call police officers on their soon to be ex-husbands in order to gain leverage for a future custody battle. He saw how the powerful owned the powerless by offering help and then threatening to call police and report the person for stealing from them if they bit the hand that fed. This went against every fiber of his personal code and he let people know about it. He crossed many powerful people and treated them as he would have the homeless man on the street that begged for help. No one different. No one special. Everyone the same in his eyes. Gray would never compromise himself for a paycheck.

"Is there anything else," Maria asked.

"That's all I'm willing to say right now. Just make sure that you report it correctly."

"You have my word, Gray."

"By the way, don't use my name. Say something like it was a source close to the investigation."

Maria smiled as she gathered her purse and coat, "Now you want to be protected?"

"I don't need protection from this maniac or from the police Maria, but I'm not stupid. You'll get more when I know you can deliver."

Maria felt a bit insulted, but she knew that this relationship with Gray was new and he needed to know she was good to her word. She dawned her coat and walked out of the bar; the wind caught her by surprise and she instantly shivered against Mother Nature's chill. The sun was going down and the temperature went down with it. She needed to be quick, she now had two dates tonight: one with the producer and one with Adam.

Gray sat at the bar and finished his club soda with lime. Sasha walked over to him and offered a refill.

"Another drink, soldier?"

Gray was impressed by her observation. "How'd you know?"

"You're walk. Back straight, shoulders back, hands to your side. Gaze fixed. Obviously prior service."

"No thanks, Marine. I've got work to do and very little time to do it. Oh, it was the eagle, globe, and anchor under your watchband that gave that away."

"You saw that, huh."

Gray put his coat on and pushed the chair back into place. "You shouldn't hide it, Sasha. Honorable service should always be recognized, even if it comes from a grunt like me. Semper Fi, Marine."

"Semper Fi," Sasha responded.

He walked out into the same elements that he watched Maria brave not two minutes before and jogged to his truck. The engine kicked over, and it took a while for the cab to heat up. The warmth of the vehicle's interior would soon be in stark contrast to the weather outside. Gray didn't mind the cold, especially on this night. He felt that this evening's journey wasn't over and knew that Maria wouldn't hesitate to let the world know what she found out. As the heat began filling the cab of his vehicle, he decided to make a call.

"Hey, it's me. The reporter is in play. We should know something soon. I'll contact you later." Gray hung up the phone and drove out of the parking lot. He knew that the other person on the phone understood what he was doing. Was it the best move? Probably not, but Gray needed to make a play to draw this person out.

****

"Got it." Tyler hung up the phone.

"Gray," Kap asked.

"Yeah. The reporter is in play. He said to wait for his call."

Kap chuckled at the words, "You know he's not gonna call. He doesn't want to expose us."

"You're probably right," Tyler agreeingly stated to Kap. "Has Phoenix been activated yet?"

"Yes, Phoenix was put in play about 12 hours ago. Desormeaux made the call and Gray accepted the package."

"Jesus, Kap. There are too many moving parts. Donaldson is getting close. Gray is protecting the team. What are we doing? Nothing. Fucking nothing! This is something else."

"You're worried," Kap said. "We trusted Gray in the past and we should trust him now. We owe him that much for what he did for me and you and the team. Let's just continue to run interference with Donaldson. Did you get the file?"

"Yeah, I got it."

"Good. Send it to Gray and let him loose with the information. Did you read it?'

Tyler looked at Kap, "No. Couldn't bring myself to open it. This should be for Gray's eyes only. He bore the cost of our sins and he should be the only one to see the file. Shit, he lived it."

Tyler sent the file to one of Gray's personal e-mail accounts. Gray set up several, but the one that was selected was for compartmentalized information. An old REAPER e-mail account. It hasn't been accessed in years, but the account was still active. Six were active at one time, now only three. Only one other knew of the accounts and he wasn't saying anything. He had to remain in the shadows until this was over. The trouble from this would resonate throughout the state and this man would be the only way to clear it up if all else failed.

****

Donaldson dispensed himself into the files before his eyes, not just the court case involving his suspect, but also his suspect's confidential personnel files. His connections ran deep, but still he is missing something. He was missing the story behind the night that changed Gray's life. He still detested the man, but he wasn't foolish enough to test him again without information against him.

"Dear God, what hasn't this guy done," Donaldson marveled. "Who are you, Silas Gray?"

The phone near Donaldson's hands rang and he picked it up without missing a beat.

"Donaldson."

"Hey sweetness! How's the arm?"

"Lt. Castile, to what do I owe the honor?"

"Eh, call me Rod. I'm just checking on ya. Making sure that Gray didn't hinder your personal play time with that stunt you pulled earlier. Which leads me to a serious question: are you a righty, left, or switch hitter?"

"What do you want, Lieutenant," Donaldson asked with a tone of irritation.

Rod couldn't help but laugh a bit, "I'm just playing with you, junior. Listen, the Chief wants an update on what you have so far. He asked me to call you to set up a meeting with you, me, and him. How does two hours sound?"

"Listen, I'm still…"

"Now don't you say nothin' stupid, sugar. If you thought Gray was bad, then you should see Chief when he's pissed. I liken it to a hurricane, minus the federal relief that comes at the end of it all."

Donaldson didn't have to do anything that was requested of him but believed that he would be able to draw information out of Rod and Desormeaux. This could be a golden opportunity to gather more knowledge on his target. He believed in his ability and superiority over the two men.

"Sure. Two hours. I'll meet you at your department."

"Outstanding. I'll make sure that the interview room is closed. Wouldn't want you to relive bad memories and shit. Bye, bye now."

"I hate that man," Donaldson said slamming his phone on the desk in front of him. "When I'm done with Gray I'm going after this department. They will respect me!" Donaldson was coming unglued at the seams. He couldn't believe that he was being treated this way and couldn't believe that these men weren't considerate of his deep influence in the state. He was nearly beside himself with rage and would have his vengeance on all of them and the department that they held so dear. They would forever remember his name when he was done with them. Gray, Guthrie, Rod, and Desormeaux, all were in his crosshairs.

****

"Well, that's that," Rod said as he leaned back into his office chair. "What's next, boss?"

Desormeaux was amused by Rod's delivery of his message and believed that the man on the other end of the phone couldn't resist the chance to "share" information. He'd known this type before: young, impulsive, inexperienced, and dangerous. He needed to see what the kid knew or at least get as much information as he could. Gray needed the help and Desormeaux would be there as he had so many times before.

"Now we wait, Rod. We have to play this kid just right. He may be a lot of things, but he's not ignorant."

"I understand, Chief, but what aren't you telling me," Rod questioned, his tone much more serious than before. "There's a lot movin' right now, boss. I'm with you and Gray and Sean, regardless, but this in-the-dark shit isn't my jam."

"Rod, you know I trust you as much as anyone in this world, but there are some things that have to remain hidden until it's time to use it. In this case, I have to play my cards close to the chest, the same way Gray is playing his. It's all about timing right now."

Rod saw that keeping whatever it was secret was eating away at Desormeaux. He also knew not to push. He trusted the man in the chair in front of his desk and knew that all would be revealed soon.

"Ok, Chief. I still got your back. Now, let's go get a sammich. Big Homie don't wanna face that ass hat on an empty stomach."

XIII.

5:56 PM

Maria finished her recorded report just in time for the 6:30 broadcast. The facts were as accurate as she could make them and her delivery devoid of the usual overemphasis so common with the news today. She delivered the facts, just as Gray asked. She needed him to trust her and believed that this olive branch would prove her trustworthiness.

"Maria, how good is your source in this," her producer asked.

"My source is beyond reproach and extremely close to the investigation. They asked for nothing in return, only that the facts be delivered as they are."

Maria's producer rubbed what little hair he still had on his head out of existence. He was nervous about airing this information. The legal ramifications alone sent a chill up his spine, but not as much as the description of the crime scenes provided by Maria's source.

"This better be right, Maria. If it's not, then I'm afraid I won't be able to cover you on this one."

Maria heard concern in his voice when he said these words. It was a fatherly concern like what her dad would say to reporters in the field.

"Trust me, this is legit. This source is literally a part of the investigation." Maria looked to her trusty sidekick, Tom, with a bit of nervousness. She wasn't demanding anything at this point and was, for the first time in a long time, asking permission rather than forgiveness. The gravity of this moment was not lost on Maria's boss.

The producer looked to Tom and handed him the recording that he was holding, "Run it. Top story at 6:30. Go!"

Tom grabbed the recording and ran to the production room. Both Maria and the producer were certain that Tom hadn't moved like that in years. This was no time for hesitation.

"Maria, this better not bite us in the ass."

Maria smiled, "It won't."

Maria turned and started to walk away. She was very pleased with herself as she got what she wanted, again. Only this time she asked nicely.

"Hey, where are you going? Don't you want to watch the report?"

"Nope," Maria said, "I have a date tonight."

Maria walked out of the building and called the man that she knew as Adam, with no answer. Adam's voicemail message was pleasant, and she was thrilled to hear his voice, even if it was only a recording.

"Hey, it's me. I'll meet you at 7:30 at the usual place. See you then. Bye."

Maria carried herself a bit taller after leaving the message. She knew that tonight was going to be a great night with a guy that she really liked and wanted to know. She wasn't too sure what the evening would bring, but she was positive that it would be a night to remember.

****

Hey, it's me. I'll meet you at 7:30 at the usual place. See you then. Bye.

The Artist heard the phone call, but his attention was focused on movement. He was able to complete his work and needed to put his canvas in a place of honor for the guests that would be arriving soon. The area assigned for the gala this evening was set up a day in advance and was empty. Servers, bartenders, and guests would arrive soon, and he had to move quickly. He retrieved a dolly from the gallery and moved his canvas using Rose's elevator, being careful not to spill any paint. He placed his new creation in the middle of stage area and covered it with a large black velvet blanket used to cover works of art prior to their public appreciation. Still, he had a moment to listen to his voicemail and a moment for Rose before he completed his ritual of cleaning up, policing evidence, and leaving to prepare himself for Maria and the gala.

"Oh, Rose. My love awaits. She will be here with me, in your gallery. The world will see you as you are, and I will be among those that will love and appreciate it. The evening will be glorious. You will be appreciated always."

No response from under the velvet coffin.

"Don't be shy, Rose. You know you want to thank me."

Still no words, only a low mumble.

"You know, my dear, this lack of interaction could be considered extremely rude. I thought you of better stock than this."

The Artist was irritated with the nonexistent response from his newest work. she was obviously there in body. At the very least she could nod her head, but that would prove impossible as he previously replaced the restraint on her head. Also, the mass of humanity that he held in his pocket prevented the spoken word. Regardless, he was still incensed by her lack of courtesy.

"Rose, you are selfish and ungrateful for what I have given you. You have repeatedly scoffed at my generosity. This, certainly, will not do. Your guests and my Maria will see the true person that you are. My friend, Silas Gray, will also see this as I am sure he's putting the pieces together as we speak."

A noise was heard under the blanket. The name jogged her back into partial consciousness. She knew that name well and knew what it meant. Horror must have filled her body when she heard it and The Artist took notice.

"Oh, you remember him. Truthfully, he would be hard to forget. He is a great man deserving of my gifts. You should've seen him all those years ago. Poised, thorough, painstakingly precise, and undeniably deadly. He is my friend and I'm doing this for him. He deserves this truth and never deserved your truth. I have other names, as well: Lanier and Duplantis. Do you remember them as well?"

Again, a soft pained sound could be heard.

"I thought you would. Do you see my generosity now? I have brought so many people together and you can't even manage proper decorum. By the way, there's one more on the list, but that will be my secret. Besides, you wouldn't know him. He's new to the family. Now, I'm sure that you will want this, so I will give it to you. Unfortunately, you'll be unable to enjoy your fans when you are unveiled, but such is life. I'll see you later, Rose."

The Artist produced a prepared syringe and its content: a toxic dose of heroin. He lifted the safety cap off the syringe and felt for Rose's throat through the covering. Once found, he injected the substance into her neck. Death was now painless and almost immediate. He left his new gift and returned to Rose's now vacant apartment in order to finish his cleanup, which he did with the same attention that he gave in other studios. Once finished, he left the apartment the way he came, using the dual-purpose elevator's discreet entrance. Soon he would be at home preparing himself for the gala and soon after that, meeting Maria.

****

Sean returned to *Hostile Downtown* shortly after receiving the phone call from Bianca. Bianca sounded nervous and this fact made Sean believe that she was on to something. He parked his car a couple of blocks away from the Bianca's establishment and walked in. The sun was setting low and the wind that everyone felt over the last two days had no signs of letting up. He was near chilled to the bone when he walked through door, but this served to quiet the fire inside of him. He didn't let go of things easily.

He walked into the bar area and saw Bianca performing her hostess/bartender/owner thing; serving people, small talk, glad-handing the regulars. She was a natural social butterfly and it served her well in this business, but moreover it served to glean information from people. She saw Sean and motioned him to meet her in the office. As soon as both entered the office Bianca shut the door behind them and sat down. She was obviously troubled by what she believed she had.

"What do you have Bianca?"

Bianca retrieved a bottled water from a small refrigerator in the office and took a small swig before saying anything. "I asked around about the guy that you told me about. I also asked around about why you would ask me for information, no names of course. One of my regulars is a crime scene tech and he told me a little something about a yesterday. What the hell, Sean? You didn't think it was important to let me know that this guy is literally tearing people apart!"

"You're right, Bianca," Sean said as he hung his head slightly, "I should've told you, but I didn't want to scare anyone. How wide did that info go?"

Bianca took another gulp of the drink, "He said he only told me. He trusts me and knows that I would only ask for a reason."

"Besides the mouthy crime scene tech, what else did you find out?"

"I got a lot of responses, but only one that seemed to be what you were looking for. One of my friends at a bar not too far from here said that he saw someone like what you described about three weeks ago. Fit, good looking, and all that. The guy ordered a club soda with lime and struck up a conversation with a young couple."

Sean's ears perked up a little. Club soda and lime was Gray's usual drink when they would meet at the bar with other co-workers. Gray didn't drink in public, only at his house.

"What did the couple look like?"

Bianca described a young couple, late twenties or early thirties, beautifully put together and in every way complimenting one another, both physically and in personality. Both had brown hair and were obviously fans of their new acquaintance.

"What did they talk about?"

"He didn't remember specific details, but the guy meeting the couple apparently talked about art and my friend thinks that he and the couple left the bar together. He doesn't know where they went afterward."

"Bianca, does your friend remember the guy's name."

Bianca again took another drink, "No, but if you go to the bar, he may be able to pull up security video from that night. The system over there usually has about a month of backup. He works tonight at 7 and I told him to expect you. He'll have the video queued up."

Sean put his hand on Bianca's shoulder. She was obviously frightened from the situation and still a bit upset with Sean for not telling her the depth of his request.

"Thank you, Bianca. No more digging. This is mine now.

Promise me! No more digging. Where does your friend work?"

"I'll answer if you do one thing for me: you promise to be careful, Sean. I'm not burying a friend for Christmas." The concern in her eyes told Sean everything he needed to know. She believed that returning the kindness that Sean once showed her was the least she could do, but the danger that her friend placed himself in shook her to the core.

"You won't. Where do I meet him?"

"He'll be at *Fracture*. Ask for Nolan," Bianca answered, finishing the rest of her bottle water.

Sean left the office and Bianca. Bianca wouldn't exit for a few minutes. She was overwhelmed with a sense that something bad would happen to Sean. Sean, however, had a different sense. He was going to that bar when Bianca's friend arrived for his shift. This will be over soon, and he would have his partner by his side to end it. He walked out of the bar and toward the direction of his car. The cold no longer bothered him. He was on fire and turned this fire into determination. He and Gray would ride or die, or more appropriately do something that would result in an ass chewing; as they had done so many times before. He accepted that Gray was trying to protect him, but Gray wasn't going at this alone and Sean would be there with him. Punch for punch. Round for round. Shot for shot.

Sean sent a message to Gray: *Meet me in the Fracture parking lot, 8 pm. Bring party supplies and a dress coat. Should prove interesting.*

****

Gray returned home after his meeting with Maria and began reading the unredacted file sent to him from Tyler and Kap. This was the same file that Donaldson had, but with certain amendments that Donaldson didn't have and wouldn't get for a few more hours. Neither he, Kap, nor Tyler could prevent complete dissemination of what Donaldson wanted, but they would delay it as much as possible without exposing themselves. The REAPERS needed to remain a secret. The pilot program was confidential and went against normal convention. If their actions came to light, then many would suffer the consequences. As it stood, Gray was the only one alive who suffered for their perceived "sins," albeit the cover up of that night was a thing a beauty and the outcome of the events predetermined. Gray's personal phone alerted him to a text message as he continued to read through the court documents that had his name all over them: *Meet me in the Fracture parking lot, 8 pm. Bring party supplies and a dress coat. Should prove interesting.*

"God damnit, Sean!"

Gray tried to text back and then call, but neither attempt went through. Sean must have shut the phone off after sending the text. Something that he and Sean had done many times before. They usually did this with people above their pay grade to prevent a direct order to stand down. They would always blame it on service or an old phone, despite having no such issues. Gray called the only person that could probably reach him.

"You on the phone with Big Homie! Whatcha need, sweetie?"

"Rod, Sean found something. He sent me a message to meet him at Fracture at eight. Don't know what he found, but he told me to bring party supplies and my jacket." Rod knew what that meant as he and the guys used a code to keep people from knowing what they were talking about, especially if they had to make a call in the public eye.

"Like I said, what do you need," Rod asked again.

"Leave a care package at the back door. Party poppers, big

and small. I've got the rest covered."

"Is that all," Rod remarked, "I thought you were gonna ask for something difficult. Am I gonna get anything back?"

"We'll see but try to get Sean on the line. He doesn't know what he's getting into."

"All right, but I got something to say. You and Chief are keeping shit to yourselves and it's driving me nuts. Big Homie knows English, Cajun English, and profane English, and you two about to get the latter, ya dig. We three gonna have a talk after this!"

"Deal, Rod. Just contact him as soon as possible. I'll be by in twenty to pick up the care package."

XIV.

6:25 PM

"Where is Rose," Rose' assistant asked the caterer.

"Don't know. I haven't seen her. I thought she was here with you."

Rose's assistant felt the pressure as guests would arrive soon and expect to see their hostess in her full glory.

"I'll call her again." The assistant's call went unanswered as it had several times before this call. "Damn. Voicemail again."

It was then that the assistant heard music to his ears: his text alert. The message was simple, understandable, and came from Rose's telephone number: *I'll be a little late tonight. Entertain ours guests and make sure that the no one looks under the black cloth. If I'm not there by 8:30, make the reveal. I should be able to make it. Remember, 8:30, not a minute before.*

"Who was that," the caterer asked.

"It was Rose. She said she'll be late and didn't say why. Probably high somewhere. Screw it. Make the preparations and make sure no one goes near Rose's "big surprise" for the evening. I have to handle the front door."

****

The Artist stood in his apartment, freshly out of his second shower of the evening and was very pleased with himself. He used an internet-based phone app to send the message to Rose's assistant. He would follow her orders to the letter. He was not like The Artist; he was a beta, The Artist an alpha. The former does what he is told, and the latter does what he wants. He knew no one would be able to trace where the message came from.

"I love the internet, my dear. It offers anonymity when you want it. The police will think that the true murderer took Rose's phone. The unintelligent pretending to be superior. Fools, every one of them. Except for my friend. He is an artist, much like me."

He continued to marvel at himself as he stood in front of his closet. Every piece of dress clothing perfectly fitted and current. For this evening, he chose a classic tuxedo. This was a formal occasion and he must look the part. He took extra care to rid the rich man's uniform of any imperfection. His chosen accessories were tasteful, among which were his cufflinks with the initials "A.S." inscribed on them. He wondered what Maria would wear for their second meeting. He was sure that she would be just as breathtaking as the moment that he first saw her.

While preparing his selected garments, he decided to turn on his television and watch the news. He had no doubt that the report would have the mayor as the main story. It was all anyone could talk about. He remembered hearing people talking about it at the gym earlier. It was quite the event and in that he felt pleased with his contributions to the community.

Breaking News. Thank you for choosing KNAC for this evening's new. Tonight, we start with an update of the story that has shocked the area, the murder of Lafayette Mayor Duplantis. Our very own Maria Gomez has the latest. Viewer discretion is advised as these details may be too graphic for some viewers.

The Artist couldn't believe this woman's drive. Determination in spades and a dogged reporter regardless of day. As soon as he saw her appear on the screen, he could tell this was prerecorded, there was no live icon to be seen. She had a date tonight.

A source close to the investigation has told this reporter that the recent murders of the Lanier family and Mayor Duplantis appear to be linked. The bodies of the Lanier's and Mayor Duplantis and one of his coworkers were found to be cut to pieces and placed in patterns. There are no specific details as to what these patterns were, but the source stated that interior walls of the scenes were spattered with various designs that reminded investigators of childish finger paintings.

"What?!" The Artist was beside himself when he heard those words. His rage overtook him, and he felt all control begin to fade away from him. "Childish finger paintings! You are fucking fools! That is art! You sons of bitches will appreciate all I have done!"

His rage subsided for a moment.

The suspect is believed to be a male of considerable size. The suspect is also believed to suffer from severe mental illness as this is the only way that many close to the investigation could justify the extreme nature of the crimes.

"Mental illness. You motherfuckers! How dare you describe my genius as something as repressive as mental illness! Whoever is forcing you to lie, my love, will pay for their crimes against me!"

Again, he contained his rage.

The source also indicated that the suspect may have a history of sexual deviance as the bodies located at the scene bore signs of sexual assault. Investigators are asking that anyone with information regarding these crimes should call the police with information. Please stay with KNAC Channel 4 News for breaking news and updates, I'm Maria Gomez.

The Artist couldn't believe the words coming out of his love's mouth at this moment. He couldn't believe that such filth could flow from her beautiful mouth, a mouth that he longed to kiss. He believed that she was deceived into these words and would never have said such hurtful things if she knew who completed these master works. He was able to compose himself long enough to dress himself, mumbling profanities toward whomever gave Maria such false information. As he finished combing his hair, he felt imperfect. Everything in him told him that he was the pinnacle of humanity, but these words unhinged him. All he could concentrate on was Maria's words spewing lies. This ran through his mind as he took one last look in the mirror. He couldn't stand what he gazed upon at this moment. Every perceived flaw exacerbated by hateful words.

"FUCK," The Artist yelled as he smashed his hand into the mirror. The shards fell to the ground and small cut appeared on his knuckles. He sucked on the knuckle to stop the bleeding, which was minimal.

He grabbed his overcoat and walked out of his apartment, slamming the door angrily as he walked through the portal. His blood still boiled as he walked through the door-lined corridor, into the stairwell, and then into the garage that shielded his vehicle. He believed that all he needed was to surround himself in luxury to get past Maria's forced lies and his car was the first step in that mission. He felt some small comfort sitting and listening to talk radio, but that only lasted for a few seconds. The radio station only played the audio of Maria's broadcast and the usual talk show hosts provided their own two cents on what was revealed.

"STOP! YOU ARE FUCKING IDIOTS! YOU WOULDN'T KNOW ART IS IT BIT YOU IN YOUR IGNORANT ASSES!"

He was surrounded by the lies and this consumed him more than ever. He changed the station for the first time in years and heard other local disc jockeys commenting on the breaking news. The lie was with him; around him; and inescapable. He desperately needed composure and turned to his master works: Mozart, Handel, Chopin. They were artists that would have understood his genius. He let their melodies sooth his soul as he drove to meet Maria at the "usual spot." By the time he reached Maria, he would have calmed down. They would enjoy a few drinks with Sasha and then be on their way to the gala.

"I will not let lies interfere with my love. This will still be a great night and Maria will tell me who told her these fabrications. I will deal with them later."

****

Maria waited for Adam to arrive and was greeted by Sasha. Sasha didn't disappoint with her astute observations and smart-ass comments.

"Twice in one day, Gomez, and you're all dressed up tonight. Must be something fancy by the way it looks. Who's the lucky guy? The gorgeous creature from last night or the brooding and rugged soldier from earlier?"

Maria chose an elegant, but comfortable floor length evening dress with a deep neckline. The emerald green dress was complimented by a single gilded locket given to her by her father. The locket contained pictures of her parents, both now well retired from their respective fields and enjoying their retirement travelling.

"The "creature" from last night has a name: Adam. And he and I are going to Rose Claxton's gala tonight," Maria said as she sipped her freshly poured bourbon.

"Well, looks and money. Seems like a winner there, Gomez. What's with the guy from earlier? Gray something?"

"Huh, Silas Gray. He's a detective from a nearby town. The murder on Hillside, that was his before the State Police came in. He was giving me some insight into the case."

Sasha was a bit surprised by this. "This guy is a cop. They don't just volunteer information. Didn't you find that a bit strange?"

"Yeah, of course I did. He seemed angry about the way his case was taking a back burner to the mayor's case. He told me that the two were related."

"I saw your report. Powerful shit, Gomez."

"You think," Maria asked, with a hint of a smile on her face.

"So, where is Adam? Running late I guess."

"Nah, I just came here early. I said to meet up at seven. He still has five minutes before he's officially late." Maria finished her drink and Sasha poured another.

"Gomez, this Silas guy. What's his story?"

"Easily one of the most frustrating men I've ever met, but he has a strong sense of himself. One second, he's complete ice and the next second, he all passion. What's interesting is his absolute control. If I didn't know it any better, I would say that he may be the most terrifying man I've ever met and, yet, I'm attracted to him. I want to know his story and I know I'll never get it."

"I meet those Jekyll and Hyde types every night," Sasha said.

"I don't think that's it. There's no real evil in him. I've interviewed evil men and he is not one of them. He seems tormented, but grounded. He carries the weight of his and others' sins and doesn't fall to pieces. He's driven by it."

"You admire him, I see."

"Wouldn't you?"

Both women lifted their respective glasses and finished the rest of their drink. Sasha looked at her watched and saw that the hour of Adam's arrival had come. She looked to the door and saw the man that Maria met the night before, dressed to the nines and looking better than she remembered, if that were at all possible. Maria, too, saw Adam as he walked in and was immediately struck by his presence.

"I hope I didn't keep you waiting, Maria. Took me a minute to figure out "the usual spot"." The Artist had calmed down a lot between his apartment and the bar. The masters always had a dual effect on him: intensity and calm. The latter was needed before meeting his love. He kissed Maria's hand and formally introduced himself to Sasha. His character was still intact.

"Excuse me, Adam, you wouldn't happen to have any sisters, would you," Sasha asked.

"Sasha," Maria exclaimed, looking directly at her as she said it. Adam laughed at the comment.

"No. Only child," Adam said between smiles.

"Eh, can't blame a girl for trying. What are you drinking tonight?"

The Artist order his usual club soda and lime and Sasha was happy to make it for him. She commented on the fact that this was the second time that day that she made this drink for a Gomez mysterious man.

"Oh, who was the first," The Artist asked.

"Gomez can answer that question for you," Sasha said slyly, dismissing herself as she said it.

"I met with a source or should I say he met me earlier this afternoon," Maria replied, somewhat surprised by Sasha's lack of candor.

"A source," The Artist inquired, faking intrigue, but secretly desiring the answer.

"Yeah. You know I'm a reporter and we have sources of information. He was giving me some inside information on the recent murder investigations in the area."

The Artist feigned surprise at this fact. "Really. Who was he? A cop or something?"

"More like a giant question mark," Maria answered. "He's a new source and I didn't expect him to talk to me at all. Especially after I kinda ambushed him the last couple of days."

The Artist asked no more questions after hearing this. He knew that his friend, Silas, gave her the information that was reported. He was deeply hurt by this revelation. He was giving himself generously to his only friend and the best that his friend could do was provide lies to the woman the he loved. His heart was breaking within his chest. The one person that he thought would appreciate what he'd done, and Silas tried to fit him into a criminal profile. The Artist had no profile. His art knew no bounds and could not be defined. The feeling faded as quickly as it came when he realized that his friend would soon see another canvas that would redefine the lies told of him.

****

Rod and Desormeaux waited for Donaldson in Rod's office. Both men were fearful of what Donaldson knew, but they needed his insights.

"Did Gray pick up what he asked for, Rod."

"Sure did. About thirty minutes ago and sent me a text after he'd done it. Bastard didn't even come into to say hi or thank you or kiss my ass. That's just rude, Chief. I'm gonna mandate sensitivity training for him and Sean. Big Homie has feelings., ya know."

A knock on the door told both men that someone arrived, most likely Donaldson. Desormeaux met with the man and escorted him to Rod's office. Being in this building again made Donaldson uncomfortable, but he had to play it just right to get the information he needed.

"Chief, Lt. Castile. Listen, we got off on the wrong foot. We all have the same goal and that is to catch the person or people responsible. I was out of line earlier and I apologize." Donaldson's delivery was as practiced as the sincerity that accompanied the statement. Still, he hoped that this olive branch would work toward his ends.

"We all fuck up, junior," Rod said. "We just learn and move on. Now, let's talk."

XV.

7:35 PM

Sean met with Nolan at *Fracture* and the two men retreated into a private office where Sean could view the video. Nolan offered a chair and Sean politely refused. Nolan excused himself from the room after showing Sean how to access the video and he devotedly reviewed the video from the night three weeks ago. He keyed in on every person that walked through the door, watching interactions and dismissing them just as quickly. He was looking for something, an attractive couple with dark hair and a stranger interacting with them. Bianca was good for information, but there were times that she could only get so much. That's where the detective side of everything came into play.

"Shit! Could be anyone," Sean said to himself as he decided to finally sit down.

Sean rubbed his eyes, the stress of the last couple of days accompanied by lack of sleep was beginning to take its toll on him. He decided to turn his phone on and, as he expected, had multiple text messages and voicemails from Gray and Rod. He didn't bother with the voicemails but read the text messages. Most of the messages said the same thing in a different way: *Wait for Gray.* His eyes then met with the flat screen in front of him. He continued to watch hoping that some small detail would open the case. Sean was realist, though. He never held on to hope or luck, just in-depth investigation. It was at this moment two ghosts appeared on the video screen.

"Jesus," Sean said under his breath as he continued to watch.

The couple appeared happy with their evening banter with multiple people. This was obviously a place that they frequented, or at the very least visited enough to be remembered.

Sean left the room and retrieved Nolan. Nolan, as with many people assisting with a police investigation, arrived quickly and was more than happy to assist in any way that he could.

"Do you know these people," Sean asked directly.

Nolan watched the video intently for a few seconds. "A little, they would come in occasionally. This was the couple that I told Bianca about. Another person should be coming in soon and he strikes up a conversation with them. There he is."

Sean nearly pushed Nolan away from the screen and through the door when the pixelated image of the figure joining the couple became clearer as he approached them. He was tall and obviously fit. He wore a short-sleeved, very fashionable shirt and had a considerable beard on this day. Obviously, this day was much warmer than the past few days. Much of his face was covered by facial hair and his forehead covered by a Newsboy cap. The man approached the couple and they appeared to talk for some time. Sean increased the playback speed and observed that all three left the bar about forty-five minutes after meeting. Sean rewound the footage and tried to get the best shot that he could of the mystery man and took a photo of the man with his phone. Sean also uploaded the file onto a thumb drive that he always kept with him.

"Thanks, Nolan. Keep this between us and if Bianca asks, tell her to remember her promise and I'll remember mine."

He walked out of the office and into the bar area. The bar was busier than usual, but many people were off of work for the next few days and decided to start the holiday early. He exited the building and the cold inundated him, but like the time before he felt nothing. He was still burning. He walked to the parking lot and saw a familiar face waiting for him.

"You're early," Sean said.

"You're an ass," Gray retorted.

The two men shook hands and embraced as friends often do. They may have had a recent hiccup, but brothers forgive one another soon after a falling out. No ill feelings and both men understood what each other was trying to do.

"I have something for you, Gray. I have a feeling that we may have the first glimpse of our killer."

"Show me," Gray said, intrigued by the statement.

Gray viewed the photo on Sean's phone and was confounded. He'd never seen this man before and the photo wasn't the best quality as it was a camera phone taking a picture of a television screen. Still, he was sure that this was a new player in this game.

"No, don't know him," Gray started, "Do you have anything else?"

Sean produced the thumb drive containing the video. Gray retrieved a laptop from his truck and both men watched the video, Gray for the first time. Both were still outside of the refuge of the vehicle's cab and the laptop sitting on the back seat revealed the mysteries of the video.

"I see you brought the party supplies," Sean said as he looked into Gray's truck. "I thought you'd show up in your department vehicle."

"Nope," Gray responded while watching the video, "Don't want anyone tracking me, especially Donaldson." All Sean could do was smile at the logic.

"Holy shit!"

"Yeah," Sean agreeingly said, "I felt the same way when I saw it."

"Why didn't you say anything earlier?"

Sean smiled, "I wanted to see your reaction when you saw them."

Gray keyed in on the couple with the well-built bearded man. He still didn't recognize the man, no matter how many times he saw the same images. He did, however, recognize the couple. He was recently acquainted with them. Rick and Sarah Lanier alive and enjoying themselves.

"Has anyone else seen this?"

"Just the guy who queued up the video, but he doesn't know anything."

"Send this to Rod and Chief," Gray said. "After that we need to talk. It's time that you knew what was going on."

****

Donaldson unveiled his theories to Rod and Desormeaux and both audience members were impressed with the depth of the investigation this soon after finding the bodies. Donaldson had obviously done his homework and there was a brain that seemed to work, at least on this level.

"So, you believe that Gray is involved with the crimes," Desormeaux asked.

"Yes, Chief. I do. Either directly or indirectly, he knows something, and he won't tell me what his connection is."

Chief Desormeaux looked over the evidence against his trusted detective and friend. It appeared that Donaldson had a pretty solid case against Gray, but Donaldson could neither put Gray at the scene, nor did he have enough to arrest him. The case was circumstantial, at best, but that wouldn't stop Donaldson. Desormeaux saw his type many times before; the type that would make the evidence fit suspect, rather than the suspect fitting the evidence. Donaldson was a dangerous man and both Rod and Desormeaux knew it.

"What if you're wrong," Rod asked. "You could potentially destroy a man's life and career. My input: you need more, much more."

Desormeaux agreed with Rod. They saw Donaldson mulling over something. What? They didn't know. He struggled with his next decision as it would reveal his hidden ace. *Should I reveal what I know or let it be?*

"Do you have anything else," Chief asked.

"I do, Chief." Donaldson made the choice. "But I have to tell you that this information cannot go anywhere. If it should get out, then both of you would face prosecution for obstruction. Do you agree to these terms?"

Both men, without hesitation, agreed to this. Donaldson now had leverage against Rod and Desormeaux and turned one ace in the deck into three.

"This is a sealed court file, unredacted, for the *State of Louisiana vs. Silas Gray.*" Donaldson revealed the specifics of the case file alleging the Gray murdered Garrett Boudreaux, the Bayou Teche Butcher. Witness lists, attorney's names, evidence, and statements made at the scene by Gray were contained therein. The witness list only contained letters: Witness A, Witness B, and so forth. Four witnesses in total. The case made no mention of the REAPER unit and its compliment. That would require more digging; digging that was being done as Donaldson briefed the two men. What caught the most attention was the name of the prosecutor, Roger Duplantis, Jr., the recently departed mayor of Lafayette.

"What about the witnesses? Any word on who they are," Rod asked.

"None, but I'm sure that their revelation will prove more

interesting than this. I initially thought Gray was involved because of the message left at the first crime scene and that was the reason for my initial aggression. I believe that Gray is making it known that he is responsible. This is his vengeance for the way he was treated."

Both Desormeaux and Rod thought this to be preposterous. Gray was not prone to fits of mindless vengeance and he was not one to hold a grudge, unless someone absolutely deserved his due attention. One of these men knew that the case Donaldson presented was a farce and the outcome known before it even started.

"You know, junior, I had higher hopes for you than this," Rod stated with contempt in his voice. "You are still unwilling to see that this may actually be a setup. Gray had nothing to do with this and now you're reaching. Everyone knew that Duplantis was a prosecutor and any one of his convictions could've done this. You have a better chance of pinning a medal on Jell-O."

Donaldson's switch now flipped, and his anger was evident.

"I agree with Rod, Donaldson," Desormeaux said, "This is weak, and you need to open up to the idea that Gray had no involvement in these crimes."

"You two are fools!" Donaldson exploded in anger. "You can't see that you have a fucking murderer working with you and now you're questioning me on the evidence that points to him. His name was at the first fucking crime scene and he had an axe to grind against Duplantis. You two had better stay out of my way or I'll have both of your badges hanging over my mantle! Do you understand?!"

Desormeaux had been quiet for long enough and was now face to face with Donaldson.

"Pay attention to me, Donaldson. Do not presume to order me to do anything. You are a guest in my house, in my city, and in my world. If you ever threaten me or any of my men again I will, I promise, bury you. I'll run you over so quickly that you'd swear that God himself came down from his throne and bitch slapped you into non-existence. Now, do you get me, junior?"

Donaldson looked into Desormeaux well-worn eyes and knew that this man meant every word of it. His delivery was calm, but extremely aggressive. The experience written in the wrinkles in his face told the story of a man of violence and his manner indicated comfort with this fact. It reminded him of the same delivery that Gray used when he was taught his lesson earlier in the day, except Gray's tone was more terrifying. For the second time in less than a day, Donaldson felt a real sense of fear.

"Gentlemen," Rod broke the brief moment of awkward silence, "I suggest that we adjourn this meeting and go our separate ways. Donaldson, you leave first."

Donaldson gathered his material and placed them into his bag. The previously composed man that delivered the evidence to Desormeaux and Rod was gone and only the familiarity of an impudent child remained. He was literally taking his ball and going home, which suited the other two men just fine.

"You two had better..."

"Walk away, junior," Rod interrupted Donaldson, "If you thought Gray was bad, just imagine what Chief and I will do to you when there is no one to stop us and no witnesses. Now, get!"

Donaldson bored a hole through Rod and Desormeaux as he turned to leave the building. The sound of the closing door and the close circuit camera feed on Rod's computer confirmed Donaldson's departure, as it had done the previous evening.

"That's right, Chief. We're making friends and influencing

people. We should write a book: *Big Homie's Guide to Friendship*."

"Rod, this man is sniffing to close to the truth, and you deserve to hear it. It's the only way that we can stay ahead of him."

Rod showed legitimate confusion at this statement. Gray told him about his last case in Iberia Parish, the case that ultimately led to his moving away from there. Desormeaux, however, knew more, much more, and Desormeaux believed that it would change the dynamic between himself and Rod. Yes, Rod was his employee, but he was also a voice that he'd come to trust. He worried about how this would impact their relationship as they have worked with each other for years. It was his moment to bring the dead back to life.

"Hey, Chief, before you say anything, Sean sent me an e-mail. Looks like a video of some kind. I figured you wouldn't want Donaldson to know, so I held off telling you until after "Donaldson the Dick" left."

****

The Artist looked at his watch: ten till eight.

"Hey, as much as I love having Sasha entertain us," The Artist said as he winked in Sasha's direction, "We have to get going. The gala starts in a few."

"Ok, if we have to," Maria said. "What do I owe you, Sasha?"

"Nothing, Maria, I've got it," The Artist said.

Maria protested, but The Artist insisted on paying. He had an old-fashioned streak in him. He paid Sasha the balance of the drinks and tipped her generously for the entertainment.

"Oh, well you can come back anytime you want to, Adam."

"I may have to, Sasha. You have a great night."

Maria and The Artist made their way to their respective

vehicles. Maria wished to take her vehicle to the gala in case she was called into work, or at least that's what she told Adam. The real reason was so that she could leave if Adam wound up being a creep or something akin to it. Regardless, they entered into their respective cars and left the parking lot going in the same direction. This would be a date that Maria would remember forever.

XVI.

Gray raised his weapon to the target. No feeling. No remorse. Only the mission.

BANG

The sound shocked his senses, but it was not of his own making. The butcher let go his grip and Mags fell to the ground in what appeared to be slow motion. The bullet struck Mags in the neck and she began to bleed profusely from the wound. She clutched the wound trying to stop the bleeding.

Gray's weapon was still trained on the target, the safety off, finger squeezing the trigger. At the moment the shot broke, the man before him looked as though he was about to raise his hands in surrender. That didn't matter to Gray and only the butcher and God would know what could have happened in the next moment. Gray's weapon fired rapidly and with precision, each round striking its intended target. It was a burst of firepower so overwhelming that it tore through Boudreaux's flesh and forced him into immediate submission of Gray's will. There was no trial in the courtroom for this animal, only trial in the street. He would face his eternal judgement alone, knowing that the reaper among REAPER's sent him.

"MAGS!"

Gray reached his fallen sister and applied pressure to the wound. The blood was dark and soaked through his gloves. He reached for his blowout kit and pulled out a pack of gauze. He immediately began driving the gauze into Mags' neck.

"You're gonna be Ok, Mags. Stay with me!"

Mags' eyes were wide and she stared directly at him as he fever-

ishly fought to stop the bleeding. The resignation that she had in her eyes while in the butcher's grasp fully came over her now. She was ready for her end, but Gray wasn't.

"God damnit, control! Where the fuck is medical! Mags is down and bleeding out," Gray yelled into his throat mic.

"They're at your location, Romeo one."

The REAPER medical team arrived and took over where Gray began. Gray stood there and watched a highly trained medical support team tend to the wound and begin an IV on her.

"She's critical, we need to get her to a hospital," one of the medics said. They loaded her on a stretcher and carried her away from the scene. She was unconscious at this moment and her limbs limply hung as she was moved from the shooting scene to a dark van that medical personnel arrived in. No markings, just a nondescript Mercedes Sprinter. The remainder of the medical team did the same for Tyler and Kap, except their injuries were minor by comparison. They were loaded in another vehicle identical to the first.

"Control, Romeo one. Initiate Cerberus. Agents moving in now to secure remaining members."

The Cerberus protocol was three-pronged much like the three-headed beast it was named after: evacuate, cover, and educate. The bodies of the fallen would be immediately evacuated from the scene, dead or alive. If alive they would be treated and provided a cover story for their injuries. If dead, then their loved ones and agencies would be given a story that would make sense. Each team member agreed to be cremated in the event of their death and no autopsy would be performed. Gray was sure that the bodies of Tony and Jacques were removed rapidly so he didn't bother to look. The cover aspect would be the cover story for the incident itself. In this instance, Gray was working late when he spotted a man acting suspiciously. He attempted to ascertain what this man was doing when the suspect opened fire on him. He engaged the threat and was forced fire upon the man in self-defense. It would be later that *the suspect would be identified as the Bayou Teche Butcher. Gray would receive more instructions from his appointed attorney prior to being debriefed by the Officer Involved Shooting Team. The final phase was educating. Gray would supply the prepared story to the grand jury. Located witnesses would be called, and he would be subject to prosecution, just like anyone else involved in a homicide. The outcome was already known, but the motions had to be seen. Jury members would be carefully selected as would the judge presiding over the charade. Gray didn't fear what was to come, he only feared the loss of those he held as family.*

"Control, Romeo one, are you direct?"

"Romeo one, Control, direct. Initiate Cerberus."

"Control, Romeo one. Cerberus initiated. Good luck, old friend."

With that the REAPERS were no more. Everything that one would expect from an in the line of duty shooting occurred, except Gray knew the outcome. The shooting would have been justified if he testified as to what really happened, but the truth would've exposed the team.

Gray knew that Tony and Jacques were dead when he found their bodies behind the rest area in the plaza. Their families were told that they died in a tragic fishing accident. The boat capsized and their bodies weren't located until four days later, preyed upon by local wildlife and carrion eaters alike. He attended their funerals a week after the shooting and mourned with the families of his brothers, albeit from a distance. The U.S. Marshals gave them full honors for their service and Gray was assured their families would be taken care of.

Mags' story was that she died on her way to the hospital. Her cover was that she died rock climbing in north Louisiana. This story was also in line with her passion for the outdoors. Her funeral was simple, but touching. Her would be fiancé, Jimmy, cried on Gray's shoulder for what seemed like hours. Gray, in turn, would cry privately. He had to be strong for Mags' parents. He wanted to visit the headstone erected for her, but he knew she wasn't there. It wasn't the way he wanted to remember her. He missed his friend terribly, especially the talks that they had.

Tyler's and Kap's injuries led to some ribbing by their fellow troopers. Both were driving from a training event in their issued police unit when they "hit" a dear crossing the road. The car wound up in a ditch on the side of I-49. After a while, the ribbing stopped and each man promoted to their current positions. Their promotions were to keep them in line with the protocols of the REAPER unit and to assure they would be taken care of in some way.

Gray bore the brunt of attacks against his character and his name. Some media portrayed him as a cop doing his job, others called him "Judge Gray" for being judge, jury and executioner of sentence on the spot. The inevitable "No True Bill" came down and the prosecution of the State of Louisiana vs, Silas Gray ended. The records, sealed. He later resigned his commission in Iberia Parish and started working as a detective under Chief Desormeaux. His reward was far from fair, but it was necessary to protect the team.

****

8:03 PM

"And that's it, Sean. That's the story of Silas Gray."

Sean stood for a moment, speechless at what he'd just heard. The REAPER team, control, Mags, Jacques, and Tony. He stood there, his mouth agape at the revelations that his friend, the man he trusted his life with on more than one occasion, was someone that he barely knew. He no longer felt untrusted, but he felt betrayed by his partner. This was now a secret that he had to bear for as long he or Gray worked in this business and beyond.

"So, Tyler and Kap have been in on this the whole time," Sean stated.

"Yeah, they were called in when the Chief had me removed,

but they didn't know it was related to the team until Duplantis' body was found."

"What about Rod?"

"Rod only knows what I told him. I was involved in a shooting and no longer wanted to be in that parish. The truth would only complicate matters."

Sean was still angry that he didn't know this about Gray, but now understood why. Gray's team was on the hairy edge of law enforcement. The edge where the lines were fuzzy and the gray area was a way of life. His partner was a sin-eater and he continued his mission without asking for reward or recognition.

Gray's phone chirped. It was another e-mail from Tyler. The subject: Witness List – Confidential.

"What is it," Sean asked.

"It's the witness list from my grand jury." Gray read the list and was suddenly struck by what he saw. He never knew the names of the "witnesses" at his grand jury and didn't care to after his trial was over. A real fear ran up his spine and he was now placing the final pieces together. The feeling struck him like a lightning bolt and now he and Sean had to be somewhere.

"Shit," Gray said, "We have to go, now. Suit up and follow me."

Both men shed their jackets and replaced them with body armor. Pouches filled with ammunition, communications equipment, and first aid kits. Gray thought to himself that the two must have been a sight while gearing up in a parking lot, but screw whoever saw it. The mission was now clear.

"Gray, where are we going," Sean asked.

"1201 Rue Royale. We have to find Rosemarie Claxton."

God, let us be on time for this.

****

Maria was taken by the opulence of the scene before her. The gala area of Maison du Luxe was decorated to resemble something out of a fantasy novel. Large drapes hung from the floor to ceiling windows, statues of Greek and Roman masters followed the walls, and paintings worth more than she made in a year hung in gold trimmed frames. It was truly a sight to behold.

"So, what do you think," The Artist asked.

Maria was still taking it all in. "It's a bit overwhelming. This place is amazing, and I would kill to interview half of the people in this room."

The Artist laughed at Maria's reaction to her surroundings. He was more taken by her reaction and for a moment forgot about the lies that she was "forced" to say about him. He, too, was taken in, but not by his surroundings, but by Maria. He saw that she fit in with the elegance that surrounded them, more so than anyone else. At this moment, she was perfect in his eyes and in her true element. His element. The elite.

"Look, it's Senator Mitchell. And that's Congresswoman Brandt. Jesus, that's Governor Dubois. I feel a bit out of place."

"You are exactly where you need to be, Maria," The Artist told her. "You are the best person in this whole room, and everyone would be in awe of you."

Maria blushed at the compliment. "Adam, that's sweet, but these are very powerful and influential people. Who am I? I'm just a reporter for a local news station."

The Artist looked deeply into Maria's eyes, "You have something that no one in this room possesses: truth. These people think that that their money, position, and influence give them standing or power. You're the only person here that won't lie to themselves. Take the senator over there, he funnels money from his campaign fund to pay for two children that he had out of wedlock. The congresswoman over there got drunk one night and killed an innocent bicyclist when driving home. She reported that her car was "stolen" the next day and the case was never solved. Last, but not least, our beloved governor. He used his position to funnel hurricane relief fund…"

"I know," Maria interrupted, "He funneled the money to family members so they would receive jobs from relief efforts."

"That's partially right. The companies were umbrellaed under an LLC based in the Caimans. Guess who owns that? His subsidiary companies are in everything. His family and friends get the bids and he will receive a kickback on the legitimate end. That doesn't include his "extracurricular" activities. By the time he leaves office, he'll be one of the wealthiest men in Louisiana."

"How does he keep that a secret? Surely someone must know something."

"Sure, they do, but he employs well-placed and trusted hatchet men and women in positions to gather information should the day come that someone wishes to turn on him."

"I think I know one," Maria said, "His nephew is running the murder investigations of the Lanier's and Mayor Duplantis. If my sources are to be believed, then he would definitely be one of them."

"Oh, who might that be?"

"A State Police detective, Gary Donaldson. Supposedly, he's a real piece of work."

The Artist sipped his club soda and lime as she imparted this information. He knew that someone would take over the investigation as soon as Silas' namesake was located at the first scene, but he didn't think it would be one of the governor's sycophants. This was unacceptable to him. This man, Donaldson, was neither worthy of his brilliance, nor *his* Silas, even if Silas poisoned Maria's mind against his genius. To The Artist, only Silas was worthy of all of his talents. Donaldson was a problem and he wouldn't have his masterpiece interrupted before it was finished.

"Maria, what time is it, I seem to have forgotten my watch."

Maria retrieved her phone from her clutch and announced the time to The Artist.

"It's 8:26. Why? Have a hot date?"

The Artist laughed at the comment, "I've already got a date, just didn't want to make a getaway before it was polite to do so."

It's almost time.

XVII.

"Sean to Gray," Gray's earpiece crackled.

"Go ahead."

"What are we looking for?"

"Rosemary Claxton. Female, white, mid-thirties, blonde hair. She owns the gallery."

"10-4."

Gray and Sean raced through the city like they were being chased by an invisible foe. The roar of their vehicles' engines was the only sound that either could hear, unless one said something on the radio. Gray attempted to get the city police to join them in their endeavor as they were outside of their jurisdiction. The response they received was that a unit could be at the location in ten minutes. Gray knew that time was not on their side.

****

Rose's loyal assistant still hadn't seen his boss and it was 8:28 PM. He would have to unveil Rose's surprise without her if she didn't show up and he was getting nervous. He wasn't used to being the center of attention. That was Rose's job.

"Where is she," he asked himself as he feverishly texted Rose.

The caterer that he spoke to previously showed up and told him that Rose was nowhere to be seen. This drove him to the realization that Rose was not coming. He checked his watch again: 8:29 PM.

"Well, here goes nothing."

****

Maria and The Artist watched as a young man entered the public stage and made his way toward a microphone set beside what many assumed was a statue covered in a large black cloth. The moment that The Artist hoped for was upon them and soon the world would see his work. He couldn't take credit for it immediately but would savor the moment that every eye was upon his creation.

"Who's that, Adam?"

"That's Rose's assistant. Every year Rose makes a big reveal and every year is better than the last. Last year was a Monet on loan from The Musee Marmotten. It's always something, but I wonder where she could be. I haven't seen her all night."

"Me neither," Maria agreed.

The young man appearing before the large group of socialites and power removed a prepared statement that he'd written. Everyone in the room could tell that this young man was not accustomed to speaking in front of large crowds, as evidenced by the beads of sweat suspiciously present on his forehead.

"Ladies and gentlemen," the assistant began, "On behalf of Rosemarie Claxton and Maison de Luxe, I'd like to welcome you to the annual…"

****

"One minute out," Gray sounded off.

"*10-4. One minute. Any word on backup?*"

"None. Call Rod let him know where we're going to be," Gray responded.

As Sean raced through the last few blocks, he called Rod. "Rod, we need additional units to 1201 Rue Royale, now! The next target is Rose Claxton. Gotta go, Gray and I are about to hit it." Sean hung up without a single response from his supervisor. He was sure Rod would hammer the message home with whomever he spoke to.

Both men now pulled into the parking lot of the gallery and parked their vehicles near the entrance. People were taken aback by the speed at which they parked, but more so by the speed at which both men exited the vehicle with what appeared to be automatic weapons at the ready. The word PO-LICE emblazoned on their external vests only added to the temporary hysterics of the moment.

"On me," Gray yelled. Sean followed without question.

They approached the front door and met with doorman, demanding the location of the gala and more specifically the location of Rosemarie Claxton. The doorman was obviously flustered by the two intense individuals in front of him and was speechless for a moment.

"Tell me!"

"The gala is in the reception area, off of the main gallery," the doorman responded to Gray's demand, more rattled than ever.

Sean and Gray disappeared into the gallery and were in a full sprint. Unlike The Artist who admired the works earlier in the day, Gray and Sean raced through and paid no attention to the masterpieces that surrounded them. The upper crust that saw them running through the spacious gallery didn't know what to think of this very strange happening. Some stood and stared, and others paid due attention and returned to their free high-end booze. The door to the reception area was in sight, guarded by two security professionals, both dressed in tuxedo's and both with ears pieces. They didn't have the look of mall cops, more likely personal security for one of the powerful people in the room. The guards took notice of the two men sprinting their way, weapons in hand and both drew their weapons immediately.

"Stop," yelled one of the men.

"Detectives Gray and Guthrie open the door," Gray yelled back.

"Stop or we will shoot!"

"Police, God damnit! Open the fucking door! Someone is in danger!"

****

"It is my pleasure on behalf of Ms. Claxton and Maison de Luxe to present to you, on loan from The Louvre, *The Winged Victory of Samothrace*."

The crowd applauded at the very sound of the description. This was an ancient piece of art that depicted the Greek goddess of victory, Nike. The head of the sculpture was no longer, but the body and outstretched wings were in fine condition for a sculpture over 2,000 years old. Some have classified the work as the finest of Hellenistic culture.

"She really outdid herself this year," The Artist remarked. "This is really something."

Maria saw the elation in Adam's face and smiled at his boyish reaction. This was a side that endeared him to her. He may have had upscale connections and knew powerful people, but he was in the moment and at this moment with her. Both about to see a masterpiece. The Artist lost himself in the and paid no attention to the affection in which Maria projected upon him. This was his moment in the sun. *This is it my coming out party!*

The crowd watched at the young man proudly grabbed onto the black cloth. The anticipation of the group grew. They waited to feast their eyes on an ancient piece of history. Admiration of the craftsmanship would soon follow. With a firm tug of the cloth the sculpture was reveal to everyone in attendance.

****

"Listen, my name is Silas Gray and I'm a detective with…"

His explanation to guard standing before him was interrupted by blood curdling screams the likes of which no one present in this small group had ever heard before. It came from within the gala and was accompanied by many more screams and a sudden rush of footsteps coming toward the door.

"OPEN IT, NOW," Gray demanded.

As soon as the guards opened the door to engage whatever threat was within, they were met with a sea of humanity. Men and women dressed in their finest attire and dripping in expensive accessories began rushing toward the men as they entered. Gray and Sean led, while the two security guards following them found their prize, the governor, and escorted him from the room. The governor's face was frozen at the sight of the horror before him. Gray and Sean were now able to see what drove these people away and a man holding a black cloth that was near catatonic and covered with a mist of red.

The image before them was grotesque, an exposed limbless woman attached to an ancient sculpture via thin nylon straps. Tourniquets placed on each of the blood-stained nubs left in the absence of arms and legs. Her face bore the likeness of terror, a deep laceration that extended from each side of her mouth to her ears, and no tongue. Another deep, but unopened wound could be seen extending from her pubic area to her neck. Most disturbing was the placement of the limbs, or more fittingly the way the limbs were shaped. Her left arm and left leg hung from one of the angel's wings from high strength wire and were shaped in the letter "T." The remaining limbs hung on the opposite wing shaped in the letter "J." The blood however was minimal when compared to the what they saw, this sick form of crucifixion as it were. This was Rose-marie Claxton, or what remained of her.

Gray and Sean trained their weapons on the man and de-manded that he drop the cloth. They repeated the command two more times before he was snapped back into reality and threw down the fabric. Sean scaled the stage area and placed the man into a set of flex cuffs.

"Gray," a voice yelled through the rapidly emptying crowd.

Gray turned his attention to the voice and saw Maria and a man standing next to her; shear panic in the man's face. He made his way to the two, unknowing of what to expect.

Sean turned his attention from the man on the ground to the body of the woman mounted on the angel. He didn't see any signs indicating that she was among the living, but he had to check. He slid his index and middle finger to the woman's throat to feel for a pulse. As soon as his skin touched her, she jolted back to life, bloody remains of her arms and legs dan-gled from the angel's wings like some demonic baby mobile.

"She's still alive. Call EMS," Sean yelled.

The Artist was amazed by this turn of events and stood there before his love and his friend, still feigning disgust but secretly enjoying this canvas evolving into performance art. He believed that the dose of heroin that he'd given was enough to finish the job but didn't realize that her tolerance to opiates was more substantial than he believed. Still, he gazed upon the defenseless woman with great fascination. *This is more glorious that I could have imagined.*

Sean attempted to calm the woman, but to no avail. Panic set in and she was near uncontrollable. "Ma'am, stop! Ma'am," Sean pleaded with the woman before him. She continued, at-tempting to scream through the wounds that she suffered.

It was only when she observed the man standing next to the

other detective and the woman in the emerald green dressed that she suddenly stopped. Her eyes were fixed on the man that she previously knew and invited into her home. His eyes met hers and both were now locked on, unable to break from mutual stares. The Artist knew that everyone was fixed on her and broke character in order to give her a smile that would haunt her last moments. Her eyes then shifted to Sean. She knew that there wasn't much time. Sean's eyes met with hers and then her eyes immediately returned to the man next to Gray. The communication was unmistakable. Sean looked to the man and caught a glimpse of the smile before reverting to immediate shock. The woman then became limp as she resided herself to the unavoidable.

"Gray, we need medical!"

"They're coming in right now," Gray yelled back.

"Stay with me," Sean yelled as he rubbed her breastbone furiously with his knuckles in order to bring her back to consciousness. This motion had an unexpected result, as the deep incision opened just below Sean's hand and the contents of the now dead Rose emptied onto the floor below the statue. Sean was shocked by the turn of events and pull his hand away. Nothing more could be done. A medical team arrived just as Rose's insides revealed themselves, but there was no recourse. One of the responding medics had to excuse himself after seeing the depravity of the situation.

"Dear Jesus," Maria said. She was visibly shaken by the sight and remained remarkably composed. Her job experience trained her for the grotesque nature of humanity, but this pushed those limits.

Gray stood beside Maria and her date, stone-faced and calm, but taken by the sight of Sean standing next to Rose. Whatever her sins, whatever her way of life, nothing deserved the butchery that was before him. The public display of this event was over the top, even for the person responsible for the previous scenes of violence. Gray turned to Maria and her date.

"Maria, sir. I'll need both of you to exit the room."

Maria heard the words and motioned to Adam to come with her. His rehearsed reaction still visible as he stood their motionless.

"Sir," Gray started, "Do you need help? Medical assistance? Anything?"

The Artist snapped out his daze and made eye contact with his friend, Silas, for the first time. He was instantly magnetized by the piercing blue eyes filled with intensity. He couldn't reveal himself in this moment but was tempted to do so. Consequences be damned. Still, his work wasn't complete. His gift to Silas was unfinished.

"No, thank you," The Artist responded. "Please, call me Adam."

"Ok, Adam. Please go with Ms. Gomez and wait outside in the gallery. An officer should be with you shortly."

"Thank you, Mr..."

"Gray, Silas Gray. Please, follow Ms. Gomez." Gray's voice was calm at this moment. He needed to be calm for those who were shocked by this experience. Gray pointed the direction for both Maria and Adam and both followed the instruction without hesitation.

"Maria," Gray called out, "Expect a call later."

Maria nodded her head in silent understanding. She knew that Gray would call her but for now she needed to tend to her shock at the sight that was exposed to her and see to Adam. He, in her view, was not climatized to such things. She and Adam then disappeared beyond the doors and into the presence of responding uniformed officers.

Sean met with Gray in the middle of the reception hall.

"How did you know," Sean asked.

"She was a witness for my trial. Witness A, as she was listed." Gray retrieved his phone and showed the e-mail that required their frantic race through the city of Lafayette. The witness list was read off by Sean: Rosemarie Claxton, Rick Lanier, Sarah Lanier, Colby Lanier, Samantha Graves, Brian Hammond.

"Who's Brian Hammond? We need to find him and get him to safety as fast as we can," Sean said.

"Brian died of a heart attack two years ago. I worked with him in Iberia Parish. Can't say I liked him much. He was an ass that would throw anyone under the bus for an extra stripe."

"What about the T and the J on the angel," Sean asked.

"Tony and Jacques," Gray said somberly. *My team.*

XVIII.

9:48 PM

Rod and Desormeaux arrived at the gallery about thirty minutes prior. They weren't allowed within the primary crime scene: the reception area. Donaldson wouldn't allow it. Since this was the call, the two men stood in the gallery near the door of the reception hall, staring at closed doors. Gray and Sean were on their own with Donaldson. The only comfort that either man had was that Tyler and Kap were in the room with them. Even then, Donaldson smelled blood in the water; Gray's blood.

"What do you think junior is doing in there, boss," Rod asked.

"Don't know," Desormeaux responded, "But I am sure he's not trying to take Gray's gun away again."

The two men stood amongst a sea of officers. The inner crime scene was mobbed by officers and crime scene techs from the appropriate jurisdiction, as well as invited state guests. This was an unfortunate string of events, but Rod and Desormeaux knew that their guys could handle it and would brief them later.

"Hot chocolate, Chief?"

"Eh, why not," Desormeaux answered.

The two men left their space and made their way to the now thrice used mobile command center. The usual assortment of snacks and hot beverages met them upon their arrival.

****

"You two sons of bitches are in deep shit now! I own you and you will tell me what you know or so help me I'm…"

"You're gonna do what," Sean interrupted Donaldson. "Bark like psychotic Chihuahua. Fuck you!"

"Now, Sean, that was rude of you," Gray added. "He's more like a Pomeranian or a Boston Terrier."

Kap attempted to interrupt the argument between the three men, without much luck. Tyler was content to keep his hands in his pockets and watch the show. Either way, this meeting of the minds was going to happen, regardless of referee. Donaldson, now pointed in the faces of his two targets, continued his loud discourse.

"Obstruction of justice, interfering with an investigation, malfeasance in office, accessory after the fact. These are just some of the things I can do to you. Do you understand me! I own you and there is not a god damn thing that either one of you can do about it!"

Gray's patience with he and Sean's collective pain in the ass was wearing thinner than it had in the past. He tried to be cordial, or at least his version of it. He tried to be convincing. Neither attempt appeared to work. If Donaldson provided the correct provocation, then it would result in a drastic measure.

"Donaldson," Gray said, "Remove your finger from my face. That's your only warning, junior."

Donaldson's anger with the man in front of him took over his common sense. The lesson of underestimating the target that Gray taught him earlier that day appeared to vanish from his memory. He hated this man with a passion.

"Oh, shit," Tyler said to Kap.

Donaldson balled up his fist and swung it at the man before him, aiming at one of the two blue eyes looking at him. As suddenly as the punch was thrown a connection of bodies was felt. Gray was now inside of the Donaldson's haymaker, powerful arms wrapped around the trunk of the assailant. Gray moved with a quickness of man ten years younger and slipped under one of Donaldson's arms and immediately had the man in a full-nelson hold, Donaldson's arms now prevented from throwing another punch. Donaldson was now lifted off the ground and moving in the direction of the recently deceased Rose. Crime scene personnel moved as the now floating body of Donaldson approached them. Donaldson now knew where he was going and where he was going to land.

"Did you photograph this shit, yet," Gray asked, receiving a host of assurance that it had been photographed.

"Good," Gray responded.

As suddenly as Donaldson was lifted off the ground he was planted, face first into the bloody refuse that decorated the floor beneath the recently unveiled ancient statue. Donaldson attempted to break the hold, but he was no match for the man in control. Sean, Kap, and Tyler didn't interfere. There was no point and, collectively, they wished to see this happen.

"Final lesson, junior," Gray said, again his tone calm and he rubbing the man's face in the remains, "If you even think of charging me or Sean with anything, if you direct an accusation in my direction, if you get in my way, then I will end you. No calls to your uncle or the fact that you're another cop will stop the hell that I will rain down on you. Do you understand?" Gray locked in the hold to an unbearably painful extent.

"Yes," Donaldson yelled, his voice giving up his obvious agony.

Gray pushed deeper into the back of Donaldson's neck, applying more force into the hold and shoving his face further into the bloody mess, "I said, do you understand?"

Donaldson felt both shoulder near disconnection. The tendons and muscles were now at the point of no return.

"YES, I UNDERTSAND," the agony now unmistakable.

"Good." Gray left lifted Donaldson out of his predicament and firmly slammed him back into it. The impact of the blow forced more of the bloody puddle to splatter on whatever surrounded them. Donaldson fell to the ground, now well below the stage where his previous resting area was. Donaldson now looked like the survivor of a horror movie. He seated himself, not bothering to say anything. He was dazed, but still coherent.

"No more lessons, junior. You and I are done."

Donaldson looked at the man before him. The blood that splashed onto Gray's clothing from the previous act of aggression was nothing compared to the blood that Donaldson saw in Gray's eyes. Donaldson realized that there was no victory here, not with this man, not ever. The previous lessons may not have stuck with him for very long, but this will remain with him for a lifetime. Gray was the better man. He had to submit to this. He had to submit to Gray's will.

"Sean, we need to leave."

Gray walked to back to the three men enjoying the show.

"Was that necessary," Kap asked.

"No," Gray responded, "But it felt good. Take care, Kap."

Gray looked at a chuckling Tyler and nodded his head. The motion was returned in kind. Sean and Gray now took leave of the scene. They had work to do; work that Donaldson was incapable of finishing.

****

Maria and Adam stood in the gallery answering questions from a detective. Neither one was a suspect, but any information, however minute, could break a case wide open. Maria wished that she could help. Adam offered much of the same. Adam was answering one of the detective's questions when the doors of the reception area opened and Gray and Sean appeared from the opening.

"Gray," Maria said, trying to get his attention.

Gray looked at Maria with the same look that she saw at the Lanier house: intense, but worried. She then saw the blood on his clothing. She knew something happened. Gray gave no verbal response and continued walking with his partner, weapons in hand. Sean, too, gave no response, but looked to see the man that previously caught his eye. These men were in another zone and there was nothing else but the work. She placed herself in a position to see into the reception hall and observed a man, picking himself up off the ground and covered in blood. Obviously, not his own. She realized it was the governor's nephew, Donaldson.

"Oh, shit, something happened."

"What," Adam asked. The Artist now placed himself near Maria and saw what she saw. He smiled at the sight, albeit covertly. He felt a rush of excitement run through his body. His gift to his friend appeared to have an impact, but moreover this sight told him that his friend was coming back to him. It didn't appear that he'd lost a step, either. This is what The Artist wanted, his friend at peak performance. He wanted the inevitable clash of masters and needed Silas at his level, or more appropriately, the level that his friend should have been throughout the entirety of this master work. *Masters rarely reveal themselves until it's time.*

The doors closed and The Artist and Maria continued to provide information to the detective. As soon as the investigator was finished asking questions, she handed them a card and told them to call her should they remember anything else. She confirmed their individual contact information and went to the next pair of gala attendees.

"What do you think that was all about," The Artist asked.

"Don't know, I'm sure I'll find out later."

"Are you ok, Maria."

"Yeah," Maria said, "Let's go somewhere else. Anywhere else but here."

"Sure. I'll take you to your car."

"Sounds good. I'm sorry that the night has to end so suddenly."

The Artist smiled and held Maria's hand as they began to walk.

"Don't apologize, this isn't your fault. I'm sure that whoever did this will be found by your friend. He's quite intense."

"I wouldn't say that we're friends," Maria said, the statement accompanied by a nervousness. "But intense is as good a word as any."

"What do you mean by that," The Artist asked.

"Oh, nothing. I will say that I almost feel sorry for whoever he's chasing. If his reputation is true, then he's already decided to set a meeting between whoever is doing this and the grim reaper."

The Artist faked a bit of intrigue at this declaration, but the irony of her statement didn't escape him. *How appropriate, a date with a REAPER.*

Maria and The Artist walked through the gallery and into the cold of the evening. The LED lights of police cars and lights from several sources, not the least of which were news cameras, turned the night into day. They would be bombarded by reporters for information, especially Maria. The made their way through the growing crowd and were able to secure themselves in their individual vehicles.

"So that's what that feels like," Maria quipped to herself.

The Artist started the engine of his vehicle. He and Maria left the latest showcase of a master.

****

Gray and Sean met with Rod and Desormeaux at the command post. Rod saw Gray's clothing and couldn't help but wonder what occurred in the closed room.

"Should I expect a complaint, sweetheart?"

"No, I'm sure you won't," Gray responded.

"Do I even want to know what happened in there?"

"No, I'm sure you don't," Gray answered.

"Outstanding," Rod exclaimed, "The less I know the less it will hurt. One question: Is pretty boy still alive?"

Gray looked at Rod, a sly expression in his eyes, "Yes, restraint got the better of me."

Desormeaux listened to the exchange and smiled as he drank his hot chocolate. He'd seen this type of reaction before and knew that Donaldson would no longer be a problem, at least not a problem to Gray and Sean. He was, however, still concerned with the recent events.

"Gray, a word please," Desormeaux asked.

Gray and Desormeaux excused themselves from Rod and Sean. They found semi-quiet place to recluse themselves from the controlled chaos of the crime scene. Neither Rod, nor Sean knew what the two men conversed about, but they did know that something was afoot, something they were holding in reserve. The meeting was brief, never more words than necessary between the two men, and they returned to their compatriots.

"Mind filling us in boss," Rod stated.

"Just a little information exchange. Nothing major, Rod. Let's go."

Rod and Desormeaux left in Rod's SUV. Gray and Sean were again on their own to do their own thing and began walking back to their vehicles.

"What'd you see in the room, Sean?"

"If you're asking if I saw what happened between you and Donaldson, then I didn't see shit."

"I appreciate that, but you picked up on something. I know you did."

Gray was right, Sean saw something that seemed out of place. He couldn't understand why the man standing next to Gray and Maria smiled when he attempted to revive the victim of this tragedy.

"The guy with Maria seemed a bit out of place," Sean said. "I could've sworn I saw him smiling when Rose died and then as soon as I saw it, he went right back to shock. It was weird. Also, I swear I've seen him before. I just can't place him."

"A nervous smile, you think?"

"I don't think so. There was something about it that didn't sit right with me. Can you call Maria and see what that was about?"

"Sure," Gray responded, "I'll give her a call. They were talking to a detective in the gallery. Ask her for the guy's personal info and run him. First name is Adam. I never got his last name."

Gray and Sean both doffed their vests and weapons and were immediately met with the nature's fury of cold. They quickly retrieved their jackets and retreated to the respective missions: Gray calling Maria and Sean finding the detective that spoke to Maria and her date.

Gray called Maria. Voicemail.

"Maria, call me back when you can. It's probably nothing, but I need some info. Bye."

Gray completed his task and went back to the command post to find Sean, but he wasn't there. Tyler emerged from the gallery and walked in his direction. He had the look of a man that had something on his mind.

"Gray, what's the play here?"

"Don't know yet. Still wondering why this is happening and how the team is involved."

"Are we exposed," Tyler asked, worry heard in voice.

"Not that I'm aware of. It seems like they're going after anyone involved with the grand jury. That's the only thing I can think of. You and Kap need to keep Donaldson in line. He's gonna fuck this up."

Tyler smiled, "He finally got the message. I don't think he's a problem anymore."

Sean emerged from the gallery and saw Gray talking to Tyler. Tyler and Gray shook hands and Tyler went back into the gallery. Sean saw this exchange and immediately thought that something was going on. He now knew the history between these two men; a history forged in conflict and blood. He would be remiss if he didn't feel uneasy about this fact, but he was trusted with a secret and that counted for something. He met his partner. Tyler quietly excused himself.

"The man's name is Adam Singleton. Here's his information."

Sean handed the pocket notebook to Gray. No bells. No recollection. Nothing from the words written.

"Run him and see if he pops on anything. Let me know what

you find out."

"Did you get in touch with Maria," Sean asked.

"Straight to voicemail. Can't say that I blame her after everything that happened. Being my friend isn't easy."

"No, I can't say that it is," Sean said bluntly.

Sean started to walk to his vehicle when Gray stopped him.

"Sean, that conversation between Tyler and I was about the team's exposure. Just thought you'd like to know."

Sean smiled at the statement. He knew that Gray completely trusted him at that moment with everything. If there were questions before, then there were none now.

XIX.

11:01 PM

Donaldson was still reeling from the latest Silas Gray lesson. His blood-stained clothing had since been replaced with a t-shirt and a pair of jeans that he always kept with him in case he had to get dirty. By the looks of the clothing that he now wore, he didn't get dirty very often. The crime scene was still quite active, and the body of the late Ms. Claxton removed, including as much of her last surprise as the coroner could scoop up. The statue remained, stained a deep red.

"You OK, Donaldson," Kap asked, an insincere tone accompanying the question.

"I guess, sir. This hasn't panned out very well." Donaldson's delivery was devoid of the typical haughtiness and condescension. "Part of me still believes that Detective Gray is a part of this, but his latest "lesson" showed me a man of deep conviction."

"You mean when he slammed you into a puddle of entrails," Kap added, "Twice."

"Yeah, that would be the one," Donaldson said.

"Listen, kid," Kap's voice now softening, "Silas Gray is not the man you're looking for. I've known him a very long time and he is as good a man and cop that I've ever had the pleasure of serving with. Trust me on this one. He's not your guy."

Donaldson keyed into one thing that Kap said, but he kept that to himself. He wondered what the phrase, "the pleasure of serving with," meant. To Donaldson's knowledge, Kap and

Gray never served with each other. Kap was a career trooper and Gray a non-state law enforcement officer. His initial reaction was to dismiss the phrase as the two would have had professional interactions with each other over the years, but the way that the men talked to each other showed a familiarity beyond the office. Tyler was the same way. There was a friendship between the men. Still, Donaldson needed to be careful.

"You're right. You and Tyler told me to lay off, but I didn't listen."

Kap was surprised at the candor. He didn't trust the man beside him, but every man had a point of enlightenment in their career. He hoped that this was Donaldson's moment.

"Good to hear, Donaldson. Now go get the bastard doing this," Kap said.

"Yes, sir."

Donaldson dismissed himself and left the reception area. Kap's statement still ran through his mind. He began to make associations between Gray, Kap, and Tyler. He believed in his own ability and now he had a gut feeling of the situation. This feeling would stay with him throughout the walk through the gallery and his eventual arrival to his car. There, he would make a phone call.

"Uncle Luke, are you ok?"

He was assured by his uncle that no harm was done and told him that he had every possible tool at his disposal to stop the monster who was responsible for this crime.

"Great! I need the personnel files for Kaplan Rodrigue and Tyler Fontenot. I appreciate it, Uncle Luke."

Donaldson was assured that he would receive those files within the hour.

****

"Nothing, nada, zip, zilch. In other words, there ain't shit else on this guy!" Rod always knew how to deliver news, good or bad. In this case, the news was less than good, but not that bad. It just meant a dead end.

"Rod, check again," Sean insisted. "There has to be more."

"When I tell you it's not there, it's not there. Big Homie knows where to look and if he can't find it, then no one can. Got it? Good. Now for my next impossible trick I'll try to figure out why Reality TV is so popular."

Rod had a point and Sean knew it. They searched every database available to them, trying to find the name Adam Singleton, or at least something more substantial than a driver's license or a social security number. This man was a ghost three years ago, not even a utility bill; the. suddenly he existed.

"How is that even possible, Rod?"

"Don't know. Have you even seen Survivor? My wife can't get enough of it. It's shit!"

"Not that," Sean said, now becoming irritated.

"I know what you meant. Sit yo hyperactive ass down before I choke you."

Desormeaux entered Rod's office. He heard the two men fussing and, if he were honest with himself, rather enjoyed hearing it. This was normal for Rod and Sean: Sean would get frustrated and Rod would settle him down. That's exactly what he needed at this moment.

"Am I interrupting, gentlemen?"

Rod and Sean stopped arguing for a moment to acknowledge the new member to the group.

"Not at all, boss. Sean and I were having a bit of civil discourse pertaining to the big pile of horse shit that we currently find ourselves in."

"Well, I'll leave ya'll to it then." Chief began to walk away when Sean stopped him.

"Chief, what do you know about Gray and his team?"

Desormeaux froze and Rod's eyes fixed on the man who just revealed something that very few people knew about. There was only one person that could have told him about Gray's team, outside of Desormeaux. Desormeaux only filled Rod in on the secret a few hours prior. This was something that neither expected, especially Desormeaux. He turned to face Sean.

"Gray told me, Chief."

"What did he tell you, son? As much as you can remember."

Sean regurgitated he story that Gray told him, almost as if he'd lived through the events himself. Garrett Boudreaux, Tony, Jacque. How Gray treated Mags' wound before she was hauled off, only to be told that she died. Kap and Tyler's cover story. The funerals. Cerberus. Everything. Sean's memory was always excellent, but this was another level of detail. Gray felt Sean needed to know and Sean wouldn't forget the trust that he placed in him.

"Sounds about right, detective," Desormeaux said, now sitting in the chair opposite of Sean. Rod sat there in silence. He knew what the Chief told him previously, but a near first person account of the hell Gray went through brought the normally jovial man into a deep somberness.

Desormeaux stood from his chair and excused himself from the office. He was moved by the trust that Gray placed into Sean, but more than that he realized that the normally stoic Silas Gray was finally trusting someone else, just as he did his former teammates. This realization made Desormeaux smile, something else that he needed at that moment.

"Sean," Rod said, "Go get some rest tonight and we'll pick

this up in the morning. You need the rest. Adam Singleton can keep till morning. I'll keep digging to see what I can find."

"Rod."

"That's an order, dummy! Go home and rest."

Rod's order didn't sit well with Sean, but he was right. Sean had barely slept in the last 36 hours and his body was feeling the strain of fatigue. He and Rod stood up and shook hands.

"See you in the morning," Sean said.

"God willing," Rod responded.

Sean exited the office and walked through the halls of his second home toward the exit. The door opened and he was once again met by the cold of the evening. The temperature dropped, again, and the wind still hadn't tired. He looked at his watch and saw that Christmas Eve was only a half hour away. There was some solace in that. Maybe the killer would be inclined to take a day off, but Sean knew better. Still, the memory of Adam Singleton's smile haunted his thoughts. He knew him from somewhere.

"Why can't I remember," Sean mumbled to himself.

****

Maria found herself in the Adam's bed again, but this night was much different than the night before. Maria didn't want to be alone tonight and met Adam at his apartment after leaving the gallery. She and Adam laid in bed and she was fast asleep next to him, holding onto him as of holding onto a life raft from a sinking ship. He was her security this night and he was more than happy to provide her much needed protection.

The Artist arose from his bed and walked his usual path. The shattered mirror was previously cleaned up. He told Maria that it was an accident and that he'd lost his footing when walking out of door. Maria seemed to buy the story and though that his clumsiness was more endearing. Still, he felt guilty for lying to his true love about something so trivial. He arrived at his refrigerator and pulled from its belly a high-priced bottled water. He had no patience for anything less than the best of everything, even water. He now faced the black granite countertop. He had one more folder: red.

"Reveal to me your secrets, my dear," The Artist said as he retrieved the final canvas of his masterpiece. The seal was removed, and the contents splayed before him. This one would be easy to find and, unless he missed his guess, this canvas would come to him. He left enough clues to reveal himself to this one. He didn't completely reveal himself, but he knew that this man was bright enough to discover who The Artist was.

"Oh, my friend Silas will love this final piece. I was mad at you before, my friend, but no longer. You truly are an artist. You nearly drove me to make a mistake with the lies that you told about me. It took me awhile, but I understood what you did. You are a genius, my dear! Here I am trying to give you the best of me and you are reciprocating. You are a true friend to me."

This folder was of the same thickness as the other two and its contents enlightening, albeit unnecessary at this point in the game. He studied the photograph and knew that this man would prove difficult to subdue. This man is the reason that he trained so vigorously and why he felt it necessary to remove all thoughts of pain from his mind. This canvas will not give up his brush stroke easily. The Artist placed the folder back into its bag and finished the rest of his water. He needed his rest this evening as the coming day would prove his most important. He slipped back into bed with Maria and she held onto him again. As he laid in the bed staring at his ceiling he thought of his new canvas and whispered a simple sentence.

"Detective Guthrie. I look forward to our next meeting."

"Adam, did you say something," Maria mumbled, half

asleep.

"No, my dear. Go back to sleep. You need to rest."

****

"Norm, I'm getting sick of cleaning up after you, but in your defense, this is more my fault than yours. Daddy's sorry for keeping you cooped up all day."

Gray couldn't be mad at his Boxer pup for very long. The goofiness of the breed alone precluded any anger to remain for an extended period of time. The unconditional love of his little buddy showed made the homecoming worth every ounce of frustration. He hated to admit it, but this dog was growing on him. He only wished that Charlie and Simon were with him. There was a knock at his door. He thought that it might have been Maria, again, but she knew better by now. He also entertained the idea that it might have been Donaldson. That thought quickly left when Gray didn't hear the rattling around of a tactical team that would have accompanied him after their last meeting. He peeked through the blinds of his door and immediately opened the door.

"Hey Chief, what's going on?"

"May I come in," Desormeaux asked.

"Of course, come in."

The two men took seats opposite one another on the large sectional sofa in the living room. Norm no longer had an interest in his master and rushed to the newcomer. Desormeaux was taken by surprise by the energetic pup and started petting the youngster.

"Would you like a drink or something, Chief?"

"No, thank you. And stop with the Chief shit. We're off duty. That's an order."

"What brings you here, Roger?"

"Sean told Rod and I about your revelation to him. You seem to have a left a couple of things out. Why is that?"

"I trust Sean with my secrets, but other things aren't mine to reveal. Everything in its own time and in its own way."

"What about Kap and Tyler," Desormeaux asked, "They have a lot to lose as well. I'm not sure that they'd appreciate the exposure."

"True, but I trust Sean. Besides, you and I know there's still a final card to play when or if it's needed. They'll take care of it all because they know that they owe me for what I did that night and for everything that happened afterwards."

"Well," Desormeaux began as he stood up, "You've always been a good judge of character. I trust we won't use that card unless we have to."

"I hope we don't have to, old friend," Gray responded.

The two men embraced before Desormeaux left Gray's house. Gray found this moment deeply disturbing. He knew that if Desormeaux was concerned, then that meant something was very wrong. In all the years that he knew him, he'd never seen the man rattled. This was an extraordinary time and the circumstances may dictate the use of a trump card. A card that would unleash a flurry of confusion.

Keres

DAY THREE

"I define a 'good person' as somebody who is fully conscious of their own limitations. They know their strengths, but they also know their 'shadow' – they know their weaknesses. In other words, they understand that there is no good without bad. Good and evil are really one, but we have broken them up in our consciousness. We polarize them."

-John Bradshaw

I.

December 24th

7:04 AM

Maria opened her eyes and saw Adam sleeping peacefully next to her. The experience from last night was fresh in her mind, but at this moment it was a thousand miles away. He didn't push for anything last night last and only wanted to be there for her. This man, whom she admittedly barely knew, was too good to be true. Attentive, mannered, respectful of her wishes, obviously attractive and brilliant. She didn't read deeper into it that for fear of finding something that wasn't there. It was only the moment that mattered to her. She grabbed her phone and saw that she had several missed calls: her producer, Tom, Sasha, and one from Gray. He promised to call later, but she wanted to relieve herself from the horror of that evening. She would call him back later. She decided that she would prepare coffee for she and Adam. She, again, took one of Adam's shirts and made herself at home, or at least more decent. She approached the island with the black granite countertop; immaculate and everything on it in its own place.

"Where's the coffee," she asked herself.

She searched the cabinets looking for the granules that made all who consumed it much more pleasant.

"Nope, next cabinet."

Her search was proving to be an endless discovery of order and a surprising lack of comfort foods. She admired a man who looked out for himself, but even this was a bit unusual, especially for a bachelor.

Her attention was now drawn to the island's built-in drawers and cubbyholes. More of the same order. One area held spices, another had padded mitts for holding hot pots and pans. She felt she was getting closer, but her prize eluded her. As she opened one of the cabinets, she discovered what she was looking for, medium roast coffee from her favorite company.

"Yes!"

She removed the package and discovered another; much larger package hidden at the far end of the area. It was something that is not typically placed in the kitchen: a black leather bag. Her curiosity was piqued at this moment.

"Well, what have we here. Secrets?"

She looked around the apartment to see if Adam awoke from his slumber. All clear. She could make coffee and find out more about this man in one fell swoop. She assumed it was his work case. She remembered seeing him the previous day in the kitchen reviewing work, despite his claim of not having to work for the rest of the year. The feeling overwhelmed her and she needed to know. Nature or profession, she couldn't tell. This was her opportunity to get to know the man better.

Maria pulled the bag forward and immediately noticed its superb quality and was confused why such an item would be hidden from view. It was lighter than she anticipated. Not may secrets to hide, she assumed.

"Let's see what we have here."

She unzipped the satchel and saw what she believed were work folders, three in total and color coordinated: green, yellow, and red. Each appeared to contain a similar number of documents. She then noticed ribbons that she presumed bound each folder separately. Affixed on one of the ribbons was a symbol that she saw at his apartment the night they met. An Ankh, emblazoned in wax.

"Hmm, this is, well, something."

She was about to open the green folder when she heard a noise. It was a person and it emanated from the bedroom. She quickly pushed the folder back into its place and pushed the bag in its original place. She rose from her knelt down position.

"Maria," Adam said. "Hello?"

"Adam, I'm in the kitchen."

Adam entered into the living area and saw Maria, running water into the coffee pot, the freshly found bag of coffee sitting on the black countertop. He smiled and met her at the sink where Maria was cleaning out the pot.

"How are you feeling," Adam asked, kissing her forehead as he finished the question. Maria smiled at the gesture.

"Much better, now. Coffee?"

"Sure. You need help?"

"No, I think I can manage," Maria said.

She prepared the coffee as Adam sat himself in barstool on the opposite side of the island. He watched her every move, taking in the scene of the beautiful woman before him. He felt that everything was right at this moment. Maria was with him and stronger than even he could imagine. Most people would've broken at the sight of his canvas, but not Maria. She was too strong for that and didn't mention it first thing in the morning. *This is my love, my only love!*

"Would you like me to turn on the TV? There might be an update on what happened last night," Adam asked.

Maria turned to look at Adam, sitting there and watching

her prepare their coffee.

"Nah, let's just enjoy each other's company."

The Artist was pleased with her attention wanting to be on him and he was more than happy to devote his full attention to her. Despite his pleasure with this turn of events, he still knew where Maria found the coffee. He placed it there himself. There was something else in the compartment that held more importance that anything else in his life: his canvases. He wondered to himself if she saw the bag containing his art or if she was loyal only to her mission. This thought didn't bother him as much as it should have, but it was still there. Gnawing at him. *Did she see it? No, not my Maria.*

****

Gray enjoyed his first cup of coffee with his little buddy, Norm. It was the first time in two days that he was able to relish the morning before all hell broke loose, or at least that's what he was thinking. The local morning show played clips of Maison de Luxe exterior shots while the morning anchor provided the voice over. The name of the victim was released, but the details of her demise kept secret. It was too graphic for most to stomach, but secretly everyone would have wanted to see it. Human nature can't help itself but to see what is not supposed to seen. A sense of decency meeting morbid curiosity, as it were. Still, Gray wished to enjoy some peace before he decided to go hunting. The peace of the morning was then broken by a text tone and a vibrating sweat pant pocket.

"Oh well, that's that I guess," Gray said, looking at norm laying on his side at his feet. Norm paid no mind to the tone and continued with his leisurely morning.

The text was from Sean: *Unlock your door. Be there in a minute.*

"Shit, Sean! Don't you ever relax?"

Gray removed himself from his claimed and well-worn spot on the large sectional. He walked to the kitchen and retrieved a coffee mug from the cupboard. This was not the first time that Sean arrived on short notice, and it would not be the last. Gray was just happy that he didn't have to warn Charlotte put her robe on this time. Gray prepared the cup and placed creamer next to it. He finished the setup when he heard a distinctive knock on the door and the chime of his home security system.

"Hey, hey!"

"Kitchen! Coffee's ready!"

Sean walked through the living room and into the kitchen, patting the now sitting pup on the head as he passed. "Don't mind if I do." Sean made his coffee and both men sat at the dinner table.

"What's going on, Sean?"

"Adam Singleton. Something isn't sitting right with me. The thought kept me up most of the night."

"What's bothering you so much," Gray asked, "The smile you told me about?"

"Yeah, I mean, who smiles when someone's insides just fell out of them. There's something wrong with that. I mean, shit, even I was shocked at that one."

Gray lifted the drink to his face and nodded. "You're right, that kinda got me, too. Here's what we'll do, you follow up with Singleton and I'll get with Maria. Same plan as last night. At the very worst, we add him to our list of sickos."

"Sounds good," Sean said, putting his cup of coffee on the table and beginning to stand up.

"After our coffee. Sit."

Sean sat down and both men continued their morning

coffee. Sean was a go getter and Gray admired that, but for the moment Gray wanted to continue the normalcy of this morning. The insanity of the day can wait a few minutes.

Gray decided to text Maria, despite his annoyance at such an impersonal form of communication: *Meet me. Tell me where and when.*

****

Donaldson barely slept a wink that night. He'd been running himself ragged for two days chasing after a man that he knew was involved with the recent rash of violence; the same man that challenged his belief in his own superiority. Gray had become the object of his obsession, but he had to be careful. Gray was dangerous, possibly the most dangerous man he'd ever met. He had to change tactics.

Just like the previous day, he read through personnel records, this time these records were for two of his own: Kap and Tyler. He knew of them and worked under them at times, but he didn't truly know who they were. Their pasts. The reason for their rapid ascensions into their positions. Most importantly to Donaldson, their connection to Silas Gray. He observed that the three were close, but the reason for their bond eluded him.

Reading through their files enlightened him. Both were top performers in their academy classes. Both attended training in tactics. Violent offender task forces. All were in line with what he knew. Their records were spotless until they were involved in a car accident about three years ago. The timing of this accident coinciding with Gray's shooting. Very coincidental, if he believed in coincidence. He also noticed that several years before that they were assigned to a seemingly innocuous post with the Department of Public Safety. Barely any records existed of their activities and those that did exist had vague duty assignments.

As he connected the dots between the three men in his sights, Donaldson couldn't help but remember Gray's words to him: *No calls to your uncle or the fact that you're another cop will stop the hell that I will rain down on you.* He knew Gray meant every word and he persisted with his crusade against him, regardless. This was in no way a professional pursuit. He wanted to destroy this man and would use his friends to do it.

"Captain," Donaldson said as the cell phone in his hand connected with the top cop of his Troop, "Could you have Lt. Rodrigue and Sgt. Fontenot meet me at the office? I can't get in touch with them. I'll be at the office in an hour."

The Troop commander granted the request, as if he could possibly say no to a man with Donaldson's connections. The investigations team wasn't working this day, officially recognizing the unofficial state holiday. This was his way of letting them know that he was in charge. He placed the phone on the table before him and continued to read.

"You two will know who I am at the end of this day."

****

Tyler's phone provided notice of his impending meeting with Donaldson. That notice was then followed by a call from Kap.

"Hey," Tyler answered.

Tyler noticed that Kap's delivery contained a nervous tone. This was unlike Kap. He was typically calm, and stress never really got to him. Donaldson had him shaken.

"Kap, I'll meet you in the parking lot at the office. Donaldson is grasping at straws and you and I both know that Gray would never give us up, especially not to him." Kap agreed with Tyler, but it still didn't diminish the mind playing tricks on him.

Tyler hung up his business phone and retreated to the office area of his apartment, specifically to his desk. He retrieved a key from his pocket and opened one of the lower drawers. This drawer hadn't been opened in some time. He removed a lockbox from the drawer; a box he secreted away several years ago and hoped that he would never have to open it again, but he had to. Within it was the same picture of the REAPER team that Gray had and under that pictured an envelope with his name on it, still sealed. Donaldson's persistence with this case forced him to open this envelope. This wasn't a hasty decision. His nature precluded rashness in all forms. The contents of the envelope revealed themselves, ten digits. He dialed the number and a voice on the other end responded.

"Name and access code."

"Fontenot, Tyler. Romeo four," he responded.

"Access granted. State your request."

"Request Keres."

"Standby," the voice on the other end of the line stated and then dead air for several seconds. "Keres protocols initiated. Standing by for additional actors' directive."

"Romeo four, direct."

Tyler hung up the phone and sealed the lockbox, all contents minus the envelope included. He placed the envelope in his shredder and proceeded to gather his things for the meeting with Donaldson.

II.

07:59

Kap and Tyler arrived at the office and were not surprised to see that Donaldson beat them there.

"What do you think this is all about," Kap asked.

"Don't know, don't care. I'm getting tired of him," Tyler responded.

"Anything from Gray?"

"Nope, and I don't expect there will be," Tyler said in his usual aloof style. "FYI, I opened my envelope. You should do the same."

Kap nonchalantly turned to Tyler and gave no outward reaction, despite his growing fear within him beginning to take over. He couldn't believe what he heard. This was like opening a portal into the past. A past that he wished never to relive. Still, he was not angered by this. Tyler was more relaxed than anyone he'd ever met and this was not an action that he would perform without every known variable taken into account.

"I'll do the same when this is done," Kap said. "I trust that you've thought this through."

"Yup. Been chewing on it since last night."

"Well, then. Let's get to it." Both men walked into the building side by side and Donaldson was there to greet them. He was dressed smartly.

"What's going on, Donaldson? Why are we here on our blessed day off," Kap asked.

"You two are here to answer my questions. I'm here to ask those questions. Should you fail to answer any of these questions, then you can consider yourselves suspended pending internal investigation." Donaldson's attitude was smug. An attitude that he dared not use against Gray.

"I see you got the intestines out of your hair," Tyler said mockingly. "How long did that take?"

"Sgt. Fontenot, you're first. Come with me." Donaldson wasn't amused by Tyler's lack of respect.

Tyler followed Donaldson into one of the building's interview rooms. Tyler was very familiar with these rooms and was never the questioned, only the questioner. He knew that Donaldson found something, but he was unconcerned with this man's questions. He sat in the room and awaited Donaldson to do the same.

On the table before Tyler sat an open personnel file with his name on it, opened to a certain page containing his assigned positions.

"Sgt Fontenot," Donaldson started, "What can you tell be about you and Lt. Rodrigue's assignment with DPS main office?"

"Kap and I were assigned to DPS for the purposes of auditing violent offender task force operations," Tyler responded, refusing to add anything else.

"And then?"

"Kap and I requested a transfer after our car accident. The hours were too long."

"How do you know Silas Gray?"

"Gray was assigned to the violent offenders task force for his region. We met with his task force periodically."

"So, you, personally, never did any field work?"

"No," Tyler responded.

 "No field work whatsoever?"

"No."

"What kind of auditing did you do for the task force?"

"We monitored activities, equipment, training, et cetera, et cetera. Nothing to write home about." Tyler sat back in his chair and was more relaxed than before he entered the room. He knew that if he kept his answers short, then this would go by quickly.

Donaldson couldn't read the man before him. His answers were to the point and made sense and he showed none of the physiological signs of deception – movement in the seat, comforting actions with hands, nothing. He knew that Tyler was not going to crack.

"Sgt. Fontenot, May I call you Tyler?"

"No, you may not," Tyler answered.

"As you wish," Donaldson relented, somewhat shocked at the lack of professional congeniality. "Is there anything you'd like to add to your previous statements? Anything at all?"

"Nope."

Donaldson was frustrated with this man. Nothing came. He didn't clear his throat, look around the room, scratch his balls. Nothing. If nothing else, this man was as loyal as it came to whomever he owed that loyalty.

 "Well, Sgt. Fontenot, if that's it then I guess we're through."

"I guess we are," Tyler said while rising from his seat. He started to walk to the door when Donaldson's evermore annoying voice disrupted his path.

"I suggest that you do not discuss this with anyone. Just a warning." The tone was cocky, filled with whatever false bravado Gray hadn't knocked out of him.

"I suggest you stay away from Silas Gray. Just a warning if you haven't figure that out by now," Tyler replied. His bravado neither forced, false, nor lacking in abundance.

"Send Lt. Rodrigue in here on your way out," Donaldson demanded.

"Fuck yourself, Donaldson," Tyler replied as he walked away, never making eye contact with the man.

Tyler entered the hallway and saw his friend sitting in a cheap, state purchased chair. He saw that Kap was calm and collected on the surface. He knew better. Kap was worried about Gray as much as he was. Donaldson was sniffing closer than ever. He was now close enough for Kap to hear his words, but far enough away from Donaldson's hearing range.

"Kap, make the call soon," Tyler said as he walked past his friend. He saw the look of concern in Kap's eyes and he was sure that Kap saw his concern as well.

Donaldson appeared from the interview room and motion for Kap to join him. As Kap entered the room he observed the table with the personnel files. Tyler's under his own. He was asked to sit, which he did. Kap had a bad feeling, especially since Tyler's interview was so brief.

"Lt. Rodrigue, shall we begin?"

****

Sean had been researching Adam Singleton since arriving at he and Gray's office. He attempted the usual methods: NCIC, AFIS, internal and external databases. Nothing. The only thing that he could find was a social security number and a driver's license. He saw that the driver's license was less than four years old. This intrigued him.

"How does full grown man just appear?"

"Easy! He doesn't." Sean's tunnel vision negated the observation that Rod had walked into the room.

"Hey Rod. Didn't notice you coming in."

Rod immediately recognized the irony in that statement. "What's got your brain burnin' this early in the morning, baby?"

"Singleton," Sean replied, "He just appeared out of nowhere. His apartment was purchased in cash three years ago and he's got no social media presence whatsoever. This guy is not in any database that we have access to. No criminal history, nothing."

"What about bank records?"

"I wouldn't know where to start. There are so many banks in the area and there's no time to call them all, Rod. Besides, they won't release shit without a court order and good luck finding a judge on Christmas Eve."

Rod sat in a well-used chair in Sean and Gray's office. Sean continued his search for Singleton, but no more information could be found that proved to be useful.

"Sean," Rod started, "What about obituaries or the coroner's office? Have you checked those?"

"You think he would have assumed an identity?"

"Big Homie seen stranger things. Just give it a try," Rod replied.

Rod sat back in the chair and placed his hand over his stomach. He shut his eyes and listened to Sean type on his computer and heard mouse clicks as Sean received results. This went on for a minute or two.

"Holy shit! Rod, you're a genius!"

"I know," Rod replied. "Please expound upon the depths of my brilliance."

"This website was started nine years ago: www.locateadamsingleton.com, listed an Adam Singleton, age 28, missing from a small town in Kansas. Vanished without a trace. No cell phone. His vehicle was located at his apartment. Wallet still on his nightstand."

"Pull it up. Let's see what we have," Rod said.

Sean clicked on the website and saw that the picture bore little likeness to the man he saw the previous evening. Eye color, hair color, height, weight, nothing appeared to match. This was just another dead end.

"Fuck," Sean yelled. "This is getting annoying."

"Slow your roll, Little Homie. Go through the website and see what pops. Maybe there's something connecting your Singleton with this Singleton. Just because it ain't him, don't mean it ain't him, ya dig?"

Sean read the main article aloud, "Missing, Adam Singleton, beloved son and friend. Disappeared from Gardener, Kansas, on December 22nd. Born on March 17... Rod, you're a..."

"I know I am," Rod interrupted. "So, we have a person missing from Kansas on December 22nd, and our homicide happened on December 22nd. The dates are significant. Look up the winter solstice for this year and the year that he went missing."

Sean, somewhat confused, again researched the dates and saw that both years had the annual occurrence on the same day.

"Same day for both years, Rod? Why?"

"Lemme educate you some. Some pagan traditions celebrated the solstice as a time of rebirth," Rod said. "Our guy seems to have done the same. Maybe he assumed the identity and this was his way of being "reborn.""

"That's a bit farfetched, don't you think," Sean asked.

"Maybe, but look at the crime scenes. The guy is sending messages to Gray in grizzly, but unusual ways. The walls of the Lanier's house and Duplantis' love shack was painted with Christian and demonic symbols. We both know that a lot of that history came from Pagan tradition. Claxton was strapped to a headless statue of a Greek goddess. Whoever this is knows the meaning of the date and the meaning of the symbols. The way he displayed the bodies was meant to evoke a response."

Sean still believed this theory was beyond rational thinking, but he couldn't dismiss it out of turn. Rod always saw things in a different light than he and Gray. Still, Sean was intrigued by the statements and knowledge.

"How the hell do you know this shit," Sean asked.

"Ah, I probably read it somewhere once and didn't need to use it until this moment. It's what I do," Rod answered. "I could be wrong, but I doubt it. Big Homie knows all, you just remember that."

"Ok, so what's the next step."

"The next step is that I'm gonna go to my office and talk sweetly to Big Momma. You're gonna see if Singleton is fakin' the funk and if he is, then you ask him why he's using a missing man's name and birthday."

"On it," Sean said excitedly.

Rod stood up from the chair and started walking out office. He then turned.

"Oh, one more thing. If you go by yourself and without back-up, I'm gonna put my foot in your ass."

"I know," Sean said.

"I mean it. If this guy is related to the missing person and possibly the homicides, then this is gonna get sporty. Get back up!"

"I got it. You sound like my mom."

"That's exactly what I am, Sean. I'm yo momma, and you don't cross momma, dummy."

Rod knew his guys and knew them well. This was a statement that he often made. They were go-getters and tracked leads no matter where they led. Often, they asked for forgiveness, rather than permission, but they weren't foolish. They were trained professionals and could handle themselves, but that never prevented him from worrying about his boys. They were his family.

Sean gathered whatever notes he took and packed them up in his bag. He had a target and he would find out as much as he could about this man calling himself Adam Singleton. He didn't contact Gray immediately. Gray was still trying to get in touch with Maria. He would be solo for now.

III.

9:00 AM

The Artist enjoyed his morning with Maria, but the necessary activity of the day must take precedence. There would be enough time for love after his gift to his friend was completed. He no longer felt ill will toward Gray for the things Maria reported. Those were his words in her mouth. She would never say such things unless she was misinformed. Not "his" Maria. Not the woman sitting next to him on his exquisite designer love seat.

"Maria, I'm going have to get ready. I have a meeting with some people about last night. Rose's death definitely makes this part of my work a bit more interesting."

Maria thought this was odd, but she didn't question it. He was a bachelor with no family to speak of. He never mentioned holiday plans and she didn't see any photos of family or friends in the apartment. She had already changed into the previous evening's attire, after an extended and satisfying breakfast for two.

"That's fine. Do you need me to leave," Maria asked.

"No, not all. Stay if you'd like. I have to shower and dress. I'll be gone for a few hours, but you're welcome to stay." The Artist leaned in and kissed Maria. He felt the rush of love and he knew that Maria felt the same way. "I hope to see you when I get back. If not, then we can meet up later."

"Ok," Maria said through her smile. She felt the passion in that kiss and longed for more, but she understood that he had to take care of things.

The Artist excused himself from her presence and walked to the bathroom. She heard the shower come to life and thought to herself that this would give her time to entertain her curiosity about the leather bag in the black granite topped island. She waited until she was sure that Adam was in the shower. The sound of pressurized water being interrupted by a body assured her that she had time.

She hastily removed herself from the couch and in seconds was reaching for the mystery bag in the island. She opened the bag, not needing to unzip it this time because she forgot to do so last time. The contents were there just like before and she opened one of the folders; the green one. She saw the bank documents and personal information for what she assumed were clients. She then saw the pictures of the clients. An overwhelming sense of dread filled her being. There they were. The Lanier family. Still photos of the two married couples. Places that they frequent. Notations as to their day-to-day routine. She then noticed a court document:

Witness List – State of Louisiana vs. Silas Gray.

She saw the names of the three Lanier's and Samantha, the future Lanier. She couldn't believe what she was seeing, and it overwhelmed her.

She looked up to concentrate on the sound of the shower; water was still interrupted by Adam's body. She placed all the documents back into green folder and retrieved the yellow folder. The contents of this folder sent a very real chill up her spine. Duplantis' information was on display for her to see. Five of the seven victims of the killer were in this bag. In these two folders. Another court document:

16th Judicial District Court

State of Louisiana

Parish of Iberia

Roger Duplantis - Prosecutor

Maria heard the water no longer running and panicked. She hastily placed the paper into the yellow folder and placed the folder into the bag. She stuffed the bag back into its position, again forgetting to zip the bag. She was terrified at this moment, but she couldn't show it. She had to be calm. She made her way back to the loveseat and assumed a normal position of comfort.

"Keep calm. Breathe," Maria whispered to herself.

The Artist opened the door and saw Maria sitting in the spot he last saw her. He emerged from the bathroom wearing a towel around his waist.

"You're still here. I guess that's a good sign."

Maria's self-preservation instinct was in overdrive. She knew that she had to keep it together and she had to appear genuine.

"Yeah," Maria replied, "Just wanted to see you before I left. I, too, have to go to work. My producer wants the info on last night and he's not one to keep waiting." This was believable considering her profession.

"You want to meet up, tonight," The Artist asked.

"Sure, the usual place?"

"Sounds good. I'll see you then."

Maria stood up and walked to The Artist. Their lips met and they both felt a connection. The connection was less passionate, but neither said anything about it. The Artist didn't feel it necessary. *She's probably upset that she must work today. My poor Maria.*

Maria walked out of the door and immediately began to walk faster through the hallway. No time for the elevator. She needed to get to her car quickly and the stairs provided the quickest route. She reached the stairs and let her feet and gravity dictate the speed at which she traversed them. She never looked back. Maria's mind ran to the possibility of Adam finding out about her discovery. Regardless, she was in a full panic by the time she reached her car in the parking lot. The temperature was below freezing at this point, but this was the farthest thing from her mind. She needed to leave as fast as possible and call Gray. At this point, he was the only person that she could trust. A turn of the key and the Chevelle's engine roared to life. All muscle, no fluff, and she would use every bit of it to flee from a man that she once felt safe with.

****

The Artist was now dressed and ready for the day. Both his gym bag and his tools were packed for the day's excursion. It was going to be a special day for not only him, but his friend. He reached for his masterwork of information and found the bag that held all that was dearest to him. He saw that the bag was open.

"Interesting, I know this was closed last night."

He inspected the contents and found that the papers in the green and yellow folders were in disarray. "NO! THIS CAN'T BE!"

For the first time in a very long time he felt something: heartbreak. It almost more than he could bear.

"No. Not her, my dear. Anyone but her. She is the only light that I will have left after this day. This is Silas' doing! He turned her against me!"

The Artist's rage was met with pain, the pain of loss. There would be no returning to the innocence that was he and Maria's love. She would see him as a monster instead of what he truly was: a generous humanitarian. His contributions served to help a friend in need of rebirth, much like he had some years ago. His falling in love was never in the plan, but his heart was hers and now it was broken.

"I must show her that I am still the man she loves, my dear. When she sees what I am willing to do for my friends, then she will know that I will do much more for her. Our love is pure and I will not let her go. I must show her that I am everything I say I am and much more than that. For now, there is no more time."

His determination was steeled more now than ever. He still didn't worry about finding his next canvas. Sean would come to him. He had to be ready for this. He knew Sean was formidable and would not be easily influenced to give up his paints. This is why he trained so hard and studied his canvases thoroughly. He knew their weaknesses. Sean's weakness was also his greatest strength: his tenacity. He had to have the answers to whatever vexed him.

"I shall wait for you nearby, Detective Guthrie. This will be finest canvas, but first there is still preparation."

He gathered his things, leaving the leather bag near the island, and made his way to the door of his apartment dedication and pain felt the entire time. He stopped before leaving and looked around his inner sanctum for what he hoped wouldn't be the last time, but he knew it would be. His refuge from the hideous world was compromised. The luxury of this space met his needs, but now it was time to evolve and become the man he always knew he was. A master, and nothing more.

****

Gray's phone rang. It was Tyler.

"Hey Tyler. What's going on?"

"Donaldson is questioning Kap right now. We were both called in this morning by the commander." Gray heard concern in Tyler's voice. This was unusual for him.

"Are we exposed," Gray asked.

"Unknown. Donaldson and Kap have been in there for about 45 minutes. My questioning wasn't nearly as long. Keres is in play."

Gray felt the sudden rush of his past flooding in. Keres was his brainchild, his contribution to the REAPER program should the team become exposed. It was to be used in emergency situations where team members would be targeted by someone or something or become exposed. Only he and one other knew the full extent of it and they never told any of the other team members of its composition or full measure. The team only knew that it needed to be initiated unanimously by every member or surviving member of the operational team. Thus far, only one team member, the most stoic of the group, felt the need for its coming to life.

"Does Kap know?"

"Yes, I suggested that he call in as soon as possible. Donaldson is too close to this," Tyler responded. "The decision will be yours in the end. This wasn't an easy call, boss."

"I know it wasn't, Tyler. This is something that may have to happen. The team cannot be exposed and we both know why."

"Gray," Tyler's tone now more somber, "Did we do the right thing by not backing you up with... you know? Do you need us now?"

Gray thought for a moment. This was a loaded question between men who lived on the fringe for years, combatting monsters that the public never knew existed. Monsters that would have carved a swath of destruction that would've made the most hardened cop fall to pieces and killers cringe in fear.

"You and Kap did what I told you to do. Never doubt that I knew you two were always there when or if I needed you. We stood up when others sat down and watched. This is my burden again, Tyler. One more time, I need you and Kap to sit."

"Gray, you don't…"

"I've made my decision," Gray interrupted. "This is mine and mine alone. I know you and Kap will be there for me if I need it. Please, just stay away from this. I will end it, no matter what it takes."

Gray heard Tyler's sigh over the phone. Tyler didn't like it, but he knew that Gray was going to do what he did best: hunt. "You call me if you need me, understand?"

"I do, Tyler. This will be over soon. Let me know when Kap makes the call."

"I will, but I'm sure he'll let you know himself. Good luck, boss." With this the call ended and Gray was on his own, left to his own methods.

He had a tendency of walking around when he was on the phone. He hated being stationary. By the time he placed his phone back in his pocket he was standing in front of his equipment; the tools of the lead REAPER. His prey wanted the man that he was, and Gray would grant that wish. He prepared himself for this moment; the moment when he would have to stare into the abyss and hope that the abyss wouldn't overpower his sense of duty and honor or right and wrong. Legal and illegal was an afterthought. Seven people were now dead, and they died horribly. He wouldn't allow another innocent person to suffer because of his decision to protect his team and his community.

The text alert broke his concentration for a moment. He was happy to see that it was Maria finally contacting him. The text appeared urgent: *WE NEED TO MEET, NOW!!!!! WHERE ARE YOU?*

Gray texted her back: *At my house.*

Maria replied: *Be there in five minutes.*

This turn of events perplexed him. The urgency of the text told him something was wrong, but what?

IV.

Sean arrived at Singleton's apartment building thirty minutes prior and parked his vehicle in a way that he could observe the comings and goings of the tenants. Despite the limited information on his target, he was able to get Singleton's registered vehicle information from one of the databases. He kept a keen eye on the parking lot's exit for a black Mercedes E Class sedan. He had to admit, Singleton had taste. This position also allowed his to watch the building front door. On foot or driving, he would see the man, unless he went out of the back door. He noticed a beautiful muscle car driving away from the building at a high rate of speed, but this was of no concern to him. He was out of his jurisdiction and completely unconcerned with traffic laws.

Stakeouts were always a crap shoot. Sometimes they were successful and sometimes they were not. Either way, the enemies of the activity was boredom and a wandering eye. Sean was different. He rarely broke away from his focus. He was a machine and that led him to many successful surveillance operations. A recent operation tasked him with finding a suspected human trafficker. He spent two days watching house in the middle of a sugarcane field at three hundred yards. It was a warner day, then, and he was able to identify several members of the ring. He found out later this when Homeland Security struck, they found 23 women, most under age, living in squalid conditions. He was happy to do his part and asked to be left out of the press conference. He was just content to do the right thing, regardless of praise. That's why he and Gray were so effective together. They preferred the shadows over the limelight.

He took notes during his reconnoiter, as he typically did with everything else. It was then that he saw a Mercedes leave the parking area. He compared the license plate with what was on file. It was a match. It was now a cat and mouse game.

"Gotcha."

He waited several seconds before he started the engine of his vehicle. The cold weather mixed with a running engine would've given away his presence. This was something that he could not allow, no matter how cold it became. He pulled away from his position and followed the sedan at a discreet distance. The cold weather kept many people in-doors, but last-minute Christmas shoppers provided enough cover to get lost in the traffic of the day.

His target left the downtown area and travelled toward the Evangeline Thruway, a part of town known for older houses and short streets. A left turn on the Thruway and they would be closing in on the interstate, which was where Singleton would go.

"Where are you going," Sean said to himself as they merged onto I-10 and headed west.

Singleton drove the speed limit, maybe a few miles over until he reached the Acadia Parish line, the parish butting up against Lafayette. Soon they were off the interstate and turning into a more secluded area, far away from dense populations. This is where following a target would prove difficult. People here know when someone is coming.

The Mercedes was made a turn into a business, an industrial area with several buildings, many of which stood unoccupied on this day. Sean passed the area and saw Singleton drive toward the rear of the businesses. It was unusual. His would be the only vehicle on the lot that didn't have a business emblazoned on the side of it. Sean made a U-turn a quarter mile from the entrance and backtracked, a fairly standard tactic. The thought of calling Gray or Rod crossed his mind, but he needed to see what the man was doing.

He entered the business and followed the tire tracks on the frost covered concrete. The trail led to the storage buildings. Sean parked his vehicle out of direct sight of the buildings and hoofed it, following the last few hundred yards in the frigid weather. Sean then saw it, the black sedan in front of one of the buildings, the lock securing the entrance of the metal building undone and the door open. The hair on the back of his stood up. This was unusual and he trusted those hairs. He drew his weapon and made a silent approach.

The car was empty. No movement was heard. He then made entry into the building, quietly. He was on Singleton's turf. The building was well lit and open. He saw something in the background. Four large white boards with something on them. The closer he got the clearer the boards became. Words, pictures, yarn connecting everything to a central point. In the middle of everything was a picture, someone that he knew well. A brother and partner. He followed the yarn from the epicenter and saw more people he recognized: the Lanier's, Duplantis and his lover, Rosemarie Claxton. His hunch led him into the lair of the beast.

The final yarn had another image of someone that he knew better than anyone else. He sees this person every morning in mirror. His face on the board before led him to the realization that he fell into a web laced by a master spider.

"Good morning, Detective."

Sean turned and saw nothing. The omniscience of the voice was magnified by the insulation lined metal walls. He scanned in a 360-degree circle, making sure to remain calm enough to avoid tunnel vision associated with hyper vigilance.

"You won't be needing that, Detective."

The statement was followed by a singular, precisely placed gunshot. The pain felt in Sean's hand as the bullet struck his weapon was overwhelming. The polymer and metal of his firearms was now useless as it flew from his hand.

"Shit," Sean yelled.

"Now, Detective. That is no way to speak in civilized company."

The Artist was enjoying his game. The thrill of his newest canvas fully aware of his existence prior to his brush strokes was more than he could have hoped for. Still, he was not finished with his newest muse.

Sean continued to scan his surroundings. He was at a disadvantage. Singleton had him, but no additional gunfire. Sean pulled a knife from his appendix area. A five-inch karambit knife. The talon-like blade was honed to a razor's edge and Sean was very astute with this blade. He'd carried it for years and was intimately aware of its lethality.

"Now that's better, Detective. I accept your gentlemanly challenge."

From whence Singleton came did not matter to Sean. All he knew were the footsteps that now approached him came from his left side. The steps were slow and methodical. The concrete floor only helped to aid with the sound bouncing off of the walls surrounding him. This was it. Two men will engage each other.

The Artist emerged from his place and allowed Sean the respect of seeing his approach. The firearm that he had in his possession was not in sight. He'd laid his piece down several yards away from his current position. This was a matter of honor and he will not have it any other way. Hand-to-hand combat would be his workout for this day.

"Detective, you have chosen your blade well. So have I." The Artist pulled from his jacket a six-inch tanto style knife, itself razor sharp. The ancient Japanese design was, in The Artist's mind, flawless. It has withstood the test of a millennium of battles and was still a formidable weapon.

The two men now faced each other, weapons in hand. Sean gripping his in a reserve grip, almost as if he were ready to throw a devastating punch, and The Artist gripping his in a similar fashion near his waist.

"Who are you," Sean asked.

"I am an Artist, Detective. These canvases are my contribution to the arts of humanity. You will be the final mark of my masterpiece. Don't worry, I will make sure that my friend knows what you've done for him. You have my word."

"What friend?"

"Silas, of course," The Artist responded. "All of this was for him."

"How do you know Gray?"

"I find it very distasteful that you refer to a man of his caliber by his last name! He, like me, is an artist. Despite the lies that he told my Maria, he is still my friend."

Sean was confused. "Maria. What does she have to do with anything?"

"She, Detective, is my truest love and Silas told her lies about me. When she reported those horrible fabrications, I knew that those words were forced. Imagine my surprise when I found out it was my dearest friend poisoning her mind."

Sean smiled at this statement. "Gray fed her that shit to draw you out. It worked when I saw you last night."

The Artist stared at the man before him. Sean's gaze was as

intense as ever and the words sincere. He thought for a moment and was then consumed by laughter. He nearly doubled-over from the words that Sean just uttered.

"He truly is an Artist and you truly a worthy canvas. His plan worked to enrage me and you caught the subtle hint that I threw your way. Bravo to you both. You two are truly worthy of my talents. Silas more than you, but I digress. Shall we?"

"I thought you'd never ask," Sean responded.

****

Maria sat in Gray's living room for the second time, but this time she asked for a drink. Something hard and preferably above 90 proof. Gray poured a glass of bourbon and handed the glass to Maria. He wouldn't partake. He needed his wits about him after hearing the tale told by his guest.

"I know it sounds crazy, but I know what I saw. Those folders had the Laniers and Duplantis' information in them. There was a third folder, but I didn't have time to look into it. How could I have been so fucking stupid?"

Gray listened while preparing his gear. His focus now precise and clear. He saw the man last night, up close, and he didn't recognize him. He'd never met the man before, but the man obviously knew him and his team.

"Gray, are you listening to me? Adam may be your killer!"

"I heard every word." Gray pulled out his phone and tried to call Sean. No answer.

"What are we going to do," Maria asked.

"I am going to Singleton's apartment. You're going somewhere safe. I'll set it up." Maria didn't say a word to this. Arguing with Gray wouldn't do a thing to change his mind.

Gray made a call and told Rod to expect company. Rod was happy to entertain guests. Gray retreated into his bedroom and emerged a few minutes later, warm clothing and shoes in hand. It was some of his wife's clothing. Maria needed something more substantial than the evening gown she currently wore. She couldn't go back to her apartment to retrieve clothes in the case that Singleton lied in wait for her. Charlotte would understand after some explanation.

"I think they'll fit. Here, put these on. Bathroom is down the hall." Gray turned from Maria's direction and tended to his equipment.

Maria retreated to the bathroom and gray finished his preparation. One final piece and he would be ready for battle. A dark gray t-shirt, the symbol of the REAPER extoled upon its front. His team would be with him on this hunt. His battle belt was affixed, Gladys in her place on his right hip and extra magazines on his left. His jacket would hide her existence, for now. Maria emerged from the hallway dressed in Charlotte's clothing.

"Do you think your wife will be upset," Maria asked.

"Oh yeah," Gray responded. "But she'll understand after a lot of explanation and a glass of wine. We need to go."

Gray patted Norm on the head and he and Maria exited. Norm, now completely exhausted, decided to lay his head down on the couch and fell asleep. He was the master of the house for now.

****

Kap exited the interview room and was completely exhausted from nearly two hours of questioning. He answered Donaldson's questions about Gray and Tyler. He stuck with the story that he was supposed to tell and never deviated. Donaldson's assault on him was more than he expected, it was impressive. If he could find more people this tenacious, then the case closure rate for his section would be nearly 100 percent. Despite his exhaustion, he had to complete his task, the task that Tyler started. Tyler was convincing, but Donaldson pushed him over the line. He needed to get back to his house and fulfill his obligation.

He exited the building and saw Tyler's vehicle still in the parking lot. Tyler appeared to be playing a game of some kind on his phone. He was seemingly unphased by the morning's events. Kap raised his hand to knock on the passenger door, but Tyler unlocked his vehicle before any contact was made. Kap took the invitation and sat in the warm vehicle.

"So, how'd it go," Tyler said somewhat playfully, his eyes never leaving his cell phone's screen.

"You were right. Donaldson is too close right now. How in the hell did he get our records and how the hell did he get an unredacted sealed grand jury transcript?"

"His connections, I'm sure. That's the only possible answer. I'm sure that the fact that the governor was at the gala last night only added to the ease of obtaining information." Tyler always had a flair for the obvious.

"Yeah. Did you talk to Gray?"

"Sure did. He's aware that Keres is in play and that you're gonna call as well. We've been instructed to stand down."

Kap didn't like the last part. Gray was his friend; his brother in arms. Tyler read the reaction and knew that Kap would fight it, but it wouldn't make a difference. If Keres was initiated, then REAPER hierarchy would come back to life. That meant that Gray was in charge and his word was final. There was only one person that could countermand the order, and they wouldn't dare challenge Gray. He was owed too much by everyone involved.

"I guess there's no point in arguing," Kap said.

"No, Kap. No point at all."

Kap exited the vehicle without another word. He needed to

get to his house and unlock his past, just as Tyler did. His present was owed to a man that earned and commanded that his wishes be respected. His future would be in the hands of that man. If history was a precursor of things to come, then this man would stop at nothing to save his team, old and new.

V.

The two men were nearly spent from what seemed like a marathon of violence. Sean would attack and The Artist would counter the move. The Artist would aggress, and Sean would deflect. Both were skilled with the blade, but neither skill level could avoid the inevitable lacerations that they now suffered, mostly flesh wounds that looked worse than they were. Blood soaked through various parts of their clothing. The fight would continue until one was dispatched or died from the exertion of battle.

"You're looking tired, Detective. Would you like to yield?" The heavy breathing made The Artist's delivery slower and he held his left side. He was wounded, but the wound was more superficial than anything. *I need to exploit this.*

"I was about to say the same to you. By the way, fuck yourself!" Sean remained defiant, his focus unshifted throughout the previous volley of steel and limbs. He hunched over attempting to catch his breath.

The two men stared at each other after the brief exchange. Despite their overt differences, there was a respect that developed through the course of the altercation albeit a respect for each other's skill. Neither would quit and neither would go softly. This was now a battle of wills and the outcome would be decided by whomever made the first big mistake.

"Just one question, Detective?"

"Go ahead," Sean said in between heavy breaths.

"What did you think of my artwork? Did you enjoy the way they were presented? I assure you that it wasn't easy, especially when the Lanier brothers watched as their wives were bent to my will."

The Artist knew Sean's sense of chivalry couldn't handle such words. He always did his research. He knew of the incident between the bigots and Bianca. Sean's honor would have drawn him to the females' suffering. What The Artist would view as artistic expression, Sean would view as an absolute violation of his principles. A violation worthy of extreme punishment.

"And Rose," The Artist continued, "Did you see the fear in her eyes as she looked at me? Or was it wonder? Did you feel her pain? I myself was enthralled with the sight of it. She wasn't supposed to survive the overdose, but such is life."

Sean's rage built up within him with every word uttered by the man before him. The apparent pleasure that he took with expressing himself sickened Sean. This man was not human, he was something else. Regardless of description, Sean heard enough. It was time to put this "thing" down, forever. Sean clenched his blade in his hand, blood dripping into his grip from a wound that suffered at the hands of his target. Sean saw his opponent favoring his left side, a wound that he inflicted during the fight. It wasn't deep enough to incapacitate, but it was something he could take advantage of.

The Artist saw the fury in the man's eyes as he attacked. Sean movements were exceptional, he was in control of himself, but not completely. His carefully selected words worked. Focus shifted slightly to favor aggression, rather than technique. Still, The Artist was impressed with this side of Sean. The animal within him unleashed and he responded in kind. The final clash of these two men would find one on the ground and the other victorious. This was The Artist's chance to finish his masterpiece and Sean's chance for vengeance.

****

Gray and Maria walked through the parking lot and were met by a steel door.

Beep, Click Entry approved.

"Well if it ain't the happy couple. How's the morning treating ya," Rod yelled from his office, observing them via his closed-circuit live feed as they walked down the hallway. Maria and Gray entered Rod's office and he immediately stood up in the presence of a lady.

"Hello, I'm…"

"Maria Gomez," Rod said, extending his hand. "I know who you are. My wife and I are fans of your reporting, especially the exposé you did last year on the Clerk of Court's Office. That was good shit!"

"Thank you. It's nice to see that not everyone was upset about that."

"Oh, no. Not upset at all. The only people that upset me is the man standing next to you and his partner in crime. Please, have a seat."

Rod looked at Gray and smiled a bit as he sat himself in his chair.

"So, what can Big Homie's Security Service provide on this wonderfully cold winter's day?"

"Go ahead, Maria," Gray said. "Tell Rod what you told me."

Maria recounted what she saw a few hours earlier. The account was nearly identical to the one that she provided to Gray, no embellishment or marked delineation. Gray was very impressed by her consistency and recall. In another life, she would've made a great investigator.

"Well, I'm sold. What shall we do next," Rod asked, his joviality still intact.

"Maria will stay here with you and I'm going to the apartment to find the evidence," Gray said, seeing that Maria didn't like that plan at all.

"Wait, I'm going with you. You're not leaving me here with him," Maria pointed at Rod. "No offense."

"None taken and yet I'm feeling unloved," Rod said, seeing Maria crack a smile. "Listen, just stay here with me. Trust me, you won't win this one. Gray is the most stubborn man I've had the pleasure of being pissed off at, but he's better on his own. Twice as good with Sean. Let them do what they do. What do you say, Gray?"

Silence filled the room, no response. Gray slipped away while Rod and Maria had their heart-to-heart. All they heard after the brief silence was the revving of an engine and the sound of a vehicle leaving the parking lot. Gray was gone.

"That's it, he's going to Big Homie's School of Manners. Lesson one will be don't ghost me while I'm trying to make a point! That's just rude."

"Sorry, Rod," Maria said. "I have to go. This is something that I can't miss." Maria stood up and made her way to the door when Rod stopped her with two words.

"Judge Gray."

Maria turned and saw the look of deathly seriousness in his face. The cheerfulness in his eyes gone. He knew something that she didn't and this intrigued her more than the Gray's destination. She needed to know what he meant by that.

"Excuse me, what do you mean by that." Maria walked back to the well-worn chair and focused on Rod's face.

"Maria, what do you think is going to happen, hmmm? Do you think he's going to get a search warrant and invite others to his party? Do you think he's going to read Miranda to this man? What do you think he's going to do to the man that slaughtered seven people in the most perverse ways that I've ever seen? This won't end with a trial in a courtroom. Whoever did this called him out and used his past to do it." Rod saw that Maria understood his words and soaked them in.

"What do you mean his past? The trial?"

Rod nodded his head. He just revealed a huge piece of the puzzle that she'd been missing throughout the past few days.

"Gray is a man that lives by his convictions and all he longed for after his time in Iberia Parish was to do his job and find as much peace as he could given his profession. You may not know it, but inside of that man is a monster that we in this business need. Now he's let loose and believe me it won't be something that any of us wanna see."

Rod's words made her remember the night that she and Gray first met, how she was drawn to him and how she saw that darkness that Rod just revealed to her. Rod was right. The beast within Gray was caged for a time, but no longer.

****

Kap stared at the still sealed envelope. He contemplated the repercussions of opening the very simple enclosure. Within it lay the groundwork for resurrection. It was a decision that he had to make, regardless of Tyler's suggestion. He knew that Gray would have to make the final decision, but this moment was his. He sat in his home's dining room, his wife and children gathering their things for a long weekend full of holiday cheer. The packing was complete and they were making the final rounds for odd and ends. A toothbrush here. A phone charger there.

"Kaplan, we're all set. I'll get the kids in the car."

"I'll be there in a second, hon," Kap replied to his wife. The door to the garage shut behind her and he heard the engine start. The garage door would be next. Kap had little time left and the decision was made.

He tore the end of the envelope and blew into the now open end, expanding the still sealed sides and exposing a slip of paper within. This paper, like, Tyler's paper, contained ten digits. He'd come this far and now he would go farther. He picked up the phone in front of him and dialed the numbers on the paper. A woman's voice answered

"Name and access code."

"Rodrigue, Kaplan. Romeo Three"

"Access granted. State your request."

Kap thought for a moment. Was he doing the right thing? Was this necessary? He felt that it was and took solace in Gray's decision to either use this or not.

"Sir," the voice said, "State your request."

"Yes," Kap snapped out his brief deep thought, "Request initiation of Keres protocols."

"Standby, Romeo Three." A pause and silence for several seconds made Kap somewhat uneasy. "Request granted. Keres protocols initiated. Standing by for final confirmation."

"Romeo Three direct. Send my regards to control."

No response from the voice and the beeping of a disconnected phone line indicated that his part was over. He was on the bench, as it were; relegated to being a spectator to this unfolding drama. He placed the numeral printed paper back into the envelope and placed the envelope in his jacket pocket. He would dispose of it at his parent's home, preferably in their fireplace. He walked through his home and exited out of the garage entrance and met with his family, who were now very warm in their SUV. His wife observed the look of worry on his face.

"Everything ok, babe," she asked.

"Oh yeah. Just letting mom and dad know that we were on our way."

Kap knew that this ruse was transparent, but his wife never asked when he told her something that was obviously false and work related. She was a cop's wife and she knew that he wouldn't speak of work, at least not the heavier subjects in her presence.

"Ok. Have you talked to Silas? Wished him and Charlotte a Merry Christmas."

Kap smiled. She knew him better than he knew herself, "No, I haven't. I think I'll have to do that."

"What would you do without me?"

"Apparently I would forget to send messages to Silas and Charlie," Kap responded playfully. Kap's wife hit him on the arm lightly and turned to make sure that the children were buckled up safely. Kap simultaneously retrieved his phone and texted Gray: *Keres in play. Call if you need me, brother. - K*

"There. Done," Kap told his misses, placing his pone back in his pocket.

"Really, Kaplan. A text message? I swear, you have to work on your people skills. How has he been your friend for this long?"

"I guess it's the sweet messages that I send to him all the time," Kap said smiling. "Besides, he'll know it was your idea."

"And that's why he likes me more," Kap's wife said.

"No doubt. Let's get going."

Kap's worry grew as he left his home; wife and children in tow. He would be three hours away from Gray if he needed him, but all he would've needed was a phone call. For the second time he would leave the man that saved his life to fend for himself, albeit in accordance with his wishes. He hated this and promised that he would one day repay him for all the special moments that he got to spend with his family since that late summer night. Unfortunately, this wouldn't be that time.

VI.

11:00 AM

"No sign of Sean's car." Gray was concerned. His phone then alerted him. He hoped it was his partner.

Keres in play. Call if you need me, brother. – K

Gray was sitting in his truck across from Singleton's Apartment building when he read the text message from Kap. The decision was now his to make. This second Keres confirmations placed all responsibility on him. Again, he felt the weight of command across his broad shoulders. He would provide the final confirmation when necessary.

"Ok, Singleton. Let's see what you got."

He exited his truck and used the parking lot entrance to enter the building, taking the stairs to his apartment. Maria gave him the apartment number, but he didn't need it. Sean told him prior to meeting with her. Sean always did his homework. As he approached the target door, he felt the thrill of the chase, adrenaline, and nervousness. He was accustomed to this. He swiped away the right side of his jacket, exposing his only backup, Gladys.

Knock, knock

"Mr. Singleton. It's Detective Gray. I'd like to ask a few follow up questions from last night." The deception was common, especially when victim or witness became a suspect for something. No response from the other side of the door. No movement.

Gray analyzed the locking mechanism and noticed it to be a common door lock with a deadbolt. The latter didn't appear to be engaged and Gray took advantage of this. He concealed Gladys and reached for his wallet, pulling out a Miranda Rights card provided to him early in his career. The sides of the card showed signs of bending from carefully applied used. He always felt it ironic that this card was sturdy, yet thin enough to perform unintended actions. He slipped the card in between the door frame and the locking mechanism, pushing the door as he did so. There was no click when the lock disengaged, there never is when this worked. That was ridiculous movie magic, in Gray's mind. The door opened slightly and Gray again reached for his weapon, fully exposing the firearm.

He entered the apartment silently, weapon drawn. Scanning and dismissing, the light attached to it destroying and creating shadows. No one was home. He closed the door behind him, still leveling his weapon at any potential threat. Maria told him that the bag was in a kitchen island, the island not more than thirty feet in from of him. Uneasiness fell upon him. Gay held his weapon nearly flat against his chest, the barrel of the weapon facing down. It was a technique that he'd learned years ago and now it was habit when making an approach to something. There it was; the bag sitting on the kitchen floor, some of the contents in open view.

Gray holstered his weapon and inspected the contents, most of which were in a kind of disarray. As he read the papers and looked at the pictures, he knew that he'd found the man terrorizing this area. He saw living pictures of the Lanier family, one of which was with a man with a beard, a fashionable shirt, and a Newsboy cap. Obviously a selfie from a cell phone.

"I'll be damned," Gray said to himself as he made this realization. "The man from Fracture. You son of a bitch."

A series of photographs showed a living Duplantis; some of them with his lover in what they believed was a moment away from prying eyes. These were taken from a distance as if Singleton was a private investigator.

The final documents were still neatly bound in a red folder. Maria's recall continued to impress him. She was remarkable accurate to the details. He opened the folder and saw the documents before him. The homework that this man did on his victim's astonished him. That astonishment left when he read the name associate with the papers: Sean B. Guthrie. He couldn't believe what he saw and tore through the documents. Bank records, gym membership, martial arts records, a DD-214 from his military service.

"Jesus, Sean." Gray reached for his phone and called his partner. The phone rang and no response. He tried again. Same result, except he left a message for Sean to call him immediately. Gray then texted Sean. Even though he couldn't reach him, the phone ringing and text delivery confirmation convinced him that the phone was on. He decided to thoroughly search the apartment for more clues as to where he could be.

****

Sean was strapped to an ornate wooden chair, unconscious. The chair befitting The Artist's tastes: solid and exquisite. Sean was bound by something unequal to the chair: duct tape. The final clash between the two resulted in both men being injured, but Sean being defeated. No smelling salts were need as Sean began to regain consciousness. His blurred vision cleared quickly, but the pain in his back and head remained. He was bound in a way that would preclude escape. The light in his face nearly blinded him. He couldn't see past it. He wasn't, however, resigning himself to death.

"Singleton, where the fuck are you?! Show yourself!"

"Detective Guthrie," the voice of Sean's captor was soft. "What have I told you about the course language? Now, keep a civil tongue or I will remove it. Also, please forgive the object of your bindings. You deserve something better than duct tape, but sometimes you must improvise. That's what an artist does."

"Oh, ok. How about, FUCK YOURSELF!"

Suddenly a hand from behind him covered his forehead and he felt cold steel against his neck. The steel was sharp and cut him slightly. The movement was violent and convincing. Sean was at a severe disadvantage.

"Go ahead, chicken shit! Do it!" Sean remained defiant. Some would say that this was a false courage in the face of danger. To those who knew him, this was Sean being Sean.

The Artist laughed and removed the tanto from his neck. A drop of blood adorned both Sean's neck and the freshly removed steel. *This man is cut from the same cloth as Silas.*

"You know, detective, I admire you more than I did my other canvases. The Lanier's were up to my exacting physical specifications. Young, fit, beautiful. Duplantis met my need for power. I mean, who better than he? The governor? The president? And Rose, my sweet opiate addict. She met my need for elegance. Detective, your role is simple. You're the emotion of my masterpiece. Look at you: all fire. I can see why Silas likes you. The same way he liked Mags and Tony and Jacques. They were passionate about what they did, each in their own way. And now there's you. Gray's emotional center. He'll do anything to save you, including facing me directly."

The Artist moved the light from Sean's eyes and pulled another chair in front of his. He also retrieved a medical kit for the multiple lacerations that he suffered at Sean's hands. He began to bandage his side. The wound was deeper than before. Sean's stroke was devastating, but not devastating enough.

"That looks like it hurts," Sean said sarcastically, "How about you untie me and let me look at it."

The Artist looked up and smiled, "No thank you, detective. I appreciate the offer." The Artist continued to tend to his wound.

"So, why haven't you killed me?"

"Simple questions, detective. How disappointing," The Artist said, toying with Sean. "You are alive, for now, because you didn't hurt my dearest friend the way that the others did. The pain that I saw my friend go through was unbearable. I almost stood up to help him myself, but I knew that he would weather the storm. He always had that talent."

Sean was now interested in this man, beyond wanting to kill him.

"How did you know about Gray's team? That was classified."

The Artist laughed and was then pained by the laughter.

"Please, don't make me laugh. This little gift you gave me hurts enough without you making jokes." The Artist dabbed a tear that formed and looked at Sean. The question was sincere, and he realized that he was being a poor host. "I apologize, detective. I thought that was funny and I see that I was mistaken. The answer is quite simple: this is Louisiana. Everything can be bought for the right price or the right campaign contribution. I do love your corrupt little state. Corruption is in the air you breathe and the water you drink. Think about it. Every guilty person getting a slap on the wrist; every law amended to serve a particular representative or their contributors; every loophole in the statutes. Corruption is all over. As for Silas, you provide the right amount to a low-level clerk of court and there you go."

"Wait, you knew about…"

"Oh, yes, detective," The Artist interrupted, "I knew of the activity going on in the clerk's office well before it became public. I didn't realize it until recently, but my Maria brought the clerk's indiscretions to light. She's quite impressive."

Sean couldn't help but agree with some of this man's logic. He and Gray spoke about this very topic many times when they were frustrated by the bureaucracies that existed in the legal system.

"You know," Sean said, "You still haven't answered my question. How do you know Gray? This connection you claim to have is more than something that just caught your eye."

The Artist was now more convinced than ever that Sean was the perfect canvas. Not only did he leave him with future permanent reminders of their meeting, but now his intellect was proving to be as much a match to his.

"Bravo, Detective Guthrie. You are more than I could've hoped for. You are correct, I said a lot and revealed very little. Unfortunately, I will only reveal that little secret to you with Silas' permission. Please understand, I'm not trying to be rude, but it would be bad form of me tell you outside of his presence."

Sean's text alert went off. It had been going off throughout the conversation, but neither man gave much thought to it. Both were trying to play each other, and their game proved to be exhilarating to both.

"Oh, allow me to answer that," The Artist said, reaching into Sean's jacket to retrieve the phone. "It's our mutual friend. I think we should call him back. It's poor manners to keep him waiting."

"I agree, we should," Sean said. "I would like to say something before you call him, if you please?" Sean picked up on his air of superiority and was now playing his captor's game, using his high self-opinion to his advantage.

"Of course, detective."

"My friend, Silas, will find me and then he will find you," Sean said, observing that The Artist was listening intently. "If I'm dead, then he will make you suffer. If I'm alive, then he will make you suffer. There is no way out of this that doesn't include you suffering at his hands. Bluntly, he's going to tear your fucking head off and there is nothing that will stop him. The thought of you begging him for mercy will make me smile."

The Artist saw Sean's conviction grow with every word directed toward him. Truth was in every syllable. He studied his Silas from a distance for a while, but the man before him worked and bled with Silas; befriended Silas; saw every aspect of Silas' personality. This was a truth formed by close proximity, a truth that caused a slight anxiety.

"Detective, thank you. Your honesty, albeit course and unrefined, is something that I truly needed. Yes, Silas will hunt for me and he will most likely find me. The outcome, however, is far from determined. We shouldn't keep him waiting any longer."

****

Desormeaux was out of the loop for a moment. He didn't like it, but he needed to be removed from the situation. His guys were doing what they do best, but this time they were off the grid and out on the hairy edge. This was nothing new to him and nothing new to his men, but he still couldn't help but be concerned for the outcome. He felt alone. The photograph in his hand only cemented this fact. He loved his guys, his family. The two men in the field right now were cut from the same cloth as the six people in the photograph, except one of those men appeared in the photograph now worked directly for him.

"I can't take another loss," Desormeaux said to himself, sipping his coffee at his home. "Time to get to it."

He was alone, the wife, kids and grandkids out shopping for last minute gifts. His house was abuzz with activity just hours prior. Now, there was just he, a photograph, and a freshly opened white envelope. The number on the sheet of paper differed from the number on Tyler's and Kap's sheet. It was a number specifically for him. Specifically, for Control.

One ring and female's voice, "Name and access code."

"Desormeaux, Roger. Control Primary," he responded.

"Access granted, Control Primary. Please hold for Keres control." Desormeaux waited for a moment and was immediately connected.

"Hello, Roger. It's been a long time." The voice was raspy and distinctive. It was a voice that was a joy to hear, but very different than he remembered.

"Yes, it has, kiddo."

"I assume that you're calling regarding the protocol and not to wish me a Merry Christmas."

"Can't I do both?" Roger smiled, it's been a long time since he'd spoken to this person, but he still felt a deep connection. A connection formed in violence and blood.

"For you Roger, I'll make an exception. The protocols are in place and are waiting for final confirmation from Romeo One."

"Do you think he'll confirm?"

"I...," the silence on the phone was telling, but the person on the other end knew Gray as well as Desormeaux and the answer was never simple, "I think he'll do what he does best. He'll protect the team. I have to get everything ready for Gray if he calls. Please give Margaret and the kids a hug for me."

Roger smiled hearing this, "Love you, kiddo. Be safe out there."

No response, just silence and dead air. Roger threw the

paper into the fire in front of him and sat back in his chair, fighting back tears after speaking to his past. He knew that Gray would be taken care of and Keres would be the one to take care of him. Much like the namesake, Keres would be there in cases of violent death. Roger knew that this would be the case. There was no other way, not with Gray. The only question was which soul would be escorted to the gates of the afterlife: Gray or the killer.

VII.

11:43 AM

The answer eluded Donaldson. He sat in the interview room, frustrated and wanting more information. Never in his professional life had something dodged him like Silas Gray. The man was an anger inducing enigma. He had personnel files for Tyler and Kap. Both files seemed to be in order and neither showed any major inconsistencies. Gray's file had conspicuous gaps in them, and his former employer only knew that he was part of a violent offender task force. He made a few inquiries, but no one seemed to know the mission of this task force, not even his superiors.

Donaldson knew he couldn't intimidate the man and he knew that he couldn't control him. His friends were covering for him, or at least he believed they were. He had no leverage. It was now that he decided that following this man would be the next course of action. A quick phone call would provide the man's location instantly.

"Hi, this is Donaldson. I need to get a ping on a cell phone. The target number is…"

****

Singleton's apartment was a black hole. The search for anything else that would indicate his location was fruitless. There was nothing. Gray, tired and frustrated, sat on the love seat in the living room area and thought for a moment. For all intents and purposes, this place was clear of any further information. His phone then vibrated in his pocket. It was Sean's phone number. He found it odd that the call was a facetime call, but Sean always did things that were out of the ordinary. He accepted the call and what he saw horrified him. Sean was tied to a chair in what appeared to be an industrial site's building. His friend, his brother was wounded and in pain. This unnerved him.

"Greetings, my old friend. I hope I have your full attention," a voice said, emanating out of view of the camera, "This is my final gift to you, Silas."

"Sean, where are you?"

"He can't speak right now, Silas. He's a bit unconscious now. Don't worry, I used a sedative and, no, I didn't cut his tongue out. He doesn't deserve that." The voice was calm throughout.

"I know it's you, Singleton. No need to hide anymore." Gray anger grew inside of him. The camera angle changed, and he was now face to face, so to speak, with the man he'd hunted for days. The Artist smiled at his friend as he observed Gray's backdrop.

"I see that you are in my home, Silas. Do you have a warrant to be there?" The Artist couldn't help but laugh. He knew better, but he wanted to play. Gray was in no mood.

"Tell me where Sean is and I'll make it quick."

"Now, Silas, that it no way to speak to a friend. It's been so long since you and I have been able to communicate, and this is how you treat me. I understand your tone and I forgive you." The Artist's tone was melancholier at this moment.

"I don't know you! You're no friend to me, asshole."

"Silas! That was rude and rudeness is unacceptable. For this, you must be punished."

The camera angle switched again the focus was on Sean. Gray could see that the man holding the phone was walking toward and was eventually over Sean.

"This is what happens when you treat friends with such contempt, Silas."

Gray saw as the tanto blade entered the screen. The shine of the blade emboldened by the bright light in the room. He watched as the blade ran softly against Sean's neck and chest, but it didn't cut into his unconscious form. The blade then retracted and reentered the screen with great speed. Gray watched as the steel entered into his partner's abdomen. Sean never moved. The sedative proved to be more powerful than the strike. The knife was left in Sean's body and blood loss from the wound was minimal.

"YOU SON OF A BITCH! I'M GONNA KILL YOU," Gray yelled into his phone. The camera angle again switched and Singleton's face was again visible.

"Again, with the language, Silas. There are consequences to uncivil discourse, and this will not be tolerated. Don't worry about Sean. The cut isn't deadly for now. He'll die eventually, but he has time if the blade stays in him. He'll bleed internally for a while, but for now we have all the time we need to speak."

"You have my attention," Gray said, staring a hole in the phone he held in his hand, "So, talk."

"How's Charlotte and Simon? Simon had to be what six, seven by now."

"If you go after them....," Gray's fury was now at a boiling point.

"I would never harm them, Silas! How dare you even think that I would go after a man's family! My friend's family! Who do you think I am?" The Artist was genuinely insulted by the merest insinuation.

"You're a psychopath that gets off on the power of killing. You're nothing special! You're just another...."

"DON'T YOU DARE, SILAS," The Artist interrupted, obviously insulted, "I am special and nothing like other men of my proclivities. I'm an artist and as such beyond normal man's comprehension. Don't you dare try to fit me into a category! I'm a goddamn genius in my chosen medium and you've benefitted greatly from my work. This has all been for you and deep down inside you know you enjoyed it! Look where you're at right now. In my apartment with no warrant and no back-up. You have been reborn into your former self. "The Silas Gray" has come back to me." The rage in his face was plainly seen by Gray. A nerve was hit.

"You're insane," Gray responded, "Completely insane."

"No, not insane. I'm inspired, specifically I'm inspired by you. Don't you see, you and I are not normal people. We are both artists. I create the art and you interpret it for others to understand. You were off the last time, but only slightly."

"What do you mean by, 'the last time'," Gray asked.

"You were so close. I watched as you inspected crime scenes after everything was done. You walked those scenes with Mags and discussed your theories with her. You were inspired by my artwork. Let me guess, you felt eyes on you. I saw as you looked around, hoping to find the creator of these visions. I swear, I thought you saw me once. It was thrilling."

It was then that Gray knew he was talking to his past. Only he and Mags walked those scenes together and, to their knowledge, no one else. He couldn't say anything after he heard these words.

"I will say, Silas, that I was a bit insulted that you would think that I would resort to raping the last victim. That is, to me, highly offensive. If imitation is the highest form of flattery, then I was rather insulted by Mr. Boudreaux. It's a shame really, he had potential, but he couldn't help himself. He had to have more." The Artist saw the lightbulb in Gray's mind shine brighter than ever.

"You bastard," Gray exclaimed.

"Now you see our connection," The Artist's smile was wider than ever before, "I am the reason that your team is no longer. I am the one you chased for those many months. Don't get me wrong, Garrett Boudreaux was a rapist and a murderer and deserved every ounce of your vengeance, but he was an amateur trying to duplicate a master and he paid the price for it."

The anger on Gray's face gave way to deathly calm, but steel blue gave away his true intentions. He thought he'd killed the man responsible for the dead bodies along the Bayou Teche, and in a way he did. But that man was only responsible for one. The Artist saw the quiet resolve and calm demeanor.

"You and I, Silas, are Artists. The likes of which this world has never seen."

"We are not alike."

"Really, then explain the way that you came roaring back to life after seeing Rose. I saw the look in your eyes when you saw her and how the façade fell away and the real Silas resurrected before me. You crave the darkness, just as I do. You seek out the demons, just as I embrace them. You want to find me so that you can be yourself once again. I did all of this for you, to bring you back from the brink of the mundane world that I know you hate. Face it, you live for this and there is nothing that you wouldn't do to hold onto this feeling. You have been reborn and that is my gift to you. My masterpiece is your renaissance."

Gray stood motionless in the apartment; a familiar rage inside of him giving itself to a familiar focus. The Artist, although wholly insane, was right. He did miss this feeling. The thrill of it. The taste of it. The old Silas Gray was awakened and the new Silas Gray dormant for the moment. The darkness consumed his every molecule and he was, once again, home.

"Adam. May I call you Adam," Gray asked calmly.

"Of course. That's not my real name, but you may call me that if you wish." The Artist was amused by this turn.

"Adam, Boudreaux killed that woman and members of my team. He deserved to be put down. Between you and I, I savored his end."

"Finally," The Artist exclaimed with excitement, "Honesty among friends."

Gray's eyes then turned colder than the weather outside of the apartment he stood in. "As for you, my friend. You wanted my attention. You had it then and you have it now. I, too, have a gift for you."

"I'm all ears, my dear," The Artist said, seeing the man on the screen becoming a familiar monster.

"You will die, very badly; preferably screaming in pain as I tear your heart out. That's my gift to you." The inflection in his calm voice never changed.

The Artist found this statement exhilarating, but more exhilarating was the lack of emotion in Gray's voice. He meant every word and would do everything in his power to keep this promise. The Artist never underestimated Gray's artistry, but he didn't realize until now far he was willing to go to uphold his moral code. His friend, Silas, would do as he promised, but The Artist still had an Ace to play.

"Silas, I believe that you will do exactly as you say and because of your honesty, I will offer you a way to save Detective Guthrie."

"Ok. How can I do that," Gray asked, his demeanor still eerily calm.

The Artist lifted a folded piece of paper near his face so that Gray could see it. No words were seen, but Gray knew it was important. "This piece of paper has Detective Guthrie's location written on it. For you to get it, you'll have to take it off my body. Don't bother trying to ping Detective Guthrie's phone. Measures were taken to ensure his complete privacy."

"How do I know that his location is on the paper," Gray asked.

"Silas, I have never and will never lie to you. That is my promise to you, and I am a man of my word, regardless of what you may think of me at this moment." The Artist placed the paper in his jacket pocket and patted the outside of his jacket. "I would say that he has several hours before he expires, but just in case I'll make sure that he lasts long enough to ensure a fair chance of you finding both he and I. It's only fair"

"I'll be seeing you soon, Adam."

"I have no doubt. Oh, and it's just you and I. No one else is worthy. If I see anyone else with you, then I'll leave Detective Guthrie's head on your front doorstep, minus the tongue of course. Until then." Gray's screen went black. Contact was terminated.

"FUCK! FUCK! SON OF A BITCH!" Gray fell to his knees and punched the floor repeatedly. His legendary control had all but left him at this moment. The memories of his fallen brethren now at the forefront and Sean would be added to that number if he couldn't find this lunatic. It was time that he found an ally in this fight. Someone keener on locating the killer than he was, or at least someone who believed that he knew who the killer was.

Gray again accessed his phone and, for the first time in years, turned on the GPS tracking system. The person looking for him was smart enough to attempt a ping, or at least he hoped he would. This was an extreme measure, but it was a risk that he was willing to take. He wasn't prepared for Keres, yet.

"Here's your chance Donaldson. Come and find me."

****

"Donaldson, what do you have." The phone rang for less than a second before he answered it. The look on his face indicated that he was receiving good news. "Great. Send the address to my phone and no additional units."

He could hardly believe his good fortune.

VIII.

1:13 PM

Rod stared in Maria's direction, hoping that his next move would prove beneficial. Maria sat in front of him, stone faced.

"Do you have any eights," Rod asked.

Maria smiled, "Go Fish!"

"Damn. Here I am holding half the deck and you have one card left. This isn't fair and I'm filing a protest." Rod grabbed the last card from the pile, dejected by his turn of bad luck in he and Maria's highly competitive game.

"Rod," Maria said, "We haven't heard from Gray or Sean. Aren't you worried?" Maria saw that Rod never took his eyes off the cards he held in his hands.

"I am worried, more than you know. Those boys are a pain in my ass at times, but they're my family. Family worries about each other and this situation causes Big Homie much by way of stress."

"You still haven't filled me in on Gray's trial," Maria said, reminding Rod that he promised to give her information.

"You're right. I owe you something after beating me so many times at this game." Rod placed his cards face down on the desk in front of him and reclined in chair. He needed comfort when revealing some of the secrets. Maria also laid down her card.

"I'm listening."

"What I'm about to tell you is off the record. I will deny it if it comes out," Rod told Maria, specific emphasis on the off the record part.

Maria shook her head, "I understand."

"The trial was a result of the last case that he and some other officers worked. They tracked the guy and cornered him in a restroom in Iberia Parish. Obviously, it went sideways and Gray was the sacrificial lamb, so to speak."

"So to speak," Maria repeated, "What do you mean by that?"

"It never got past grand jury and wasn't going to. No indictment, no trial, and no open court testimony. The Lanier's and Claxton were witnesses and Duplantis the prosecutor on the case."

Maria looked confused for a moment and then understood what Rod was telling her. This was something that could blow up into either the biggest story of her career or a quagmire to end her career.

"Rod, why are you telling me this? This is some serious shit and something that could prove damaging to everyone involved."

"Because this is something that you are now involved in. You are in danger because of what happened in the past and you deserve to know because of the that. I trust that this won't go anywhere," Rod's face was serious at this moment. He studied Maria and she seemed to understand the gravity of this information. Gray was a good man and Rod knew it. Now, Maria knew it too, although through a heavily redacted version of the events.

"You have my word, none of this is going anywhere," Maria stated reassuringly. "Now, do you have any Queens."

Rod picked up his cards and reviewed them.

"Damnit, woman," he exclaimed as he slammed down the card, "

Maria smiled as she picked up the card and placed a pair of queens down in the desktop.

"Looks like I win, again."

Rod smiled and then decided that he would not accept defeat, again. He began to shuffle the deck and Maria was savoring the chance to beat him yet again. Rod's phone rang and he announced the caller to Maria.

"Oh, look. If it isn't the man of the hour." He accepted the call, "Hey sweetness, we were…."

The interruption shook Rod to his core and he became as somber as any single person could be. This was something that he didn't expect to hear and hoped that he would never hear. One of his guys, his family was taken. His heart nearly shattered in his chest knowing that Sean was in the hands of a serial killer.

"Do you know where he is," Rod asked. The answer only deepened his swift depression. Maria looked at Rod and immediately knew something had gone terribly wrong. She couldn't tell which of the two men was in trouble, but Rod's concern filled the room.

"What can I do?" He listened to the Gray's voice, concentrating on every syllable. "Gotcha, call you back in a few."

Rod began calling Desormeaux but was interrupted by Maria.

"What happened," Maria asked.

"Singleton has Sean," Rod answered bluntly

"Jesus, Rod. Is he…"

"He's alive and from what Gray just told he's in bad shape. Your boyfriend is holding him somewhere and wants Gray to find him and then Sean." Rod called chief.

"Hey, Chief. Singleton is the man we're looking for and he

has Sean. If anyone else gets involved, then Singleton will kill Sean." Rod listened to Desormeaux's words as intently as he listened to Gray's words.

"No, Chief. Gray said to stay out of it. He did ask me to ask you if you made a call. He didn't say what that meant." Again, Rod listened.

"Got it. I'll let him know. Chief, he was adamant that no one else be involved and that this was unfinished business from three years ago. He said that you would know what it meant." The response was brief, but completely understood. Desormeaux would stay away from this.

****

Desormeaux nearly collapsed from impact of Rod's phone call. He was calm during the conversation, but he was soon overwhelmed by the enormity of it all. The realization that Gray's last mission never ended. This was something that he wasn't prepared for. He had to call Gray and see what was going on. He made the call and set the phone on the counter before him, his hands were shaking so much that he feared he'd drop anything he held. Gray answered immediately.

"Silas, I sat on the sidelines once before. I can't do it again. Let me help you," Desormeaux pleaded.

"Roger, I'm ordering you to stand by. You know that the protocols are in place to protect those whose involvement was beyond classified. You were chosen as the original control because of your position as chief of police could explain away the absences and you were the best man for the job. My job is to protect the team and that includes you." Gray was direct. His authority in this matter superseded everyone else, regardless of rank.

"Screw protocols! Sean needs all of us," Desormeaux's temper got the best of him.

"Roger! Calm yourself. I will get Sean back. You must trust me. This will not end well if you don't."

"Trust you like you were trusted on the last mission you ran," Desormeaux said spitefully and without thinking. The silence on the other end of the phone was deafening. Roger composed himself, realizing what he'd just said. "Silas," Desormeaux said remorsefully, "I'm sorry. You didn't deserve that and I'm wrong for saying it. That... that wasn't your fault, and neither is this."

"I blamed myself for a long time for what happened that night and, in a way, I still do," Gray said. "That night nearly destroyed us all, but we must complete the mission for the team. I will find Sean and I will end this, tonight."

"Silas, you boys come back to me in one piece. I don't think I can handle the loss of either of you, let alone both of you." Roger felt a tear fall from his eye as he said these words. He loved his people, but Gray and Sean were special to him, even though he'd never admit it publicly.

"You have my word, old friend. Both of us will be alright. I have to go."

"Silas, before you go, Keres said that everything will be ready when you call. They're waiting for final confirmation."

"I'll make the call when it's time. Take care, Roger."

The phone went dead and Desormeaux stood at his kitchen counter trying to hold in the emotion of the moment. His family would be home soon, and he needed to be there with them, and not with his boys. This would be the longest day of his life.

****

Donaldson arrived at the location indicated by the GPS ping he received. The ping itself was useful, but the margin for error was still several hundred meters. The only indication that he had that Gray was in the area was that he saw Gray's truck parked near the apartment building. He parked his black Charger near Gray's truck and continued to scan the area.

"Where are you," he said to himself.

Donaldson was cognizant of his surroundings, more so than he had been in his prior dealings with this target. He began scanning the interior of the parking area when he saw the familiar figure of Silas Gray. Gray's profile was seen near the entry/exit door to the apartment building. Donaldson had the element of surprise. This was going to be his moment.

"Gotcha."

Donaldson exited his vehicle and made a silent approach. The excitement built up within him, the same way that the Christmas season builds the excitement within children anticipating gifts. He thoroughly remembered everything that this man had done to him over the last few days and now had the opportunity to give Gray a taste of his own medicine. His excitement continued to build. Gray didn't see him yet. Donaldson's issued Glock pistol was at the ready and now was the time to jump his quarry.

"State Police! Show me your hands!" Donaldson's voice echoed through the parking lot and Gray turned his head to see him. "Show me your hands, God damnit!"

Gray saw that Donaldson jumped the gun to early, a rookie mistake. Gray knew Donaldson was approaching him and acted as if he noticed nothing. He anticipated this mistake and left himself a way to show Donaldson the true monster. After seeing the man, Gray turned toward the door and ran inside, Donaldson would follow. The chase was on.

Both men flew up the stairs, Donaldson two to three levels below Gray the entire time. Gray entered the hallway on the seventh floor and would soon find himself in Singleton's apartment, the door partially ajar. He made sure to give himself enough space for Donaldson to stay behind, but not enough to lose him. Gray's trap was set and any pain that Donaldson felt would be based on Donaldson's cooperation.

Donaldson entered the hallway and saw nothing. He scanned the doors.

"No... No...," he said as he saw closed doors lining the corridor.

He saw then slightly ajar door and the thrill of chase immediately went into overdrive. He opened the door with his non-weapon hand and saw the open space. There weren't many places to hide in the area. His focus was before him as he walked through the door. Tunnel vision took over as his adrenaline spiked. Without warning, he felt something foreign to him; it was cold and metallic and press against the right side of his head.

"Don't move, junior," a calm voice told him. Gray reached for Donaldson's weapon and Donaldson immediately reacted as Gray thought he would: no reflex action, nothing. Gray took the weapon from Donaldson without a problem. It was practically given to him.

"Please," Donaldson pleaded, "Don't kill me. I have..."

"Shut up, Donaldson!" Gray expected a little more from another cop, but he was disappointed, yet again.

Gray took the muzzle of his weapon away from Donaldson's head and circled around to the front of his target. Donaldson was terrified and Gray the object of his terror. Gray held Gladys at shoulder level, pointing her at the man's face.

"Detective Gray, if this is about what I said to you or what happened last night, then I'm...."

"Jesus, Donaldson. Shut up," Gray interrupted.

Donaldson's whimpering was beginning to work Gray's last

nerve. Gray would never admit it, but he secretly enjoyed the weakness before him. This was the most genuine that Donaldson had ever been in Gray's presence.

"Ok, just don't kill me," Donaldson replied, nearly crying as he spoke.

"Walk to the island in the kitchen." Gray's tone was cold.

Donaldson began walking to the island and Gray kept his weapon trained on him. As Donaldson approached, he saw what Gray wanted him to see. Three folders: green, yellow, and red. Confusion and fear were written on Donaldson's face.

"Open the green folder."

Donaldson did as he was told and began looking through the folder's contents.

"Duplantis and his lover. What are you doing? Bragging before you kill me," Donaldson asked, his voice still trembling.

"Now, open the yellow folder."

Again, Donaldson performed the action without hesitation.

"Rosemarie Claxton." Donaldson's tone began to change from fear to intrigue.

"Now open the last one," Gray said, now lowering his weapon slightly.

"Detective Guthrie. What's going on here?" Donaldson was now more confused than anyone. *Would the man before me kill his own partner?*

"What about the Lanier's?" Donaldson saw that the weapon was no longer trained on him. Gray looked relieved at the turn events.

"Finally, you're asking the right questions. Look in the leather bag sitting on the island," Gray said.

Donaldson opened the bag and saw the remaining documents. On the top of the documents was the picture of two members of the Lanier family and the bearded man wearing the Newsboy cap. Donaldson had seen this man before, but for some reason couldn't remember where.

"Who's this," Donaldson asked.

"That, junior, is the killer. He goes by the name Adam Singleton. You saw him last night before I taught you your "lesson." He was being questioned by another detective." Gray now holstered his weapon, but kept Donaldson's weapon just in case Donaldson was feeling a bit full of himself again.

Donaldson was not amused by the reminder and the look on his face only added confirmation of this fact.

"Where is Detective Guthrie?" Donaldson saw that Gray's stillness transformed into concern.

"I don't know. Singleton has him. He said that I would have to pull his location off his corpse and that's what I intend to do."

"Why show me this? Why are you telling me this? Of all people, why me?" The look on Donaldson's showed that he was bewildered by this turn of events.

"Because, I need your help. I left a note of what I need on the counter. Do what it says and call me when you have the information. My number is on the paper, as if you really needed it."

Gray began walking toward the door, disassembling Donaldson's weapon as he approached the door. He wasn't going to give Donaldson even the most remote chance to shoot him in the back.

"And what if I don't do what you ask," Donaldson yelled back at him.

"Then the next conversation that you and I have will not end as well as this one," Gray shot back, walking out the door and dropping the pieces of Donaldson's weapon on the floor. "Good luck, junior."

Donaldson turned his attention to the documents in front of him and Gray's handwritten note. He finally realized that Gray was giving him the opportunity to solve a major case, several for that matter. Gray, however, was not to be crossed. Donaldson read the note and deemed the request to be reasonable. Whether as a matter of course or self-preservation, Donaldson would help Gray and, in turn, help himself.

IX.

"Ok, detective. That should do it. Now, I apologize for your accommodations, but I hope you understand that this is all very necessary."

The Artist viewed his latest work and was instantly thrilled with the potential for his final master stroke. He took pride in his preparation. Sean was still seated in the chair with an IV connected to one of his arms. He viewed this as fair enough. Sean was wounded, but not near death, yet. If The Artist decided to remove the knife from Sean's abdomen, then there was a possibility that he would bleed out rather quickly. Sean was still unconscious, so it was decided to wake him. The smelling salts did the trick and Sean slowly regained his faculties.

"Detective, I'm so happy you could join me," The Artist excitedly said as Sean became more aware of his dilemma.

"What are you putting in me?" Sean was incensed.

"That, my dear, is something that will allow our friend time to find you."

Sean moved to lunge and was immediately met by a sharp, almost intolerable pain in his stomach. Sean looked down and saw the knife's handle exposed, but no blade. He realized that his situation was more dire than he believed. His wrists bound to the ornate antique chair.

"Don't hurt yourself, detective. Any movement could prove detrimental to your health. The IV is there to make sure you don't bleed out before my masterpiece is completed. I'm nothing if not magnanimous." The Artist beamed with pride at this and made sure that Sean saw him.

Sean sat back and calmed himself. He was at the mercy of this man and his wound. Any unnecessary movement would cause extreme pain and possibly end his life prematurely. He had to survive so that he could have the satisfaction of knowing that Gray killed this monster.

"I'm sorry to leave you, detective," The Artist started, "but I have a previous engagement that I must attend to. I don't mean to be an impolite host, but there are more guests that require my attention. I'm sure you understand."

"Of course," Sean said as he nodded his head, his sense of humor apparently returning. "Just one more thing before you go."

"What's that?"

"Don't die, too quickly." Sean remained defiant.

"Funny," The Artist said amusingly, "I was about to say the same thing. You have a wonderful day. By the way, I'll be borrowing your phone. Wouldn't want you to cheat Silas out of his adventure."

"Fuck off," Sean said, returning The Artist's pleasantry with his own.

The Artist walked away and could feel Sean's cold stare burning through him. It was time that he left his canvas and returned to the task at hand: the joyous reunion with his old friend. His friend now knew who he was, and they'd met the night before, but now was the time for a proper reunion. He closed the door behind him and intentionally failed to lock it. He wouldn't want Sean to die because he didn't make this as fair as possible. He entered his Mercedes and was met with his adored talk radio when the engine started. He didn't pay much attention to the current topic. He was preoccupied with his friend. He also thought of his beloved Maria. The Artist wouldn't be without her, despite her discovery and despite her obvious misconceptions of the man he is. Still, he would stay a while longer and enjoy the entertainment.

"You and I will be reunited soon, my love. Now that my guest is well taken care of, I can focus on my friend and our relationship."

The black Mercedes pulled away from Sean's location and he began his journey back into the city that he held in the palm of his hand. As he saw it, there would be no true happy ending. He would have his love by his side, but he would most likely lose his only friend. Still, there was no time for self-pity. He wasn't finished with his work. Entering the city limits of Lafayette held an excitement that The Artist yearned for. He knew that law enforcement was capable of tracking license plates using license plate readers, or LPR's as many called them. He didn't bother to change the plates on his vehicle. He believed his friend wouldn't ask others to finish the work that he started. This was more than professional, more than personal. This was vengeance. Vengeance would only be enjoyed by the one seeking it, and nothing would stand in the way of satisfaction.

"What will you do, old friend? Your next move should be interesting to say the least." He smiled at the thought of their future encounter. "Will you invite others? No. This is a reservation for two, my dear. You and I. The masters of our respective crafts. I with my paints and you with your hunt."

The road home was always familiar. So many ways to get home and so much time to get there. The holiday traffic added to the commute, but that was of no concern. He didn't concern himself with the masses shopping at the last minute or visiting family. These basic activities were lost on him.

"Look at them," he said aloud while staring at families in

SUV's and spouse's turning into parking lots, "A city of sheep. Never realizing the magnitude of their brush with greatness. All of them consumed in their mundane, boring lives. Fascination with holidays that have lost meaning. My God, if there is one, how pitiful you all are. None of you are worthy of my talents."

Each passing block brought him closer to home. Each streetlight more familiar than the previous one. He would be home soon, or at least as soon as traffic would allow.

****

Gray drove to the only place that held solace at this moment: his office. His focus was not on the mission, but on a man. His friend, his brother in arms. This situation wasn't his fault and he knew that, but this held little comfort. He stared at Sean's desk for what seemed like an eternity; the mess of files and sticky notes that adorned his partner's computer screen; the photo of Sean and his mates at Camp Pendleton; he officer of the year award that Sean received three years prior. He felt that he led his partner into a trap set by someone less than a man, but more than a monster. Gray was in familiar darkness and he secretly loved it.

"What are you doing," Maria asked softly.

"I thought you were with Rod."

Maria smiled, "I was. He needs to lick his wounds from the ass whoopin' that I've been putting on him. Cards really aren't his thing."

Gray didn't turn. "I can't believe this is happening again. This was over years ago." Gray didn't need to face her to know that Maria was confused by this statement.

"I don't understand, Gray. What do you mean years ago?"

Gray turned his well-worn chair toward her. The look on his face was that of a man possessed by years of fighting the monsters that few ever see, and fewer had the courage to hunt. His eyes still piercing and ferocious. Maria sat in the chair in front of him. This chair was also well-worn by those who sought comfort and condemnation, alike, but today was different. Gray and his partner often referred to this chair as the "confessional." Some would say that it was sacrilege to label it as such, but it was appropriate due to the amount of truth that came from the conglomeration of fabric, wood, and steel. For now, it was Gray's turn to confess and Maria to be the keeper of secrets.

"The night we met, you called me a name that I believed was long dead. I reinvented myself over here; in this place and in this office. I became the detective that I wanted... needed to be, away from the violence of my past. I felt that I became a better version of myself in this place."

Gray looked down at his hands, the instruments that dealt both comfort and punishment. He lifted them to his face. Maria saw the scars of battle across each knuckle. Some wounds fresher than others. These were the hands of man experienced in love and pain, capable of gentle support and extreme brutality. The contradiction wasn't lost on either of them.

"My past, it seems, will not die." Gray interlocked his fingers and sat his hands on his lap. He fixated on a small water stain on the ceiling tile above him. He leaned back into his chair and closed his eyes. He was exhausted. Thoughts raced through his mind: Charlotte, his son, Sean, Rod, Kap, Tyler, Mags, Chief, all of it. Everything interconnected in a cacophony of violence.

Maria saw that the man before him was somber, but not near broken. The intensity she previously saw in his eyes contradicted the sorrow in his voice. This wasn't self-loathing, it was preparation for what was to come. She sat still, just listening.

"Maria, I don't know how this will end, but it will end. You need to know the truth in the case that I don't make it out of this," Gray told her, his posture now changed to sitting upright. His eyes now fixed on his audience of one. His hands still clasped together, but now sitting on his desk.

"Why me and why now," Maria asked.

"Because you have proven that I can trust you. This story needs to be told. Needs to be brought to light, but you have to make me a promise." Gray's voice was now as intense as his gaze.

"Of course. Anything."

"Promise me that if I don't make it out this that you will tell the story accurately, but if I do make it that you will never utter a word of this to anyone. The people involved have too much to lose if this goes public and I'm still alive."

Maria looked at Gray and saw that he was still protecting those he cared about, despite his world crumbling around him. This was a promise that she intended to keep.

"Gray," Maria started, outstretching her arm and placing her hand on his, "I promise that this story will either be reported accurately or forgotten. You have my word."

This was the first touch of sincerity that Gray felt since this all began. His natural reaction was to recoil from her touch, mostly out of respect for his wife, but this was not an intimate contact. This was an assuring touch, no more than that of a friend placing an arm around his shoulder or a colleague patting him on the back. Much needed human contact, but nothing more. He knew that Maria would do as he asked. It was time to reveal the inner workings of this drama to someone outside of the circle. Gray removed his hands from Maria's assuring touch and sat back in his chair. *A history lesson from a contemporary will now commence.*

"Several years ago, I was recruited to lead a team of law enforcement officers with a singular mission: seek out and recover the most dangerous that this state had offer. We were good. Damn good. But that ended July 17...."

****

Donaldson continued to pour himself into the information before him. The note that gray left for him remained folded. His laser-like focus negated any request, even one from Silas Gray. For the first time in nearly three days, Donaldson was getting the answers that he sought. He didn't disregard Gray's request, much to the contrary. He was distracted by what was before him. A habit that proved useful in the past, but would soon have dire consequences.

His phone rang, but his focus blocked out the sound. He couldn't take his eyes off the pictures, research, and other papers hidden away from the rest world.

A second call, still no move to answer.

X.

4:57 PM

"Jesus!" Maria's exasperation at what she just heard was both understandable and warranted. She'd never heard anything like it. Secret task force. Serial killers. Gunfights. It was almost too much to believe, but the man telling her these things was both trustworthy and not prone to exaggeration. This was the complete truth and every fiber of her confirmed this.

"This is insane," Maria said, an amazed look on her face.

"I know." Gray's tone was as calm as ever.

"What does Adam want from you?"

Gray exhaled, "I don't know and I don't care. All I want is to find out where Sean is and if that means that I have put him down permanently, then that's what I'm going to do."

Maria saw through the calmness of this statement. She knew that Gray was in pain, but he would never admit it. She watched him as he again sat back in his chair and let the problems of the world seemingly flow over him. This was a man that was in full control of himself or at least he appeared to be.

Beep, click

The door opened.

"Well, isn't this cozy. I got a detective sittin' back in his chair like ain't shit goin' on and a reporter staring at him like he's about to do a trick." Rod's presence immediately lightened the mood.

"Did you try to call Donaldson for me," Gray asked.

"Sure did. Twice. And got nothing. Whatever he's doing is apparently more important than answering the phone."

"Donaldson," Maria said, the confusion in her voice was evident. "Isn't that the guy that…"

"…that Gray gave an intestine facial to last night," Rod interrupted. "That he is, baby. That he is."

"What does he have to do with this, Gray?"

"Junior and I came to an understanding earlier today and he decided that it would be in his best interests to assist in my investigation rather than be a hindrance," Gray responded, never moving from his laid-back position. "I'll text him to see what's going on."

Gray sat up again and picked up the phone in front of him. He entered the characters and then placed the phone back on the desk in front of him, face down. Gray then resumed his previous state.

"He'll either respond or he won't," Gray said in a matter of fact tone. "Either way, I'm sure he'll wind up pissing me off with his answer."

"Uh, do I even want to know how you got him to cooperate with you," Rod asked.

Gray propped his head up ever so slightly and gave Rod a look that he'd seen before. It was the "Don't-Ask-If-You-Don't-Want-To-Know" look that he'd seen too many times before from both of his detectives.

"You know what," Rod said as he stood up and began walking out of the office, "Forget I asked. Actually, forget everything. I'm getting to old and grumpy for this shit. I swear you two will be the death of Big Homie and then you'll have to face Big Momma. She'll be your problem 'cuz all my worries will be gone. Crazy sumbitches." The door secured door closed behind Rod and both Gray and Maria could hear his mumbling as he walked away.

"Thanks, Rod," Gray yelled, a slight smirk evident on his face.

"Kiss my ass," Rod yelled back, the words muffled but understandable.

The moment of levity between the two friends was needed, but the worry soon rushed back to Gray's mind. Why didn't Donaldson answer his phone? Is he pursuing this monster on his own? Was he doing anything with this knowing that Sean's life hangs in the balance? These questions played with his mind, but he didn't show it. He still sat there, in his chair. The calm exterior contradicted the war inside of him.

****

Sean sat in this chair for what seemed like an eternity in his mind. The ornate wooden chair proved to be more of a challenge than he'd expected. His bindings were tight and solid, but the constant motion began to roll the tape at either end. Despite his situation, he continued attempts to free himself, only stopping when the pain of the knife protruding from his stomach became too much. He'd passed out a few times from the pain, but his will to free himself and exact vengeance was too great to keep him out for long.

Adapt and overcome. Adapt and overcome.

Sean continued his movement, rocking each arm back and forth as he'd done before. The edges of the tape on his right arm beginning to roll a bit more with each movement, more so than on the left arm. His improvised manacles were good, but improvised, nonetheless. The continued motion began to loosen the silver bindings. He presses his hand against the hairs solid oak arm and was able to lift it ever so slightly. The pain that coursed through his body was breathtaking. The slightest movement of the knife was excruciating.

"Come on you son of a bitch! Just a bit more!"

His continued effort allowed his right arm to slip free. Sean gasped as he gained an increase in his freedom of movement. He was near exhaustion and bleeding more than he had before, the knife still firmly set in its place. It was then that his rage became uncontrollable. He paid no mind to the pain anymore as he clawed at the duct tape on his left arm, the slow trickling of blood from his abdomen become more pronounced. A minute of this and his other arm was free. His legs would be next. The angel of death hovering over him couldn't hold back the rage of a Marine on a mission.

As he stood, Sean felt every inch of the steel within him, his joints cracked, and his mind began to wander. He saw the door that he entered and knew he had to make it out. Beyond that door would be another journey: his vehicle. His assailant took his car keys and his phone. He was sure that as gentlemanly as The Artist was, he was no fool. This would prove most difficult.

"Okay, let's get this going."

Sean was cognizant of the fact the that IV attached to him was a lifeline. He detached the plastic bag from its perch and rolled the top of it, making sure to apply the right amount of pressure to keep the saline flowing through his body. His injuries were evident, his drive defined by his situation. He would not be stopped from completing his mission. Singleton was on his mind, but his mind began to wander again. To the common man, he may have appeared as a drunkard would after a night a revelry. Sean, however, knew that he needed aid and needed it quickly.

He approached the door and was surprised when he found it unlocked, but more surprising was the wind and cold that greeted him as he exited his temporary prison. The unrelenting cold front that consumed the region over the last few days was now in full force. Sean's lungs consumed the air. He felt it burn just as he felt the blade still cutting away at his insides. His hands shook. Partly from the cold and partly from shock, still he approached the vehicle that he left out of sight of the buildings in the yard.

"Shit," Sean said to himself as he thought about the distance to his car.

Every step that followed became more painful than the other. The cold did nothing to ease his discomfort. The bag in his hand still flowing the elixir that would keep him alive. Finally, he reached his car and was met with another challenge: door locks. He looked through the window and saw that nothing was disturbed. Still he had no key and the psychopath still had his phone. His only hope was now technology, his radio in his vehicle. He kept his portable radio in the card, behind the seat.

Sean looked for something, anything hard enough to break the window and was in luck. The derelict area provided broken concrete, concrete that was once well maintained and trod upon by steel horses. He couldn't help but think of the irony of this moment. A detective breaking into a car. In one hand he held his IV and the other a piece of concrete large enough to break glass. The throw caused more pain than he'd experience up to this point. He nearly fell to his knees as he watched the block bounce off the window.

"God damnit!"

Again, he picked up his newest hope and threw it with everything he had. The result was the same. A small scratch on the window and a small piece of concrete chipping off its larger brother. Sean fell to his knees again, nearly blacking out from the combination of exertion and pain.

"God, if I ever needed you, then this would be the time to show up."

Sean picked himself up and grabbed the larger piece of concrete remaining. Every muscle in his body screamed for him to succumb. To quit. The trickle of crimson from his belly was now pouring down his leg and pooling at his feet. He squeezed the remaining fluid into himself as fast as he could. His lifeline was now a simple piece man-made stone, ancient in design and now useful for another purpose. All his being was forced into this throw and it left his hand bearing the weight of every last hope Sean had for survival. The tempered glass didn't stand a chance against such passion; such anger; such hope. The shattered window was now a portal to his savior. Sean reached into the car, unlocking the door. he seated himself into driver's seat and reached behind the passenger seat for his radio.

"Please be there. Please be there."

The hard-plastic shell of his Motorola radio met him. It was cold, but feeling it warmed him to the core. He turned the power knob and the device came to life, evidenced by the green screen bearing in name and call number. Each radio assigned to an individual officer. By the antenna was an orange button: the emergency button. He pressed the button and waited for a response. The voice on the other end was angelic.

"Bravo 15, echo, Bravo 15 echo. Are you code 4?"

Sean held the transmit button, "Negative, comm. Officer down, I repeat officer down. GPS my location and send available units and rescue. I've lost a lot of blood. Knife wound to the abdomen."

"10-4, Bravo 15. Stay with us. Acadia dispatch has the call and units are on the way."

"Direct, comm."

Sean could no longer hold onto his consciousness. The cold gave way to a new warmth that he'd never felt before. A soothing warmth inviting him to sleep. He likened it to being surrounded by a warm blanket that was fresh from the dryer.

Thoughts of his service to his country and community flashed through his mind. Bianca, Rod, Chief, Maria, and Gray. Friends, old and new. He thought of his parents and how proud they were of him and his path in life.

"I think I'll just close my eyes for a moment," Sean said to himself, the green glow of his radio's display shining near him.

"Bravo 15……Bravo 15……Respond, Bravo 15….."

****

"Have you received the call yet," the deep authoritative voice asked.

"No, not yet," the dutiful assistant responded. "No word from Romeo One."

"I'll advise Keres of the situation."

The suited man exited the dimly lit communications room and walked down a hallway adorned with the symbols of the state: a pelican here, a Fleur de Lis there, pictures of authority figures past and present. He approached a heavy wooden door that separated the outside world from the secrets held within. The bracelet on his wrist granted him unfettered access into a room where very few had entered, and even fewer knew of its reason for existence. He was immediately confronted by a woman; brunette and very well maintained.

"Access code." The blank stare of the woman would have turned most into stone, but this was a normal occurrence for both.

"Sierra 6. Authorization Tau."

The young woman before him entered the code into the computer on her desk. She waited for the response. What the man before couldn't see was the firearm lying beside it. Any move without authorization would result in a tragic out-come.

"Access granted," she stated to the man before her. "Keres is waiting for an update."

"Yes ma'am."

The suit left the gatekeeper of the office and entered a larger, more utilitarian office. Only one picture adorned the office and it faced his boss. No one else knew of the image it held. His boss had their back to him and was staring out of a window directly behind the desk. The dark silhouette commanded respect and would receive that respect from anyone who entered, regardless of position or title. This was a person of importance and secrets. No one would dare stand against this office, let alone its sole occupant.

"Do you have an update?" The voice was raspy and calm. It was distinct, yet mysterious.

"Yes. Detective Guthrie just made an officer down call. Local authorities and rescue are on their way?"

"His situation?"

"Dire," the man responded. "He's severely wounded."

"And Romeo One?"

"No call yet. Should we prepare?"

The figure never moved when asking these questions. There was no need for movement right now, but a friend was in danger.

"Yes. Prepare, but no one moves without confirmation from Romeo One. Dismissed." The order was given, and it would be followed without question.

The man who paid deference throughout said nothing and turned away, leaving from whence he came. The darkness clad figure, however, never moved. *What are you waiting for, Silas? You know I'm here when you need me. What are you waiting for?*

The clock on the wall read 1815 hours, a quarter past six

o'clock to those outside of this world. Darkness had fallen in the Bayou State and it would soon consume all who engaged it.

"It's a cold night, Silas," the raspy voice said aloud. "The darkness will consume you and all in your path, as it had years ago."

XI.

6:15 PM

Winter claimed yet another day and darkness consumed the area. The only illumination to be seen was man-made. Streetlights and Christmas decorations were strewn about the "Downtown Lafayette" section. There were surprisingly very few cars on the roadway of this typically lively area. The Artist was now home and what he saw when he arrived pleased him more than any wrapped package under any tree: a black Charger parked on the street near his residence.

"Oh, my dear. Christmas is indeed a time of giving, but why are you here? You were not invited to my show of shows and yet you insist on interjecting yourself into my business. This simply will not do."

The Artist parked in his usual spot. He had no fear of what was to come and no fear of the person that he would soon encounter. The show-crasher was mentally and physically no match for The Artist. He thought of this as he walked his usual path. Everything was still and his approach just as still. His door was still open. The Artist peaked around the doorframe and peered into his home. A sudden rush of excitement and anger filled him in this moment.

"How dare you sit at my table, peasant, and view my creation. You have interfered too many times."

The man sitting at his black countertop was an annoyance at least and an obstructionist at best. He watched for a moment as the hipster-looking trespasser continued to look through pages and pages of The Artist's work. The Artist was infuriated with this offense against his brilliance. This man wasn't worthy of such perfection. He was neither his beloved friend, nor his beloved friend's partner. He wasn't worthy.

The Artist watched his prey as he slowly walked the wooden path leading to his kitchen. His target was too involved in paper and had no overt sense of situational awareness. The Artist knew how to step and where to step to avoid all noise. This place was, after all, his lair. His nimbleness allowed a silent approach to the man before. The Artist was, however, amazed at the man's singular focus. The Artist took pride in this. His material must have been something special to beguile someone of their senses.

The Artist was no longer in the man's line of sight and approached from the man's back. He drew his weapon from the custom holster on his hip, silent and efficient. The weapon was an exquisite example of craftsmanship befitting a man of exceptional taste. It was not his preferred method of expression, but the man before him was law enforcement and he would take no chances at missing his meeting with Silas. He pushed the weapon forward and the muzzle was mere inches from his targets head. As he squeezed the trigger, he felt a sudden sadness. Sadness that this would be his most abrupt and least interesting stroke. He decided against finishing the job suddenly, despite this man's futility. This was an occasion for improvisation and as such would be unique. A one-off canvas that would try him in many ways. His finger no longer applied pressure to the trigger. *This will be glorious.*

"Good evening, sir," The Artist stated calmly as be pressed the muzzle against Donaldson's head. "Any sudden movement and I assure you that you will not finish your reading."

Donaldson froze where he sat, his focus broken and his nerves firing to life. The warm sensation of danger filled every part of his being. It was the same feeling that he experienced when Gray surprised him earlier that day.

"Singleton," Donaldson asked.

"In a way, yes, and in many ways, no," The Artist said, grinning slightly.

The Artist reached for the man's holster and removed his weapon from him. The Artist also removed the handcuffs on the man's left hip.

"Now, I will put these on you and you will not fight," The Artist whispered. "If you do, I will kill you. You will be my witness to my final masterpiece."

Donaldson offered no resistance to this. If Gray were present, then he wouldn't have been surprised. Donaldson had no courage to speak of and only subsisted on the power of others. The Artist found this disappointing. The final click of the cuffs on the man's wrists confirmed The Artist's safety. Donaldson's hands were now useless and hung behind the behind back. The Artist now faced the man. The two stared at each other, but Donaldson looked away in fear after a few seconds. Tears were nearly visible.

"My dear, why have you come to my home?"

Donaldson responded with near hyperventilation, "I followed Gray to this place and he showed me these folders. He's coming back soon."

"Ha," The Artist scoffed. "That last statement is as real as Santa Clause, my dear. He's not coming here, and he won't unless I ask him to. You will provide the motivations for his return. It will be a wonderful reunion."

Donaldson feared for himself more so than ever. Gray was a controlled maniac, but this man was different. He was seemingly controlled, but he gazed upon the aftermath of his work. This situation was indefensible to him.

"What are you going to do to me?"

"I'm going to ask my friend to join us. Do not be troubled,

my dear. You are in a safe place."

****

Rod's feet couldn't carry him fast enough to Gray's office. He moved as a man on a mission, starting from his seated position in his office, through the two sets, and across the covered walkway that separated the two police department building. The final secure door was nearly ripped on the hinges as he opened it. Now there was a sharp right turn and Gray's office. Gray still in his chair and Maria still sitting in her previous position. The two were talking, but Rod's message superseded manners.

"Sean's alive," Rod exclaimed, still catching his breath. "He's in Acadia Parish. Deputies and rescue are on-scene. He's in bad shape, but still breathing."

Gray stood up from his chair and felt instant relief.

"How bad," Gray asked, his piercing blue eyes burning a hole through Rod.

"It's bad. He lost a lot of blood and is critical. He was able to get to his radio and call out an officer needs assistance."

Gray bent over and pushed his knuckles into his desk. Just knowing Sean was alive was enough for him. Critical condition was more than he'd hoped for.

"Where is he," Maria asked.

"He's being transported to Acadia General. Chief is on the way there now and I'm about to head out. Let's go!"

Gray retrieved his phone and grabbed his car keys from his desk drawer. His partner was alive. The weight lifted from his shoulders. It would be touch and go, but at least he wouldn't die at the hands of a monster if he decided to let go. He would be surrounded by people who cared for him, loved him. As he began to walk away his phone rang again; a Facetime call. The name on the caller ID: Sean Guthrie. Gray froze.

"I have to take this," Gray said to Rod and Maria. Both stood still, wondering what could stop this man from seeing his partner. Gray's finger slid across the screen and there was the man responsible for Sean's condition.

"Silas, my old friend. You look wonderful. Seriousness suits you." The Artist's tone was friendly, but patronizing.

"You lost, you fuck," Gray retorted. "Sean is alive. He survived whatever hell you put him in. You failed."

The Artist saw conviction in his Gray's eyes. This was truth, pure and simple.

"I am happy that Detective Guthrie survived his ordeal. I don't exactly know how, but he is an impressive man. Skilled in many ways. I should know. I now bear some of his work on my body. No matter, I have something even better for you."

The live feed showed Gray that Singleton was at his apartment again. His thoughts immediately went to Donaldson.

"This man," the image now on Donaldson sitting on the wooden floor in the kitchen, "Said that you invited him here. To show him my work. This simply cannot be, Silas. I told you that this was my gift to you. He also said that you asked him for a favor, but he became distracted. Too bad. You could have found me so much sooner if it were not for his ineptitude."

Gray looked at his screen and saw a pitiable man sitting. His head was low, and his breathing pained. He couldn't see Donaldson's face from the angle that The Artist provided, but he saw a familiar darkness pouring onto Donaldson's shirt. It was thick and flowed consistently.

"Quickly," Gray heard The Artist say off camera, "The audience is waiting to see your lovely face." A hand emerged from the side of the screen and snatch the tuft of hair on the top of Donaldson's head. The violent grip pushed his head backward and exposed the face of Gray's previous pursuer. He didn't like the man and had very little respect for him, but he was still human. "Do you like my work thus far, Silas?"

Gray beheld Donaldson's face, bloody cavities where eyes once were. His mouth was open and Donaldson nearly choked on the blood that was no longer following with gravity's pull. It was then that the hand let go of the hair and Donaldson fell to his side and then rolled onto his back. Blood choked the helpless man. The feed then focused on three distinct masses that laid next to the now fallen Donaldson. They formerly belonged to the man Gray taught lessons to.

"Now you get to witness my next stroke, old friend."

"Stop! You son of a bitch! What do you want?" Gray's was enraged at this sight. No one deserved this.

The video feed was now still and focused solely on Donaldson. The view from the side allowed for full view of Donaldson's head, chest, and shoulders.

"What I want," The Artist said. "I want to finish the work that I prepared for us, my dear. The artistry that you are witnessing in this moment is our creation. You supplied the canvas and I will supply the talent. This is our first collaboration."

Gray watched in horror as the psychopath mounted Donaldson, legs on either side of the chest and his full weight now on Donaldson's torso. The Artist had in his hand a simple implement: a chef's sharpening steel. A solid steel rod protruding from the wooden grip.

"STOP," Gray yelled into his phone.

The Artist ceased for a moment and The Artist dipped his head into camera view.

"Why should I, old friend?"

The Artist smiled and then his face was no longer visible. This statement was pure evil in Gray's mind. He couldn't help Donaldson. He watched the screen helplessly as The Artist gripped the sharpener's handle and slowly drove the steel rod into Donaldson's left ear. There was no screaming, only mumbling. Gray saw the animal making small circular motions was the rod delved deeper into Donaldson's ear canal. Even though the assailant's full weight was on his chest, Donaldson could be seen writing in pain. Gray stopped watching. He knew that the next ear would follow, and he wanted none of it.

"Oh, Silas," the voice from Gray's phone was playful. "Wherever did you go?"

Gray lifted the phone to his face. He saw The Artist's face. It was adorned with small specks of blood from Donaldson expectorating while being tortured. The sharpener was now lifted into Grays view. Several inches of the steel rod covered in blood.

"We have an appointment, my dear." The Artist's face more wicked than ever before. "Should I expect you or should I find more people this lovely Christmas Eve night? Perhaps I should visit a neighbor. The family directly below me has a small child that loves coloring. Brian, I believe is his name."

Gray's previous enraged state gave way to his mythic-like calm. His normally piercing blue eyes appeared to have fire in them, but he was still.

"Where," Gray asked.

"My place," The Artist responded. "You and you alone."

"I'm on the way." No emotion in these words.

"I'll be waiting."

A familiar tone and The Artist's face disappeared. The darkness that Gray feared would overtake him now filled every pore in his body. He needed this darkness. Craved it. Yearned for it. It was his and his alone. A darkness that could only be satisfied with blood. He knew that if he indulged in his addiction, then he would need help. Help that only an old friend could provide.

"Rod, You and Maria go to Sean. I have to stop this."

Rod saw that Gray was no longer the man he was just days ago. The light in his friend was gone and only the monster remained. The monster that had laid dormant for years was no standing before him. He would've offered help, but Gray wouldn't have accepted it.

"You do what you need to do, Gray. I'll take Maria and we'll meet Chief

"Silas," Maria said.

Gray looked at her. Maria flashbacked to the night that she and the infamous "Judge Gray" met for the first time. The look in his eyes was the same look that she saw when she crossed the line with him the first time. It was terrifying to her. He offered no words in return.

"End this," she said to him.

Gray put the phone in his back pocket and walked away from the two people that held his company for the last few hours. The fire in him burned with an intensity that would engulf anyone in his path. He was a man possessed. His vest awaited when he opened his truck's door. the weight of the vest was substantial, but at this moment he felt nothing. The assorted pouches were filled with extra magazines for his UMP and Gladys, two filled flashbang pouches, a tourniquet just in case he needed for himself, and a radio that he had no intention of using. The engine of his vehicle roared to life and a moment later tires squealed. There was only one more thing to do. He took the phone from his back pocket and dialed a phone number that he memorized years ago. No white envelope for this man. One ring and a voice.

"Name and access code," the voice stated.

"Gray, Silas. Access code Romeo One."

"Access granted, Romeo One. Transferring to Keres actual."

A brief pause and he was connected to an old friend that would be his guardian angel after everything settled.

"Hello, old friend," the raspy voice began. "I was wondering if you were going to call."

"It's been a long time, Keres."

"You know you can use my real name, Silas"

"Not on the phone, Keres. You know the protocol."

"You and your protocols. Fine, I'll play. What do you need?"

"I'm sure you know what's going on."

"Yes," Keres answered. "I wouldn't be good at what I do if I didn't. I'll send resources to your location immediately. We'll track your phone's GPS."

"Good. I want you there as well. I need to see you."

"Don't worry, Silas. I'll be there. If we can't find you immediately, we'll just listen for gunshots or sirens. That's always a sign that you're around." Only this friend could make him smile when he was on mission and his friend didn't disappoint.

"I'll see you soon," Gray said, hanging up the phone as he finished his statement.

XII.

7:00 PM

The cold drove most people in doors and families enjoyed Christmas Eve dinners. Very few cars rode through the streets. This area of the city was almost completely shut down. This suited Gray just fine. Fewer people meant fewer that could be caught in the crossfire. He parked his truck in a familiar spot, the same spot he parked it earlier. He saw that Donaldson's Charger was still there. Might as well have been Donaldson's gravestone; a testament to a man respected by few, but would be remembered by all after tonight. Gray didn't hope to find him alive and secretly hoped he wasn't. Donaldson was at the very least blind, deaf, and mute. The Artist assured this.

Gray exited his truck and has his weapon at the ready, portions of the worn coating of his UMP shined in the streetlights. His senses were heightened. Every sound magnified. Every movement keyed in on and dismissed in turn. The hunt was on. He approached the building the same he approached it earlier. The same path he took when chased by Donaldson. The confrontation was inevitable, but he was on Singleton's territory. His prey had homefield advantage. *Iberia all over again.*

Gray walked the flights of stairs that led to the demon's inner sanctum. He trained his weapon forward and up, looking over the sights of the German engineered weapon in his hands. His movements were fluid. The agility built over years of training and thousands of practiced runs were evident. His heart rate was low, but the adrenaline flowed freely into his veins. No shaking. Complete control of himself. Darkness was in full control.

Seventh floor. The seventh circle, as it were. Reserved for those of violence according to Dante. The epicenter of every evil that befell the Lafayette area for the past three days. *How appropriate.*

The familiar corridor met him as he exited the stairwell, doors lining each side. His destination was known and there was no hesitation. His approach to the doorway was silent. There was no need for silence, but this was his way. The door was slightly ajar, inviting Gray to enter. He positioned himself on the left side of the doorway. His left hand slowly opened the door and his right hand gripped his weapon tightly. He knew the layout of the apartment. This was his advantage, his only advantage. The obstructed view of the apartment's interior was now open. His entry was swift. The light on his weapon flashed to life. Sweep and clear, sweep and clear. He soon found that there was no need for this. The studio was open, save the bedroom. The only walled area that offered any kind of substantial concealment.

He approached the kitchen area and saw the blood that Donaldson was forced to spill, but the body was no longer there. Streaks now lit Gray's path, leading him to the bedroom. The same bedroom where "Adam" and Maria consummated their desire for another. For Gray, this would serve as Singleton's tomb.

His approach to the closed bedroom door was the same as the door before: silent and methodical. No sound. The space between the bottom of the door and the wooden floor indicated that a light was on. This suited Gray. Less he had to do. It was now time for shock and awe. Silence was out. He reached for the doorknob and found it was unlocked, but he did not open the door. There was no fear from this animal.

Gray relinquished his grip from his weapon and reach into

one of his pouches. The small tube in his hand possessed enough energy to distract anyone. The fingers on his right hand manipulated the primary and secondary safety pins simultaneously. The stun device in his left hand was now primed and awaited to removal of the spoon that held back it's explosive contents.

Gray again reached for the doorknob and open the door slightly, just enough to drop his gift. His release was perfect and he shut the door as soon as it left his hand. His hands now gripped his weapon. He waited for his cue to enter.

BANG

A brilliant flash of light and 180 decibels of sound filled the small space. Gray entered the room immediately upon detonation. Sweeping and clearing. No need for his weapon light. Every light in the room electrified. The smoke from his gift wasn't too thick and dissipated quickly. The violence of action Gray displayed paled to the violence found within this room. No Singleton, only Donaldson.

The bed was made and on it the naked body of Donaldson. Gray didn't see it immediately, but Donaldson's head was missing and only the body remained, a large open wound extending from the lower ribcage to the pelvis. His insides exposed. Each limb was tied to a post on the luxurious piece of furniture, displaying the body for all to see. The Artist didn't have time to detach the limbs, but the shock of it had the desired effect. Gray averted his attention to the lit bathroom. He enters, weapon at the ready.

Before him was the shower that this psychopath adorned with bloody handprints. Laying in the shower was Donaldson's head; face twisted in pain, but dead, pointed straight up, supported by assorted bathroom accoutrements. Desired effect accomplished, yet again. Dried and drying blood from the lifeless eye sockets, mouth, and ears added to the horror of this sight. Inside of the mouth was a white piece of paper:

high quality, rolled, and perfectly placed. Gray reached for the paper and unrolled it. The message was clear and concise: LOOK OUT OF THE KITCHEN WINDOW, SILAS. I AM WAITING.

Gray dropped the paper and made his way to the window. The same window that this monster viewed his hunting ground. Gray scanned up, down, everywhere. There he was, standing on the sidewalk looking at his apartment. Gray was lit by the bright sink light hanging above him. He caught his reflection in glass surface before him: eyes darkened, the look death in his face.

****

The Artist saw the figure in his window. Although the distance between them was no longer as far as it had been, he longed to have him by his side. His gift to Silas was complete and he wanted to have his friend express to him his brilliance. The method, the research, the execution. All of it. He was obsessed by it. No fear of repercussion. Only Silas could appreciate this work.

The Artist lifted Sean's phone to his ear and watched as the figure in the window reached for his back pocket. "Hello, my dear. I must say that you are a vision tonight. Top form. You have not disappointed me in the slightest."

There was no response.

"Come now, no words of encouragement. I did all of this for you. You, my dear, have returned to me. I see it, even from this distance, I see it. You owe all of this to me. Your new-found life, the gifts on display, everything. We are connected. I am you and you are me. Could there ever be a more perfect pairing? I don't think so. In fact, I know so."

****

The Artist's word only worked to drive Gray's darkness into

the forefront. Humanity was gone. There was only retribution. No law but the most primitive. Savage versus savage.

"I'm coming," Gray responded, colder than ever before.

With those words he hung up and replaced the phone in his back pocket. Keres would need this to find him. His movements were casual. No running. He knew that this fiend wouldn't go anywhere. Singleton wanted this. He wanted to meet Silas Gray. The reaper among REAPER's. Death, itself, was temporarily clothed in the skin of a man.

As he walked the flights of stairs, he paid no attention to the woman on the phone calling police. The sound of the flash bang startled many and it was inevitable. She dared not make eye contact with the well-armed, intimidating man that passed her. She froze, hoping that her next movement wasn't her last. The woman forced herself into the corner of the stairwell and watched as he walked down the next flight of stairs. No words, no look, just silence. Her faculties returned long enough to describe to the operator what she just saw.

"There's a man. Tall, dark hair. He's wearing a large vest and he has a gun. Please hurry," she spoke into the phone.

The woman ran away, presumably to her living quarters. Gray didn't care. She was inconsequential in his world.

****

The Artist focused his attention on the parking garage, expecting that his friend would emerge from whence he came. The anticipation of this moment was almost too much to bear. He shook with excitement as a child would seeing gifts in front of the chimney. He only regretted that their relationship would end. The cold weather and the holiday cleared the streets. Every other soul on this night sought shelter. None would see the power of this moment. Two maestros preparing their orchestras for a battle of supremacy. *Glorious.*

The atmosphere was perfect for The Artist. A venue for two. This was what he imagined. Two men, both alike in the ways that mattered in this world. Two masters facing off in their respective art forms. He dropped Sean's phone on the concrete in front of him. He no longer needed it. He gave a brief thought to Maria and their reunion after this night. The love that they shared was powerful, but he needed Silas first. Only his attention would fulfill the passion in his heart. Only his friend.

The first crack of gunfire caught The Artist off guard and broke him of his thoughts. It took him a second to register what happened. A near miss and an impact directly behind him. The burst that followed was ferocious. He scanned and saw that his friend had emerged from the front door, not the garage area that he anticipated. *My Silas, again not disappointing at all.* The Artist sought cover behind a concrete wall behind him and retrieved his weapon, the exquisitely hand-crafted pistol that Sean met earlier this day. The object that forced Donaldson's submission. He returned fired and was met with more of the same. His friend was a juggernaut. This will not stop him. The still of the night broken by a war between two old adversaries. This was a gunfight, plain and simple.

Gunfire from Gray stopped for a moment as he reloaded his weapon. The Artist peered over the concrete wall and saw the dark figure approaching, calmly walking and reloading. He was taken aback by the beauty of it all. Only his friend would unleash such a maelstrom of violence and metal with such calm and casual affair. The Artist returned the volley as the man approaching him finished reloading and again released a volley of violence in his direction. The flashes of light coming from Gray's weapon lit up his face with every shot. There was no expression, eyes devoid of humanity. He was consumed by the evil of years of violence. The souls of his team and the souls of those he took from this world accompanied him in this fight. The target is directly in front of him. Brass fell to the ground. It was music that only a master could make. *Absolutely beautiful.*

Again, the gunfire stopped. Reloading was again necessary. The Artist knew of this tactic: suppression fire. He took the opportunity to run away, firing his weapon toward his beloved friend, but his progress was halted by another surge of Silas Gray's magnum opus. Gunfire resumed as soon as he began running. Gray saw this and continued his volley, tracking the target as he ran. This was his last magazine for his UMP. The weapon was a means to an end. Confuse the enemy and suppress in order to gain ground. He unleashed this fury to gain an advantage. His target ran behind another wall. The Artist was exhilarated by this display continued.

Click

Empty, but the weapon served its purpose. Distance was no longer an issue. He unclasped the weapon from his vest and dropped it to the ground. No need for the extra weight. He would get it back soon enough. The Artist stood up and looked in Gray's direction. Both stared at each other for a moment. Love in The Artist's eyes and death in Gray's. The two only about a dozen yards or so apart. Perfect distance for Gladys.

"You wanted the REAPER and now you have him," Gray yelled.

"It's all I ever wanted, my dear," The Artist yelled back, psychotically laughing after this statement. "You've come back to me."

Gray drew Gladys from her resting place on his hip. The Artist didn't wait for her to sing the song of his death. Gray's intention was to get close enough for a personal kill. Very close. He wanted to see the life drain out of him.

This was the crescendo to the ultimate masterwork. Silas Gray and The Artist meeting in a surge of violence that only they could understand and, moreover, thrive in. Each seemingly more vicious with every shot fired. Every word spoken. The brutality of this piece would resonate through streets of this city and this state.

The chase was on.

XIII.

Frigid conditions of the evening contradicted the fire in lungs and the acid in his blood. His heart raced and his nerves steeled after nearly three days of intense investigation. *It was time this came to an end.*

His thoughts ran to the pain in his knees and the weight of vest, but the mission came first. He was in good condition, but it could always be better. Rapid footsteps and heavy breathing were the order of the moment. *Too many of these moments.*

The figure in front of him was the object of his desire. His obsession. His curse. Nothing could've filled the void in his soul like this figure. The love and hate that he had for this singular being was nothing he felt before. Graduations, wedding, birth of his first child; Nothing compared to his hunger for catching his prey. That's what it was, a hunger.

Shit, another turn. This guy must run marathons! My knees can't take this shit!

As he made the turn onto the next street, he realized one thing: I am alone. Unsanctioned. Unplugged. No backup. *Just me, my nemesis, and our respective weapons.* His weapon, a Sig 1911, at the ready. Eight rounds of department issued .45 ACP ammunition with one in the chamber. It weighed just over two pounds, but he just ran five blocks. She might as well be a bazooka. The SureFire light attachment added to the weight but provided the advantage of 800 lumens of white light. Scan, dismiss, scan again. *Night becomes day, you son of a bitch.*

Another block made; another intersection. So many hiding spots in this area: an art center; a parking garage; a glass building attempting to stay modern but showing its true age. Historic "Downtown Lafayette" provided a business atmosphere on workdays and a party paradise on the weekends, but on this day, it is still; it's eerily still. He attempted to catch his breath and believed that his target eluded him. The annual Christmas decoration hung from restored streetlights as they did every year. The glow of the holiday offered more light on this cloudless night, but this provided no advantage in locating the demon he pursued. He is exposed; open to his prey.

A loud crack, almost like a firecracker, but without the echo. No sound like it; no feeling so ominous. The sudden impact felt like a freight train hitting him in an area the size of a pencil eraser. One shot, one kill; one of phrases drilled into him at Fort Benning's Sand Hill when he was a younger man, but he never thought of being the victim of that statement. A second impact as he fell to the cold concrete floor of the urban landscape. No soft landing as his body weight and selected accoutrements forced him onto his left side. Vulnerable and unable to move. *I'm still here, asshole.*

The Artist emerged from a parking garage near one of the corners of the intersection. The object of obsession is within his grasp and in his grip is a gun. His vest stopped the bullet from piercing his heart, but the pain he felt was a possible cracked rib, maybe two. The fire in lungs escaped and his panting gave way to his lungs being paralyzed. We wanted to breathe, he needed to breathe, but for a moment his body couldn't perform a simple function. Lying on his left side was uncomfortable, but he still held onto to his lifeline, his ace in the hole, his weapon. *Breathe, but don't move, god damn it!*

His adversary approached him; each step more deliberate, a slow approach. There was no sound as he inched forward. The ominous figure was bathed in faint holiday lights, but darkened by the shadows offered by the surrounding structures. Savoring the moment when the hunter was now the hunted.

347

Two predators, now one. Nothing like the kill. The thoughts of the man that caused his premature demise flooded his mind. He'll be hailed as a hero. An officer felled gloriously upon the field of battle. They will name a school or street after him. Create scholarships in honor of his sacrifice. Folded flags and a 21-Gun salute to honor him. Valkyries will escort the warrior into the Great Hall. Valhalla awaits. *Fuck that! Just wait for your moment. You'll only get that moment.*

The prize is now over him. He raised the blued steel that paralyzed him temporarily. No face. No sounds. *Now!*

His adrenaline surged and a familiar clarity entered his mind; clarity that only battle can provide. His thoughts were untainted by family, friends, policies, procedures, commendation, or criticism. Only instinct and discipline remained. The mission comes first. Clear objective. Clear line of sight. Clear threat. All force is authorized, even the kind that the media would decry as too aggressive. Right and wrong, good and evil, antagonist and protagonist meet in the ultimate duel. In this moment there is only one outcome: one dead, one alive.

Action beat reaction. His mental clarity and his training become one. As he rolled to his right, he guided his weapon. *Stable platform.* Aim for the sweet spot on the target. *Center mass.* The bazooka in his hand became a handgun again. *Sight picture.* Two pounds of steel. *Sight alignment.* The thumb safety disengaged without conscious thought. The trigger squeeze was fluid, but rapid. *One, Two, Three.* Recoil of the weapon managed through thousands of practice rounds. *Four, Five.* Sound was non-existent, but his vision as sharp as ever. *Six, Seven.* His once piercing blues eyes now black and empty; no remorse, no feelings, just the mission. *Eight, Nine, Slide Lock, Reload.* The metal meeting the meat wasn't like the movies, it never is. The searing copper jacketed hollow-points entered flesh at just under 1000 feet per second and devastated anything in its path, but his target didn't fly backwards. This wasn't a Quentin Tarantino movie where the blood spewed forth like a deranged water fountain; just a slight pink mist. His target fell to the ground, collapsed more like it. Forward and to his right. No words, not even a grunt. Just silent death. A warrior's death. Quick and efficient.

A deep cleansing breath filled his lungs. The clarity he had in the previous moment gave way to the fog of modern society. Humming streetlights, sirens in the background getting louder, and the engines of cars in the distance. The thoughts of his wife and son rush in and grab him like a mother consoling their child. His prize lies on the ground motionless, but in respectful tranquility. A red liquid pools around and under the body of the fallen. A warrior's blood. A worthy adversary. Death came for them both, but only one would be escorted by Charon over the river and into eternity. By living, he assumed the role of storyteller and now the story of this moment was his alone. Only one other possessed the capacity to understand their game and he was no longer for this world. *Goodbye, "old friend." I'll see you in hell.*

Gaining full control of his senses allowed him to stand. He was shaken, but steadfast. He didn't gloat or curse or anything related to celebration. He stood there, quietly and respectfully, staring at the crumpled mass, still unable to see the visage of his fallen foe. He had taken lives before, but it was never personal. He felt the weight of it, but never to this extent. He was both proud of what he accomplished, but sad that the chase was over. His opponent took him beyond the limits of his mental and physical fortitude and now there was only the numbness of the moment and the inevitable aftermath; internal affairs asking the same questions over and over, scores of police officers and psychologists asking if he was feeling O.K., public information officers preening themselves for the inevitable live press conference, and cameras hoping to get a glimpse of the bloody aftermath. For now, there was peace;

peace that only death could bring.

He thinks of the last three days and utters two words under his breath, words that have a new meaning. "It's over."

He reengaged the thumb safety and holstered his weapon as he had done so many times before. He gazed at his trophy as the blue and red LED lights became brighter and sirens increase in volume, memorizing this moment like previous times before. Every smell, sound, and nuance etched themselves into his memory. The taste of iron still hung in the air where the mist once existed. Thoughts are, in this moment, his own and there is silence. His stillness would be broken by a familiar phrase and tone.

"Drop your weapon and get on the ground!"

He's heard these words before, said them many times. He felt the barrels of weapons trained on him. The fog of previous events is completely gone now. He's off the grid and just shot a man, or someone who likened themselves to a man. Reality was different and the aftershock would be immense. He turned toward the order, slowly, hands visible.

The deputy repeated his order but now sees the face of who stands before him and the word emblazoned on the front of the vest worn by the man in front of him: POLICE. Still he didn't register it immediately and began to repeat himself.

"Drop your weapon and... It's Gray! Hold your fire!" Mental registration is complete.

Sirens are still blaring at this point and all the lone figure could do was crack a slight smile. *Someone always forgets to turn off their siren.* The storm was behind him and a growing storm before him, but that wouldn't be his concern. Still, the concern of years past weighed heavily on him.

He rolled The Artist onto his back and saw that some life was still in him. The man wouldn't give up on his beloved friend. His beloved Silas. The expression on The Artist face was peaceful, save the bullet hole that tore way a part of his left eye socket. The Artist gazed upon Silas for what he hoped, believed wouldn't be the last time. Gray knelt beside him and grabbed The Artist's hand forcefully. The Artist felt the passion in Silas' grip. The Artist had something thing to say.

"You see, my dear," The Artist said, the blood in in his throat beginning to constrict his breathing, "We are the same. A shadow of one another."

Gray understood now what The Artist's true intentions were and his mission was accomplished. All remaining civility left Gray in a single moment and only the monster within him remained. Gray bent down further down and whispered in The Artist's ear.

"Yes, we are, 'old friend'," Gray said to him, contempt in his soft whispers.

Gray stood up, letting go the grip that he had on The Artist's hand. The Artist saw his friend rise above him; standing over him. The police unit's LED lights lit up his beloved's face and streetlights appeared as a halo around the vested figure. He was taken by the glory of it all. The majestic view of his most cherished and he finally together. His Silas was a man of integrity, of honor, and he was felled on the battlefield. He would be treated as a fallen enemy and soon they would be engaged with each other again. The thought of it thrilled him. Their game would begin anew in the future. The Artist felt a peace pass over him, and his countenance mirrored that peace

Gray saw this serenity on The Artist's face and felt it necessary to relieve The Artist of this repose. The responding deputies were too busy paying attention their radios to see what was happening. Gray again drew Gladys from her home. He hoped it would be for the last time. He guided her toward his fallen foe's head. The Artist's eyes widened; the look of terror now filling his expression as he saw the fires of hell reignite in the piercing blue eyes that he once held so dear. True terror, for the first time in years, gripped him and would not let go. *The betrayal of our friendship, your integrity! My dear Silas, why?!* It was then that the deputy saw what Gray was doing, but was too late to stop it.

"Gray, stop...."

One final torrent of eight shots. All of them finding The Artists head, or what was left of it after the volley was silenced. The slide locked back. The exposed barrel smoked. There was nothing left. He was finished. Mission complete, permanently.

"What the fuck, Gray," the young deputy yelled, "he was still alive!"

"Well, he won't be back," Gray responded, the comment driving a chill up the young deputy's spine.

The deputy was in complete confusion and removed his firearm from his holster. The confusion led to him not knowing what to do. Gray just shot a man eight times after obviously speaking to him. The young man said the only thing that entered his mind.

"Gray, don't move."

Gray reached down toward the now lifeless target and reached into his jacket pocket. The finely crafted ensemble was now covered in blood, bone, and grey matter. The deputy raised his weapon at Gray. Gray saw that the "rookie" was shaking. He didn't know what to expect. The deputy then saw what emerged from the jacket pocket: a folded piece of paper, blood soaked, and written on it was Sean's previous location. Gray promised to take it from his corpse and he was a man of his word. Gray again stood over the lifeless form and stuffed the paper in his back pocket, the same back pocket that held his cell phone. Gray now turned toward the deputy. The deputy's weapon shook as he trained the sights on his target.

"Put that thing away, junior. Before someone gets hurt. I didn't just chase this fucker to get shot by you," Gray shot back. As he responded to the order he walked toward the deputy, the now ammunition-less firearm raised so the deputy could see it. Obviously, no threat.

The deputy had no other choice but to comply. The man before him commanded deference through his own actions and if he wanted to harm the deputy, then he would've done so beforehand.

"Here you go. Don't get attached to her," Gray told him as he hands the deputy his firearm. The deputy grabbed the firearm from Gray's hand and stood in stunned amazement.

Gray walked to the rear of the deputy's car. The back door was unlocked. He removed his vest and placed it in the back seat. Relief filled him as the additional weight no longer rested on his broad shoulders. He saw the deputy reach for his handcuffs.

"That's not gonna happen, kid. Press the issue and you'll find me a very uncooperative." Gray's eyes now pierced through the youngster. His stare was soon broken as he felt the warmth of the car's cabin. It was inviting and calm. This was an area typically used for suspect transfers, but for Gray it offered asylum and peace.

"Hey," Gray yelled to the deputy. "Would you mind turning off the siren? It's kind of annoying."

Gray then sat himself in the rear of the unit and awaited his fate. The door closed and with its closure the sounds of the night faded. He closed his eyes and rested his head against the headrest. The deputy outside of the car just stood in shock, but eventually the noise from the siren ended.

"Good job, junior," Gray said to himself.

Now we wait.

XIV.

9:00 PM

Desormeaux, Rod, and Maria arrived at the scene. It was buzzing with activity. Crime scene techs, officers and deputies still in shock at what just happened, and multiple layers of brass bitching at one another. The argument wasn't about what Gray had done, but rather who would handle the investigation. Sheriff's claiming jurisdiction because they arrived first. Police claiming it's their baby because it happened in their city limits. Chief interjected himself into the love fest.

"Where's my detective," Desormeaux asked, his will strong and would not be ignored.

"Over there," one of the rank officers said, pointing at a sheriff's unit at the middle of the activity.

Desormeaux motioned to Rod to meet his at the specified car. Maria joined Rod and all three approached the rear of the unit. They were amazed at what they saw: Gray appeared to be sleeping. Desormeaux opened the door and the cold air hit Gray. He wasn't asleep, he was just enjoying the warmth. Gray opened his eyes and saw friends.

"Jesus, Roger. I was enjoying myself back here," Gray said.

"Really, fucker," Rod exclaimed. "We leave you alone for two hours and you decide to drop a cluster fuck bomb in the middle of Lafayette!"

"Yeah," Gray responded, "That's exactly what I intended."

"Well at least your shit went as planned," Rod retorted.

"How's Sean," Gray asked.

"He's good, he'll be out of commission for a while, but he'll make it. He said that you're a dick for not taking that guy down earlier," Rod answered.

"What's next," Desormeaux asked. "Did you make the call?"

"Yeah, Chief. I made the call. Should be here any minute now."

Both Rod and Maria looked at each other and neither could figure out what was going on. One final secret among the two men before them.

"Who should be here any minute," Maria asked.

"You'll see, or should I say you'll see and then be forced to forget," Gray responded, his eyes again closing, and his head backed against the headrest.

"And what in the hell is that supposed to mean," Rod asked. "Big Homie won't forget shit. Especially since you decided to turn downtown into war zone. Oh, and I almost forgot, there's a body over there missing most of its head. Adding to that will be the shitstorm of jurisdiction that we gonna have to deal with. Like I said, I ain't forgettin' shit."

A police officer from the city approached Desormeaux and said something to him. It must have been important.

"Hey guys, I have to talk to the brass and see if I can't smooth this out. You ok, Silas?"

"I'm good, Chief. Tell them I'm sorry for the trouble." Gray grinned and Desormeaux could only return the smile and shake his head as he walked away, muttering something under his breath, most likely profanities. Gray didn't mean it. He thoroughly enjoyed the chaos, especially when upper level administrative staff was involved.

"Now who are these uptight looking sumbitches?"

Rod's expression wasn't lost on Gray or Maria. Gray, for the first time since seating himself in the rear of the police car, exited and saw the same thing that Rod saw. Maria was drawn to the sight of it as well. Three black Dodge Durango's with blue lights emanating from the grill and windshield. The obvious answer was that they weren't local law enforcement. The three SUV's parked near the area where the chief's and sheriff were meeting. A well-dressed man in a wool overcoat exited the first vehicle and introduced himself. The distance was too great to hear words, but the power of the man's words stopped everyone in their tracks. Desormeaux looked back at Rod, Maria, and Gray and grinned in their direction.

The second SUV's front doors opened, and the occupants exited. The man from the passenger side and the woman driver who exited were just as well-dressed as the man who spoke to the brass. The imposing male then reached for the rear passenger door and opened it. Desormeaux and Gray saw her and she was a sight to behold. Exceptionally well-dressed, poised, and commanding respect from everyone around her. She was Keres. She paid no attention to Desormeaux as she passed the dumbfounded men who believed that they were in charge. As much as she wished to embrace him, she had to ignore him. She had to keep him from repercussion. Gray smiled as she approached, and his smile warmed her to the core. So much time had passed between them and yet their bond was still as strong as ever. The only thing that changed about her was the scar on the right side of her neck. Other than that, she was exactly as Gray remembered her: fit, tall, and with her dark shoulder-length hair pulled back into a perfect ponytail.

"Silas," the raspy voice said as she stood in front of him.

"Mags," Gray responded. "You sound, different than I remember."

The smile on Gray's face told the tale of years of friendship and comradery. Mags smiled back at him. She missed his dry sense of humor, but missed his presence even more.

"Mags," an exasperated Rod said, "Wait! What the hell? This is some Twilight Zone shit here! Big Homie gonna have to sit down."

Mags chuckled at Rod's statement. "I can see why you like him so much, Gray. He reminds me of Jacques. And who is this young lady?" Mags turned her attention to her newest fan.

Maria gazed upon the perceptibly powerful woman standing in front of Gray and was immediately taken by her; she couldn't resist the overt power of this woman.

"Me! Oh, my name is Maria. Maria Gomez."

"Ah, yes. The journalist. I've seen your news casts. You did great work with the Clerk of Court expose'. Very well done. I trust that this will not become public. Careers and lives of my dear friends hang in the balance."

Mags' look toward Maria froze all her thoughts. The power emanating from these carefully selected syllables told her volumes. She would keep this secret, always.

"No, ma'am. I mean, yes ma'am. No story here. None at all. Uh, Rod, I need some coffee." Maria's delivery was akin to a stutter.

"And I need Jack Daniels," Rod retorted. "But coffee sounds like a helluva an idea."

Maria and Rod walked away from the two former teammates and fast friends. They were family and that familial bond would never be broken. Mags could no longer control herself. She never could when her emotions were involved. She never learned to turn those completely off. She reached out to Gray and embraced him, driving her face into his chest. A tear fell from her eye. Gray was initially surprised by the outburst and his ribs still ached from being shot. His hands didn't grasp onto her, but then he couldn't stop himself. The pain subsided and he slowly wrapped his arms around his friend and rested his head on top of hers. They embraced each other as old friends would. Years apart held no sway in their relationship. They soon parted from each other and Mags wiped the tear from her eye and composing herself.

"When did you get so emotional, Mags? Wait till I tell Kap and Tyler that you've become all mushy."

"Kiss my ass, Gray. You know how I am," she shot back. *Just like old times.*

Mags looked around and surveyed the chaos that her closest friend and mentor dropped in the middle of the city on Christmas Eve.

"Where's the other one? Donaldson, I believe?"

"He's dead, Mags. Murdered by the man lying on the ground over there. He died putting the pieces together and helping me at the same time. Unfortunately, he wasn't good at either."

"Well, he'll be hailed a s hero after tonight. The man who took down a serial killer. I'm sure that the lack of attention will just break your heart."

Gray smirked. "I'm trying to pick up the pieces as we speak."

"Ah, sarcasm. I see some things never change."

One of the well-dressed guards approached Mags from behind. "Ma'am, here's what you requested." The man handed her an open bag. She reached into the bag and removed the contents. It was an object familiar to herself and Gray.

"Here you go, Gray. I'm sure she will be more at home on your hip and not in this bag."

Mags handed the implement of The Artist's death back to its rightful owner. Gladys was back in his hands and she wouldn't leave him again.

"It's finished, Mags." Gray rubbed the right side of his neck and Mags knew what it meant. Mags mirrored the motion. "Boudreaux was a copycat."

Confusion, however brief, set in and quickly left. The meaning of these words intensified as she felt the scar on her neck. The Butcher, the real Butcher, laid in the street almost completely headless not 30 yards from her. The debt to the reaper was paid in full. Mags nodded at this statement and her tone turned more professional.

"If you'll excuse me, I have a mess to clean up."

"I understand," Gray said. "Just one more thing, did you ever marry Jimmy?"

"You know I did, Silas. You were there."

Gray looked surprised at the statement. He attended the wedding, but was incognito and remained in the background.

"Your undercover skills were never your trademark. My only question was how you knew where it was."

"Just a lucky guess, Mags. Send him my best, would you."

Mags smiled as she turned and walked toward the grouping of brass that she previously ignored, Desormeaux still being among them. All their stares fell on this woman and only one held back emotion at the sight her. He wanted embrace her as Gray did, but he couldn't. He couldn't risk the exposure to himself, Kap, and Tyler. This was the hardest thing he did today outside of making sure Sean was taken care of at the hospital.

"Gentlemen," Mags started, "I'm sure that all of you have questions and I have neither the time, nor the inclination to answer them. I will be taking over this investigation. The rest of my team should be here shortly, and you will be provided details of this investigation at my leisure, if at all. Now, all your people will hand over any notes, videos, evidence, and anything else that they currently have and will vacate this crime scene at once. If anything is missing or 'accidentally' left out, then rest assured your respective careers will be over and you will find yourself in the unfortunate position of having to hire an attorney to defend you in your criminal trial. I thank you for your time and cooperation. Now, leave and don't say anything that you will come to regret. Good evening gentlemen and Merry Christmas."

She looked at Desormeaux as she departed their company and he met her stare. So many words were said in a look. Mags gave him a slight grin as she left his company and the grin was returned. No one else saw it, they were too busy licking their wounds after the one-sided exchange that proved Mags had bigger balls than they did.

"Nice, kiddo. Very well done," Desormeaux said to himself.

Rod and Maria saw the exchange between Mags and Gray and the look that Desormeaux gave her as she walked away. They both walked back to Gray and were full of curiosity. Gray still stared in Mags' direction. Pride filled him as he watched her lead her people. The respective law enforcement heads still stood in stunned amazement as they, too, watched her take over the scene. None dared cross her.

"Whenever you're finished daydreaming," Rod began, his accent becoming thicker, "Do you think you could let me in on how she is alive and how she is standing there giving orders and how she is going to clean this shit up. Hopefully I'll have a heart attack tonight so I don't have to answer questions. Lord Jesus, you're worse than my sister's kids. You're grounded! I can't take this shit no more!"

Gray retrieved his vest from the rear seat of the young deputy's unit without answering one of Rod's questions, only chuckling at Rod's latest soliloquy. There was nothing to tell. Mags was never here and at the end of it all she would be a figment of everyone's imagination, if they knew what was good for them. Gray then began to walk away from Maria and Rod.

"Where are you going," Maria asked.

Gray stopped. "I'm going to pick up Norm and then going to meet my family. I'll see you guys later. Merry Christmas."

"What about Mags," Rod asked.

"Who?"

"Mags. You know, the hottie that just pulled a Lazarus and scared me… I mean, Maria to death. Poor thing. Look at her, she's terrified."

"Mags," Gray said with a forced confusion, "Mags died, Rod. You should really take a day or two off. I think you're seeing things. I'll see you guys later."

Rod and Maria watched as Gray turned around and walk away from the scene. He walked under the crime scene tape and through the small crowd that gathered just beyond its border, vest slung over his shoulder. The news media paid no attention to the man passing through. If those vultures knew about his involvement, then they would've pounced. To them, he was just another low-level officer rendering assistance. *No story here.* His destination: The Artist's apartment building. His truck was still there. Rod then turned to see Mags enter the vehicle that she arrived in and that vehicle speed away from the scene. Her people remained to clean up the scene. Desormeaux still stood with the respective department leaders and feigned outrage over the usurpation of their respective jurisdictional authority.

"So, Rod, what do you think?"

"Sugar, I have no idea, but I need a drink and the bar around the corner is still serving. Would you care to join me for an adult cocktail on this lovely evening?"

"You know, Big Homie, that's a great idea."

Rod smiled and offered his arm to Maria, which she gladly accepted.

"Now, don't be tellin' Big Momma about this! She ain't hip on her love muffin courting other women, especially on Christmas Eve."

"Your secret's safe with me," Maria said, smiling as they walked away.

"I know it is, my baby. I know it is."

EPILOGUE

Two months passed since The Artist's death and Gray felt nothing more from his experience. He never gave Charlie the full story as to what happened on that night and she didn't need to know. She asked if Gray knew the trooper that was killed and Gray said that he only knew him by reputation and that he seemed like a good officer. A white lie, one of many that he had to tell in order to protect her. This seemed to suffice. She only cared that her doting husband was by her side and that their son had his father to wrestle with. She didn't need to know about the other side of her spouse. The side that terrified all who saw it. It was a quiet mid-winter day.

"Babe," Charlie said to Gray, "Could you get the mail? I thought I saw the truck pass by earlier."

"Sure thing, love. Hey, bud," Gray said to his son, "Wanna come get the mail with me."

"Yeah, I'm gonna get my flip flops!"

The child ran to his room as excited as he could be. Gray admired how the small things in life thrilled him. There was an innocence is every adventure, real or imagined.

Knock, knock

"Hey, hey," the familiar voice said as the door opened. Sean needed no invitation. He was always welcome.

"Uncle Sean!" Simon no sooner retrieved his preferred foot-wear when he heard his favorite "uncle" come through the door. The little one couldn't help himself but to jump into Sean and wrap his little arms around his neck when Sean caught him. Sean groaned a bit, still suffering some of the aftereffects of his fight with The Artist.

"Guess what, Uncle Sean. Me and daddy are gonna get the mail. I wonder of there will be lions and tigers."

Sean was amused by the imagination on this kid. "What about bears," Sean shot back.

"Oh, my," Gray said, completing the classic line from the old Hollywood movie.

"You three are a mess," Charlie said to the group. All three stared at her as she made the statement and she saw the blank expressions on their faces. "Yep. A complete mess."

"Hey, Charlie," Sean said as he walked over to her and gave her a friendly kiss on the cheek. "How's everything?"

"I was gonna ask you the same thing. How are you after your accident?"

"Oh, I'm good. My car not so much. It definitely taught me to not drive while I'm tired, but here I am and here I'll remain."

"Yes, you are. Now go get the mail with these two heathens. They need a chaperone."

The three men in the house were powerless when the alpha female was around. They did her bidding and didn't question the queen's wishes. They walked slowly down the driveway, Simon walking several feet ahead of them and retrieving the mail before Gray and Sean were halfway to their destination.

"Got it! You two need to pick up the pace!"

The two partners smiled at the youth and accepted that they came in last place, yet again.

"Good job, bud. Bring it inside to mommy. Daddy and Uncle Sean are gonna talk for a minute."

Simon ran into the house without a word; a little bolt of

lightning. The two friends were now in the elements as they were those months ago. It was not nearly as cold or windy. Winter was still in full swing, but the temperature was mild, almost pleasant. Certain parts of the country would call it brisk. Still, it wasn't the night that they would share forever.

"So, anything," Sean asked.

"Not a thing. Mags took care of everything. Donaldson died a hero and we weren't involved in anything. Your cover story still intact?"

"Yeah," Sean said. "She came to me a few days later and told me what I needed to know."

"I know she did. She told me that you were being stubborn with the nurses and doctors."

"Mags has a big mouth, Gray."

Gray laughed at the statement due to the irony of a woman that didn't exist talking too much.

"It's a shame what happened to the assistant chief in Lafayette," Sean stated.

"I know," Gray shot back. "Soliciting prostitutes and human trafficking. Who would've guessed? It came out of left field."

Sean stopped and grabbed Gray's arm. Gray turned to his friend and looked him in the eyes. Sean froze for a moment. The steel blue gaze of his friend was soft, but still shocking despite their friendship.

"Tell me, Silas, was that Mags as well?"

"Sean..."

"I'm serious, Gray. Did Mags do that to the assistant chief?"

"The assistant chief did it to himself. Mags didn't trump up the charges on him. It's not her way and it's not the way I taught her to be. She only brought it to light. She warned them."

"And it's by sheer coincidence that he was making waves about the Christmas Eve shooting at the time Maria broke the story."

"Yeah, she did a good job on that one. Almost as good as her Clerk of Court story."

The look on Gray's face told Sean to let it go. Sean needed to appease his conscience. Both men had integrity, and neither would allow an innocent person to suffer, regardless of circumstance. In this case, each person that could've made waves about the ordeal wasn't innocent, except for Desormeaux, and Mags warned them to leave it be. It only took one to fall before the message was sent and the other men fell in line. Powerful men on their knees before a ghost. Mags was formidable, to say the least.

"It still kinda gets me that Donaldson was given credit for solving the case. This was ours, well, mostly yours."

"Doesn't bother me a bit," Gray said, "He died and we lived. I'll take that consolation prize every day of the week."

The front door opened and Charlie emerged holding a white envelope.

"Babe, this one is addressed to you. No return addresses."

Sean and Gray walked back to the front door and Charlie handed him the non-descript package. The wording on the front of the envelope was hand-written and only said two words: SILAS GRAY.

"Thanks, love," Gray said as Charlie handed him the envelope.

"You two make me sick," Sean said. "'Hey babe,' 'Thanks, love.' Kissy, kissy, smootchie, smootchie. Blah!"

Charlie shot Sean the eyes that only a woman could shoot

in a man's direction. Gray believed that every woman was capable of this look. He called it the Medusa Stare. It could freeze men in their tracks. Gray dared not look directly at her as she did this for fear of turning to stone.

"You wish you had what we have, Sean," Charlie said sarcastically. "Isn't that right, Silas?"

Gray looked startled at the statement.

"Don't bring me into this. That's between you guys. I'm just the guy holding an envelope." This was an ongoing discourse that he wanted no part of. He'd take another three days of murder and gunfights before inserting himself into this dispute.

Charlie retreated into her home and the two men were left with the letter of mysterious origin. Gray opened the letter and observed the image of a sickle; the blade of the reaper. Sean, too, saw this and was immediately intrigued. Gray unfolded the document and within it was the picture of the original REAPERS. All six of them and the original control, Roger Desormeaux. The only photograph that existed with all seven operational members. Gray believed this to be destroyed, but Mags found it and sent it to the one person that could appreciate it more than she did. She no longer needed the photo on her desk. She'd apparently made peace with herself. The letter that accompanied it was heart-felt:

> Gray,
>
> You have taught me so much and are still teaching me from a distance. This photo sat on my desk for years and it is only fair that you should keep it. You were and still are the heart of the REAPERS. I can't repay the debt that we owe you, but I can only hope to meet your expectations. There will always be a place for you here should you decide to come home. You have my number.

Love,

Mags

P.S. Jimmy sends his best, but still thinks you're an asshole for not telling him that I was alive during my recovery.

Gray stared at the photo: Kap, Tyler, Tony, Jacques, Mags, himself, and Roger. This was a great time of their lives and a dark time of the lives. The memories of their friendship would stay with him for as long as he remained in this world. Their deeds would go unsung and only rumors of their existence would remain in the halls of police departments and courthouses. The streets would also speak of the ghosts that swooped in to take those that owed a debt. That's what they were: debt collectors and the debt always needed to be paid, either in time or in blood. It was their way.

"Do you think that Mags will call again," Sean asked.

"No, I don't," Gray answered. "She'll wait for my call. If it never comes, then her successor will wait for my call."

"What about you? Do you think that you'll go back one day?"

Gray thought for a moment; such a simple question with such a complex answer. "The REAPERS were my team, Sean. My family. There is only one left that could keep it alive and he's at peace."

"And if he's needed again," Sean asked, his inquisitive nature taking over.

"Then... then he'll come back. Family has to be protected at all costs."

Sean accepted this and pushed no further into the conversation. The darkness felt by The Artist was explained to him in graphic detail by Rod, albeit with the flare that only Rod could deliver. His friend, his partner, his brother was a man like none other he'd ever met. Violence defined him and enduring peace eluded him. He wanted his brother in arms to find reconciliation between the man and the monster, but peace could only last for so long for men like him.

The two friends walked back into the house. Both were content.

****

"Delivery is complete, ma'am."

Mags sat in front of her desk, a dust imprint where the picture of her team once sat left a void that would not be covered. She sat on her throne of secrets. No one would dare challenge her and only a handful ever called her by her real name. The head of a group that didn't exist that performed missions that most never knew. The worst of the worst was the mission and only men and women of unshakable integrity would be among their growing ranks. Violence hadn't ceased. The absence of the REAPERS only guaranteed this fact. They had to evolve, but they needed their guide. They needed their heart and soul.

"Is everything in place," Mags asked.

"Yes ma'am. We await your approval."

"Tartarus is a go. Authorization: Keres actual, Romeo 2."

The young woman left the room without a word. Mags was alone with her thoughts. The new mission would soon begin, and it would be marathon, not a sprint. The titans of crime had to be stopped and the preparation to ensure their downfall was methodical; agents imbedded, assistants bought, and plans were set in motion that wouldn't be stopped. This would be the bloodiest fight yet. The fallout from such an ambitious mission would reverberate through the state, possibly the nation. Still, her thoughts were with her friend and how this new mission would affect him. She was in a state of melancholia as she stared at the blank space where the picture one sat, as she typically did during times of deep thought. The image that brought her comfort in these times was gone, but she could still see the faces of her beloved team, she and Gray in the middle with big smiles on their mud-stained faces.

She stood from her desk and looked out of the window, the same window that she would often look through when she waited for something important. She surveyed the world that she ruled in the shadows. A concrete landscape filled with homes, interstates, and structures dedicated to man's vices and hubris. Among them a tall, almost obelisk-like structure not far from the Mississippi River. It stood above all other buildings in the area. It was a titan among lesser gods: the capitol building. Her gaze fixed on its concrete façade. The windows surrounding the building like the eyes of Argus – the mythological giant said to have one hundred eyes and was all-seeing. She didn't care about power, only about what was right. She kept their secrets and it was nearly time for a reckoning. A debt that must be paid.

The REAPERS were no longer. There was only Sierra Division; the progeny of the original unit. The compliment of this evolved unit referred to it as SCYTHE. The few who knew of the original membership called it "Silas' Bastards," a moniker fitting a unit that didn't exist that comprised of people with no origin. Newer members of this unit only recently found out who the father of this nickname was and were not disappointed by the revelation. His name was uttered with reverence, if uttered at all.

"I'm sorry, Silas," she said to herself, still staring out of the window, "But I'll need you very soon. I need the darkness that follows in your wake. I hope that you'll be able to forgive me, old friend."

She would patiently await his call. The call from the reaper himself.

For now, Silas Gray will rest.

Made in the USA
Coppell, TX
19 May 2020